'CALL RITA GOMEZ.'

I watch as the state's case takes the long walk from the back of the room to the stand. She forces herself to keep her look straight ahead, wobbling unsteadily in her new, unaccustomed high heels, scrupulously avoiding eye-contact with any of the bikers. Lone Wolf is staring at her with singular intensity, an almost palpable heat radiating from his eyes.

'Keep it locked up,' I caution.

He's still as a statue, his eyes boring in at her. Sooner or later she's going to have to look at him; when she does she might explode. The others stare at her, too. She was prey to them before, a defenseless muffball in the company of mean, off-the-wall predators; now she's the prime threat to their lives, the door between them and the free world, and they only know one way to react to something that basic: eliminate it.

J. F. FREEDMAN

Against the Wind

A SIGNET BOOK

SIGNET

Published by the Penguin Group
Penguin Books Ltd, 27 Wrights Lane, London W8 5TZ, England
Penguin Books USA Inc., 375 Hudson Street, New York, New York 10014, USA
Penguin Books Australia Ltd, Ringwood, Victoria, Australia
Penguin Books Canada Ltd, 10 Alcorn Avenue, Toronto, Ontario,
Canada M4V 3B2
Penguin Books (NZ) Ltd, 182–190 Wairau Road, Auckland 10, New Zealand

Penguin Books Ltd, Registered Offices: Harmondsworth, Middlesex, England

First published in the USA by Viking 1991
First published in Great Britain by Michael Joseph 1992
Published in Signet 1992
1 3 5 7 9 10 8 6 4 2

Printed in England by Clays Ltd, St Ives plc

To my father—
one terrific lawyer

ACKNOWLEDGMENTS

This novel was begun in a UCSB extension class taught by Shelly Lowenkopf. Mr. Lowenkopf's guidance, support, and ongoing enthusiasm helped me start this book and, more importantly, see it through to its finish.

My brother, David A. Freedman, who is a practising attorney in New Mexico, has been a helpful source of local information, as well as assisting me with the legal and technical language and passages.

Jerry Adler, Jack Laird, Ronda Gomez-Quinones, Abby Mann, Howard Krakow, and Norman Powell have been especially supportive at different times in my life, when being so was not always easy or popular.

Most importantly, my wife, Rendy, has always been there for me, during the bad times as well as the good.

PART ONE

MY ARM IS KILLING ME. I force open my eyes enough of a slit to admit light. The shades are up, I neglected to pull them last night, the sun blasts through the windows, through my encrusted eyelids right through the retina into the back of my brain. Jesus that hurts, I'm a pathetic ball of pain this morning. I broke my newly self-imposed rule last night and went bar-hopping, that much I remember, but subsequent events are vague, to put it mildly. They're so damn vague they're a blank page. Getting drunk and hitting on women I've never met, whose sexual history is suspect at best, could and has turned out to be detrimental to my health. The last time I ventured out like that, two weeks ago Saturday night, I got the shit kicked out of me. Had to show up in court that Monday morning with a butterfly bandage over my right eye, my face an unsightly mass of lumps, bruises and contusions. My client, a devout pacifist, freaked; I was forced to ask for a continuance. Fred Hite, one of my partners, took her over, mollified her, but the incident didn't make me any new friends in or out of court.

I'm going to open my eyes and sit up and there's going to be a soft explosion in the back of my head like a watermelon being dropped off a third-story roof from all that house whiskey I undoubtedly drank and have no memory of and I deserve it for being such a dumb self-pitying ass and my arm is still killing me.

Maybe I broke it. Maybe I'm in the hospital. That would tear it.

Her hair is brown, but the roots are gray. It's a tangled mat, like balled-up baling wire, and about the same consistency, as if she'd given herself a home permanent and got talking on the phone too long. She snores gently, her head resting on my shoulder like a bowling ball. Dear God tell me I didn't. This one is major coyote arm, the only way I get out of here alive is to chew it off while she's still sleeping. In my own apartment yet.

"You got coffee?"

"What?"

"Coffee. Just tell me where you keep it. I'll make it." She's staring at me like you look through the bars in a zoo. Her eyes are bloodshot, bright red, unnaturally so, cartoonish.

I wave my free arm. "Above the sink." She blinks, hoists herself to her feet, pads stark-naked towards the kitchen. I look at her receding back, her sagging ass. I know I was drunk but was I blind too? Jesus what else happened last night? For all I know I committed three ax murders. I'm dead in this town if anyone I know saw us together.

She's in the bathroom. I listen to her doing her toilet. I roll over, grab her purse off the floor, rifle the wallet for her driver's license. Doris Mae Rivera. From Truchas. Forty-six years old. Patricia (Mrs. Alexander numero uno) and I didn't have any money, we were too new out of law school and then we had Claudia; but Holly and I, that was the society page. Successful lawyer and his attractive, devoted wife (okay, the second marriage for him and third for her, but who's counting?), active in community affairs, we were Mr. and Mrs. Hot Shit: the ranchette north of town, the twin BMWs, the Taos ski condo. Now I'm lying on sweat-soaked sheets I haven't changed in weeks in a rented condo a welfare mother would turn her nose up at, going through the wallet of Doris Mae Rivera (acquired last name, obviously, no Hispanic woman would be christened Doris Mae), a forty-six-year-old currently unmarried woman who probably lives in a house without plumbing; Truchas is famous for the view from its outhouses.

She flushes and I drop the wallet back into the purse. She emerges wearing my velour robe, the midnight-blue number Holly got me last Christmas from the Sharper Image catalogue for a mere two-seventy-five. One of that year's minor gifts. Her hair's wrapped in a towel; she must've looked in the mirror.

"How do you like your eggs?" she calls, rummaging in the refrigerator. Coming to the bedroom door, smiling coyly, almost shyly. Maybe we got married last night, anything's possible.

"I don't." I untangle my pants from the pile on the floor, pull them on, stumble through the living room to the kitchen area; it's all one big room, a mess. I've got to get a cleaning lady in here or I'll turn into something out of Kafka. I'm close enough already: this is a sign.

"Get dressed." I brush past her, take the O.J. from the refrigerator, drink it straight from the carton. She turns to me, her mouth a small oval. Her hand involuntarily drops, cracking the egg in the fry-pan. I reach over and turn off the gas. She looks at me, her expression pained. One drunken encounter and she's already proprietary.

I close my eyes, take a deep breath. I shouldn't ask but I have to know.

"Did I . . . ?" I choke on my own tongue.

She smiles. "With all your heart," she rhapsodizes, actually closing her eyes. "You have the most sensual mouth. I can still feel it all over my . . ."

"Thank you." I cut her off, turning away from her eager, treacly smile.

She misses the point.

"Oh God. I know exactly what you're thinking."

I turn back. No you don't. Unless you're a mind-reader. She is kind of dark; maybe she's part-Indian, a spirit woman.

"I'm completely clean," she swears hastily. "No AIDS, herpes, nothing like that." She smiles, having cleared everything up. "I'd never do that to you, or any man." She pauses. "I don't get that many offers that I don't (very softly now, almost a whisper) appreciate it."

"You have to go. Now."

"But . . . what about breakfast? Coffee? I could make you a jalapeño and jack omelet." Spatula in one hand, Melitta pot in the other. I'm a lucky man; New Mexico's answer to Julia Child is standing in my very own kitchen.

"There's a McDonald's two blocks down. They serve up a mean Egg McMuffin." I'm back in the bedroom, scooping up her clothes, undergarments, shoes, purse. Dropping it all on the living room couch. "You're out of here. Get your clothes on."

She starts crying. Not a put-on like the numbers Holly used to run on me, this is real: big round tears, shuddering sobs. I grasp my head in my hands, hold on tightly.

"Hey, I'm sorry. Really. But I've got to get to work, I'm already late. Don't you have a job you have to get to?"

"I'm on unemployment," she sobs. The towel's off her head, she's buried her face in it, her hair hangs wet and stringy. "I've been laid off fourteen weeks."

Very careful now. Sit her down on the couch. Take off the robe. Slide her panties up her legs, up over her ass. Slip the dress on. No chance with the bra and pantyhose, they go in her purse. Put her shoes on.

"Can I use your bathroom?" she asks weakly. "I don't want to walk out of here looking like this." She turns, looks straight at me. It's unnerving. "Believe it or not, I do have my pride left," she adds in an attempt at self-respect.

"Sure." I'm discombobulated. "Take your time. I'll make the coffee."

"I knew you weren't all that mean," she says, sliding back into romance-novel coyness as she sashays into the bathroom. From behind, with her clothes on, she's not that bad. I catch myself; I'm becoming a master of sublimation. You fucked up, man. Don't compound it.

She comes out a few minutes later, having put on her bra and hose and makeup, brushed out her thick hair. Better; still no beauty, but I don't have to flagellate myself all day: in a dark bar she'd have a certain low-down easy charm. She puts a folded piece of paper on the kitchen counter.

"My phone number," she tells me. "In case you reconsider and feel like calling."

I nod. "Sure." But don't give up your day gig to wait by the phone, I'm thinking. Then I remember: she's unemployed. She can baby-sit the phone all day if she's of a mind to.

She starts to leave, quickly turns back catching me off-guard, kissing me full on the lips, open-mouthed, grinding up against me. She's good at it; somehow I'm not surprised. I linger with it longer than I want to before I break it.

"Too bad you were so drunk," she says, standing in the open doorway, "we were actually good together. A shame you don't at least have a nice memory of it like I do."

THEY HIT ME WITH the good news before I get to my first cup of coffee.

"Come on in the conference room. We've got to talk." This is Andy Portillo, my other partner; from one of the old northern New Mexico land-grant families. Big, husky fellow, a couple years older than me, looks like a picker you see sitting on the tailgate of a '52 Chevy half-ton eating burritos off the roach-coach. Looks, of course, can be deceiving: his plain dime-store black frame diplomas read Oberlin College and Columbia Law School, along with dozens of prestigious awards and honors. He's our corporate guy, the back-room genius. Fred handles the civil stuff. I'm criminal law, a couple years back one of the heavyweight law journals came out with a survey of the best criminal lawyers in the country, state by state. I was one of a handful from New Mexico. When I get rolling in a courtroom I can be pretty impressive; some of my jury summations are local legends.

"You're fucking up, Will," Fred informs me without preamble.

"I know. But I can handle it." The best defense is a good offense. "Come on guys, what is this shit, I haven't even had my first cup of coffee." I flash the famous Alexander rogue smile, the courtroom closer, the one people tell me reminds them of Jack Nicholson. It ought to; I copped it from watching him.

They're not buying it; they've known me too long.

"Do you remember Mrs. Taliaferro?" Andy asks rhetorically. "Mrs. Ralph Taliaferro, that sweet little old lady from Pueblo who has this firm on a thirty-five-thousand-dollar yearly retainer just so we'll be there in case she needs us?"

I groan. Susan comes in with my coffee. I scald my lips, spill some on the mahogany. She wipes it up, leaves as fast as she can: the thunderheads in the room are low and sinking.

"What time was the meeting?" I'm having a difficult time retaining these days, I'm burning gray cells by the thousands daily. I glance at the wall clock: 10:45.

"Eight-thirty," Fred answers. "It's been on your calendar for two weeks." His hand drops to my shoulder. It's not an altogether friendly gesture. "She flew in for a partners' meeting, in her own private Lear. *All* the partners, and since it's a criminal matter, her idiot son having gotten his tit caught in the wringer dealing to a DEA agent, she was especially interested in talking to our criminal law specialist. Unfortunately, he was indisposed."

"I'll talk to her. I'll fly up this afternoon." Hell, I'll fuck her if I have to, I'm getting to be an old hand with the geriatric set.

Andy shakes his head. "She dropped us. Dixon's firm called fifteen minutes ago. They're sending a messenger over for her files." He turns away, looking out the window at the statehouse across the street.

"I'll fix it," I promise him hastily. My gut's churning. "Dixon's a hack, she's a smart lady even if she did mother a tribe of morons, she'll smell him out in a week."

The room is quiet. Fred snaps a pencil between his fingers. It sounds like a gunshot; despite the grim news I'm still fighting this hangover, I'm going to need a pot of coffee before lunch.

"Sit down, Will," Fred commands. "Come on, man, we've got to talk," he continues, softer. He looks drawn; they both do. We're all close friends, we've been in practice together almost ten years, we were the coming firm that actually arrived.

"It's gotten out of hand . . . I'm talking about your behavior."

"I know what you're talking about," I tell him. I'm testy, I don't like being lectured, especially when I deserve it.

"This isn't the first time, Will," Andy says. "Or the second. You're out of control, man. You're . . ." He hesitates. "You're not doing yourself much good these days. Or anyone else."

"Andy and I've talked about it," Fred jumps in, a shade too quickly. "With the associates, too, they're part of this, but ultimately it's got to be our decision. The partners. The three of us."

I drink half a cup. It helps.

"What exactly are we talking about?" I ask. I'm not sure I want to know the answer.

Andy sits next to me, leans in close. He's a bear, this guy, a big warm bear, I love him, he's the best friend I've ever had in my entire life.

"You're no good to anybody right now, Will, especially yourself."

"Hey I'm having some problems okay? It's not the end of the world."

"We want you to take a leave of absence," he tells me out of left field.

I've been sucker-punched before; it always takes your breath away even when you should see it coming. I breathe deeply; I look at him, at Fred. Give them credit: they hold my look. It can't be easy.

I finish the rest of my coffee in a swallow. "I can't. Not now. You know I can't now." Then it hits me: my partners, my best friends, are kicking me out of my own firm. Alexander, Hite, and Portillo. It's my goddam name that's first on the door. I explode.

"What is this shit!" I yell. I'm up, pacing, getting the old courtroom adrenaline flowing. I always think better on my feet.

"Calm down Will," Fred says. "You want the whole building to hear you?"

"Fuck the building," I tell him, "and fuck you. Both of you." I'm pacing, I'm sweating, I'm cooking, but I'm scared, too. "I'm going through the worst goddam time of my life right now, I've got a divorce settlement coming up with Holly that's going to wipe out my assets, I've got a daughter who needs three grand worth of orthodontia, that's the tip of the iceberg, there's a million other important things on my mind, and you're telling me because I miss one lousy meeting you want to kick me out. Thanks, guys. I need your support and instead you turn your back on me."

I slump in a chair. Jane, the *Michigan Law Review* editor we hired as our latest associate last year right out from under the noses of two major Wall Street firms, sticks a quizzical head in the door. Andy waves her out impatiently. She jumps; that's not at all like him. The entire office must be feeling the tension.

They turn to me. They are my friends, and they're concerned. And I'm not helping them. I can't. If I lose the firm I lose the only anchor I've got left.

Fred speaks first: we don't call him 'The Knife' for nothing.

"You're hurting the firm." Simple, direct, and lethal.

"It's out in the open," Andy adds. "People are talking."

"So let 'em. So what? I do the job don't I?"

They don't answer.

"Okay . . ." Carefully now, these are your friends, and partners, a lot's at stake, don't push them into something we'll all regret later. "I've fucked up, maybe more than once, definitely more than once, but that's behind me, on my word, I'm lining up my priorities, I'm going to take care of business. It's going to be strictly business, I'm not drinking, I haven't had a drink for a week (okay, one white lie, I'll fix it retroactively) . . ."

"You were drinking last night," Andy informs me coldly, catching me in my lie immediately. He leans away from me; not so much the big, friendly bear now. "You were drinking with Buck Burgess at the Longhorn during happy hour. Now cut the bullshit and get straight with us or I am personally going to throw you out this window."

"That was beer, for Christsakes, one lousy beer." I almost shit with relief; for a moment I thought I'd done real damage, somebody'd seen me in a forty-five-degree weave with the lady from Truchas. "Okay, to be technical it was two beers but they were light beers," I point out quickly, a lawyer's mind is never at rest, "beer isn't drinking. Hell," I add, trying on a grin, "I get higher drinking iced tea."

"Then you'd better add iced tea to your list of don't-dos," Fred says. "Look, Will," he continues, "you've got a choice: take a leave and work out your problems . . ."

He pauses. Even for him, a guy who relishes a confrontation, this is painful. I don't help; they're going to have to play this hand out, I want them to show me what they're holding.

Andy doesn't blink. He's a killer poker-player.

"We don't want to buy you out, Will. But we will if we have to, if it's the only way. But we don't want to. For sure that's not what we want to do."

We have this clause in our original partnership language: if any two of the original three partners feel the third is harming the firm to the point where he's causing irreparable damage they have the right to buy him out at current book value plus work in progress. It's a lot of money; none of us ever wanted it before. Now it's in front of us. We sit in putrefactive silence.

I blink first.

"For how long?"

Fred shrugs.

"A week? A month?" I ask.

Andy shakes his head. "A month won't do it, Will." He leans back towards me, the conciliator again. "It's not just you, although," he says diplomatically, albeit a shade too facilely, Andy's not good at being slick, his bedrock honesty is his calling-card, "your well-being is the most important thing to us."

"You're talking about the integrity of the firm," I finish for him.

They exhale; I'm not going to be a hard-case.

" 'Cause that's where the money is," I continue. They're wrong; I'm going to make it miserable for them. "Can you even afford to buy me out?"

"It'll be a bitch," Fred says. "But if we have to—if that's what it comes to: yes."

I'm the buccaneer in the group; if they say they can it means they've already worked it out.

"So what're we talking about? Three months? Four?" I'm sweating freely now.

"At least," Andy answers, on sure ground again. "You need to cool out, Will. You're burnt out."

There it is.

"How do we work out the money?" I ask. "We can't afford to pay me if I'm not bringing in business; not for that long."

They stare at me. Jesus, I'm slow this morning.

"You fuckers."

"You just said it," Fred answers in a tone that implies he's the wounded party. "You take a big hit, bro. No way we could carry that. We'd want it the same way if it was one of us," he adds unctuously.

"We'll find a month," Andy says. "Maybe two." At least he's having a harder time than Fred. I'm beginning to wonder if I ever deep-down liked Fred. I don't think so.

"What if I flat-out say no?" My back is up, these miserable two-faced sons-of-bitches, what kind of bullshit is this, we've been partners, friends, out of the blue they're putting a loaded gun to my head?

"Don't." Andy's tough now, his voice flat, emotionless.

I sag; they see it, I can't hide it, not in the condition I'm in this morning. It's a palace coup, bloodless, over before it's started.

"How do we work it? I'm not going to take any public humiliation," I tell them. "I'll bring the firm down first," I add, staring defiantly back at them.

"You've asked for an extended leave," Fred informs me. They've worked it all out, the pricks, they've probably got papers for me to sign. "You've been under intense emotional pressure with the divorce, you've been a lawyer almost your entire adult life, you need to step back and look at the big picture. We're reluctant to do it but in the long-range interests of the firm, and for your own well-being, we're going along with your desires. We wish you the best of luck, hope the trout are biting or whatever it is you'll be doing, and eagerly await your return to the firm of which you were an original founder."

I breathe an audible sigh of relief; the door isn't completely closed. Maybe they're right, maybe I should take some time off. So what if it's a rationalization; rationalizations have a kernel of truth.

"How do we know when it's time for me to come back?"

"We'll play it by ear," Andy says. "No guarantees."

"So there's a chance I'll never come back." Great, I think, forty years old and starting over in a town where there are no secrets. This whole sorry mess'll be on the streets by tomorrow.

"Let's don't think negatively, man," Andy says, "we really don't want this. We need you, Will, you're our star, we're going to lose half our trial business right off the top, some of it we'll never get back."

"Then why the goddam draconian measures?"

"You've forced them on us, Will. We don't think the firm can survive otherwise."

Jesus, has it really come to that? I close my eyes, take a deep breath, exhale. Should I apologize? No; if I'm going out I'm going out in style, my style. Of course, if I were to apologize, they'd really feel like turds.

"I'm sorry. I don't see the gravity of it but I've obviously hurt everybody pretty badly."

Bull's-eye. The grief on their faces is genuine. Fred puts an uncharacteristic hand on mine, an oddly inappropriate yet touching, old-fashioned gesture.

"You'll be back," he soberly informs me.

I nod equally soberly.

"What about Susan?"

"We're taking care of her," Andy says, quick on the draw. "We've already spoken to her . . ." his voice suddenly falters as he picks up on the fuckup, but he catches himself adroitly, presses on, no looking back now: "informally, of course, we mentioned you might want to take a leave, let it fly as if it was your own idea. She'll be a rover, we'll keep her busy. She agrees," he adds. "She's been concerned about you for some time."

That's probably true. Susan's the cliché secretary in all the best senses. Thank God I was never drunk enough during office hours to make a pass at her.

"Who gets my office?" I've got the primo office, the corner with great views out of two sides.

I thought I'd catch them but they don't bite. I wonder if they rehearsed this.

"No one," Andy answers. "It's yours until we all come to a final decision."

"Good," I say. "I might want to use it from time to time . . . for personal business," I add with a defiant twist.

They glance at each other.

"Sure." Fred nods approbation. "Just don't camp out okay?" He winks; it's a big joke, a chummy conspiracy, we're all in on it together. I just happen to be the butt.

Andy doesn't smile; he's taking it harder, I knew he would. He steps forward, offers his hand.

"Not too many hard feelings?"

"I don't know yet," I answer. "Probably."

His hand drops. "If it's any consolation this wasn't easy . . . for either of us."

"You're right. It's no consolation."

"If you need money I want to be the first one to hear from you," he offers. I know he's sincere.

Fuck them and their feelings. "If I do I sure as hell won't come to either of you."

We look bleakly at one another. By one of those foreordained coincidences we're standing on opposite sides of the conference table: the two of them solid on their side, me fighting to hold it together on mine.

"I'll clear my personal things out of the office by the end of the week."

"No hurry," Fred says, magnanimous now; I didn't throw an embarrassing tantrum. Civilization as we know it has been preserved. "Susan'll take your messages."

"I guess that's about it, then," I tell them. "I'll spend the rest of the week clearing my calendar."

"Keep in touch, Will," Andy says. Without realizing it he's already regarding me in the past tense. Fred's preoccupied with the view outside.

There's nothing more to say; they leave the room. I slump into a chair. My head's really killing me now and I can't rationalize that it's a hangover anymore.

The bikers should be high, stoned, blown away. They've been doing tequila shooters since they came in three hours ago. Before that, before they rode down from Taos, they'd had a taste of crack, some Maui Wowwee mixed with hash, bootleg quaaludes somebody'd stashed years ago and brought out to impress them (and keep them on the good side), as well as a handful of designer drugs rumored to be 3,000 times the potency of morphine, stolen from a local anesthesiologist. Any normal human being would be wasted beyond oblivion; these four are still on their feet, sliding through the scene.

The patrons in this low-rent bar are your basic kickers, lean mean bastards, but even the toughest of them gives the bikers a wide berth, 'cause everyone knows these dudes are crazy, Jack. So it's a couple hours of drinking and eyeballing and listening to the house band recycle Bob Seger and Willie Nelson before it mellows out, before some of the boys mosey over and starting talking bikes (which means Harleys of course, none of this rice-burner shit), panheads and knuckles and suicide shifters and if you never rode an old Indian, man, you don't know what it is to get your kidneys scrambled permanent, and then some of the ladies start hovering (all the world knows ladies love outlaws), rubbing their nipples through the tank-tops up against those outrageous tattoos, playful grab-assing, shit these guys're just good ol' boys, fucking aye, straight society can't handle the truth they lay on the world so they've got to cut them down, categorize them, call them outlaws. Anyway so what if they are outlaws, that's the American way, who would you rather fuck darlin' (this is Lone Wolf, the leader of the bikers, talking), Jesse James or Dan Quayle? Short-dicked little faggot.

It's getting late now, playing out the night. The girls are going home with their husbands and boy-friends, "No shit, darlin'," this 38-D cup is overheard telling one of the outlaws, "I wish like hell I could ride out of here with you right now but tomorrow you're a memory and he's nasty-jealous." It's fun to shuck and jive with friends around for protection but taking off with these dudes? They've heard the stories about how bikers initiate mamas, real horror shows, they don't need this ticket to ride.

Last call, triple shooters of Commemorativa, lots of money floating around, money's never the problem, what we're talking is pussy and the lack of it.

"Anybody need a ride?" Lone Wolf asks. Almost plaintive, soft, no threat.

"Me. I do." From the back of the room, behind the pool table where the light drops off.

"What's your name?"

"Rita. Gomez."

"Step out here where I can see you, girl," Lone Wolf asks. By nature it's a command performance. She walks into the center of the room, where the light's better. Some of the other women instinctively back off; this girl is too dumb and too drunk.

The bikers check her out. About twenty-one, twenty-two, dark, not bad once you get past the pockmarks, good firm little tits through her T-shirt, nice tight ass.

"Where you going?" Her voice is deeper, huskier than it ought to be, askew with the rest of the package.

"Any place your little heart desires."

"Old Adobe Motel. On the East Side?"

"You visiting?"

She shakes her head. She's drunk; she stumbles, catches herself. "I'm not drunk."

"Didn't say you were."

"I work there. They give me a room. It's got a kitchenette and all." She takes a deep breath. "I need fresh air."

They kick over their motorcycles, eardrum-splitting exhaust blasting the stillness. After two in the morning and it's still blisteringly hot. She climbs on behind Lone Wolf, wrapping her arms around him, laying her head against his colors. He can feel her nipples through the denim; he hasn't been laid in three days, it's an instant hard-on, this is going to be all right.

The motel's on the right, a block ahead past the light. $24 a night. Adult cable. The neon sputters.

"That's it!" she yells into his hair over the blast coming from the wind, pointing. "Pull in behind the back, the manager don't like bikers, especially ones like you. I got two quarts of Lone Star stashed in the refrig."

They roar through the intersection against the red, not even slowing as the motel flashes by.

"Hey where you going? You just passed it."

"No shit."

She turns, looking back. The motel recedes behind her, its sputtering neon blending with the halogens spread out along the highway. For a moment she feels fingers of fear, making her want to pee; then they're gone, swallowed up in the pool of whiskey that's still sloshing around in her belly.

By the bikers' standards it's a short train; there are only the four of them, and they only fuck her twice apiece. Lone Wolf does her first, of course. He's the leader, he gets the prime cut, the good loving: french-kissing and full-in deep-throating. She doesn't know what's coming, that's how drunk she is, by the time she figures out it wasn't what she wanted it's way too late, she's along for the ride, floating above it all. Drunk or sober she knows the way you survive this is to let it happen and pretend it isn't. They have a knife out for show, a mean pig-sticker, but they don't have to even threaten to use it, except to pick their fingernails. She's a good girl: compliant and tight where it counts.

They're up in the Sangre de Cristo Mountains, almost to the top. Down below, the lights of Santa Fe shimmer in the heat. The bikers drop some uppers, red hearts, 30-milligram h-bombs. They can't sleep, they've got a day's ride yet ahead of them, they've got to stay alert.

"Come here, girl." Lone Wolf pulls Rita to him, his back against a boulder, looking down at the lights. She sulks at first, but she knows not to piss him off too bad so she comes over and cuddles, her back in his chest. Her pussy hurts like hell, she's going to walk like a cowgirl for a week.

He fires up a joint. They pass it back and forth.

"That was nice. You're a good lady. I could get to like you."

"Me too." She'll say whatever he wants to hear. She's frightened, exhausted, hurting. She's been getting over a yeast infection and didn't have enough lubrication; they tore her up good.

"Maybe I could check you out next time I'm coming through. Just me you know?"

"Yeh that would be cool. I'd like that. By yourself I mean." Tell him what he wants to hear.

"Yeh that's what I mean." He takes her chin in his hand, turns her face to his. "Nothing happened tonight. Did it?"

The obvious answer dies in her throat. "No," she replies. "Nothing." You didn't fuck me, she says to herself, your friends didn't fuck me, my pussy doesn't feel like you blew up a cherry bomb in it. "You just dropped me off at my motel and I never saw you again."

"Yeh." His voice is soft, barely a whisper. "That's how I remember it, too."

He stands, pulls her to her feet. They all mount up, ride back into town. Rita clings to Lone Wolf's back. They drop her at her motel, fuck her one more time apiece. She's beyond resisting; she lies there and takes it.

It all becomes a blur; she remembers a banging on the wall, somebody shouting 'Shut the fuck up in there,' a guy she had gone out with was staying in that room, he had met some other guy earlier on at the Dew Drop who had claimed to be a dope dealer or something, one of the bikers had shouted back 'fuck you.' Finally, she passes out. She doesn't know how much time has passed when, moaning in a bad-dream half-sleep, she finally hears their choppers roar off.

She wakes with a start, her armpits soaking. Outside it's full sun, a cloudless sky, so hot already the tarantulas are looking for shade. She walks through the dingy courtyard. She's going to have to hose this down, it's filthy, shit there's condoms and everything. Right now though all she wants is to go back inside and lie down. God, her pussy aches.

Her friend Ellen, the other maid, is coming on shift. "Where you been?" Ellen asks.

"Don't ask."

"You look like shit." She squints against the sun. "What happened to your eye? Damn girl, the left side of your face's all stove in. Your eye's practically swoll' shut."

"I'm okay." Weary, so goddam tired. Got to be evasive, though. They find out she ran her mouth they'll come back and retaliate. "I was out with some guys. We went up in the mountains." She runs her tongue around in her mouth that feels like it's packed in cotton, licks her dry lips. "Too much booze. I got to cut that shit out."

"Tell me about it."

They go into Rita's room. She pops a tall boy, takes a swig to get the dryness out of her mouth, strips to her panties.

"Jesus Christ Rita!"

The front of her panties is stained with blood. She turns away, scared. She doesn't want Ellen to know.

"Must be my period."

"Your period bullshit. Nobody bleeds like that. You look like somebody knifed you or something."

She comes closer, trying to get a better look. Rita spins away, pulls on a terry-cloth robe she copped from the Ramada from when she used to work there before they caught her stealing and canned her ass.

"Let me get a look at that."

Rita's too tired to argue. She stands passively while Ellen gently opens the robe and pulls down the soaked panties. They lie in a forlorn heap on the floor.

"Damn!"

"I'm all right. It looks worse than it is."

"You got to go to a hospital."

Rita jerks away, tightening the robe against her clammy body. God, she feels like shit. She's got to get to sleep right now.

"No fucking way."

Ellen backs off, looking at Rita suspiciously. "Are you in some kind of trouble?"

Rita sits on the bed, taking a long pull from the Lone Star. "No big deal. I fucked a guy with a big dick."

"Must've been Johnny Holmes from the looks of you. Seriously Rita you should get looked at."

Rita shakes her head. "I been up all night, I got to conk out. If I'm still bleeding when I wake up, then I'll go. Grab me a couple towels, would you?"

Ellen goes into the bathroom, comes out with two thin towels, the motel limit. Rita bunches them up, folds her legs around them. She lies down on her side, her face to the wall. "Cover for me a couple hours huh?"

"Sure. I'll look in on you."

"Thanks." Rita smiles at her, rolls over into a ball. She pulls the covers up over her; it's hot out, even this early, it's going to be brutal, but she feels a chill coming on. She shivers involuntarily, feeling the wetness oozing out of her. Fuck the bikers, fuck Lone Wolf, she ain't going to be here when they come back, no way José.

At least she can't be pregnant.

Ellen takes a long pull from the Lone Star tall boy, sets it on top of the TV. As she closes the door behind her she sees Rita lying on the bed, already asleep, curled up into a tight ball like one of the homeless dogs you see down by the plaza.

PATRICIA OPENS THE DOOR. She must've just come back from running; she's still wearing a sweat-stained Santa Fe High School T-shirt, red with a blue devil on the front, Cornell-red sweat-pants with a white stripe on the leg, and off-white Nike running shoes with a red crescent on the sides, the kind with a see-through window in the heel that shows air bubbles. She's a healthy woman, she runs four miles a day, works up a good sweat. Her breasts, underarms, thighs are soaked through her gear, there's light ribbons of moisture on her upper lip and forehead under her sweatband. It's appealing; she's always had a good, athletic figure. We probably shouldn't have gotten divorced. But we did, it was so long ago that it's all amorphous now, shadow memory.

"Claudia's at Paulette's," she informs me. "They're making marionettes. It'll be a few minutes yet. Come on in."

It's the same house we bought the year we got married; she could do better, but she stays, she likes the neighbors, it's the best elementary school district in town, close to her office and Claudia's after-school care.

She tosses me the sports section. "Do you want coffee? I brewed some fresh."

"Since when are you drinking coffee?" I ask. She's a health nut from way back.

"I'm not. I thought you'd like some."

"Sure. Thanks." I flop unceremoniously on the sofa, start leafing through the sports pages, looking for the baseball scores. It's a nice little domestic scene being played out here, wife (okay, an ex) fixing hubby a fresh cup of coffee, daughter playing next door with her friend, the paper crisp and unwrinkled, the grass in the front yard is green and freshly mowed, the sky is blue with no prospects of rain; something's weird here, I've been picking Claudia up Saturday mornings for eight years now and Patricia's never offered me a cup of coffee, not once.

She places a coaster under the cup, sets it on the coffee-table in front of me.

"We've got to talk." She sits next to me, but not close enough that we might accidentally touch. Hands folded between her knees, hunched slightly forward. Her shoulders are tense; I don't know what it is, but it won't be good. Then it hits me: she's heard the truth behind my fake leave of absence from the firm, she's worried about Claudia's child support, the braces. Maybe, I indulge myself, she's worried about me.

"Okay," I say calmly, "shoot." I take a casual sip; my body language is going to be cool, I'm a master of my emotions.

"I heard about your leave of absence," she says.

I nod.

"I think it's terrific. I wish to God I could."

I shrug. "I'm not sure it'll pan out." I've got to be very careful here.

"If it doesn't you can always go back ahead of schedule," she says. "At least you've got something worth going back to," she adds bitterly. "Your own practice."

She hates her job. She's an assistant District Attorney in the appeals division. Technical stuff; she's never argued in front of a jury. She's very good, they'd be lost without her: John Robertson, the D.A., her boss (who I drink with occasionally, even though we're always on opposite sides of a case, him being the District Attorney and me a defense lawyer) tells me so all the time. She's hated the job for years.

"I hate my job."

"You're great at it. Everyone says so."

"Oh Robertson, that putz," she exclaims with considerable irritation. "He'd praise an orangutan if it could take dictation and work overtime three days a week."

"No, really." Is that what this is all about? Some stroking? "Everyone knows you run the appeals division. Rodriguez is only a figurehead."

"Great," she rejoins. "That's why he makes forty-seven-five and I'm stuck on thirty-five."

"He's due for retirement in a couple years," I mollify her. "You're a lock."

"I don't want to wait a couple years," she says. "Will . . ." she massages her temples with her knuckles, hard enough to redden them, "I am almost forty years old."

"You look great."

"Thank you"; resentfully. She presses on. "I'm stuck in a dead-end job that I hate, I'm living in a house that I hate but I can't afford to buy a new one, and . . ." here she takes a deep breath . . . "God, this is embarrassing . . ."

"What?" I'm alarmed; is she sick, has she caught some terrible disease, maybe something sexual? All these years I thought she stayed in the house because she loved it. It's what she's always told me.

"I haven't had a man . . ." again, a long pause. She's actually blushing, her neck is flushing. "I haven't been laid in over a year," she says to the ceiling.

The impulse is to offer my services, but that would be making light of it, not a clever move. I look at her; she's a great-looking woman, what's wrong with the men in this town? She can't even get an occasional mercy fuck? That's the problem; she couldn't do it that way.

"So the guys in this town are a bunch of blind assholes or gay. So what else is new?"

"That's the goddam point," she says vehemently, turning to me. "That's the whole goddam point; that and the fact that I'm going nowhere in my work. Zilch, zero, zip."

"It'll work out." It's a lame answer, but what else is there? I'm sorry she's feeling bad, but right now I've got my own problems to deal with.

"That's why I'm moving."

The cup freezes halfway to my lips. I manage to put it back on the coaster without spilling it on the rug.

"To Seattle." She's on her feet, checking her watch, suddenly fascinated with the time. "I'd better call Claudia. I don't want you to lose any of your week-end with her."

"Whoa Nelly." Now I'm on my feet, which are uncharacteristically shaky; my legs are turning to jelly. "What're you talking about?"

"I didn't know how to tell you." She pulls off her sweat-band, stretches it into a figure eight. All of a sudden my head is light, I feel a rush of air through the room. I stare at her, my brain frozen.

"Simple English'll do."

"All right." She inhales, gathering her forces. She's very competent; if our history wouldn't inevitably have gotten in the way I'd have brought her into the firm years ago; she and Andy'd make a great one-two behind-the-scenes punch. If they don't take me back she can have my place; save them some money on repainting the door, not to mention cards and stationery.

"For the past year I've been sending out my résumé," she says. "No big deal, everything on the q.t.; I was curious about my market value, I wanted to know if I had one." She hesitates.

"And?" I'm dreading where this is going.

"There are people out there who think I'm kind of special," she tells me proudly. I swear her breasts rise under her T-shirt.

"I think you're kind of special," I banter, trying out a grin; it feels lame.

She stares at me strangely. "That's funny," she says, "I've never felt that. Not professionally."

"It never came up." I don't like where this is going, I want to get it back on track. "So where does Seattle fit in?"

"Four firms seemed interested, enough so that they wanted to interview me. Two were back East; I don't want to go back there. One was in Tucson, the other was Seattle. So . . . last month I went to Tucson and Seattle."

"I thought you went to your parents in Minneapolis last month." I'd had Claudia for the entire week.

"I didn't want anybody to know."

"You didn't want to panic Robertson," I say. "Or piss him off," I add more accurately.

"In case I didn't get them," she nods, answering honestly. She breaks into a grin. "They both wanted me."

"So how come Seattle?" My mind is racing but it isn't going anywhere, it's stuck in sand. All I can think is if she moves my daughter moves, if my daughter moves I don't see her, every day if I want to, at least two or three times a week. Right now, this very moment, I am suddenly consumed with fear.

"It's beautiful," she says, "I've been living in the desert for twenty years, I want to smell the ocean. And it's filled with eligible men—nice, charming men. I had dates both nights I was there," she adds, almost gaily.

"So how come you didn't get laid?" I ask sourly. I can't believe I'm hearing this.

"I'm not a first-date lay," she says. "You know that."

"That was a long time ago." I remember it vividly.

"Some things don't change," she says, almost primly. She changes the subject. "And the money's terrific. I'm starting at seventy-two five."

I whistle; that's good money, Seattle's a major market but it's not like New York or L.A. Until I caught fire a few years ago I wasn't doing that well.

"Have you ever been to Seattle?" she asks. "Of course you have," she catches herself, "one of the seniors mentioned he knows you, you handled a case together."

"Joby Breckenridge," I answer hollowly. He's the only lawyer I know in Seattle. "Breckenridge and Hastings. Heavy-duty firm. They must have forty, fifty lawyers by now."

"I'll be number fifty-four," she confirms.

"You'll get lost." This can't be happening.

"Of course I won't." She's smiling, widely, one could almost say deliriously. "There's only four people in my section . . ." here she pauses for the coup de grace . . . "I'll be in charge. In two years I'll be a partner."

"So when does the blessed event take place?" My head is ringing. "When does Seattle's gain become Santa Fe's loss?"

"It's going to take a while," she says. "I promised Robertson I wouldn't leave him high and dry. As much as six months, maybe. I could make the move over Christmas vacation. Probably then."

"Breckenridge isn't champing at the bit?" I'm dying inside, how can she do this to me? It's a conspiracy, it's got to be, the world has collectively decided to screw me.

"They'd like me to start tomorrow," she replies with a touch of acid, annoyed at my sarcasm. "But they understand."

"How very white of them."

"Don't piss on it, okay? I've got to do this, Will, try to understand."

"Does Claudia know?"

She takes too long to answer.

"Yes."

"What does she think?"

"She doesn't like it. That's to be expected," she hurries on, "all her friends are here, it's all she's ever known. She'll adjust; ten-year-old kids are resilient as hell, much more than grownups."

"What about me? About her and me?" I hear myself whining, fuck it, what she thinks of me right now is irrelevant.

"I know."

I stare at her.

"Look," she says, "do you think I want to separate the two of you? This is the hardest decision I've ever had to make in my life; but I had to do it. I'm dying here."

She's dying here. That's bullshit; okay, it's not perfect, but it's a life. And there are men, she's too damn picky. I'm the one who'll die here. I'll be one of those divorced daddies you see standing forlornly in airports on Christmases and holidays; not knowing what my child's life is, not helping make decisions about anything basic: not being with her.

"I have joint custody," I say feebly.

"She'll be with you whenever she can. I don't want anything to come between you two."

"Then don't move."

She shakes her head impatiently. "It's done, Will. Don't guilt-trip me. I don't deserve it." She picks up the phone, starts dialing. "I'm calling her. It's a beautiful day. You don't want to waste it. Mary?" she says into the phone. "Will's here. Send Claudia over. No, right now."

I walk to the door, open it. Across the street, a door opens at the same time; we're in congruence, even in something this mundane. My daughter runs across the street, hurls herself against me. I can't conceive of everyday life without her.

"Time to rock 'n' roll," she informs me. She's been watching too much MTV. "I'll get my backpack."

She runs into the house. I turn, watching her. Her mother is watching me. I go outside. It hasn't been my house for a long time.

WE SPEND THE AFTERNOON fishing, on my friend Lucas's ranch up in the mountains. Lucas is your prototypical sixties hippie who founded a commune with a bunch of other urban back-to-earthers who wanted to 'get back to the land.' (A phrase you never hear anymore.) Unlike many of the other northern New Mexico communes that started at this time and are still alive, these city-folk eventually tired of breaking their backs trying to farm a piece of land Clarence Birdseye couldn't have made a go of. Lucas hung in—he's a tenacious S.O.B.—and bit by bit bought up their shares for ten cents on the dollar. He tried working it the better part of a year on his own before he resigned himself to the inevitable and walked into the county Environmental Planning Commission office, where with the aid of his good friend and ally Agnes Rose, the Land Resources chairman who was elected on a no-growth ticket, primarily with the help of Lucas and other rabid environmentalists, he divided up the property into five-acre ranchettes, making sure to keep the best quarter of the two thousand acres for himself. The ranchettes were rocky, barren land with but one saving grace: each had a fantastic view of the valley and Santa Fe. Within eighteen months they'd all been sold (except for one, which Lucas generously deeded over to Agnes), at an average of $60,000 per lot, and Lucas was overnight a thirty-one-year-old man of wealth and leisure. He and Dorothy ("don't call me an ex-hippie I never was one to begin with"), his sexy, bitchy, funny, social-climbing wife, are among Santa Fe's major art patrons, each year holding a big bash at their ranch to raise money for the promotion of Santa Fe art.

I'm Lucas's lawyer; for that, besides my fees, which are considerable, I get unlimited hunting and fishing privileges. (He's one client I'm not going to give up easily; knowing him, a man as perverse as I am, he'll probably tell my erstwhile partners to shove it, and stick with me.) The stream that rushes through the top quarter of his property is teeming with starving cutthroat trout from April until November; among other bait I've caught them with is tin foil, gouda cheese with the wrapper still on, and a busted tap off a cowboy boot. Claudia and I've been fishing here for years; for her sixth birthday I bought her a beginner's fishing kit, and to my great surprise and joy she fell into it immediately. Now she has her own professional outfit and can land a lure on a twig that's moving in a swift downstream current. We fish with barbless hooks, she takes maybe three or four trophies a year: she's respectful of all living things, a characteristic I find exceptionally appealing.

"I don't want to move," she tells me. We've been working around to this for about an hour. She flicks her wrist like a pro, watches her line arc lazily towards the middle of the stream.

"I don't either. Want you to."

"What can we do?" She reels in slowly; it's too close to midday, all the fish are hiding out. "Why don't you make her your partner?" she asks.

Would that I could; anything to keep Claudia and me from losing each other. Even if things were hunky-dory that would be an iffy proposition; now that door's closed and locked.

"That's not why she wants to go," I say. I pop a brew, reminding myself that beer isn't drinking. "She wants a new life with people who don't know all her moves. Santa Fe can be a pretty small town."

"She's got the middle-aged crazies," Claudia says with certainty. "She's talking about getting a boob job."

I look at her: she's growing up way too fast for my taste. She looks back at me, unselfconscious.

"How do you know about all this?" I ask, uncertain as to whether I really want an answer.

"She told me," she answers blithely. "She showed me the booklet she got from the doctor. It's gross," she continues, on a roll now, dissecting it. "They cut this little slit in your armpit (here she raises her arm, shows me exactly where the incision goes) right here, you can hardly see it, then they stick this Baggie filled up with sterile salt water I don't know if they get it from the ocean or what in the hole and they push it up into the boobs . . ."

"Okay, okay." I don't need to hear any more of this. "I get the picture."

"I told her it's a stupid idea," Claudia says. "She'll wind up looking like that old movie star . . . what's her name?"

"Raquel Raley?" I venture.

"Yeh, her."

"What's so wrong with that?" I'm not particularly a Raquel Raley fan but you have to admit the lady is still built like a teenager's under-the-sheet fantasy. "I think your mother's great-looking," I add; seeing her this morning brought me up short, sweating through her T-shirt like that, it's a hell of a lot better than what's been coming my way these days; ". . . but if she thinks she needs to help herself out why should you or I say different?"

"The human body was not meant to be a receptacle for plastic," she tells me with obvious distaste.

"Well spoken," I say. "I'll have to remember that. May come in handy in a summation someday."

She grins; she loves being involved in my work. I tell her what I'm doing, discuss my clients (often hilariously; she shares my superiority complex, but on her it's always sweet, never bitter), ask her advice.

I look out over the water.

"She wants to get married," I tell Claudia. "She's lonely, she doesn't want to grow old alone. It scares her. You think about stuff like that when you get older." I pause; should I be burdening her with this?

She takes it in stride. "Mom's got me," she says, looking up at me with those clear blue eyes that knock me over every time she stares at me with any intensity at all. She's still a kid, practically a baby yet. I catch myself, pull it back into reality; no, she isn't. I want her to be, but like lots of other things I'd like to stop the clock on it's not going to happen.

"Someday you'll be gone. I mean you won't be living with me and her anymore," I add hastily.

"I already don't," she informs me.

We pack up our gear, walk back down the trail to my car. Across the gorge near the U.S. Forest Station, in the clear mountain air seemingly close but actually several miles off as the crow flies, a small crowd's gathered. We can see flashing lights from police cars.

"Somebody must've gone over the side," she observes. "Stupid tourists."

Four or five times a year someone, usually a native, not a tourist, will misjudge the speed up here and go off one of the curves. It can be a long drop to the bottom.

We stand and watch for a minute. Even with the pocket binoculars I carry for bird-watching it's too far away to see anything. I throw our stuff in the trunk. Claudia dangles her bare feet out the window as I drive back into town.

I fire up the Weber's, wait until the coals are white, carefully lay the inch-thick salmon steaks cross-grain on the grill. As I was unwrapping them on the kitchen counter I realized with no small touch of irony they must've been flown in from the Pacific Northwest. Claudia's watching TV, an old Marlin Perkins rerun about jackals and buzzards, something vaguely educational; Patricia and I have a pact about not letting her watch ordinary commercial television. One of our few remaining areas of agreement.

The phone rings.

"Don't answer it," Claudia calls from the other room. When the phone rings on a weekend it's either her mother or a client; in either case it's a call we don't need.

It keeps ringing; it's going to wait me out. I reluctantly pick it up on the sixth ring.

"I'm not home," I tell it with as much annoyance as I can muster.

"I already know that, Will," John Robertson laughs, easily. I should've resisted the phone; talking to anyone who reminds me of Patricia, even if it is a semi-friend. (That in itself is weird, a D.A. and a defense lawyer getting along; he's never lied to me and he's never tried to railroad anyone; years ago I made the conscious decision to shelve my justifiable paranoia about prosecutors in his case, and made him the exception to the rule.)

John is *the* up-and-comer in the state, everyone's fair-haired boy, in spite of being one of those too-perfect people: All-WAC football player, a wife who looks like a *Vogue* model, kids with straight teeth. Sometime in the not-very-distant future he's going to run for governor or senator and it'll be a lay-down.

"I'm cooking dinner," I tell him. "For myself and my daughter. It's our weekend together. We value this quality time and prefer that it not be disturbed. My normal office hours are Monday through Friday, nine to six. Thank you. This is a recording."

I hang up. Naturally he calls me back immediately.

"I'm serious, John," I tell him with honest irritation. "I don't want to be bothered. What is it that it can't wait until Monday?"

"You're on a leave of absence," he informs me, as if I need being reminded. "You won't be in on Monday."

"How did you know?" Damn, word travels fast in this town.

"Fred told me yesterday."

"Where'd you see him?" I ask idly.

"He called me. Said Jane was taking your caseload. Wanted me to know personally."

That fuck.

"You okay?" he asks. He's trying to make conversation, but I can hear the concern over the phone.

I tighten up. "Sure. Why do you ask?"

"I always thought of you as a workaholic."

"I am," I say. "That's why I'm doing it. I've got to force myself to stop and smell the roses."

"Good man," he says. "That takes a lot of guts."

"Oh, it wasn't all that tough." I'm lying through my teeth. I'd better watch it; it's becoming second nature.

"How'd Andy and Fred take it? Must've shocked the shit out of them."

"Pretty good, all things considered. They'll survive."

"Let's hope not too well," John says. "Don't want 'em to think they can get along without you permanently. 'Cause they can't," he adds. "Without you they're just another gray-flannel firm."

"This is true." I'm glad he called after all. "So what's the deal? I really do have dinner cooking." Something clicks. "You're not downtown are you?"

"Regretfully so," he says.

"What's the emergency?"

"You've got some clients," he tells me. He doesn't sound like he's in the best of spirits.

"I'm on a leave of absence, remember? I just started twenty-four hours ago. They're not any of my regulars, are they?"

"Not exactly." I can feel the pause on the other end of the line.

"What does that mean? Exactly, if it's possible."

"Look, just come on down here, will you? It won't take all that long."

"I can't. I really am cooking dinner for Claudia."

"Bring her with you. I've got a new stack of comics."

"Dinner'll go bad. I'm cooking salmon steaks. From Seattle," I add masochistically.

He picks up on the joke, ass-backwards as it is. "I'm not happy about Patricia leaving if it's any consolation."

"It's not but thanks anyway."

"Take your time," he tells me. "Finish your dinner, have an extra cup of coffee, then come down here. It won't take long . . . but you're the man. You'll see why."

He hangs up before I can rebut him.

"Who was that?" Claudia calls.

"Your good friend and mine John Robertson."

"Are we going down to the jail?" she asks brightly. She loves going down there; they all fuss over her like she's the Queen Mother.

"Maybe after dinner. I'll see."

"I hope they've got some new comic books," she says. "I've read all the old ones a thousand times."

I go out on the patio. The sunset reminds me of a passage in *The Odyssey*. The salmon's beautiful, pink and moist, ready for turning. The day before yesterday it was swimming with all its heart up one of the raging rivers of the Northwest (fish don't have brains, they have to have heart), fighting for its life through explosively-roiling white-water rapids which the hairiest hot-dog rafter would chicken out from, just so it could spawn. Now it's sizzling on my barbecue. I hoist my beer, toast its hopeless, valiant effort. At least it died trying.

The bikers cruise leisurely, in ragged formation, Lone Wolf always at the point. Wherever they go they're given a wide berth, especially by other motorcycle riders who come blasting along on their high-tech high-performance state-of-the-art Japanese bikes, the ones you see ripping up the road at 110 miles an hour today and in the wrecking yard tomorrow. Fuck rice burners, fuck all foreign bikes: a real biker, and most definitely any outlaw biker, whatever colors he wears, rides a Harley. It's part of the unwritten law; you buy American and you ride American. No draft-dodging pussies here, either. Except for those who were turned down because of their criminal records, they were all in the service, Vietnam and other like shitholes, and you never heard of one of them turning tail.

They ride awhile, a couple hours, take a break. You know how you talk about a woman, Lone Wolf says, she's built for comfort, not speed? Well this ol' gal (meaning his bike, a custom '66 knucklehead) sure ain't built for speed . . . and she ain't too damn comfortable either. Laughter, patting of gas tanks, six hand-rubbed coats of lacquer, like you pat your old dog. Except for your colors, meaning the vest you wear with the insignia on it, and except for the other men who wear that same vest, the most important thing in your life is your bike; more important than your old lady, your kids, anything: it defines you, it and your colors are who you are. And who you are is a very scary motherfucker who inspires fear and envy in every man, woman, and child who lays eyes on you. You are a one-percenter, one of the chosen.

They stop for gas, then breakfast, reaching Albuquerque in the early afternoon. It's oppressively hot now, a dry wind that sucks the breath right out of you. They make their way to the Albuquerque chapter's large, heavily-guarded clubhouse. It's relaxing hanging out, swapping war stories and bullshitting with the local members, old, old buddies and comrades-in-arms. And of course there's a nice selection of women, a couple of them real beauties, all eager to party with the visitors.

The party goes nonstop for forty-eight hours. Everything is brought in: cocaine, amphetamines, grass, Mexican heroin, Chinese and Mexican food, ribs, chicken, beer, tequila, wine coolers for the women. People all over the place, coming in and out every hour of the day and night (club members and guests only, the security outside is ratcheted-up supertight, reinforced with Uzis from the club's arsenal), drinking, doing dope, fucking, sucking. They are into serious partying, one of the things they do best.

After about two days that gets old so they say their fond farewells and move on, heading south. They aren't hiding from anybody, they leave a trail a Cub Scout can follow. And they're clean; when they're on the road they're always clean because they're always getting hassled, it's one of every American cop's favorite pastimes, busting outlaw bikers; experience has taught them never leave anything to chance, nothing that will allow a local pig to make a name for himself.

So when the state Smokey stops them a half-hour short of the Texas line there's no cause for concern, except the basic one of who they are, and they can't do anything about that, not that they want to. One of them says something about the chick they'd reamed, maybe she'd talked, but Lone Wolf says no, she was a righteous bitch, besides she knew she was dead meat if she did. They aren't concerned about the cop, they're doing a law-abiding fifty-five, they pull over promptly, cut their engines, lower the kick-stands, take out their ID's in such a way that the cop has no problem seeing they aren't pulling iron on him. He approaches them warily nonetheless, his hand resting on the butt of his .44, the holster unsnapped: he's not going to wind up a statistic.

He asks them if they were in Santa Fe the other night. Lone Wolf answers that yes, they were. He then asks if they stayed at the Pink Flamingo Motel. Lone Wolf answers they hadn't, they'd camped out the one full night they were there, they'd left the following night. He even has a receipt for the campground, which he takes out of his wallet, unfolds, and courteously hands to the officer. The cop glances at it by rote; then he informs them, in cop-talk, that they are under arrest for suspicion of armed robbery of the Pink Flamingo Motel, that the owner had stated he was robbed at gunpoint by some men on motorcycles, that they fit the description.

It's bullshit. Lone Wolf states it as much; courteously, of course. The cop answers he doesn't know, he's just following instructions. They dutifully follow him to the highway patrol station back in Hobbs, where he reads them their *Miranda* rights, formally arrests them, and puts them in the van back to Santa Fe. As a consideration they're allowed to secure their motorcycles in the police garage.

CLAUDIA AND I meet Robertson in his office in the complex, across the street from the county jail. It's a nice place for a public official, built in the old adobe style. That's one thing I give Santa Fe credit for, they maintain the architectural integrity of the town. The new places aren't built the same way, of course—the days of making the bricks by hand on the site are long gone—but they look good, they fit in like a worn boot, you wouldn't know at a casual glance that they're not artifacts like the rest of the center of town. Of course, the old-timers grouse like hell about all the new building going on. They think time stopped around 1936. In some ways it's too bad it didn't.

"Where's the fire?" I ask, as Claudia and I walk in. She barges right over to his bookcase, where he keeps the comic books. She flips through a couple stacks, turns to him in annoyance.

"There's nothing new here," she says accusingly. She's going to make a great lawyer, she's hell on wheels on cross.

"Look in the top drawer of the breakfront," he tells her, pointing behind his desk. As she pulls open the drawer he turns to me. "Across the street."

She finds the books. "These are *good*," she says. "Where'd you get 'em? Some of them are really ancient."

"Glad you approve," he smiles as she digs in. "I bought a collection," he tells us. He collects old comic books, going back to after World War II. "I found some old guy up in Chama who's been saving them for when his kid comes home. His kid's fifty-six. I persuaded him the kid wouldn't miss them."

"So what's the deal?" I ask. I'm impatient; I value my time with Claudia, and the weight of Patricia's announcement is suddenly heavy on my feelings. I want to hoard every minute I can with her. "Which one of my clients fucked up this time?" I hate clients who screw up on weekends, why can't they fuck up during working hours like everyone else?

"Like I said on the phone—these aren't any of the old standbys," John informs me. "Brand-new, still in the wrapper."

"These? How many are there?"

"Four."

"How come . . . ?"

"They asked for you."

This isn't unusual. People get in trouble, they check around, find out who the main players are.

"One of them had your card," John adds. "You defended some of their colleagues last year," he finishes, seemingly reluctantly.

"Oh yeh? Who? I must've done okay by them."

"Yep," he says, turning stone-cold serious. "You walked them on a million-dollar dope charge."

"The Fresno Hell's Angels."

He nods, visibly turning up-tight; he hates being reminded of that case. I don't try to suppress my grin. The state had them dead to rights and I got them off scot-free. It served John right; I'd talked them into a plea-bargain and John had turned it down. It was one of his few bad defeats. Didn't affect our friendship, but a couple of those could derail his trip to the governor's chair a few blocks up the street.

"More Hell's Angels?" I ask.

"Worse."

"What could be worse . . . from your perspective?"

"You'll see. Let's walk across the street."

I look over at Claudia. She's hunkered down with the comics, she's fine for an hour.

"What'd they do?" I ask.

"Probably nothing," he replies sourly.

"Then how come you're down here your own self on a Saturday afternoon?" I twit him.

"When it's shitbags like these I have to show the colors," he answers. "Because if I'm not here that'll be the time one of the local TV hotshots will."

"The trials and tribulations of the career politician," I intone.

"They don't even need you and your ridiculous prices, they could cool their heels three or four days and walk it, but they want what passes for first-class representation in this state," he adds, throwing me a verbal elbow for personalizing the Hell's Angels defeat, "they want to post immediate bail."

"Everyone is entitled to an attorney," I state solemnly. I look at Claudia again. "Let's get it over with. I'll be back in a little while, honey. You okay here?"

She's engrossed in her comic, nods that it's fine. We walk across the street to the jail.

I'M LOOKING AT FOUR of the scariest guys I've ever seen in my life. I've defended other outlaw bikers, murderers, rapists, Colombian drug traffickers, mean, bad bastards of every size and description: few have chilled me as much on first meeting them as do these four now in front of me.

They're wearing faded denim jail jumpsuits, are cuffed. I'd been waiting about five minutes until they were brought down, enough time to skim their folders: the four of them cumulatively have pulled a life of hard time.

They sit on the opposite side of the table from me, four abreast, the same way they must line up when they're riding their motorcycles. I know who the leader is before any of them opens a mouth: it radiates from him. I address all of them; they're all my clients if I take them, and I will; but I talk to him.

"Before we get started formally," I tell them, "my fee is two hundred an hour, plus any personal expenses, plus outside expenses like investigators, plus whatever other expenses come up. No out-of-state checks."

The leader nods ever so slightly—he's been to this dance before.

"I'll want a thousand up front. If I don't use it all, I'll refund the difference."

Again, the slight nod. There's the faintest of smiles on one corner of his mouth, obviously his main expression. It expresses confidence, superiority, contempt, anger, all in one compact look.

"Payable now."

"Whatever you say. Just get us out . . . now." His voice is soft, almost breathy. Kind of like Marlon Brando's.

I slide a consent-to-pay form across the table. It authorizes the sheriff to give me their money, in a specified amount. He glances at it, scrawls his signature, slides it back. I tuck it in my shirt pocket. Now we get down to business.

"I read the complaint," I say, looking straight at them. "Did you do it? I'll defend you either way, but I'm kind of curious, know what I mean?"

He reads between the lines; he can lie if he has to—I'll still defend them. He doesn't have to lie. "No way." He says it with disgust; it's beneath them. "We've never been to this place, never saw it."

I glance at the charges, refreshing myself. "Such and such a date and time, etc. etc., okay, 'did enter said premises and take two hundred and fifty dollars at gunpoint from Mr. Said Mugamb, the owner and proprietor of said establishment,' etc. etc." I close the folder. "You didn't lay a gun upside this man's tonsils and take his money?"

"Fuck no. That ain't our style."

"The gun or the money?"

"Both. Particularly the chump change."

He's telling the truth. The last thing these guys want or need is exposure. And if they're going to pull something, it'll be for a lot more than two-fifty.

"For what it's worth, I believe you," I tell them. "And between us I think the law does too." Robertson and I had discussed it on our walk across the quad; he has no love for these guys, he'd be thrilled to find something that would let him prosecute. It would get four undesirables off the street, and be a publicity boon to him in the bargain. But he knows the outlaw biker style too, and the evidence is flimsy. Just the assailed party, who'd picked them out of a thrown-together lineup, before Robertson was able to get me on the phone. I could bitch about a technical violation but there was no point; they'd agreed to it and anyway it wouldn't hold up in court, not without anything to back it up. Robertson's a prosecutor, he's always been on that side of the aisle, from his first job smack out of law school, he's thoroughly indoctrinated with the police mentality; but he's too principled a man to railroad anyone, not even scum like these. He'll let them cool their heels a few days, but unless he gets something corroborating—which we both know won't happen—he'll shine it on.

"So what's the deal? When can we get out?" He looks at me levelly; he wants an answer, the right one.

"In about an hour," I tell him. "They're going to want bail, because of your priors. Can you make it?"

"How much?" he asks.

"I can probably get a group rate. Cost you a grand apiece."

He nods.

"You'll have to stick around until the preliminary. If you're caught leaving the county all bets are off."

"That's Monday?"

I shake my head. "Things don't move that swift around here." They're from urban jungles, they're used to a quick in and out. "I'll try to jam on it, get it on the docket by Friday."

They groan collectively. "We've got plans," the leader says.

"I know," I tell him. "You plan to enjoy a week in Santa Fe and keep your noses clean." I stand. "You'll be out in an hour. Here's my service," I add, writing it on a slip of paper, "call me after you're out and let me know where you're staying. It's cool," I reassure them, "by lunchtime Friday you're on the road."

The jailer swings open the metal door. I take a parting look at them through the glass insert: they're staring right back at me. As I walk outside I'm thinking I'd hate to ever get on the wrong side of my new clients.

The corpse is transported down to Albuquerque in a county paramedic's ambulance. By state law all murders require an autopsy, and in cases like this one: bizarre, heinous, possibly cultish or at the least a retaliation, they're handled at the best facility in the state, which is the university medical school pathology lab, presided over by the state coroner, Dr. Milton Grade, an old man now but still a powerhouse, a past president of the American Association of Forensic Pathologists.

It's a mutilation. The autopsy team is hardened to killings, but this one's particularly gut-wrenching. It didn't help matters that the body lay out in full unremitting sun before it was found, so that it not only was decomposing more rapidly than usual, but had swelled to the point where another day of baking would've caused the whole sorry mess to explode, which in turn would have made an accurate estimate as to the time and method of death much harder, if not impossible. Fortunately that didn't happen; the body was iced in time, stabilized, and shipped.

Grade's the last one to arrive. He apologizes, why do these things inevitably happen on a weekend? His staff laughs politely, but it is true, they get a lot of Saturday and Sunday business, it has to do with New Mexican culture which in a perverse historical way honors Friday and Saturday night drunks and their close acquaintanceship with guns and knives. He hangs his street clothes in a locker and dresses for work. Now they all look alike—a team of butchers. The long white coats are washed after each autopsy but the laundry can't completely bleach out the faded bloodstains of previous dissections.

Grade works his way down from the head, speaking into a micro tape recorder, moving smoothly and professionally, calmly instructing the assistant pathologist and lab technicians to lift a limb or turn a body part when he needs to get a better look at something.

It takes twice as long as usual to get through this section of the autopsy. Grade gives the team a short break. He stands outside the room, leaning against the tile wall, having a cup of coffee from the vending machine with his assistant, Dr. Matsumota, a young resident from Columbus, Ohio. It's quiet down here in the basement, the low-hanging blue fluorescent lights accentuating the coldness and sterile eeriness that comes with cutting up dead bodies.

"This must've been what doing the Manson victims was like," Matsumota ventures. He's new enough at this that he still gets physically sick when he works on a particularly grisly one; back in the room he'd had to fight to keep from regurgitating the #3 combination plate he'd had for lunch (cheese enchilada, chile relleno, rice and beans).

"Worse," Grade replies. He pauses. "Think how it must've been for the victim," he adds.

"But he was dead . . ." The alternative is too morbid to contemplate.

Grade drains his coffee. "I think the gunshots came last."

"You mean he was alive . . . ?"

"For some of it. He would've gone into shock before whoever did it was finished."

Matsumota starts to gag.

"I've come across it in some recent literature, maybe at a seminar, I don't remember where exactly, doesn't matter," Grade continues. "Ritual killings perpetrated by roving gangs of homosexuals. You saw the poor bastard's ass," he says, not bothering to mask his disgust, "that was pure mutilation." He stares up at the ceiling. "I hope to hell he passed out fast. God help him if he didn't."

Matsumota's already gone, running for the men's room, his hand clutching his mouth.

They gut the chest cavity, working roughly now, cracking the bones that are in their way, blood splattering all over the white butcher coats, cutting out the organs, dropping them into heavy freezer baggies, weighing them, cataloguing them. It's tedious; it all has to be done right, accurately, there will be a trial and their conclusions will be presented as evidence. When it's over the technicians lift the remains, just a shell now, into a body bag, put it into a locker. They were able to get a couple decent fingerprints, which'll be sent to the FBI in Washington, and to the Pentagon. Hopefully someone will miss him and come identify the body so he'll get a decent burial, his name spoken, rather than an anonymous grave in a state-maintained dump site.

Grade showers and dresses, goes to his office in the medical complex. Tomorrow his secretary will type up the official report; right now he has to call the District Attorney. This one doesn't want to wait until tomorrow.

"YOU'D BETTER GET DOWN here right away."

"Now what?"

"The shit has hit the fan, Bubba," Robertson tells me. "I don't want to talk about it over the phone," he continues, "it's too important. Just get down here *muy pronto*." He's sweating, I can feel the moisture through the line. That in itself is unnerving; John Robertson never sweats.

"By the way," he adds, "do you know where your biker clients are? Right now?"

"No. They checked into the Sheraton. Give 'em a call if you're that anxious, although I doubt they're hanging around on a Sunday evening." I hesitate. "Does this have anything to do with them?" That was a dumb question, I think immediately.

"We'll talk about it in person." He hangs up.

I pop a brew, strip, head for the bathroom and a quick shower. I just got in from taking Claudia back to her mother's. We'd spent the day together, hiking, swimming, goofing off, she'd run me ragged. The phone was ringing as I walked in the door, it was my service telling me the District Attorney had personally been trying to reach me for the last two hours, that I was to call his office immediately, no matter how late I got the message.

I stand under the shower longer than I have to; whatever's awaiting me isn't good news, and the idea that my new clients are involved in something else, something more nefarious than an unprosecutable armed robbery charge, is discomforting. Lawyers, defense or prosecution, are human like anyone else. We can't like everyone, even if we're defending them. The good lawyer doesn't let it affect his performance, but at the same time there are cases you wish you weren't involved in. Experience and my gut are telling me this is going to be one of those situations. So I let the shower run longer than necessary, and wash my hair for the second time today. Robertson'll be looking good, well-dressed and freshly-clean, even if he's wearing jeans. And for one of the few times when I go to the jail when it isn't working hours, so will I.

Before leaving the house I call the Sheraton. Their line doesn't answer; them not being there shouldn't bother me, but it does.

"THEY FOUND A BODY up in the hills yesterday afternoon. Some kids were hiking up by the ranger's station; they found it."

"Yeh, I know," I say. "I saw it on the news last night." That was the commotion Claudia and I had seen when we were fishing. "Sounded pretty grim."

"Pretty grim. That's an interesting way of putting it."

I'm in Robertson's office again, just the two of us, although outside there's activity, considerably more than you normally see on a Sunday night. It's almost dark, out his window I can see the sun finally melting down behind the ragged horizon.

"I'll show you the pictures in a minute," he says. "If they don't give you a negative twist on your fellow man nothing ever will."

"What does this have to do with the bikers?"

"Maybe they did it." He looks at me straight-forwardly; it's a look that tells me the fun and games are over.

"What makes you think so?" My mind's already racing, if these guys have to go up on a murder charge it's a new ballgame and I'm not equipped to play. You need a support team behind you in a case like that, a lawyer who's just been kicked out of his firm can't do the job; not the way it has to be done when your clients have an image comparable to Adolf Eichmann's.

"Dr. Grade told me," Robertson says.

"Are you out of your mind?" I explode. "That's prejudicial and you know it. How did he even know these guys were in town? Jesus Christ, John, that's inadmissible, you won't even be able to get an indictment."

"Calm down, Will. Grade doesn't know they're in town; hell, he doesn't even know they're in the state."

"Then what in hell are you talking about?" He's playing head-games with me, I don't like it. Not when there's a murder charge lurking around.

"This." He picks up a file from the top of his desk. I recognize it: an autopsy report. "He told me this. I put the rest together myself," he says. He pauses a moment; "and so will you when you see what's in it."

"I'll judge that for myself," I say, reaching for it. He doesn't let me have it.

"After they're formally booked."

"When is that?"

"Any minute now," he says, glancing at his watch. "We picked them up a few minutes ago. They're on their way in."

"From where?"

"From wherever they were. Don't panic," he reassures me, "they weren't trying to skip. They were out somewhere normal." He drops the folder on his desk. "Let's talk man to man, Will. This is really hairy."

"Off the record?"

He nods.

"Okay," I say.

Now he hands me the folder. I look at the pictures. He was right; this is truly sickening. I was in Nam, a ballsy kid fresh out of high school, I saw front-line action; I know instantly I never saw anything this barbaric.

"Jesus H. Christ." I swallow. I need something to drink, even if it's only water.

"And these are black and white," John says, indicating the photos. "Think what it must've been like in living color, with the temperature sitting on a hundred degrees. Not to mention the odor. The cops who went out on it threw up."

I force myself to look at the pictures again. The images don't improve.

"I can't blame them," I say. "But why do you think my guys did it? If anything, it points to organized crime, the Mafia, organizations like that."

"Because of the cock," he says, having a hard time getting out the words.

"Exactly. It's a common wiseguy touch," I answer. Whoever had killed this guy had cut off his dick and stuck it in his mouth. "The Mafia have been known to do that to snitches; everyone knows that. And the Viet Cong," I suddenly remember—I never saw it personally, but it was common knowledge over there.

"Outlaw biker gangs have been known to do it, too," Robertson informs me.

An alarm goes off inside my head. "I didn't know that," I say cautiously.

"Neither did I," Robertson admits. "But Grade did. He volunteered the information without knowing we had these guys in hand," he adds. I can tell from the way John says it he's attaching real significance to it. Maybe he should; there's going to be an uproar when this goes public.

"What else did he volunteer?" I ask. I'm trying to get a handle on this but I can't tear my thoughts away from those pictures.

"That he wasn't killed by the gunshots," he tells me.

If he didn't have my undivided attention before, he does now.

"Then . . ."

"He was stabbed to death," Robertson confirms. "Forty-seven times. Or maybe he was emasculated first, then stabbed forty-seven times. Whichever it was, the shots to the head were last, an afterthought," he says, bitterly.

"Okay," I say slowly. My head's starting to clear; I want to make sure what I say is to the point, which is to protect my clients. "I grant you this is hideous, barbaric, and disgusting. I still don't see anything that ties my clients to it."

"They were in town at the time it happened," he says.

"Give me a break."

"And according to Dr. Milton Grade, one of this country's most eminent forensic pathologists . . ."

"I know Dr. Grade's bona fides as well as you do," I interrupt, impatiently.

". . . this kind of ritual murder has strong homosexual overtones . . ."

"One guy cuts off another guy's Johnson you could say there was sexual shenanigans involved, so what?" I say.

". . . which has become characteristic of certain outlaw biker gang killings," he finishes. "Grade's come across it in some journals," he adds.

I hear the first shoe dropping. Now I'll be on edge until I hear the second, if there is one.

"Fine," I tell him. "That still has nothing to do with this case. What else do you have? Anything that ties the victim to my clients?"

"Not yet," he says evenly.

"Then where's your case? Besides a general fear and loathing in the law enforcement community for these kind of people?"

"That's part of it. Everyone hates scum like these," Robertson says. "Including you. Even when you're representing them."

His phone rings. "This is Robertson." He listens a moment. "Fine." He hangs up. "Your clients are across the street." Meaning back in jail.

"Are they under arrest?"

"Let's say they're under suspicion."

"What for?"

"Aggravated murder and kidnapping."

We both know what's left unsaid: aggravated murder and kidnapping in this state carry the death penalty.

MY CLIENTS ARE OUTRAGED and they're not in the least bit trying to hide it. They haven't been processed yet; it's been less than thirty-six hours and they're sitting across the jailhouse table from me again, this time dressed in their colors, which makes them especially fearsome. Lone Wolf leans towards me, his heavily-muscled arms crossed on the table. They're covered with tattoos, elaborate snakes and hawks and hearts and daggers and blood and roses, all intertwined, a living populist art museum.

"What in the fuck is going on here?" That soft, whispery voice of Lone Wolf's is ghost-like, in stark contrast to the gut-level savageness he physically projects.

"What kind of bullshit lawyer are you, Alexander?" he continues. The threat is palpable, I can feel its pulse: you took our money, you told us you were going to solve the problem. Now we're back in here.

"You called me, ace, remember?" Fuck them, if they want another lawyer let them get one. I've got enough aggravation that I've got to take, the surplus I can do without.

He stares at me. They're not used to being called out.

"Don't get your bowels in an uproar," he says. That sly grin peers out from behind his three-day growth. "We know you're the best." He leans back, withdrawing the menace. "Just tell us what's going on."

"What've they told you?"

"They didn't tell us jackshit. They paraded in where we were eating, picked us up, told us if we didn't voluntarily come in for more questioning they'd revoke our bond. Didn't leave us much choice."

"Made a big goddam scene about it," a second one chimes in. His nom de guerre is Roach, he looks like Mick Jagger with a wine-colored birthmark the shape of Florida running up the right side of his neck to his eyebrow. "Scared the shit out of the civilians," he adds, grinning. He also sports a star sapphire filling on his left eyetooth.

"They didn't even let us finish our dinner," the third one, aka Dutchboy, says. He's huge, the baby of the group. Red hair in a bowl-cut and freckles: Huck Finn in your worst nightmare. "I'm still so hungry I could eat a virgin."

They laugh; I smile along despite myself. Maybe it's because I share their sentiments that they're getting screwed.

"There're your basic vending machines in the cellblock," I tell them. "They'll have to do 'till breakfast."

Their faces cloud. This isn't going to be easy, but easy's no longer an option.

"There was a murder in the mountains north of here a few days ago," I say. "They found the body yesterday." I pause; there's no reaction. That's good.

"They're holding you for it." No point in pussyfooting around.

They stare at me, almost a classic group double-take.

"No fucking way."

"You didn't do it."

"This is getting old, man."

"I had to ask. I told you that. I always have to ask."

"Okay. I hear you." Lone Wolf's calmer now, an act of will. "We didn't do it, we don't know anything about it. That is the truth, man,

I swear to God." He's staring at me; they're all staring at me, they don't blink.

I look back at them. Not with as much intensity; you have to be somewhat crazy to have that kind of intensity. These men have it in spades. I don't; I'm glad of that. I can feel the cherries, lemons, grapes, bells tumbling around in my head, the kind of internal slot-machine that plays inside a lawyer's consciousness that comes together and tells him whether his clients are bullshitting him or being straight. There's no immediate payoff this time. When they told me there was nothing to the armed robbery charge I believed them flat-out, but I'm not totally convinced about this one, there's something nagging. I'm inclined to believe them, the absolute lack of recognition when I first brought it up can't be faked, ninety-nine out of a hundred people would've revealed something; but they're one-percenters, they survive by walking the tightrope. Maybe, even probably, they didn't do it; but it's the kind of barbaric act these men are certainly capable of.

But until they change their story, or a piece of evidence comes along that proves them liars, I'll take them at their word. I have Dr. Grade's report with me, I open it and follow it side-by-side as they recite their recollection of the events of the last few days, looking for discrepancies.

They'd been in town, they'd picked up some low-rent girl in a bar (willingly, they make sure I know that and believe it), okay so she was drunk but there was absolutely no coercion, there's a couple hundred witnesses out there to that (Dutchboy luckily kept a book of matches from the bar, it'll be the first thing I check out), they rode around a couple hours . . .

"Did you have intercourse with her?" I interrupt them.

"No, man, we sat around the campfire and read Rod McKuen. What do you think we are, faggots? 'Course we fucked her," Lone Wolf tells me, almost with contempt. "If we don't fuck 'em they ain't worth fucking."

"All of you?"

He looks around. "Anybody fake his orgasm?" They guffaw, a good belly laugh. "Yeh, man. We all fucked her."

"Some better'n others," Roach kicks in.

"You're on my list," Lone Wolf tells him, pointing a finger. I admire their composure; I don't think I could be telling jokes with a murder charge hanging over me, even if I absolutely didn't do it.

"You raped her."

This is taking a wrong turn; this girl, whoever she is, definitely won't be a witness for the defense. If I'm lucky she'll never turn up.

"No rape," Lone Wolf says emphatically. "She was hot to trot. Any of y'all hear any complaints?" he asks the others.

They all shake their heads.

"Hot for all of you? You're positive? Because if she was madly in love with three of you but didn't want the fourth," I continue, "that is rape. Uncontestable."

"She was more than willing," Lone Wolf insists. "She never once asked us to stop." He knows the jargon; he should, he's been hearing it most of his life.

I ruminate on it. It's a fine line; if an average citizen was on trial for that, he'd probably walk. There isn't a jury in this country that wouldn't convict these four.

We press on. They took the girl back to some motel in the low-rent section where she was staying (not far, I realize with chagrin, from where Patricia and Claudia live), then rode south to Albuquerque on New Mexico 14, the picturesque back road that goes through Madrid, an abandoned railroad and mining town that's now a hippie-artist tourist attraction. They'd stopped on the way for gasoline, got to Madrid around seven in the morning. I quiz them on this; how sure are they about the time? They're sure; they'd had to wait until seven-thirty to get breakfast, the only restaurant in town didn't open until then. The waitress, who was also the cook, would remember them; she was a real character, she hadn't been intimidated in the least, they'd traded insults all during the meal. They have a credit card receipt for the gasoline. Thank God for plastic, I think, pocketing the receipt: even society's outcasts use it.

They tell me about their sojourn in Albuquerque. I get them to pass over it quickly: the details are boring, repetitive, childish, they remind me of bad fraternity weekends with a lot of blood and guts thrown in. But the good thing about the yarn they're telling me, underneath all the junk, is that they were demonstrably with several hundred people, enough of whom can be compelled to testify on their behalf. In fact, virtually every minute of their time since they arrived in Santa Fe until their arrest down south is accounted for, and of greater importance, witnessed. The murder took time; the coroner's report is explicit about that. If what they're telling me is true, they were never alone long enough to have done it.

"They gonna set bail tomorrow morning?" Lone Wolf asks.

"And how much?" The fourth man, Goose, speaks for the first time. He's older than the others, probably past forty, his beard and pony-tailed hair more salt than pepper, a squat barrel who looks like a character in Disney's *Snow White*. "We ain't millionaires, you know."

"But we can cover the costs," Lone Wolf says quickly. He doesn't want me getting cold feet.

"You're going to have to cool your heels in here a few days," I inform them. "The prosecutor can hold you without a formal charge until he can get a judge to hear this on Monday, and after that he's going to press for confinement until he goes to the grand jury. So you won't skip."

"We didn't skip before," Roach reminds me.

"You weren't under suspicion of murder before," I inform him. "It won't be long," I say, trying to put the best face on it I can, "only a couple of days more than you were going to be in town anyway. You'll save money on room and meals."

They don't protest, they've been through this, they can do a week in hell if they have to.

"That should do it for now," I tell them, packing up. "I'll check in on you tomorrow."

I start to call the guard to let me out. Lone Wolf stops me.

"If worse comes to worse . . . if somehow we gotta go all the way to trial . . . how much freight do we have to pay?"

I was waiting for that. I'd hoped it wouldn't come up tonight.

"A murder case like this is normally going to cost fifty to seventy-five grand," I tell him. This isn't the time to pull punches. "Depending on what flows to the surface."

They blink, swallow hard. All except Lone Wolf, who doesn't flinch a muscle.

"Apiece," I add.

Now they react, even Lone Wolf. He tries to mask it.

"We can cover it," he doggedly assures me.

"Half up front."

"I said we can cover it." He only has one gear: forward, full-speed. The others eye us nervously, spectators in a high-stakes game.

Goose clears his throat.

"We got to talk about this," he declares.

"Let me say something first," I interject quickly.

They turn to me.

"I won't be charging my normal fee," I tell them. "I'll be giving you a special rate."

Lone Wolf stares at me.

"Why?"

"Because I believe in this case," I tell them. "Because you need me—you need the best."

Because *I* need *you,* is closer to the truth. I'm out of work, I can't afford to let this one slip away. Not only for the money, but for the notoriety, the publicity, as well. Not many cases this inflammatory come down the pike; I need the visibility as well as the hard cash.

"So how much?" Lone Wolf asks.

"I'm going to try to do the whole thing for a hundred-fifty grand," I say. "One-seventy-five tops. Anything less won't give you the defense you're going to need, if anyone tells you less they're lying."

Lone Wolf stares at me.

"We can cover that," he says. "If it won't go higher."

"We'll have to make sure it doesn't," I tell them.

They smile.

"We want the best," Goose says. "And that's you, man. And you'll have your money—that's a promise."

I'm sure I will. I don't want to know where it comes from, though. Manuel Noriega's lawyers don't want to know where their client's money comes from, and neither do I.

"Let's hope you don't have to spend much of it," I say. "Personally I think it's a long shot this gets past the grand jury."

"How long?"

I pick a figure out of the air. "Twenty to one."

That cheers them up.

"As long as you're our lawyer all the way," Lone Wolf says. "I've got a good feeling about you, man."

The other shoe drops. I know their records; they'd been bad boys and paid the price for it, but none of them have ever faced a murder charge.

"*If* they press charges," I tell them, "and *if* they can convince the grand jury to buy them, so you actually have to stand trial: I'm one of your lawyers. Or rather," I cover myself quickly before they can say anything, "I'm the lawyer for *one* of you."

"What do you mean? What the fuck do you mean?" Lone Wolf is standing, hovering over me.

"Sit down," I order. "Now, goddam it!"

He shoots me the evil look, but he sits. They're all confused, disturbed.

"Here's the drill," I explain. "I can't defend more than one of you on a murder charge. It's against the bar's code of ethics, for a good reason. It's conflict-of-interest."

"Fuck conflict-of-interest. You're the man around here. You're who we want. All of us."

I shake my head. "There're plenty of good criminal lawyers in this state," I tell them. "The public defender's office has a great criminal defense team. If it was me," I say, "that's who I'd call."

"We're not you," Lone Wolf says flatly.

"Anyway that's how it works," I tell them with finality. "Here or anywhere. And it's not like we're four ships passing in the night," I continue, "we're all in it together, we pool our strategies, our efforts. It's like having four lawyers for the price of . . ."

"Four." Lone Wolf finishes for me. He looks at the others, establishing primacy, then back to me. "If that's the way it goes that's the way it goes." He stares hard at me. "When do they get to meet the other three geniuses?"

I'm now officially his lawyer. I didn't figure it would go any other way. None of the others mouth a protest.

"Hopefully never," I say. "The grand jury can't return an indictment based on what you've told me."

"It's the truth."

"Fine. So no other representation will be necessary." I start to go, then casually turn back as if just struck by an idea.

"Just for the hell of it," I tell them, "I'll check around. Make sure the best people are available."

They're not Einsteins, but they catch the subterfuge.

"You just said we wouldn't need them."

"I know," I admit. "But I'm a lawyer; I'm trained to cover every possible contingency; it's Pavlovian, I can't help it." Are they buying it? I hope, looking at them. I don't think so.

"I'll see you in the morning." The jailer swings the door open. As I'm leaving Lone Wolf cracks a wiseguy grin.

"Not if we see you first."

The door bangs shut. We're joined at the hip now.

There's one bright spot in this: won't Fred and Andy be thrilled to see me bright and early tomorrow morning, I think gleefully as I walk across the quad in the dry evening heat.

I'VE BEEN BEHIND closed doors for two hours already, since seven. I called Susan last night, filled her in, told her to be early and to keep her mouth shut. She was nervous, but happy and combative. It's nice to know there are some things in life that aren't for sale.

They come in together, Tweedledee and Tweedledum. Fred was here first, Susan kept me informed over the intercom, but he waited for Andy. Andy and I may patch this up someday, but Fred's already a memory.

"Cleaning up some last minute business?" Fred asks benignly. They're at my desk, hovering like a Jewish mother with a bowl of nice hot chicken soup. Actually, Andy's the mother; Fred's the wart-faced spinster aunt.

I keep them waiting, the old head-in-the-paperwork shtick. Finally I look up with a distracted smile.

"New business," I say. "Don't worry," I quickly reassure them, "the world need not know I'm on the premises."

"It won't wash, Will," Andy says. He's pissed, trying to hold it in. "We talked this all out. Don't force us into doing something you'll regret."

"Like what?" I stand. I'm in the power spot, in my office behind my desk. "Come on, don't keep me in suspense."

"Jesus, Will," Fred whines, "do you have to be such a jerk?"

"Do I have to be such a jerk?" I turn my gaze to the ceiling. There's a waterspot from last year when the toilets backed up; got to get it fixed. "That's a very interesting question, Fred. Verrry interesting. Are we talking from the legal or philosophical viewpoint?"

"Will . . ." Andy's growling. I've known them forever, I know every button to push.

Now I turn and look at them, leaning forward on my antique piñon desk for emphasis. It's a couple hundred years old, belonged to one of the land-grant governors. I've turned down $12,500 for it.

"Let me explain the facts of life as I see them," I say. "You want me out of here. Fine. At this point *I* want me out of here. I'm sick and tired of your holier-than-thouness and your utter lack of compassion and continuity."

"Will . . ." Andy tries to stop me. I shake my head; I'm unstoppable this morning.

"Hear me out. Please." Damn, I think, savoring the thought, I'm a good arguer. No wonder I'm such a bitch in the courtroom.

"I am not a saint," I continue. "I am not even a wonderful person. But I am a man who has *always;* and I don't use that word lightly; has *always* backed his buddies. Like the time, Fred," I remind him, "when the Ethics Committee was up your shirt about the Indian Trust Fund."

"That was crap," Fred says hotly.

"Yeh, it was," I answer. "But you were sweating it. And who presented your case and made them look like jerks?"

"It wasn't the same situation, Will," Andy says. "Don't milk it."

"Fine," I answer. "Then I'll put it to you as dead-center as I can. I got a case over the weekend . . ."

"We know," he says. "Robertson told us."

"Then you know these people need the best criminal defense lawyer in the state *who is me* and that is who they are going to get! You don't want me associated with the firm, fine. Take my name off the door, I'll use the side entrance. I won't bother anyone in the office, I won't even talk to anyone except Susan, because she's mine, and by the way you'll have her letter of resignation on your desks by lunch."

I pause, an old summation trick; I've been going at breakneck speed, you have to let them get a breath and catch up.

"I am taking this case for as long as it goes," I continue on. "Hopefully a week, but if it drags on until Armageddon I will be on it, and

I will be operating out of *my* office. And if that doesn't suit you then file papers for dissolution of the partnership and we'll blow the whole fucking thing sky high!"

They're teetering. I'm watching it with glee. One strong breath and they'll topple over.

"My advice," I go on, "is to just let it slide. Let's not rock the boat okay? You want the world to think I'm still on my leave? Great. I'm only here because of the potential gravity of this case. When it's over I'll go back to my fishing."

They look at me. They're in a no-win situation: they give a shit, and I don't. And they know it.

"I think that's a good scenario," Andy says after a moment. "That's how this firm works. We don't abandon clients just because we have a problem."

"I agree," Fred chirps. "The firm has an obligation."

"Good." I smile at them in turn. "That's the party line. But between us and God the firm doesn't have jackshit to do with this. It's my case, I'll take the fees, and the glory if there is any. You can bask in my sun," I add. I'm gloating; I shouldn't, but I can't help it.

"Fine," Fred answers, tight-lipped. "I hope you make a lot of money off this one, Will. You might have to live off it a long time."

He turns and walks out. Andy and I are left.

"Too bad it couldn't've been him with the elbow problem," I offer.

He shrugs. "Too bad? Who's to say? But it's your problem, and from the looks of things I don't see you solving it." He pauses. "Quite the contrary."

"Maybe I will." And maybe I won't.

He looks at me. He doesn't have to say anything more. I've lost him; rather, we've lost each other. He leaves me alone. I don't want to be here right now. I tell Susan I'm leaving, and exit through the side door. Nobody sees me.

ROBERTSON UNCHARACTERISTICALLY KEEPS me waiting half an hour. When I finally get in to see him he isn't alone; Frank Moseby's with him at the opposite side of the room, leaning against the credenza. He smirks at me.

Frank Moseby is an asshole who wears a face. He's tall, stoop-shouldered, overweight, doughy, with chronic B.O. His shirts always tell you what he ate for lunch, and to top it off he's a racist. Most New Mexicans are fiercely proud of their Spanish cultural heritage, but down south, where Moseby comes from, it's still strictly redneck; land-grant families that've been important in the state for hundreds of years are cholos.

Despite what for most people would be lethal drawbacks, Frank's become the top gun in the prosecution division. Sure, it's partly attrition; most good criminal lawyers his age have moved into private practice, but he likes the action he gets in his job; and his personality would kill him in the real world. But there's more to it than that. He's a hard-shell Christian who believes with all his heart that most people are scumbags and criminals, and that it's his job, his duty, his holy obligation to put as many of them away as possible. He's a lay preacher in one of the local conservative churches, and he brings the fervor of the preacher into the courtroom. It's corny sometimes, it probably wouldn't play in New York or Los Angeles, but out here it's effective as hell, even in a supposedly sophisticated oasis like Santa Fe.

What makes it all perversely effective is that Moseby knows and cultivates it. He's reveled in being the lone redneck homeboy among a covey of slick modern lawyers for so long it's second nature now.

His presence here means two things: he's being assigned to this case, and Robertson's taking it seriously.

"My compliments to your tailor," I tell him.

He flips me the bird. If there's one thing about Frank I do like, it's that you know exactly where you stand with him.

"When are my clients going to be charged?" I ask Robertson, getting to the point of my visit. He's sitting behind his desk, leaning back in his chair like a slim blond Buddha, staring up at me through narrow-lidded eyes.

"When I've got something to charge them with," he answers calmly.

"And when will that be, pray tell?" I ask, wishing he wasn't being so cute. Bail can't be set until they're charged, and he can request denial of bail; with the new criminal justice code it's easier to do, especially in a capital case with defendants who have records and bad reputations: defendants like mine.

"Well," he says, leaning forward, "the statute says it has to be pretty soon. Unless I can talk the judge into extending," he adds.

Which means if he doesn't have enough hard evidence to take to the grand jury by then that's exactly what he's going to try to do.

"You're not playing by the rules, John," I say.

"Whose rules?" he asks.

"How about the state of New Mexico's?"

"Little early in the game to tell me I'm doing something wrong, isn't it, Will?"

"I just want to see how the land lies." I glance over at Moseby. He's still wearing his smirk, flashes it at me.

"Like this," Robertson answers. "I think these parasites are guilty, Will." He stands up, facing me. "I feel it in my gut, real strong. And I am going to do everything I can to find evidence that'll prove me right."

"My gut tells me the exact opposite," I say. Right now my gut is churning to beat the band.

"Fine. But let me warn you: I'm going to throw everything I can at this case. Frank here'll do his usual first-rate job, and I will personally be in that courtroom, especially when the time comes for summation. Goddam it, Will," he tells me with honest conviction, "they did it. And I know it. And nothing will turn me around until you prove to me they didn't."

"You mean they're guilty until proven innocent."

"They'll get a fair trial."

"And then you'll hang them."

"I hope so."

First Andy, now him. It's been a wonderful morning.

"And don't forget, Will," Robertson reminds me, "bail can be denied on a capital case. Usually is."

The bastard's reading my mind.

"Good luck," he throws in. "You'll need it . . . all the way through."

"And may the best man win," Moseby throws in.

What a schmuck. I can't help it; I break into a grin.

"In that case," I tell him, "it's a lay-down."

Frank Moseby is sitting in the bar of the Freeway Ramada Inn with Luis Sanchez and Jesse Gomez. Sanchez and Gomez are senior deputies with the county sheriff's office. They've been assigned to this case: Moseby asked for them specifically. They've both been cops for over twenty years, they hold no illusions about the nobility of the criminal justice system, in fact it's the opposite: laws are a nuisance to them, to be obeyed when it's convenient, skirted when it's necessary. This doesn't mean they're crooks; it means they understand the job.

They're off-duty, so they're drinking draft Michelobs and scarfing bar nuts. Moseby's beverage of choice is Diet Pepsi; his church forbids consumption of alcohol. Gomez chain-smokes Salems, a habit he picked up in the army. His eye is on the waitress, a full-figured woman he guesses is in her early forties. He likes them stacked, he likes the way she looks good in the uniform of the day: high heels, old-fashioned seamed black mesh stockings, mini-skirt, low-cut peasant blouse. In a little while he'll make an excuse that he's got to go to the john so he can find out what time she gets off. From where he's sitting she isn't wearing any rings.

"So you hooked a big one, eh?" Sanchez is saying. "A regular barracuda."

"A whole school of sharks," Moseby says.

"Now you gotta reel them in." Gomez brings his attention back to business.

Moseby nods. He chugs the last of his Pepsi, swirls an ice cube in his mouth, crunching it loudly. Spittle forms around the corners of his lips. He holds his empty glass high in the air. What a pig, Gomez thinks. The guy has absolutely no class at all. And some poor bitch has to lay this dork. He wonders idly what Moseby's wife must look like. Not like this waitress, that's for sure.

"Another round?" She's standing over them. He looks up at her. She's practically falling out of her blouse, goddam what a set. She's smiling, she likes him, he can tell. A lot of them like him, he's famous in the department.

"What do you think I've got my hand up for, to air out my armpit?" Moseby says. He's a solitary laugher at his own bad taste. She blinks; Gomez winces. He catches her eye, winks conspiratorially: you and I know he's an asshole. She smiles back. He drops his arm nonchalantly off the top of the booth so it accidentally brushes the side of her calf. She doesn't back off. His fingers trail the seam of her stocking. She bites her lip.

"I'll be right back with those drinks." She sashays away.

Moseby cracks the ice cube with his teeth. "That's your job," he says. "You two. I figure if anybody can find something we can pin on these lowlifes you can."

"You figured right," Sanchez says with ease. "If there's anything out there we'll find it."

Gomez lights a Salem, floats a smoke ring, which drifts up towards the fake wood-beamed ceiling. "What *do* you figure is out there?" he asks. "Why are you holding them?"

"Because Robertson wants to," Moseby answers honestly. "Because a truly awful crime was committed and they were in town."

Somebody's punched up "Third-rate Romance" on the jukebox.

"So it's political," Gomez rejoins sourly. He doesn't like that; it means the heat'll be turned up to find something on these bikers and fast, even if the evidence out there isn't choice. If in fact there is any evidence out there.

"Partly," Moseby admits. "Because there's nothing concrete that ties the victim and these bikers together so far. But the profile points to them, and the profile is usually pretty much on the money."

"The profile's a computer," Sanchez scoffs. "The profile ain't human."

"It helps," Moseby retorts. "But you're right, it's only a real smart machine. All it can do is point the way. Human beings have got to do the work. I've got faith in you two. If there's anything out there, you'll find it."

The waitress is at the table, setting down their glasses. Gomez lets his fingers walk her leg again out of view, just firm enough so she can feel it. She spills a little beer on the napkin as she puts his glass in front of him.

"Let me know if you need anything else," she tells the table, looking at him. She drifts back to the bar, glancing back. He returns her look long enough to let her know he's interested, then turns back to the table. Sanchez gives him the eye: he blows on his fingertips. Moseby's unconscious.

"You're right," Sanchez tells Moseby. "If there's anything out there to be found, we'll find it."

Moseby swallows half his Pepsi in one gulp. "Make sure you do," he says. "And make sure it's sooner than later."

MONDAY NIGHT, so I do what comes naturally: I go out drinking. The Dew Drop Inn, the bar the bikers sent me to, is the prototypical low-rent place the Chamber of Commerce keeps out of its brochures. You come here for two good reasons: to drink and to find somebody to take home for the night. Or if you're with a date or your old lady, you come here to drink and show off. Occasionally you come to fight; that works, too.

Normally I'd have a PI doing this work, but Al Collins, the firm's regular investigator, is on vacation, and anyway I can't afford him, not cutting my fee like I've done. It's like I'm starting all over again; not an entirely comforting thought.

I've always felt at home in joints like this. They're second nature to me, cousins to the bars I used to hang out in when I was a kid back in Kentucky. People who drink in places like this make their living mostly with their hands. They drink whiskey, out here a lot of it tequila, and beer. These days some of the women drink white wine, that's okay. And everyone smokes, if anyone's heard of the Surgeon General it's that he's the guy who's pushing rubbers.

That's the one thing everybody knows; AIDS awareness is universal, it's permeated everywhere. Men and women still go home with each other, but they talk some first, at least the women make sure the guys aren't gay, the guys ask about who the women have been sleeping with, meaning if you're a fag-hag thanks but no thanks.

Rita wasn't cautious. Several of the regulars vividly remember her going off with the bikers. I've been here an hour by now, nursing my beers slowly because I'm on duty, long enough to have struck up some easy conversations.

"She was drunker'n hell, ol' Rita." I've become friends with a bottle-blonde who looks like a semifinalist in a Dolly Parton look-alike contest. She's got a steady but it's my good fortune (or dumb luck) that he's pulling nights this month. My kind of woman at times such as these: a cheap date (house white wine) with a motor-mouth.

" 'Course being drunk's one of the few things Rita excels at," she adds cattily. "I don't know what it is she's trying to forget but she sure works hard at it."

"How much time had she spent with them before they all took off together?" I ask. I want to try to put this rape situation to rest.

"About ten seconds. She's not exactly known to be discriminating."

Well, shit I reckon. A girl who has a reputation as a loose drunk and goes off with four strangers whose intentions are obviously not pure is bad news; first because of what she represents to the straight community, and second because she was visibly impaired, a couple hundred people saw it, she was incapable of making an informed decision. I make a note to quiz my clients more forcefully about her condition at the moment of truth; I also have to hope I find someone who saw her sober near the time it all happened.

"Wasn't the first time, either," Dolly prattles on. "Or the second. Kind of trash that woman is makes us all look cheap," she says. "I mean it's okay to find an attraction with some decent guy," she continues, her Calvin Klein label is rubbing up against my 501 patch, it's getting crowded in here now but not that crowded that I'm about to give her the benefit of the doubt, "we're all only human, right? A friendly neighborhood place like this is just as legitimate as a church basement, right . . . ?"

"Right," I answer. How right you don't know, I think, remembering. I met Patricia in a bar much like this one; I was by myself and I turned and saw this stunner standing next to me and her beer glass was empty so I poured half of mine into hers and . . .

". . . after you get to know each other and find you share common interests," she finishes her thought.

She's read a book. I wonder what the title is. Men or Women Who Love or Hate Somebody or Something.

"I've always been fascinated by the law," she confides in me.

"Is that so?"

"Definitely. Ever since I was a kid and watched Perry Mason. I love 'L.A. Law,' that's the one night you won't catch me out. I read in *People* that more lawyers watch it than any other show. Did you read that?"

"I must've missed it." I'm on a seesaw, I was down and now I'm coming back up, lovely Rita went off with anyone who asked. And more than likely did what they asked, and willingly. Not a swinging strike; at best a loud foul.

"What time was that again?" I ask.

"What time was what?"

"When she and the motorcyclists went off." Come on, lady, don't go airhead on me. Not yet anyway.

"Are we still talking about that?" She tries on what means to be a pout.

I swallow the bottom of my glass in lieu of an answer. The bartender materializes out of nowhere. I nod; what the hell. She slides hers over automatically.

"Closing time," she says. "Two. Way past my bedtime," she adds. "Normally."

"Yeh, mine too," I say. That was the wrong thing to say, I know it as soon as I hear the words come out of my mouth.

She slips her hand in my arm. As far as she's concerned it's official. I'm a good-enough-looking guy, but I'm not going to flatter myself, it's the occupation *lawyer* she wants to go home with.

"I didn't bring my car," she tells me, nailing it down. "I came with a girl-friend."

"Aren't you afraid she'll tell your steady?" I've always had this inability to just say no, I don't know if it's fear of being thought unmanly or not wanting to hurt anyone's feelings. I catch myself: that's bullshit, if she was a pig I could and would say no. She's a good-looking woman with a certain obviousness and a very large chest. I'm turned on by women like her; it's my working-class upbringing.

"She hates his guts," she says. She's leaving nothing to chance: "It's way out of her way to take me home."

I finish my beer. By coincidence she's finishing her glass of wine.

"Can I give you a ride?" I ask.

"Thanks. I'd appreciate that."

We're all over each other in the parking lot.

"I'd rather not here if you don't mind," she says when we come up for air, grinding against me.

"I can wait," I say, grinding back. "Barely," I add, wanting to make sure her feelings aren't hurt. Besides, it's the truth. Partly.

"I'm not far," she reassures me.

"I'm glad to hear that. Otherwise . . ." I grab for one of her tits. I'm slightly high, right where it feels good. She twists away, giggling.

"Come on," she says. "What is this, a BMW?"

"Yep."

"Very classy." She's in the front seat. "Take a left, three blocks, then a right."

I pull out. It's late, there's almost no traffic. Without warning her head drops below the level of the window.

"You keep your eyes on the road," she admonishes. "I'm just going to have an aperitif."

Somehow I manage to keep the car on the right side of the double-yellow lines.

"You're not going to stay?" Her name, I've discovered, is Lori.

"I've got a busy day. If I stayed here all night . . . besides I'd hate to be here if your steady walked in unexpectedly."

She pauses; the idea doesn't go down too well with her either, since I've brought it up. But now I'm here and he isn't. "You're sweet," she tells me. "That was very nice."

"Very nice?" My feelings are hurt. "The earth moved for me."

"Extremely terrific. How's that?"

"Better."

She watches me as I dress.

"I didn't think I'd pull this off," she tells me with an honesty that belies her tough veneer. "I thought you were just pumping me back there at the bar."

"I was," I admit. "And I'm flattered you were so persevering." It's so easy when you don't have to lie.

She's looking at me in a warm sort of way and I'm looking at her the same way and it hits me. "That steady of yours. We're not talking in the present tense, are we?"

"No." Simple and direct.

"Then why the subterfuge?"

"The what?"

"Why did you tell me there was when there wasn't?"

She's embarrassed, but she comes clean. "I thought you'd find me more attractive," she says, "if you thought there was another guy in the picture."

I've never heard it put that way before, but it does make sense in a lefthanded kind of way.

"I wouldn't've cared," I answer honestly.

"You're the only one," she rejoins, unsuccessfully trying to keep the nervousness and bitterness out of her voice. "A woman in this town's washed up at thirty-five unless she's got the bucks."

An honest-to-God wave of sadness washes over me. For her, yes, and others like her; but more for Patricia: attractive woman, capable lawyer, mother of my child. Thirty-nine and with less then five thousand dollars in her savings account. How can I think about trying to stop her from leaving?

"Hey," she says, brightening, "I got a good time out of it. We both did."

"Absolutely."

"Maybe we'll even see each other again. At least I don't have AIDS," she throws in. Is that how people say 'I Love You' now?

"Maybe we will." No promises, no bullshit.

She accepts it, taking what she can get for now. "That was a bitch about that kid, wasn't it," she says, shifting gears. "The one who was murdered," she continues. "I mean that *is* why you were asking about Rita, isn't it?"

"Yes," I answer, noncommittally.

"Because she knew him, right?"

What the fuck?

"Right," I say, trying to recover. "Because she knew him." I hesitate a moment. "How well *did* she know him?" I ask, trying to sound casual.

"I don't think they were getting it on or anything," she says. "Not like on a steady diet. But it was pretty common knowledge he was staying at that motel she works at. She brought him around a couple times. I don't really know his story. He was probably just crashing there for a few days."

"GOOD NEWS, GUYS."

They sit up. It's five after seven in the morning, the earliest I could get in to see them.

"The chick you fucked?"

"Yeh?" Lone Wolf, as usual, speaks for the group.

"And the guy that was murdered?"

"Yeh?"

"They knew each other, asshole! He was living at that motel where she worked."

I'm on my feet. I don't know how I feel; livid, outraged. Betrayed.

"Want to tell me about it now?" I slam my fist so hard on the table they jump. "All I ask is the truth," I yell. "The simple, unvarnished truth. I'd defend you with the truth, even if you're flat-out guilty. But now I can't."

"We told you the truth." Lone Wolf stares up at me.

"My ass." I close their folder. "Call some other chump. I don't tolerate being lied to."

"We told you the truth," he repeats, staring hard at me. "We told you the fucking truth!"

We're both on our feet now, screaming at each other.

"You're a lying sack of shit!" I yell at him. "All of you!"

"It's the truth!" he yells back, equally enraged. "We don't know what the hell you're talking about."

I look at the others. They're pale, silent. I don't know if this is an admission of guilt, of being caught in the lie, or the shock of hearing what I just told them about the connection between Rita and the murdered man.

"You took her up to the hills," I say.

"That's right."

"Where the victim was found."

He stares at me. "We don't know anything about that."

"And then you brought her back to the motel," I press on. I'm racing. "And you fucked her again; with her consent, of course," I add, biting it off.

"Yes."

"And during all this time you never saw the victim. Richard Bartless."

"Is that his name?" Goose asks, almost timidly.

"*Was*," I correct him.

"We didn't do it." Roach speaks up. "We didn't. On a stack of Bibles that's the truth."

They're in county jumpsuits again. They look scared.

"It's too coincidental," I say, shaking my head; is it distrust or is there also panic in all this: my panic at trying what might turn out to be a hopeless case. "I just don't know how I can believe you."

They sag; even Lone Wolf.

"I've got work to do," I tell them. Christ, when Robertson finds out about this, which he will and soon, I'll be the laughingstock of the entire state. The idea of having to look at Andy and Fred is excruciating.

"What're you going to do?" Lone Wolf asks.

"I don't know." I look at them. The anger's subsiding, a slow, petering-out leak.

"You gonna quit us?"

"Give me a reason why I shouldn't."

"Because we didn't do it."

We stare at each other. The four of them, behind bars. Me, looking through them.

"I'll talk to you later. If I have anything to talk to you about." I scoop up my papers and leave them.

The truth is, I can't quit. If things were on an even keel at the firm, and if Patricia hadn't exploded her bomb in my face, and if I wasn't about to finalize with Holly (I was moronically generous; Fred, who was handling my side, told me I was crazy, but I just wanted it over, how was I supposed to know the bottom was going to drop out?), and if all the other things that've come up to conspire to destroy me weren't present, maybe I would. But these four are all I have now. Their case'll carry me financially (a shitty, unjustice-like thought, but there it is), and buy me time to figure things out. Deep down I know it'll never be the same with Andy and Fred. Even if I hadn't blown them out in my childish fit of self-righteousness and one-upmanship, the door had been shut as soon as they did what they did. I'm going to have to start fresh, not the worst thing in the world given my reputation as a trial lawyer, but scary all the same.

Besides, I don't like to abandon clients. I never have, even when I had every right to a couple of times, when their lies blew up in my face. I still believe that old bromide that every client deserves the best defense he can get, no matter how society views him. And I like this kind of case: I like clients like these, dangerous fringe players, who stand for so much we abhor, who scare us, make us want to run for cover. I run for cover as much as the next guy, so when I have the chance to stand on my hind legs and howl a little I go for it; it's liberating.

And maybe they are telling the truth. That's happened before, too.

MY CIRCLE IS DRAWING increasingly closer. Patricia's house, the bar, the bottle-blonde's place, now the motel where Rita Gomez works. I thought I'd escaped all this; if not twenty-odd years ago, when I left home without ever looking back, then certainly when the partnership came together.

Like everything else about my life these days, I was wrong.

I park along the side, out of sight of the office, locking the car with the alarm, something I rarely do. I don't want to deal with the management; they'll bullshit me and if they run true to form they'll can the girl for bringing trouble around. As I'm the bikers' lawyer, she's not going to cotton to me anyway; that's enough reason not to alienate her any more than she already has been.

It's an old-fashioned auto court, sixteen units, kitchen included. All in need of paint and sundry repairs. I smell the septic backup. Later in the day, when the sun's had a chance to bake it, it'll be inordinately fragrant. The place reminds me of summer vacation trips, when my father would pile us into his Hudson and we'd go to what's now called the Redneck Riviera, the north Florida, Alabama, Mississippi Gulf Coast. I hear it's chic now; then it was where you went if you were from that part of the country and had nowhere else to go but thought you had to get away and see water. It bought a vacation so similar to what was at home that except for the sand, which oozed tar-oil from the pumping platforms miles off, faint in the hazy distance, and the tepid, mosquito-ridden water, you couldn't tell the difference. After three of them we stopped going and bought a color television instead.

Inside an open door I see a young woman vacuuming. She senses my presence but chooses to ignore it.

"Hey," I call out. I can't play games with her, I've got to get this thing going.

She squints out at me. With the sun at my back I'm a dark shape to her. Even so, she knows I'm not a customer: I'm too well-dressed and I'm not with a woman.

"Yeh?" Her voice is whiny, belligerent, cautious.

"Can I talk to you?"

"What about?"

"If you shut that goddam machine down I'll tell you." Jesus Christ, do I have to eat shit from everybody?

She shuts it off; there's authority in my voice, she's not going to push it further.

"Thank you." Just enough tinge of sarcasm to let her know I know she's playing a game.

"What do you want?" she whines. "I got work to do, I'm behind already, I'm the only one on today, bastards left me short."

"I'm looking for Rita Gomez," I say.

She stares at me. I've scared her.

"Are you her?"

She shakes her head, fast. "Do I look like her?" she offers.

"I don't know," I tell her. "I've never met her."

"How come you're looking for her then?"

"I've got some questions to ask her," I say. At this rate we'll be here until sundown. "Just a few, it won't take long."

"You a cop?"

I pause. "No. Why?"

"Then what do you want her for?" she says, throwing it back at me.

"Because I have some questions and I think she might have some answers. Why would you think I'm the law?" I add, starting to grow more suspicious than I already am. "Don't regular people come to see her? Her friends?"

"You don't look like any friend of hers."

She isn't giving an inch. If she'd been casual and told me Rita wasn't around I probably would have turned and left. Now I have to press.

"Do you know where she is now?" I ask, trying a different tack.

"No."

"Doesn't she live here?"

"Yeh, she lives here. But she ain't here now."

"When do you expect her?"

She shrugs.

"When does she have to be at work?" I press.

"Right now. Why do you think I'm so far fucking behind?"

"So she's AWOL," I say.

"She's what?"

"Not here when she's supposed to be."

She smiles. She never had the benefit of three thousand dollars' worth of orthodontia.

"Yeh," she says.

Enough of this. I walk into the room, shut the door. She backs away from me. It's dark, the floor-length curtains are closed against the heat.

"You're not supposed to be in here," she tells me. "That door's supposed to be left open when I'm cleaning."

"For the last time. Where is she?" I ask, louder now. "Don't make me play bullshit games. I don't have the time and you're not worth it."

She's scared; she holds the vacuum hose like a weapon.

"I don't know. Honest. I don't know where they took her."

Bingo. On somebody else's card.

"Who? Who took her?"

"I don't know."

"What'd I just say?" I take a step closer.

"Some guys," she says quickly, almost stumbling as she moves away from me. "Two of them."

"When?"

"Last night. Around ten or eleven."

"Cops?" I ask.

"I don't know." She hesitates; I take a step closer. Now she's cornered. "Yeh. They didn't say; but they were, for sure."

This is why I'm in the position I'm in: last night while I was drinking and getting laid, pretending to be working hard and getting information, two cops did the job the way it's supposed to be done and got to Rita Gomez first.

"And you don't know where they all went?" I ask.

She shakes her head.

"I thought they were taking her to jail."

"Jail?" How far behind am I? I think. Maybe Fred and Andy are right, maybe I really am losing it.

"For questioning about Richard. You know," she says, her voice heavy with disgust, "the dumb shit who was sniffing around her and got his sorry ass killed."

What kind of man was he, I think, that this girl should be so contemptuous of him? That even to someone like her he should be such a loser?

The police go through Santa Fe like a whirlwind. Every bar, motel, homeless jungle, blood bank, temporary employment agency, street corner, the works, they move through the city in waves, Moseby coordinating it, Sanchez and Gomez are the lead-team but every available cop is requisitioned, thrown into the mix. If they can hang the bikers so much the better, it would make for a more politically spectacular trial and ensure attention, and ultimately, conviction: Moseby knows without Robertson's having to tell him that if they can put together enough evidence to go to the grand jury and come out with an indictment the rest will be a downhill slide. But the main thrust is to find the killer. So far there hasn't been undue publicity. Robertson makes sure the proper spin is put on it: internal gang-style warfare that got out of hand and resulted in unfortunate but predictable retribution. He keeps the more grisly details away from the public. The press has bought it for the present; once an arrest is formally made and pre-trial gets underway the manipulation will begin, until, by the time the trial starts, the accused will be seen as a social pariah, a mad dog fit only for slaughter. This scenario is common, it's always played out this way in this type of murder. No one, except the accused and his defense attorney, ever questions it. And their reasons, of course, although most of the time futile, are obvious and self-serving.

As it turns out, Sanchez and Gomez are the ones to hit the jackpot. They'd gone to the Dew Drop Inn but struck out; they were cops, they didn't hide it, nobody gave them the time of day. They left knowing the bikers had been there (almost meaningless, as the bikers were in dozens of places in the general time period) and took with them some girl who did or did not work in a motel, depending on who contradicted who. And that maybe the victim and the bikers had all been in the bar the night before, and maybe got into a beef about a bad dope deal, and maybe went outside and discussed it further; this was very much in dispute, it could just as easily have been somebody else who went out back with the victim, on a different night altogether. It was remembered that the victim's mouth made promises his fists couldn't deliver.

The ninth motel is the payoff. The girl is in terrible distress, she can't stop the hemorrhaging, she's tried home remedies because she was afraid to go to the hospital and have to make up a believable story about what happened. They dutch-uncle her, she could've died, didn't she realize that? She's too weak to resist, yes they're cops and of course they'd appreciate any help she could give them but their main concern right now is getting her taken care of.

At the hospital, where you absolutely can't fix the records, they fix them. (To guarantee, they tell her, that her assailants can't find out she went to the authorities.) So when she leaves with them several hours later, weak but professionally patched-up, carrying a plastic bag stuffed with antibiotics, she's never been there officially. And since she's never been there officially, no one's officially questioned her, gotten any information from her.

And then she disappears, and for five days nobody sees her.

ROBERTSON CALLS ME UP. "They'll be arraigned tomorrow morning."

"It's about time," I tell him, somewhat testy and not bothering to cover it. "This could've been done three days ago."

"Three days ago I didn't have a judge." The bastard's so damn calm; I can feel the chill over the line.

"What's the charge?" I ask. I know he doesn't have anything, the grand jury hasn't been convened.

"Accessory to murder."

"That's bullshit!" I explode. "You don't have a goddam thing do you? You're just hanging onto them so the papers don't cream you. Goddam it, John," I continue, lowering my voice and attitude, "this is wrong. You know it. This isn't like you. Why are you doing this?" I don't want to say 'to me,' but it's there, hanging in the space that's between us and growing wider.

"Don't take it so personally, Will," he admonishes. "You'll be happier and probably live longer."

"I'm not sure I want to live longer," I say. "Come on, John. If you don't have anything on them don't do this. It's beneath the dignity of your office, as well as your own personal code," I add, trying to guilt-trip him just a smidgen.

"Accessory to murder," he repeats, not taking the lure. "We have enough to book them on those charges as defined by the state. And we're going to do better than that," he adds with equanimity.

The only thing better than that is murder one, but when a prosecutor, especially one who's ostensibly a friend, quotes scripture, you roll with the punches. What bothers me more than anything is that John is by nature a cautious person. That's why he's on his side of the law. He rarely goes out on a limb; so his telling me as forthrightly as he's doing that he thinks he can bring murder one is unnerving. Maybe that's the intent: he knows I'm vulnerable right now, maybe he's setting the groundwork for a plea-bargain.

"Okay," I relent. "What's the tariff?"

"I'm recommending a million."

"What!" I scream.

"Cash bond. Apiece. I'm reasonably sure the judge'll see it that way. These are dangerous men, Will, we don't want them skipping on us."

I exhale. My clients have as much chance of posting a million-dollar cash bond, singularly or collectively, as I do of being the first astronaut to go to Saturn.

"Why do you have to be such a prick about this?" I ask when I've calmed down enough so I don't rage anymore over the phone.

"Because they killed a man," he answers. "And I want to make sure they stick around to pay the price."

"State your name for the members of the grand jury please."

"Rita Gomez."

"Your age."

"Twenty-two."

"And your occupation."

"I'm a maid at the Old Adobe Motel."

"In Santa Fe?"

"Yes sir."

"And where do you live?"

"At the motel. They been letting me use a unit, seeing's how they don't usually fill up this time of year."

"How long have you lived there?"

"About three months."

"And before that?"

"Las Cruces. That's where I'm from. Originally."

"In your own words, Miss Gomez, would you please tell the members of the grand jury what occurred on the night of July twenty-first of this year."

"Yes sir. I was out at this bar. The Dew Drop Inn. I went with Richard but he got ornery and had to leave."

"Richard Bartless? The murder victim?"

"Yes sir. He'd been staying at the motel a couple days so we got to know each other."

"Continue please."

"Anyway Richard was with this other guy who claimed to be a dope-dealer or something and Richard started giving these guys some shit and they called him out . . ."

"These guys? Are you referring to the four men commonly known as Lone Wolf, Roach, Goose, and Dutchboy?"

"Yes sir. Those four."

"Go on."

"So they were out in the parking lot and he saw he wasn't gonna do nothing but get his ass kicked for him so he ran off and left me there. So then everybody went back inside and hung around until it was time to close and the one they call Lone Wolf said does anybody need a ride home? And I said I did 'cause they'd scared Richard off he was my ride so Lone Wolf said he'd give me a ride home back to the motel so I went with them."

"Did they take you back to the motel?"

"No sir."

"Where did they take you?"

"They took me by the motel and I said this is it but they didn't stop they kept going. Up to the mountains, they didn't stop until we got up there about halfways so then they stopped."

"And then what happened?"

"They did me."

"They raped you."

"Yes sir."

"All of them raped you?"

"Yes sir. Two times each."

"Did you try to resist?"

"You think I'm crazy? Getting raped's bad but getting killed's worse."

"So you consented out of fear for your life."

"For sure."

"Go on."

"So then they took me back to the motel and we drank some beer then they started fucking me again . . ."

"Raping you . . ."

"Yes sir. So then Richard comes in, he must've been sleeping next door where his room was and heard them and me 'cause I was yelling for them to stop 'cause it was hurting me and he came in and told them to stop, couldn't they see they were hurting me, so they told him to go fuck himself and get out of there but he didn't leave."

"He wasn't scared of them?"

"Probably but he was trying to help me. He'd probably smoked some weed, he had some righteous weed he was trying to sell."

"Go on."

"So they didn't like the way he was ranking on them, like I was his girlfriend or something, I wasn't, I was just his friend, so he kept on ranking them and they started beating up on him. So then he pulled a knife out of his boot like one of them Green Berets and tried to come at them with it and that really pissed them off so they took it off him and starting really wailing on his ass, beating him up fearsome. He was really yelling, you could probably hear him clear across the highway. So they got nervous somebody would hear him and call the cops, so they got some of the clothesline out of the washroom where the laundry machines are and tied him up with it, real tight, they didn't need to tie him that tight, it was practically stopping the blood in his hands. So after they tied him up they threw him in his car and drove up to the mountains where they had been with me."

"You went with them?"

"They made me. They were afraid I'd call the cops. I would've too."

(She takes a drink of water.)

"Go on please."

"So then when we got up there it got real gnarly. I mean it was rank. First two of them fucked him in the ass . . ."

"They anally raped him?"

"From behind, yes sir."

"Do you remember which two?"

"Let's see . . . it wasn't Lone Wolf . . . it was the old one, Goose. And not the kid . . . Roach, he was the other one . . ."

"Please continue."

"Richard was screaming like crazy and they told him to shut the fuck up but he kept screaming so they said fuck this. So then they had this fire going, they held him down and they stuck his knife in the fire until it got hot, then they stabbed him with it a whole bunch of times. They'd heat it up every couple of times, maybe so's it would go in easier, I don't know. All I know is they kept stabbing him. So by the time they were done stabbing him he was dead, no question."

"What were you doing during this time, Miss Gomez?"

"Praying. That they wouldn't kill me. Especially not like they killed him. It was the most horrible thing I ever saw."

(She takes another drink, composes herself.)

"Continue whenever you can. Do you want to take a break?"

"No sir. I'm all right. It's just remembering all that is really awful. Especially the next part."

"I understand . . . continue please."

"So then they took the knife . . ."

"Maybe we should take a break . . ."

"No I want to finish . . . so they took his knife and they cut off his dick and they stuck it in his mouth."

"They emasculated him."

"They cut off his dick, yes sir. And stuck it in his mouth."

"Like it was part of a ritual?"

"Yes sir. Like that voodoo stuff you read about."

"Go on please."

"So then we all hung around for a while, like they were figuring out what to do next, so then Lone Wolf gets out this gun out of his pocket and he shoots him in the head . . ."

"The victim who was as far as you could tell already dead."

"He was definitely dead, for sure. So he shot him a bunch of times in the head and one of the other ones says what're you doing that for and he tells him so it'll look like he got shot first and then stabbed. So the cops'll think it was a gang-style murder and get thrown off the trail."

"He said that. The one you knew as Lone Wolf."

"Yes sir."

"Go on please."

"So then they threw his body into the bush down the slope and they put me in the car and drove me back to the motel."

"And they let you go?"

"Yes sir. First they talked about killing me so I wouldn't talk to the police but I promised them I wouldn't talk to the police so Lone Wolf said okay we don't kill her she ain't talking are you and I said no. 'Cause he knew I'd be too scared to 'cause they'd come back and really would kill me. So they just fucked me instead . . ."

"All of them?"

"Yes sir."

"Go on."

"Then they left on their motorcycles. That's all. That's the whole story."

"IT'S COMPLETE BULLSHIT," Lone Wolf tells me defiantly. "You want to know why?"

"As a matter of fact, I would," I say in response. I don't know the particulars yet, that'll come out in discovery, drop by excruciating drop, however Robertson wants to play it, which will be as close to the vest as possible. That's okay, I know how the field is slanted now, I'll make my adjustments. What I have been formally presented with is that this afternoon the grand jury, basing its decision solely on testimony by Rita Gomez, the motel maid who to my chagrin and profound embarrassment turned up as suddenly as she disappeared, brought open-charge-of-murder counts against my clients, all four of them, which can in theory be anything from first-degree murder, with aggravating circumstances, to involuntary manslaughter; but I know Robertson's going for the Big Enchilada, he'll only drop down if that becomes an absolute impossibility. The state wants my clients to die.

"Because if we'd killed the fucker, and she was there," he replies, "we'd have dusted her, too. Over and out."

There's a certain irrefutability to that. I haven't seen her testimony, of course, but she had to have claimed to have been at the killing, because no one would've believed her unless she was there.

"Maybe you took pity on her," I throw back at him. "Maybe you thought she'd be too scared to talk."

"You gotta be shitting us, man," he says, almost laughing out loud at me. "You think we're gonna take pity on some cunt that could fry us? Jesus H. Christ," he continues, shaking his head in disgust, "maybe you *ain't* the lawyer for us. You sure as hell ain't showing a lot of brains about this."

I'm stung. A glib retort fires from my cerebrum to the tip of my tongue. I manage to choke it off, probably the most mature act I've accomplished in recent memory. Let them have the skirmishes; I want to win the war.

It's quiet. We hear each other breathing, we merge into a single entity, inhale, exhale, in unison. It's after midnight, the jail population has long since been put to bed, but I have access to my little band twenty-four hours a day and I wasn't content with delaying this until morning (which is what Robertson assumed I'd do when he waited until nine-thirty to inform me of the charges). Last week I probably would have; but I've been burned too many times recently, on this case and everything else, to let something this important slide. I'm going to set the agenda now, or at least try to. And one thing's for certain: I'm not getting off this case.

"Your choice," I say calmly.

The other three panic; Lone Wolf smiles, more broadly than I've heretofore seen. Now I know why he's called Lone Wolf.

"Just testing," he says with an admirable lack of fear under the circumstances. "You ain't getting off that easy. You're in here with us, lawyer man."

The others aren't sure; I keep them on the hook for a few delicious seconds before I mercifully let them off.

"Fine," I say to all of them. "I'm with you."

The relief is genuine. It makes me feel good, partly because of the control factor, and partly because they really do want me; and need me. Their aloneness hits me: I'm their only link to the other side of the cage they're in.

"Under two conditions," I continue.

"Whatever," Lone Wolf says, a bit too hastily. He had his moment; now the precariousness of their situation is too important to play with any longer. I'm glad he's feeling desperate, but a part of me wishes he wouldn't show it. I like the absolute bravado in his nature.

"Make sure you hear this," I tell them. "All of you. Your lives are going to depend on it."

They're waiting.

"That under no circumstances do you lie to me," I say, holding up a pinkie. "None."

"We haven't," he answers.

"The consent or lack of it with the state's witness is questionable, my friend," I reply, "but we're past that now. And two," I say, taking a breath, an honest one, because this is all of it, and I want them to understand that, "is that you're innocent. Maybe I could've finessed it before; I can't now."

"We are," Lone Wolf says without flinching.

I look at each of them in turn. Either they're the greatest ensemble of actors since *One Flew Over the Cuckoo's Nest,* or they're telling the truth.

"THEY WAS A CAUTION, them boys." Her laugh, completely spontaneous and of equal enjoyment to sender and receiver, is deep and rolling, like a hollow barrel tumbling down a long tunnel incline, echoing and echoing.

"So you do remember them?"

"You don't forget four mugs like those," she tells me. "You know me," she continues (I do, as a matter of fact, but she'd say the same thing to a perfect stranger), "I don't *never* forget a face. I could tell you exactly to the quarter inch how long Elvis's sideburns were and it's been a good twenty years since the last time that boy set foot in here, God rest his soul. Liked his hamsteak practically burnt and mashed a bowlful of salsa in his grits. Righteous guitar player, too. You been down to Graceland yet?"

I don't reply; it's not expected. I'm sitting at the counter of the only coffee shop in Madrid, a captive audience. It's white Formica, highly polished, an old soda-fountain counter, complemented by tall bolted-down stools covered in fading but unripped and untaped red Naugahyde.

It's blisteringly hot outside. The old window air-conditioner, turned up to high cool, is wheezing and coughing for all it's worth, which isn't much but better than nothing.

Maggie's across the counter from me, leaning on her elbows, a smoldering Lucky stuck in the corner of her mouth like Ida Lupino in *High Sierra*. She's wearing a Grateful Dead tank-top, Levi cutoffs, and high-heeled bedroom mules with pink fluffy toes. Her own toes are painted with metallic green polish. She admits to seventy, and her outrageously dyed carrot-red hair has a royal-blue punk streak right down the center. An on-the-spot gift from a recent customer.

She refills both our cups. I'm her only customer at the moment.

I left Santa Fe early this morning, following the bikers' trail. New Mexico 14's a pretty road, old and picturesque, the now-overdone stuff of postcards and slick magazine ads. It winds past the state penitentiary, down through Madrid, past Golden, whose authentic trading post was commonly acknowledged to have the finest selection of turquoise jewelry in the country, until the owner died a few years back and his heirs didn't keep it going, at length bisecting Interstate 40 east of Albuquerque. Maggie's cafe is one of the 'must' stops for locals; not for the food, which is standard diner fare and half of that defrosted, but for Maggie and her wild stream-of-consciousness off-the-wall conversation and philosophizing.

"Didn't they intimidate you?" I ask. "Just a smidgen?"

"What for?" she says in genuine puzzlement.

"Because they scare the shit out of most civilians, that's what for," I answer. "That's their stock in trade, among other things."

"You're joshing me," she says. "Hell those boys were pure pussy-cats. Rode some boss motorcycles, too. Ain't nothing like a Harley to get your juices flowing. My third ex-husband rode a Harley. Rode it 'till the day he rode it right off a cliff out there by Jemez Pueblo. Wasn't hardly enough left of that machine to fill a baby's shoebox. He was a handsome devil, that one. Wasn't the same after that crackup, though," she adds. "Ever'thing got all bent up, even his dingle. I couldn't look at the poor thing without breaking out in sheer hysterics. Reckon that's why he run off with some half-Navajo woman. She must've featured the angle of his dangle. He sure enough was a handsome man 'till then, though." She pats her hair in place, glancing at herself in the back-bar mirror. She's been known to hit on the occasional retired RV tourist who's fallen in more or less by mistake, with or without his wife standing by.

Some pussycats, I think. Mountain lions maybe. I can't imagine anyone conjuring them as cuddly little fur things.

"And polite, too," she adds. "Excellent manners. Reflects well on their mothers."

"They show you their tattoos?"

"A choice selection of them. Those you can show in mixed company," she says primly. "And I showed them one or two of mine back!" she roars, laughing that wild laugh again. "They was mighty impressed, let me tell you. Said mine was better, right to my face they did. It's true, too. Some of theirs were home-made jobs, what you call jailhouse tattoos. All of mine are professionally done," she adds proudly. "Lyle Tuttle did my heart and my butterfly when he came through here. I wouldn't serve him 'till he promised to do me. You see him written up in that *Rolling Stone* anniversary issue by any chance? That boy's the Rembrandt of tattoo artists, doctor."

"I must've missed it," I tell her, leafing through my notes. She refills my cup, adds a precise amount of half-and-half, stirs it in for me. I look up. "It was Saturday morning when they were here. You're sure?"

"Damn straight I'm sure," she replies with indignation. "I said so didn't I? Well didn't I?"

"Of course," I reply quickly. Maggie's not someone I want to pick a fight with. For one thing, it could keep me here a couple hours extra, and I've got places to go and people to see.

"Do I look like I have Alzheimer's disease to you?" she continues. "Do I? My mind is so sharp," she goes on, not waiting for an answer, "that a professor from MIT, that's the Massachusetts Institute of Technology to you, doctor, told me he wanted me to come back to Boston, Massachusetts, to study me. My brain. He said I had the most accurate brain of any mature person he had ever encountered. Yes, it was Saturday morning. Bright and early."

"Do you recall how early? When they showed up?"

"They was setting on the front stoop when I opened up." Maggie lives in a little apartment in the back. She showed it to me once. It's decorated in mostly Hawaiian tourist style.

"Which was when?"

"Seven-thirty. Regular as clockwork. Not seven-twenty-five," she says forcefully. "Not seven-thirty-five. Seven-thirty. A.M. amen."

I jot down the information in my notebook. The bikers had told me the same story: after leaving Santa Fe before sunup, they'd ridden south, stopped for gasoline and a couple six-packs at an all-night mini-mart north of Cerrillos, and got to Madrid about seven, where they'd camped out on Maggie's porch until she opened. The station attendant, a teenage boy with a severe case of neck boils, had remembered them vividly. Maggie might think them pussycats but they'd definitely scared him, four apparitions riding out of the night on low-slung hogs: the stuff of American nightmares. They drank one of the six-packs while they stood there filling their bikes, no more than fifteen or twenty seconds to the can. It was right before six when they got there; the boy remembered it precisely because while they were doing their business he'd turned on the TV to catch the first news and it ran a color-bar for about a minute before the six o'clock program came on. I'd showed him a time-coded credit card receipt Goose had signed. That's the one, the boy had said affirmatively. I'd also shown him pictures, Polaroids I'd taken the day before. It was them, no doubt about it. You don't forget four strangers like that, not hardly.

"What'd they eat?" I ask Maggie. I don't really care, I just want to test that so-called brain of hers. I drain my coffee; it's cold, acidy-tasting under the sweet cream. My back is getting cold from the air-conditioner blowing on my wet shirt.

"Bacon and eggs over medium, grits, wheat toast. Ham and easy over, hashed browns, biscuits. Bacon and scrambled hard, hashed browns, white toast. French toast, bacon. Four milks, three coffees. The kid didn't drink coffee. And four large O.J.'s," she concludes, trumping me.

I put a dollar on the counter, wave her off from making change, close my notebook.

"You bailing out on me, doctor?"

"Places to go and people to see," I reply.

"Don't take your time coming back. And bring your little girl with you next time. She like them castanets I gave her?"

"She loves them," I tell her. "Practically sleeps with them." I'd stopped in about a year ago with Claudia, and Maggie had insisted on giving us the grand tour. Claudia's eye had caught an old pair of Spanish castanets sitting on Maggie's bureau, a gift from an old admirer, and Maggie had made her a gift of them there and then. I didn't think Maggie needed to know Claudia had lost interest by the afternoon and shortly after had misplaced them, never to be seen again.

"Well tell her hello for me," Maggie says, beaming. "Tell her there's another present waiting for her with her name on it."

"I will," I say. "And thanks."

I walk to the door. I can feel a blast of heat on the other side.

"Them boys," she calls out. "What kind of trouble they in, doctor?"

"Big trouble," I tell her.

"They kill that man up in the mountains I saw on TV?" she asks querulously.

"The law says they did."

"They did not kill that man," she tells me with certainty. She hesitates. "You lawyering for them?"

I nod. She nods too, somehow reassured.

"You think they killed that man?" Her voice cracks, slides; the old lady underneath she can't repress at this moment.

"No," I answer. "They didn't kill him."

She's the first noncombatant who's heard the words come out of my mouth. She's the first to ask me.

THE FIRST BEER of the day is always the best. I sit in the dark bar in a booth near the back, drinking a long-neck Budweiser that came from an old ice-cooler. They always taste better when they're long-necked, and they're always the coldest when they've been hibernating under chunks of ice floating in dark-green water.

The biker from Albuquerque sits across the table from me. His name is Gene. He's president of the Albuquerque chapter of the Scorpions, the same national organization my clients are from. He's six feet six, an Arnold Schwarzenegger in outlaw biker colors. He's been Lone Wolf's best friend since they met as teenagers in a Pittsburgh reform school.

"Lone Wolf," I muse. "How'd he get a handle like that? Sounds kind of romantic for a one-percenter."

"Kind of pussy, you mean?"

I half-shrug—he can say that, I don't dare.

"Some chick laid it on him. Must've been reading one of them romance novels."

"Nobody's ever ragged him about it?" I ask.

"Fuck, yes," Gene says. "'Till he busted this one motherfucker's forearm up into toothpicks one time. After that nobody seemed to find it particularly strange."

He takes a pull off his brew, regards me.

"Figure this out," he drawls. "What kind of dumb fuck who has two prior convictions and just got off parole kills somebody and leaves the body and a witness to tell the tale?"

"The kind of dumb fuck who thinks he's above the law," I answer. "The kind of dumb fuck who picks up a drunk girl in front of two hundred witnesses and gang-rapes her. That kind of dumb fuck."

"They got 'em up on a rape charge?" he asks.

"You know they don't," I reply testily, knowing he knows where things currently stand.

"Then they're the dumb fucks, 'cause they messed up on the charges. Anyway, she's a known whore and a common one at that," he informs me, "she'd fuck a syphilitic dog in a Juárez whorehouse. I personally know seventy or eighty men who've fucked her and survived."

"Are they all Scorpions?" I ask.

"Mostly," he grins. "A few Hell's Angels and Bandidos."

"All prepared to testify on their behalf?"

"If it comes to that." He leans forward, caressing his beer bottle, which is barely visible in his enormous hands. "What do you think?" he asks, suddenly serious.

"About . . . ?"

"What's going to happen."

"The verdict."

"Yeh." He drains his beer, walks over to the cooler, comes back with four more in one hand. He church-keys the tops off two, sets one down in front of me.

I drink in long swallows, feeling the cold going down the back of my neck. There are times when I think about cutting back, for my own good. This isn't one of them.

"It's going to be an uphill battle," I tell him honestly. "I don't know who all the state's witnesses are yet, but they're going to be buttoned up tighter than a nun's asshole. If I work hard and get lucky I'll find a crack in one of them and get inside and break it up."

"What about your own evidence?" he asks.

"I'm developing it," I say. "That's why I'm here."

"It's going to come down to somebody's word against somebody's word."

"That's usually the way it works," I say. "I'm sure you're no stranger to that."

"Not hardly. And what I also know is people like us usually come out on the short end of the stick."

People like us. In one form or another I've been hearing that phrase my entire professional life. Is there some kind of secret underclass that's never been defined sociologically? I'm not talking about the usual groups that commit the majority of violent crimes: the fatherless families, the beaten-down ethnic minorities, usually black or Hispanic, the battered inner-city rubble, the hardscrabble rural, the alcoholics, the junkies, the mentally ill. They generally have one thing in common: poverty. I'm not talking about that. It's something else, the feeling that there's society and then there's you, outside of society. I was relatively poor growing up, but I never had that feeling. I felt I belonged, in or out of trouble. But there's millions of people out there who feel they're not part of the basic community; even if they manage to become middle-class in the economic sense they still feel estranged, apart from the rest. And if you're not part of the group, why abide by the group's laws? I think that most of these people believe they never had an option; it's like fourth-generation families on relief, it's all they've ever known. But others, like these bikers, choose to be apart, outside. And in the past few days, since the charges were brought against them, I've been wondering why.

"Why is that?" I ask Gene.

"Because in this society," he tells me, suddenly earnest, "somebody's got to lose. I mean this idea about winners, right, the American way, winning, winners? Well, if there's got to be winners, if you got to have winners to make the system work, then you got to have some losers, too, right? And to Joe Mortgageholder out there, who's been brainwashed his whole life that if you do this and this and this you'll be a winner, people like us, who think the whole goddam thing's a crock of shit and say so in a big loud voice, well we're fucking losers, right? And the winners got to get the long end of the stick, right?, so people like us, designated losers, we get the short end."

"So you admit you're all a bunch of losers," I say.

"Fuck you Jack." He finishes his first new beer, drains half the second in one gulp. "*You* admit we're losers. 'Far as we're concerned we're the biggest winners of all time. This thing about a jury of your peers?" he continues. "Ain't nobody on that fucking jury's *my* goddam peer. You give me a jury of my fucking peers, Jack, I'm outa there."

It's a novel concept. I'll have to try it out sometime; maybe in this trial. Wonder how the legal community would react to that gambit?

"I don't think I can sell that," I tell him. I start on another beer. It's comfortable in here. I'm out of the heat, I'm drinking cold long-neck Budweisers on somebody else's tab, and I'm conversing with a person of reasonable if not high intelligence.

"You ever read Karl Marx?" I ask idly.

"Cover to cover," he answers with a trace of a smile. "And Veblen and Hoffer and Frantz Fanon, among others. Milton Friedman, too, although I think consensually he's pretty well discredited by now. Fucking Reagan," he growls contemptuously, "bastard made Nixon look good."

Jesus. I'm drinking beer with a radical socialist economic political outlaw biker with two priors and three hung juries who uses words like 'consensually' in everyday conversation.

"Tell me about Lone Wolf and the others," I say.

"What do you want to know?"

"Anything I can use in their defense."

He makes his way methodically to the cooler, comes back with another half-dozen cold ones. This is definitely going to be my last interview of the day. We toast each other with raised bottles. He leans back, thinking of what he can tell me that'll save his friends' lives.

"He's done some mean shit in his life but he never killed nobody. Lone Wolf that is. None of the others ain't never killed nobody, either, to my knowledge."

"That doesn't help very much."

"You mean was he a boy scout or something? Pulled an old lady out of a burning building, that kind of shit?"

"Wouldn't hurt," I say.

"He was in Nam. Field hospital in Da Nang. Won two purple hearts. Bronze star."

Now that's something. I jot it down to check on later. I like this guy sitting across from me but he could be jerking my chain.

" 'Course they were giving medals out at the end in Nam like Hershey bars," he informs me. "Trying to find any way they could to put a heroic face on it you know what I mean?"

"That's still good. Juries love war heroes. What else?"

"He had a brother that was homosexual."

"Had?"

"He's dead. 'Least that's what the Wolf says. I don't know none of the particulars. He don't talk about it, and nobody's ever been dumb enough to bring it up."

The mind reels. How many doors am I going to be opening here? And this is just one of four defendants.

"That ain't common knowledge," Gene adds. "You best check with him about whether he wants going public on that. He ain't going to be happy I even told you."

"Don't worry, I will," I say; "check with him." I pause. "You're his friend, you know his mind. Has that made him more tolerant?"

He shakes his head. "The opposite," he tells me. "He hates faggots with a passion. Not that any of us love 'em," he adds, "but the Lone Wolf's got a particular hair up his ass about queers. He almost killed one once he thought was hitting on him. Bought ninety days for it."

I'm on the worst rollercoaster of my entire career. I was almost euphoric earlier, becoming more convinced of my clients' innocence, accompanied by a growing outrage at the social forces judging them. Now I'm faced with a piece of evidence that forces me to examine the alternative: there's no question that the killing, if not an outright homosexually oriented murder, had strong homosexual overtones.

And now his best friend tells me my client has a pathological hatred and aversion of gays. If Robertson and his boys find out about this tidbit it'll be another brutal hurdle to overcome.

"Look," I tell him frankly, "this is a major bitch. If this piece of information ever gets out it could help put Lone Wolf and the others on Death Row."

He nods.

"Don't get me wrong, I'm glad you told me," I continue, "and I will talk with him about it . . . but I've got to try and keep this quiet."

"If anybody else asks me about this I don't know shit, that what you're saying?" he asks.

I drink some beer. "You ought to think about going to law school," I tell him, half-serious. "You'd make a pretty good lawyer." It's really the beer talking.

"I tried it," he answers.

"You went to law school?"

"Case Western Reserve. In Cleveland. A semester. Wasn't for me. My last futile attempt at living the straight life."

I look at him. Maybe it's the beer, I don't know. But I've got to ask him.

"You're an intelligent man," I tell him sincerely. "Why have you chosen to live this way?"

"That's a dumb fucking question." He starts on another beer.

"Humor me."

"Not everybody can live the way *you* want 'em to," he tells me straight-forwardly. "Or ought to. Anyway," he adds, "you don't really want to know."

"I just asked, didn't I?"

"Come on, man. Get real with me, okay? I know how the straight world works. It romanticizes men like me. Well that's dangerous, 'cause we're dangerous men. I mean, look . . . I ain't as bad as people sometimes make me out to be, but I ain't America's sweetheart, either. I mean I ain't Peter Fonda in *Easy Rider,* hear what I'm saying? I been in the joint myself. And you know what? Guys're in there for a legitimate reason. They did something bad, probably violent. It's something in their heads all the time, the violent stuff. Like if they ain't thinking about fucking some cooze they're thinking about kicking the shit out of some civilian, more'n likely. So what I'm saying is, man, don't fucking romanticize any of this. It could blow up in your face."

"I certainly don't want that," I say. This man does not pull his punches. "But I'm still curious . . . why pick a life-style that makes you a punching bag?"

"Maybe it picked me."

"You don't strike me as the passive type. Lone Wolf either."

He looks at me; he pins me with his eyes.

"I'll tell you a little story," he says. "I went to New England last year. First time back east in fifteen years. In the fall, the leaves turning, the whole bit. Just me and the old lady, like a couple of straight tourists. No chopper, no colors. Invisible."

He polishes off another beer. I wait. He doesn't seem inclined to continue.

"And?" I ask finally.

"Didn't feel right, the invisible part," he says. "But that's not what it's about. We were in New Hampshire . . . damn beautiful place. You ever been there? In the fall, the leaves, all that good shit?"

"Once," I reply. I went up to Winter Carnival once when I was in college. I don't remember it well, I was drunk most of the time, like everyone else there.

"Real pretty. My old lady about creamed over it, talking about moving there and all. I told her wait until you're ass-deep in snow for a month, then tell me about moving. Anyway, they got a slogan on the license plates in New Hampshire. It really hit home to me. You know what it says?"

I shake my head.

" 'Live Free or Die.' That's me, man. That's Lone Wolf, the other bro's. That's what we stand for." He looks across the table, levelling his gaze at me. "I'd eat a ton of shit for the chance to taste an ounce of freedom," he says. "What about you?"

I HAVE TO KNOW the truth about Lone Wolf's gay brother. So I go to the source.

"I don't talk about that shit," he tells me harshly.

"You do with me, ace," I say. "This murder had homosexual overtones. If you've got skeletons in your closet I've got to be prepared for them."

He buries his head in his hands. It's the first honest show of human emotion I've seen in him.

"He's dead." He looks up at me. "He died a long time ago."

"How?"

He shakes his head. "It was a long time ago. Let it go, okay?"

"What about the rest of your family?"

"There is no 'rest.' Lone Wolf, man—that's my name. That's who I am."

CLAUDIA'S SLEEPING. I hold her in my arms while I wait for Patricia to open the door. I want Patricia not to have heard my deliberately soft knock, to be on the phone in her bedroom in the back, talking long-distance to her mother, with the television going. I want to stand here like this until dawn. It's bone-dry even at this hour, not a trace of humidity; it's been this way all summer. Butterflies move through the hot still air in clusters, attracted by the smell of jasmine and honeysuckle. They form a halo around my baby's head.

Patricia opens the door without making a sound, a mother's way.

"Why did you bring her back so late?" she whispers, making sure the peevishness in her voice comes through so I don't miss it. I may have the world by the balls (so she thinks), but she has our daughter and she doesn't want me to forget it. "She has a swimming lesson at eight in the morning."

"We were having fun," I protest. "She wouldn't leave; I had to wait until she fell asleep."

"Okay." She nods. She knows. She can be gracious; it's truer to her nature.

I carry Claudia through the small house to her bedroom, lay her on the bed, gently strip off her shoes, socks, shorts. She can sleep in her T-shirt and undies. I cover her with a sheet, less for warmth than for protection, against what I don't know. Not true; I know, more than anything in the world I know this. Because *I* need to protect her, to feel I'm her protector, that it's necessary. She curls into a ball on her side, her mouth slightly open.

"Would you like a cup of tea before you go?" Patricia asks. She's sitting at her breakfast-nook table in shorts and a T-shirt, making notes on a brief. She's taken to wearing reading glasses, tortoiseshell half-frames. It somehow enhances her sex appeal; like looking at a woman in a lingerie ad wearing glasses, the juxtaposition of sex and intelligence. It reminds me of how long it's been since I had intelligence in my sex life.

"Do you have a beer?" I ask casually. It's still hot enough out that I can ask for a beer without looking bad.

She shakes her head. "I don't drink in the house anymore," she tells me, glancing up. "I don't like that image for Claudia."

Has Claudia been talking to her about my drinking? I wonder. She sees me doing it but she's never said anything about it. I think back; how much do I drink in front of her? Not counting beer, of course, it's almost nothing; maybe a Scotch or two while I'm cooking dinner. I'm not a solitary drinker, I usually find my trouble in large groups of strangers.

"A cup of tea would be nice. Don't bother getting up," I say as she starts to, "I know where it is."

"That's okay. Let me."

I sit at the table while she fills the kettle from the tap. Her work is spread out, the brief and her scribblings on legal pads. I glance at it: a utilities case in its fourth year of appeals. The kind of boring shit I hate. I understand why she wants to leave. I would, too, if I had to do this kind of work day in and day out. She's right; she's underpaid for a job that requires constant reading of this stuff. If you're going to lose your eyesight it should at least be from reading exciting material.

"Regular or herb? I've got Sleepy-time, Peppermint, Earl Grey." She holds up the boxes to me.

"Whatever."

"Earl Grey. You'll sleep through it anyway."

She sets the cup down in front of me with the bag still in it, freshens her own. She's drinking herbal tea; she's always been a restless sleeper, caffeine would probably keep her up all night.

"Interesting?" I ask, referring to her work.

"No." She pencils a question mark in a margin. "Do you know how many law school graduates cannot write? I mean a simple declarative sentence. It's appalling. And the worst-written briefs seem to invariably wind up on my desk."

"Pretty soon you won't have to put up with it anymore."

"It can't be soon enough for me."

I was fishing, hoping she'd tell me she'd changed her mind and wasn't taking the Seattle job. She took the bait and calmly spit out the hook.

"So how's your preparation going on the murder case?" she asks off-handedly.

"Good, good," I tell her.

She looks up. "Oh?"

"Yeh, better than I expected actually, at this point anyway. I've got some pretty good people lined up for the other three defendants, we're getting together formally next week to start plotting strategy. But the best thing," I tell her, "is I'm finding holes in their case you can drive a tank through. By Robertson's own construct the whole timing is off. Look," I say. "Listen and tell me if I'm crazy."

She looks at me as if I am crazy. I ignore it and press on.

"They left the bar at two. Dozens of witnesses confirm that. They took her up to the mountains. That's a good forty-five-minute ride, you know that, you know the area. They all fuck . . . have intercourse with her. Twice apiece. With me so far?"

She nods. She's starting to listen with interest.

"Okay," I go on. "Let's say ten minutes a pop. Then they take her back. So that's an hour and a half travel time plus the same amount of time playing doctor. It's five in the morning already; oh, I forgot, two more pops back at the motel, another fifteen minutes, they were probably quickies, now it's a quarter after five. At five to six they're in Cerrillos, I've got a receipt and a witness, and an hour later they're in Madrid, again with a witness. Now you tell me: when did they take this guy back up to the mountain, stab him countless times, shoot him, emasculate him, and get her back to the motel? It doesn't track, Pat. It's a physical impossibility." I beam at her. God, this feels good. Saying it out loud confirms it. "Unless I get a real curve thrown at me I have a damn good chance to walk these four. I'm talking completely."

She stares at me. Like I did something wrong instead of proving my case beyond a doubt.

"What is it?" I ask. I sip the tea; it's not bad, although a beer would be better.

"Nothing."

"What? Tell me."

She pushes her work aside, takes off her glasses. It's a classic move, done unconsciously of course, but nicely executed. She's never tried a case in her life but I'll bet she'd be pretty good at it.

"Don't take this the wrong way," she tells me.

Whenever somebody says that to me I know I'm going to.

"What?" I ask again.

"I'm only telling you this because I think you should hear it."

"What, already?" I hate procrastination; I do it enough myself that it grinds me when it comes from someone else.

"I heard what you said and it sounds good, Will. But the word on the street is this is a hopeless case. That you're tilting at windmills."

I explode inside.

"What kind of bullshit propaganda is Robertson spreading?" I demand of her, my voice rising with my temper. "That bastard," I fulminate, "he's trying to rig this fucking thing. You see," I say, pointing a finger like a schoolmarm, "this *proves* he's nervous. He knows he's already got problems and he's trying to win it outside the courtroom. You just heard it," I say, "you can see I've got genuine goods."

"Please don't yell at me," she says softly. "I'm not accusing you of anything."

"Sorry, babe, sorry. But I hate that kind of shit. It's a typical prosecution ploy, but I've never known John to resort to it."

"He doesn't want to lose."

"Of course he doesn't want to lose. I don't want to lose either but I'm not playing head-games on him, trying my case outside the courtroom."

"He especially doesn't want to lose this one. It's all over the office," she says. "He's convinced beyond a shadow of a doubt that they're guilty and he can't stand the idea that four scumbag bastards—those are his words not mine—might walk away because of some devious lawyering, his words again," she adds quickly, "not mine."

"It's not the way you do it," I tell her. "You know that. It's unprofessional."

She puts her hand on mine. It sends chills down my back. I stare at the two hands.

"Will . . . I'm warning you, that's all. At least listen to that."

"These men are my clients," I tell her with conviction. "They deserve the best defense they can get. Especially," I add, "since I'm convinced they did not murder that man."

"Okay. I said it. It's over."

"Thank you." I'm touched. "I appreciate it. I really do."

Actually, I'm bothered, a lot; she wants me off this case too much. Everyone does. They all want my clients to lose, and they're afraid I'm going to go down in flames trying to stop it.

"You are my child's father," she reminds me. "I don't want to see you winding up in an ugly place."

"I'll try not to. But I am going to conduct the best defense I can."

"You always do. That's why you're the best."

Even as I'm basking in her praise the proverbial bell goes off in my head. "Have you been talking to Andy or Fred?" I ask.

"What would I be talking to them about?" she asks back.

"Nothing. Just asking."

"Are they down on this case too?"

"Not really. They're down on me in general," I throw in, hoping to defuse the future.

"I know."

"You do?"

She nods. "It's around town."

I slump in my chair. "What exactly is 'around town,' as you put it?"

"That you might leave the firm." She actually looks away for a moment.

"You're joking."

"No, I'm not."

"That's bullshit! Stupid rumors, pure and simple," I tell her. "Because of the timing of my leave."

She nods again.

"I don't know how some of this stuff gets started," I go on. "There's nothing to it."

"That's good. It would be tragic if it was otherwise," she says.

The air's become too close in here. I've got to leave. The trouble is, I don't want to. I want to stay in this little house of memories with my child sleeping in the next room and her mother holding my hand in hers.

"It's late," I say. "I'd better go."

I'm hoping she'll stop me. It won't take much.

She nods. "I'm beat. Big day tomorrow."

I'm forced to my feet. "For me, too."

She walks me to the door.

" 'Night."

"Good night."

She leans forward, brushes my mouth with her lips. I read more meaning into it than she does, I think.

"Good luck, Will."

"Thanks. I feel good."

"Just don't become consumed with it. You can't win every time out."

"I know that." God, how I know that. Standing on this porch with her is living-in-pain proof of how much I know that.

PART TWO

I'M FLYING, mind-blown beyond belief, sitting in a sweat lodge west of Taos with my old friend Tomas Lost Ponies, the famous Pueblo shaman ("Donahue," "Nightline"), a man who is always smiling and laughing despite the fact that he and his people have been dumped on for as long as he has memory, which in his case is seventy-seven years, although he doesn't look much older than me, if at all. By strict application of the law I shouldn't be here; it's illegal for a nonmember of the Native American Church, meaning anyone who isn't at least one-eighth Indian, to participate in these rituals, especially the taking of peyote, which to the ignorant and arid world of Anglo-Saxon American law is just another mind-altering drug, intrinsically evil and abusive. And as an officer of the court, of course, I should be particularly sensitive to what is legal and what is not. But I am a guest here, it would be ungraceful of me to refuse my host's hospitality. And I know, again putting on the black robes of the legal profession, that while the law is stern she is also an understanding and compassionate mistress (at least in first-year lawbooks), and that all laws are a mosaic of events, coincidental and accidental, so that today's *Plessy* v. *Ferguson* is tomorrow's *Brown* v. *Board of Education*.

I am, therefore I hallucinate. And if anything that feels this good is illegal, fuck it.

It's past midnight. We've been tripping for over twelve hours, sitting in the sweat lodge and seeing the inner and outer worlds in the flame of a candle, the sweat pouring off our naked bodies, then going outside and dancing, first under the white glare of the sun and then for the last several hours in moonlight while millions of stars twinkle overhead, each significant, each communicating to me, me communicating back to them, reaching out to them, at various times soaring through time and space so that I am flying through the heavens alongside them, whispering out secrets to each other, the beauty of the cosmic consciousness that bonds us all and makes us one.

"Man, you are *so* ripped." Tomas is laughing. We've jumped into the lake to cool down, he and I and the other men who are partaking with us. I stayed under the water talking to the fish, beautiful shimmering fish, infinite in color and variety. The fish stare at me with their bulging eyes as they talk back in the profound way only fish can talk. God, they are so sexy, so coquettish, like that little fish Cleo in Disney's *Pinocchio*. I can stay under and talk to them because they've shown me how to use my hidden gills, my Pleistocene throwbacks which very enlightened beings can call back.

Right now I am in such an extraordinarily enlightened state. I am one with the sun and stars and life underwater.

"I'm talking to the fish," I explain. For some reason, unknown to me, this sends him into paroxysms of laughter.

"I am," I continue patiently. One must be patient when one is explaining enlightenment, even to another who is also enlightened.

"Talking to the fish." He can't stop laughing. "That's a good one."

"I am." Enough is enough with the laughing.

"A long time, I'm sure," he says.

"Long enough to learn their secrets," I answer sincerely, if a touch smugly. "And stop laughing, it isn't that funny."

"You were under less than ten seconds," he tells me. "I pulled you out. Otherwise you'd have dived for the bottom."

So? Ten seconds can be a long time. Still, it is a bit confusing. It seemed an eternity.

"Anyway," he continues, "there aren't any fish in the lake now. They haven't restocked it yet."

I smile inwardly. That shows how little he really knows. There were thousands of them down there, all colors of the rainbow, they were rubbing all over me, showing me how to use my prehistoric gills.

"Good thing I was here with you," he adds, "you probably would've drowned. Don't you know humans can't breathe underwater?" He looks at me sideways, shaking his head. "Shit, Will," he says, "you could give hallucinogens a bad name, man. Don't hippie out on me, okay?" We're standing off a ways from the others. He glances over at them. They're deep into their own rituals, aren't paying us any attention.

"I'm okay," I reassure him.

He eyes me dubiously. "The elders don't like bringing whites into the ceremony," he says. "Don't want Uncle BIA coming down on them."

"I'll be good." I giggle involuntarily. "Those fish were so beautiful. I never knew fish could be so sexy."

He laughs with me. "You got pussy on the brain, man," he says.

Pussy on the brain. Jesus, even in this stoned state this guy's got me pegged. I look at him carefully; he guilelessly, unselfconsciously, smiles back at me, and in a flash-point of misunderstanding, exacerbated by my mind being in a state too enlightened for my spirit to handle, something about that clear, innocent smile triggers a bomb that's been waiting to detonate, the bomb of suspicion I carry just below the conscious, like a permanent black cloud of unknowing. Tendrils of paranoia start creeping up the back of my brain, a purple Rorschach that suddenly, without warning, explodes inside my head, wiping out the reservoir of good feeling that's been accumulating all day and night. And then comes the awesome clarity that only a stoned mind can produce, where you can see into the past and the future and make them one. They're out to get me, all of them, with Tomas as the front man, it's been a set-up from the beginning, concocted and executed by my enemies to bring me down. Shit, how could I have been such a dumb, unsuspecting fuck? In my position you can never let your guard down, not for an instant.

"Hey Will." Tomas breaks my reverie. "Check out the shooting star." He points heavenward, where a dying light is falling. "Beautiful, huh?"

"Yeh." I'm looking up. It is beautiful. It's all so beautiful. He's beautiful and I'm beautiful and the sky and the stars and the moon, the other participants, the whole enchilada. All beautiful, all love. Fuck me and my twin curses of civilization and litigation.

They go back inside the lodge. I stay outside, alone with the night. The blanket of stars packs the dark sky. Standing naked like this, my hairy body wet with my sweat (I'm not nearly as evolved as the men inside, who barely have hair on their pubes, let alone anywhere else), my glands throwing out a primeval territorial stink, I could, to a lost traveler from another galaxy, be mistaken for the first of my species to have stood on this spot ten million years ago. I feel that old, and that young.

Across my mesa, on the next ridge, I see a lone coyote trotting along, his dark form silhouetted sharply against the indigo sky. For a moment he seems to turn and look back at me and I'm seized with an irresistible impulse to be him, be inside of him, be a coyote spirit, and without preamble I turn my head and torso skyward and howl at the stars, a long, high, piercing howl that echoes across the darkness, bouncing off the canyon walls, a howl at the stars like the wiliest of old coyotes, braying at myself, at myself and all my surroundings, now that I'm whole with them again, the positive side of the peyote kicking back in, showing me the sheer audaciousness of my silly, confusing, god-forsaken, and still extraordinarily beautiful cosmos. When your insides are peyote and your outside is a northern New Mexico night you know for sure that God has a sense of humor. He must, to forgive so easily all the bullshit ramblings of a mind raging with banalities, unable to accept basic simplicity. It flashes me to Claudia and to the poster of Einstein on her bedroom wall, with the epigram underneath: "Life should be as simple as possible, but not one bit simpler."

Howling at the moon, full blast now, really into it, like a lovesick dog sniffing around a bitch in heat. My hosts have come back out and are finding this funny as hell, splitting their sides as they pass around a bottle of wormy mescal, for religious purposes and to ward off the chill. I'm the college-educated, earth-ignorant butt of their pagan jokes. I like it, though, playing the mascot, fool to the king and his court, new kid on the block eager to please. There's nothing malicious in them and their laughter, it's the spirit of children, innocent and happy.

Sure. And all God's chillun got wings and a split-level home with a convertible in the garage, instead of a one-room cinderblock shack with an outhouse. I should be as free and knowing as these men. And as forgiving.

Dawn is approaching. We have bathed each other and dressed, and now we're on horses riding east to the top of the mesa. No one feels the need to talk; a natural state for my hosts, but even I, after a day and night of having my mind and spirit bent, altered, shaped and caressed, am happy and comfortable to be passive and let it all come to me.

We sit on horseback on the edge of the mesa and watch the sunrise: hypnotic, like waves breaking, over and over and over again. It's breathtaking, but a wave of sadness tinged with apprehension washes over me; in a short time, too short, I'll be sitting in a courtroom starting jury selection. I'll be back in the world again.

We part company. They all have a hug for me, they were all glad I was part of it. I feel like tattooing it on the back of my hand so the next time the paranoia comes I can just check it out like looking at my watch: oh, yeh, it's only my own stuff, not to worry, it'll go away.

ONE LAST PRIVATE MOMENT with Tomas, then I'm in my Beemer, heading south. It's still early, not yet seven, I'm starving, I haven't eaten in twenty-four hours. I pass a McDonald's and I'm tempted to stop, but an Egg McMuffin doesn't seem the way to break my fast.

The AM/PM Minimart has chili dogs, two for ninety-nine cents, shredded cheese, relish and onions included. I sip at a large black coffee while the owner, a middle-aged lardass with a Parris Island haircut, loads up my dogs for me. As he hands over the greasy bag and my change he cocks his head, staring. I involuntarily look behind me, then back.

"Do I know you?" he asks, his eyes narrowing.

"I don't think so. I don't recall ever stopping in here before." That's all I need, some shit-kicker who was robbed last month and harbors the fear that every off-hours customer is the perpetrator, come back to haunt and humiliate him again.

He shakes his head. "No, that ain't it." He shrugs, turns away. Then he remembers, turning back to me with a triumphant smile. He chews tobacco or dips, his teeth are black. "You're the lawyer for them bikers. The ones killed that kid up in the hills. I seen you on the news."

I smile disarmingly. "Guilty as charged."

His face darkens. "Guilty is right. They ought to take those fuckers and fry their fucking brains and you along with them."

Fuck me. That's a twist. Usually bikers are thought of as folk heroes, sort of modern-day lowrider Robin Hoods, especially to closet outlaws like this guy. If people like him are down on us it means the boys have piled up a hell of a lot of negative publicity. Not a good sign.

Still, I don't have to put up with this shit, I'm the customer. "They're charged, ace," I inform him, feeling the heat blistering the inside of my skull, "but they haven't been tried. And until they are, and found guilty, *if* they're found guilty, which I doubt will happen, they are innocent. That's the way it works. Okay?"

He scowls at me. "No. It ain't okay. They're guilty and ever'body knows it and you can take that trial shit and shove it up your ass."

"Fuck you." Now I say it out loud.

He looks for a moment like he's going to try something, but I'm half a foot taller, thirty pounds heavier, and ten years younger. He retreats behind his scowl.

"They're guilty, mister." His voice rises. "They're guiltier'n hell and the world knows it. And the best shyster lawyer, which is what you are if you're for them, can't turn that around." He shakes his head in anger that he can't clean my clock. "Now get the hell out of my store and don't show your face in here again."

I turn and walk out without a glance back, slamming the door for good measure.

Outside, leaning against my car, I find myself shaking; anger's what I feel, not fear. Pissants like him don't scare me, I've run across dozens of them, they're all mouth. It's what he represents that's frightening and sobering: the state of New Mexico has already tried and convicted my clients. It's been all over the newspapers, television, the works. It's relatively quiet now, but once the trial convenes all the hubbub will start up again, scum boiling to the top.

The hot dogs are surprisingly good, spicy. I wipe the chili from my mouth, littering the front of the store with the wrappings. Looking back, I see him glaring out at me, a rabid badger foaming inside his hole. The incident sickens me, but I know there'll be a lot more like this one.

It's hot out, the sun rising quickly, but I'm shivering in an envelope of my own clammy sweat as I drive off, heading home to decisions that won't wait any longer.

LONE WOLF FLIPS through the résumés. The others watch him. I can feel the heat rising, even though the interview room's air-conditioned to a fault. He tosses the papers onto the conference table that separates us.

"This is a joke, right? You couldn't bring us a Bugs Bunny video so you brought us this." I'm getting to hate those cold blue eyes: this guy can go an hour without blinking.

I maintain silence, cool and calm; outwardly, anyway. I've learned over the last month to cut him plenty of slack.

"A cunt, a spic, and some over-the-hill rummy who probably can't find his ass with both hands and a wheelbarrow?" he yells, pounding both fists on the table. Hard. His hands work in unison; they have to, he and the others are in full irons: arms, legs and waist. He grabs the stapled résumés and tears them in half, quarters, eighths. "Wipe your ass with this," he informs me, laying that blue-eyed devil stare on me again.

I gather up the remnants, drop them in the circular file behind me. "You're the boss," I tell him evenly. Very calmly, deliberately, I stuff their files into my hand-tooled leather briefcase, stand, take my suit-coat from where I'd draped it over the chair, shoot my cuffs, put the jacket on. Slowly, letting them see it, never taking my eyes off them for a second. I pick up the briefcase, turn towards the door.

"Where're you going?" Roach asks. He's apprehensive, his look darting back and forth between Lone Wolf and me. There's a flicker of uncertainty. I see it in the others' eyes as well; I was counting on it.

"Out," I answer dryly. "To tell the District Attorney that you no longer seek my representation. It's a formality that has to be observed," I add, "so he can go to the court and request suitable counsel for each of you."

"What in the fuck . . ." Lone Wolf starts.

"I'll have my secretary check the time I've already put in," I say. "Whatever's left over I'll refund by the end of the week." I bang on the door to let the guard sitting on the other side know that I want out.

"Wait a minute." We all turn to Goose, who's probably more surprised at hearing himself speak up than any of the rest of us. "Are you saying you're quitting us?"

"No. I'm saying you just fired me," I tell him.

"No way!" Roach is standing now, his face flushing, the wine-colored birth-mark throbbing against the veins in his neck. "How do you figure that one?"

"Ask El Jefe," I say, turning to Lone Wolf, who's staring daggers at me, "he's the man with the answers."

"Fuck you, Alexander."

"Not with your dick, mister."

It's showdown time. And I'm the only one who's holding any cards.

"Am I wrong? Did I misread your intentions?" I'm sick of this jive dance we've been waltzing around the floor with, this bullshit macho gamesmanship. He's going to learn right now that I'm calling the shots, if he doesn't we'll never get through the trial.

He smiles at me; disarming bastard. "No problema. We merely want the best."

"And that's what you got." The guard's opened the door, his head sticking in. I shake mine; he retreats, closing the door and locking us in again. "For this trial, for you—who you are, and what you're paying"—I can't not say it, we all live in a finite world—"you've got the best."

"No bullshit?" He's serious.

"No bullshit."

"Any of 'em Jews?" Goose asks.

"No," I tell him. Jesus, what is it with these guys, do they hate (or at least distrust) every minority in the world? "Why, are you down on Jews as well?"

"No, no," he answers quickly, "they're good lawyers. Best lawyer I ever had was a Jew. I mean I'd prefer one if you had one," he concludes lamely.

"Yeh, me too," Dutchboy chimes in, "they've got the smarts up here," he taps his temple, "know what I mean?"

I laugh. "Sorry I couldn't come up with one on short notice, but the lawyers I've picked are just as good. Trust me."

"We don't have a choice." Lone Wolf is serious now, all business. "Do we?"

"Not as long as I'm on this case."

"All right then."

"They're outside waiting. I'll bring them in. And one more thing . . ."

I let it dangle. Dutchboy takes the bait.

"What?"

"No more games. No more ego-tripping, playing with my head. I'm straight with you, you're straight with me. I say what and when. You say yes or no. This case is a bed of thorns, gentlemen. You've got to let me work. Agreed?"

They exchange looks; the other three looking to Lone Wolf.

"Agreed," he says.

I bang on the door and tell the guard to escort my colleagues in. Then I turn back to the bikers. "It's going to be fine," I tell them.

"We're trusting you, remember?" Lone Wolf tells me.

"I'm trying," I answer truthfully. "You don't make it easy."

The door swings open. Their eyes pop as Mary Lou is the first to walk in. Roach starts to say something (about her breasts, vagina, legs, or a combination of them), but Lone Wolf nails him with a glance that says: 'this is going to be professional, forget about your cock.' Roach turns away, flushing, his entire face turning the color of his birth-mark, as if his thoughts had been projected on the blackboard on the wall. Mary Lou's so business-like she doesn't even notice; or she's faking it convincingly.

She's followed by Tommy and Paul, who take seats on our side of the table. Each group looks at the other, trying it on for size. For the next several months we'll all be tighter than family.

I introduce the bikers first, saying a little about each in turn, noting that I've prepared informational files on all of them. That's not the purpose of this meeting; this is so we can see each other, put faces with names, make it about people, not abstract numbers and charges on a bill of particulars.

Then I introduce the lawyers to the bikers, just the facts, not bragging on them; but the facts are solid, these are all quality people, the bikers see that right off—they're going to be in good hands: it had taken me a lot of soul-searching and not a small amount of arm-twisting to put this combination together. I wasn't sure who I could enlist in the cause. Your better lawyers don't build careers and reputations on long-odds cases; Perry Mason and all the other hot-shot television lawyers to the contrary, good defense lawyers want to win their cases, the majority of them anyway, they want to know going in they've at least got a decent shot at it. That's how they become known as good defense lawyers. They only want it to *appear* that they're bucking the odds; even your flaming ACLU types are conservatives at heart, dikes against the oceans of anarchy, otherwise they wouldn't be lawyers. And given the personalities and the situation, a decent shot wasn't the way anyone was characterizing this case.

I knew I would pull one member of the team from the Public Defender's office, not only to cut costs, but because they're experienced in this. The third would be an up-and-comer from one of the established firms that was willing to take a flyer on making a future partner's reputation with an improbable win; a can't-lose situation. As for the fourth, most probably a contract lawyer from the P.D.'s list, who with any luck wouldn't be a drunk or a fuckup. I knew I could pretty much count on the court not letting that happen; this case is too important to the state to get it turned on appeal because of incompetence or malfeasance.

Tommy Rodriguez is the public defender. He came up the hard way, one of those success stories you read about in *Reader's Digest*—born in a melon patch to Mexican parents working the bracero program, for openers. That he ever enrolled in an American school is in itself a minor miracle; that he kept going, from school to school across the south as his family came up year after year from the Mexican mountains, is overwhelming. An old-maid English teacher in Tallahassee, Florida, took him under her wing in eighth grade and became his legal guardian, and from there it was one triumph after another: top of his class in high school, full ride at Duke, UVa Law (*Law Review*, Coif, the works). When the old lady retired she moved to New Mexico for the dry air, and he came with her like the most dutiful of sons, which is why he's a New Mexico state P.D. instead of pulling down six figures from a Wall Street firm. That'll come someday; he's only twenty-six. He told me he got offers last year from firms in L.A. and New York. He's biding his time and paying some dues: when he makes his move he wants to go with clout. Being on a major murder case like this one is exactly what he's been looking for.

The rising star from the big firm—Simpson and Wallace, one of the big three in the state, with over sixty lawyers, which is gargantuan for New Mexico—is Mary Lou Bell. As my buddy Travis from Austin would say, this woman is *complete.* She's young (barely thirty), she's smart, she's competitive, she does her homework, and to top it off she's got beauty-queen looks; Kathleen Turner with a Phi Beta Kappa key. Under different circumstances I'd sniff around, make a pass, just to say I was there, like a dog leaving his mark. But I have enough self-control (I keep assuring myself) to keep from shitting where I eat, and something in her body language tells me it would be a bad move, anyway; she doesn't want picked-over goods. So we're good buddies. One of the guys, who just happens to wear skirts and high heels. As I had assumed, Simpson and Wallace is absorbing most of her fee. I didn't even have to twist their arms particularly hard; they're happy she's getting the exposure. It can only help them.

Paul Marlor is the potential joker in the group. He's a generation older than the rest of us, in his sixties I'd guess, although I don't know for sure. He was a major east coast lawyer, Philadelphia or somewhere (he's never been forthcoming with the details), dropped out in the sixties, bailing out on his wife and children, surfaced here about ten years ago with a young wife and a baby and started a single practice. He's an excellent lawyer, gets to the heart of a case with a jeweler's precision, and only works as much as he has to, to maintain a modest lifestyle; protection against burning out again. His son and my daughter are in school together, we became acquaintances through PTA. He's a good guy, holds his Scotch with the best of them, is always happy to help. There's something solid about him; maybe it comes with age, like liver spots and loss of hearing. He adds ballast to our group. The others will defer to him on procedure. He'll defer to me—it's my case. And he came cheap, a necessary consideration.

All in all (metaphorically patting myself on the back), a formidable foursome.

We meet for an hour. Nothing specific, we're feeling each other out, first-date stuff. I've already gone over the state's case with my new associates, they pretty much know what to expect.

My task today is to assign each client his lawyer; I'd made my choices before I brought in the team, but I wanted to wait to announce them on the off-chance there'd be a case of bad chemistry in one of the pairings. There wasn't; I knew each of the bikers well enough to know what was right.

Dutchboy gets Paul: the old pro and the wild kid, Mark Twain and Huck Finn. Paul will have a soothing influence on Dutchboy; probably the first stable influence in his life.

I assign Tommy to Goose, a reverse of Dutchboy and Paul. It's the kind of pairing a jury loves without even knowing it. Goose has the best chance of getting off of any of the bikers, and Tommy, being Hispanic, gets brownie points in a state that's strong in its Spanish heritage and proud of it. I could see the rapport in the way that they grinned at each other, Goose eager to please, the old dog who's been kicked around and wants a warm place by the fire, and Tommy who understands what it is to be needed.

Roach gets his wish: Mary Lou. I'd discussed this with her before I brought her in; he's going to be the one who appears to be the most off-the-wall, in some ways more dangerous even than Lone Wolf, whose native intelligence will be manifest. It's a black and white role reversal: the woman, strong and competent to be sure but also feminine and traditional (she'll always be in demure skirts and dresses, not in female lawyer's clothes and not provocative), the man bowing to her judgment, so that by the time it goes to the jury, Roach will have been softened in their minds, defanged. And I knew deep down that Goose and Dutchboy would in some way have been uncomfortable with Mary Lou; she's too much woman for them. Roach'll test her once or twice, she'll slap him down like swatting a fly, and he'll be put in his place.

We make individual appointments for tomorrow. Most of the time we'll be together under joint work-product privilege, but each man needs to know his attorney, get close. And I need time alone with Lone Wolf, because he's the case: if I can walk him, the others will follow.

The bikers are sorry to see us go. It's scary inside, no matter how tough you are. The idea that you may spend the rest of your life in a six-by-nine barred room, or worse, get fried, is enough to sober anyone who isn't crazy. And these men aren't crazy; they just act like it, and it's haunting them now.

We talk over coffee.

"They could be innocent," Mary Lou says with some surprise.

"They're certainly getting screwed," Tommy adds. "This is the most political case I've ever seen."

"Get used to it," Paul counsels him, stirring two sugars in his cup, "politics is what this trial's going to be about. A situation like this, innocence or guilt has damn little to do about it."

He's low-keying it; you learn to do that with experience. You don't judge your clients, you represent them. You don't let your emotions cloud your judgment or how you handle your defense. You do your job as best you can, and you let the bleeding hearts get the ulcers.

We'll get together tomorrow after we've met with our clients individually, start comparing notes. I'm happy that they believe as I do; that whether or not the bikers are innocent (they're all, in varying degrees, withholding judgment so far), the state's definitely fucking them. It'll give us a buoyancy and optimism that'll make preparation less of a grind and more of a crusade.

Mary Lou lingers a moment after the others leave. I'm tempted to ask her to dinner, especially when she puts her hand on mine.

"I want to thank you for calling me in, Will," she says. "I needed this. You don't know how badly." She stares at me. She's sitting close enough that I can smell her perfume. She wears Chanel No. 5. It's intoxicating.

"I'm glad that you're glad." Come on, man, I exhort myself, snap to, you sound like a dork.

"This is exciting, isn't it? The kind of case that reminds you of why you became a lawyer. Making an honest-to-God difference," she proclaims, punctuating her sincerity by whacking her palm hard on the table, "instead of all that high-priced hand-holding I have to do at Simpson and Wallace." She stares hard at me: her eyes are huge, Paul Newman–like blue (probably contacts but so what?), shining with the fervor of the committed defender of the accused.

"That's why I like my practice. What I do matters, even if only a little," I add modestly. I'm all but fluttering my eyelashes to show what a good and committed guy I am.

"Don't hesitate to call on me anytime. I mean that, Will. We're in this twenty-four hours a day."

I nod. I've got to eat, might as well . . .

"Except for tonight," she smiles sympathetically, albeit crisply. "I've got a dinner date."

"Me too, as a matter of fact." I smile back, letting her know that while I appreciate her total commitment I certainly have no intention of imposing on her private life.

Shit. That was too close.

I stand in the doorway, watching her leave. Nothing wrong with the view from here, either. Snap out of it, Alexander, I admonish myself. She's a colleague, not a potential fuck.

It would've been the wrong move, I saw it coming, and I almost hit on her anyway. Stop me before I kill again, or whatever the equivalent is for dipshits like me. I'm going to tattoo it on my hand if I have to: keep business strictly business. It'll be better all around. Safer, anyway.

"I WANT TO SHOW you something."

"What?" I'm not paying attention, it's late, Claudia and I were askew all weekend. I couldn't let go of the case, my mind kept drifting at odd times and of course she picked up on it immediately, kids have radar stronger than SAC for shit like that, they call you on it in a minute. She's older now, starting a new grade, more independent, the old rules aren't working. No more easy, absolute compliance with what Daddy knows is best, no longer am I the supreme fount of earthly information. I'm having a bitch of a time letting go, it's not enough that she's my child, I want her to *be* a child, young, innocent, needy. I realized for the first time this weekend that my needs are greater than hers; it brought real physical pain, gut-pain. She'll handle Seattle effortlessly; a month there and she'll have a new life; and I won't be part of it. Already she was talking about the new house they're going to have, the new car, new everything. Same old daddy, she'll visit me all the time, more than ever; she comforts me as best she can.

She comforts *me*.

It's going to be brutal. She's lying asleep in her bed thirty feet from me and I'm already missing her.

"I want to show you something," Patricia says again.

I look up. She's in her bedroom, framed in the doorway, the light low behind her.

"What is it? I've got to go, I've got work to do yet tonight."

"It'll just take a minute."

I walk to the bedroom door. She's by the window, her back to me. She's wearing shorts, nothing else. I feel a tightening in my sphincter. She turns to face me.

"What do you think?"

My mouth goes completely dry. I haven't been this nervous around a woman since junior high.

"They're beautiful," I tell her when I manage to find my voice.

She walks towards me until we're a foot apart. "Do you really think so?"

I nod; I can't trust myself to speak too much.

"They're not too big?"

I wet my lips, fighting for saliva. "No. They're just right. Perfect," I croak.

They're jutting out at me. When I was a kid we used to call tits like these Cadillac bumpers.

She smiles. "I was afraid of getting them too big, I didn't want to feel trashy, you know?"

I nod dumbly.

"But I figured as long as I'm doing it I might as well go for it. Within the bounds of good taste," she adds, schoolgirl-shy. "As if anything this insane could be in good taste."

"They look fine. Very real."

"They are real. I just helped them out a little."

"Yeh. That's what I mean." She's standing there with these extremely firm, large breasts pointing at me. I never knew she had such balls, not only for the operation but to stand there and let me, make me, look. She's changing her life, everything about it. She's doing it. I want to cheer.

I feel my erection. Get out of here right now. Get the fuck out of here.

"I was scared to show you," she says.

"I can believe it, knowing you."

"I thought about it all afternoon."

I'm hard. I haven't been hard around her in a long time. If she looks she'll see. It'll embarrass her; she's not forward sexually. Boost her ego, though. Maybe. Or gross her out. I don't know, not wanting an erection is a new and disquieting thought.

"But I finally thought, 'I have to show someone, why go through something this difficult if no one knows?' And you're the only one." She steps even closer. "Go ahead and touch them. I know you want to."

"You don't know that."

"Just to see what they feel like? In the interest of medical science?"

Where did she get so bold? Give a woman a new set of knockers and she thinks she owns the world. Hell, maybe she does. I should applaud that in her, she's always been such a wallflower about self-promotion.

They're tight. My fingers touch them lightly underneath, a gentle and hopefully guileless caress.

No such luck. Her involuntary moan and my rabid tumescence overlap each other. My hand jerks away like it's touched a hot iron.

"Will, I'm sorry." She's blushing furiously.

"It's okay." I've got to get out of here. Right fucking now.

I'm rooted to the spot.

"I shouldn't have done this. I don't know what came over me."

You got these great new tits, you didn't want to keep it a secret or what's the point, you have to show them to someone and I'm harmless, the eunuch ex-husband. You want to show off, you want to know you can still turn a man on. All or some of the above.

"You're proud of what you did and what you look like. I can understand that." I'm breathing easier now, regaining some control, if not of the situation at least of myself. "Do me a favor, though, put on a T-shirt."

She slips one on, holding her arms over her head longer than I think she needs to. I'm going to have the whole show, including the curtain call.

This is the best beer I've had in a long time, I really needed this beer, she went out and bought it this afternoon, knowing what was to or at least might come, if she could summon the courage. So if she was going to show me her new breasts, her new her, which she and I both know, despite her seeming ease, would be difficult for her, she was going to help me come down afterwards. It's considerate; a gesture in some ways more meaningful to me than the unveiling.

"How's the case going?" She reaches over, takes a sip of my beer.

"It's going."

"How's your team?"

"They're good. Busting their asses."

"Mary Lou too?"

"Especially her." I look up; there's an edge in her voice.

"She's a good lawyer?" A rhetorical question; she knows Mary Lou's working reputation. She wants me to demur, to tell her Mary Lou's not so great, she's just lucky. I can't. It's a lie, she knows it's a lie, and Mary Lou's my partner, I stand up for my partners. At least until they fuck me. God forbid that with Mary Lou.

"So far. She really wants it, this case."

"Who wouldn't?" The jealousy's out in the open. I choose to ignore it.

"You'd be surprised. A lot of lawyers wouldn't touch a case like this. Even if you win, it can be political shit."

"I'd give anything to get a case like this," she says. "I'd give my left tit." She laughs mirthlessly. "Even my new left tit."

"It's not what you do." Finish your beer and make a graceful exit, this conversation is going nowhere but down.

"No shit Sherlock."

"Come on babe. Don't. Everybody else is already beating up on me."

"I'm sorry. I'm jealous, I can't help it."

"Now what's the point . . ."

"The point is that Mary Lou's got the case and I don't. That's the point. The point is that she's the hot female lawyer in town, she's with the big firm, she's almost ten years younger than me, she's pretty, she's got the world by the balls. And you know what? I'm a better lawyer but she's on the fast track and I'm not and I'm never going to make it to the major leagues if I stay here in Santa Fe. That's the point, Will. And don't sit there so damn dense about it."

"I can't help any of that. And anyway she's not prettier."

"At least not her boobs. They're not world-class like these new cantaloupes," she says, thrusting them up at me across the table. She's popped her own Heineken's, takes a long pull. "Are they?"

I almost choke on my beer. "Got's to go," I recover.

"Answer my question first."

"I don't know." Occasionally I can tell the truth. "I strongly doubt it."

"You're sleeping with her."

"No. I'm not."

"All right, not yet. You will. It's a matter of time."

"Who says she would even I wanted to?"

"Can't hurt and it might help. You're the senior, you're the star, everyone likes a little star-fucking, they think it rubs off."

"It's unprofessional," I say. I hear that old Jimmy Durante song buzzing in my head: 'Did you ever have the feeling that you wanted to go, but then you had the feeling that you wanted to stay?'

"That's never stopped you before." She stands. "It's okay, I'm not judging you. Be the best loving she'll ever get." She's around the table, close to me, her nipples hard against my chest. "I know that of which I speak."

Her fingers brush the side of my neck; so much more erotic than the feel of her breasts.

We fuck like the end of the world is upon us; it's got to be a disaster, probably the stupidest, most reckless act I've ever done, so I play this jive scenario in my head: it's acceptable because you aren't going to live to regret it. What fatuous bullshit: I'm regretting it while we're doing it, before even, while we're undressing. All over each other quickly, not allowing time for thought, reflection; that would kill it, it has to be unconscious. We have to try to make it unconscious.

'I'm going to fuck the shit out of her.' 'I'm going to fuck her brains out.' 'I'm going to punish her pussy.' All that swaggering high school talk we used to verbally circle-jerk to in the men's room while stealing a smoke, the rubber forming an indelible circle in your wallet. Not love but conquest. There's no delicate foreplay, when I kiss her hard new breasts there's a real hunger; her sensitivity magnified by my roughness and her acute self-conscious awareness of them, she cries out, louder than I remember her ever doing, biting into a pillow so the sounds won't penetrate the walls into Claudia's room.

I'm astonished at her sexual energy; the polar opposite of any love-making we ever did when we were married, as if the change wasn't simply the new breasts but everything about her. She's a gumby, she's all over me. When I enter her she grabs the cheeks of my ass so hard I'm afraid she's going to draw blood. 'I'm going to bang the shit out of her.' That's a laugh; I'm fighting for survival here. We bang away at each other, the roughest ride I've ever had.

She bites my shoulder when she comes, pulling me to her with such force I could slip inside and be lost forever. Everything releases in her, orgasm, tears, sorrow, pent-up anger. Rivers of passion. It scares me.

"We can't ever do that again."

"I know that." She's naked, reclining against the headboard, her breasts sticking straight out. We drink our Heineken's straight from the bottle.

"We shouldn't have done it this time."

"Why not?" she asks.

"Come on, Patricia, you know fucking well why not."

She sits up into the lotus position. I can't stop looking at her breasts. They don't sag an inch.

"Because we're not married?" she asks. "You've laid half the un-married women in this town, Will, why should one more make a difference?"

"Because we *were* married."

"It's all right to bed down any common piece of trash that'll have you," she says, leaning forward, "but not your ex-wife? I'm lower than some pick-up in a bar?"

"I loved you," I tell her. "That's the difference."

"You can sleep with somebody you don't care about but you can't sleep with someone you love. Loved," she corrects herself.

"Something like that." I'm weary, this has drained me, I should get dressed and bail out.

"That's a sad set of principles. I'm feeling sorry for you when I hear you talk like that."

"Join the party."

She looks at me quizzically. "You can rest easy," she informs me. "It won't happen again."

"No shit."

"Because *I* won't need it again."

I look at her.

"I wanted validation," she says straight out. "The boob job was one step. To take it to completion I had to have a man and you're the only one I could trust myself with."

"Thanks, I guess," I grouse. Jesus.

"What's the matter?" she asks.

"I feel used, that's the matter. What the fuck do you think?"

"You were. So what?"

"So I don't like it. Especially from you."

She shrugs. "Couldn't be helped, Will. We all have to use each other sometimes."

"You sound like me," I tell her.

"Is that so bad?"

"Coming from your mouth it is. You used to rag me all the time when I talked like that." I'm the mercy fuck, that's what I've come down to.

"Too bad, Will. Now you know what it used to sound like to me."

Touché. I tilt my bottle in salute, drink. She joins me, a healthy swallow.

"For some reason I thought you didn't drink anymore," I inquire.

"Occasionally. If I'm going to need emotional fortification. It wasn't easy setting this in my mind," she confesses, "I was on edge all day thinking about it." She tilts the bottle. Her neck is still beautiful, long, ivory in the moonlight. She seems at ease, remarkably unself-conscious about her body; or she's a better actress than I remember. Better at a lot of things than I remember.

"I heard *you* quit completely," she adds, sighting me over the lip of her bottle.

"Not true," I answer, trying to keep my voice casual. "Where'd you hear that?"

"Andy," she replies. "He told me you'd decided to kick."

I shrug. "I was overindulging there for awhile, I'll admit to that. I'm cutting back, just beer and wine now, I'm off the hard stuff. Probably better."

"I guess I misread him. It seemed to be of real concern to him."

"He's a mother hen. It's his nature to worry."

She nods. "Think about it," she says.

"About what?"

"Quitting completely."

"Why should I do that?"

"Because you're an alcoholic or close enough that no one can tell the difference," she answers. "It's not a secret. Even Claudia knows."

"That's bullshit," I defend myself.

"It's your life."

"That's right," I reply, too hotly.

"But it's hers too," she reminds me.

"I'm fine with her." Why have I let myself get on the defensive like this?

"You're great. But she sees it. It influences her."

"If it'll make you feel any better I won't drink around her," I say. "At least not hard stuff."

"Thanks. It does." She leans over, touches my hand. "You're a wonderful father and don't you ever forget it."

I stand in her doorway. There's a strong smell of jasmine and honeysuckle coming from the side of the porch. She's leaning against the jamb, wearing a short robe.

"You're still a great lover," she tells me. "Sorry if I wasn't completely straight with you."

"It's okay," I nod. "You're terrific yourself."

"It'll be a nice memory to take into my old age," she says.

"You'll forget it as soon as a better man comes along." I've gotten over my anger at being used.

"I hope not." She means it.

It's comfortable here, standing on my old porch, looking at my former wife, the residue of sex still hovering around us.

"Will," she says in parting, "good luck with the case."

"Thanks. I'm going to need it."

She pauses a moment; she wants to say something to me but doesn't know if I want to hear it. I wait her out.

"You've got a good team," she says. "Even with Mary Lou."

"I think so."

"And I'm only jealous of her professionally—not the other way."

"You don't have to be anymore. They're calling you up to the bigs, kid, remember?"

She smiles a moment. Serious again: "Can I ask you a question? Professional?"

"Shoot."

"How come the firm isn't involved more?"

I feel the hair rising on the back of my neck. "What do you mean?" I ask cautiously.

"From what I can see, which admittedly isn't at first hand, they don't seem to be giving you much support. I realize you're on a leave and this is a one-shot deal, but still and all it's a sensational case, you'll probably get national coverage. It's like they're invisible."

A long, slow exhale. Fuck it, if you can't tell your ex-wife, who can you tell?

"There's an easy answer for that."

A smile of relief crosses her face. Goddam, she really does care.

"My leave of absence isn't voluntary."

"Oh my God!" Her hands are at her mouth, then she's smothering me, pulling me to her, against her breasts. They aren't soft and comforting, I realize nothing is perfect.

"Those bastards," she exclaims. "Those lousy shits. After all you've done for them. They'd be nowhere without you."

"They figure they're nowhere with me. And by their lights they're right," I say.

"Fuck their lights."

My sentiments exactly.

"Let me help you." She's holding my arms in a gesture of solidarity.

"No." I shake my head.

"Why?"

"Because it's wrong, that's why."

"Who cares," she answers, she's so much more practical than I am. "You need all the help and support you can get, the rest is immaterial."

I have to be as honest as I can. "From anyone else, Patricia, except from you."

"That's lousy."

"I know," I say, "but I can't see you anymore. Nada. Nix. It's got to be absolutely hands-off between us."

"Because of tonight?"

"Yes."

"Shit." She's angry. "Why didn't you tell me this before?"

"There was no reason to. Why," I ask, "would it have made a difference?"

"I don't know," she answers truthfully. "Maybe. Probably."

"Sorry."

"Who was to know?" She fixes me with a rueful smile. "I blew my shot at the big-time in Santa Fe for a lousy piece of ass."

I smile back. I'm scared inside, now that I've said it.

"If you ever want to talk . . ." She leaves it dangling.

"I'll call you."

"Promise?"

I nod. I give her a chaste forehead kiss, walk out the screen door and down the porch stairs. She's still watching as I'm driving away.

My apartment hasn't been cleaned in two weeks, the air conditioner's on its last legs, I feel unclean. If I wasn't hoarding my pennies I'd take a hotel room for the night, get a cleaning lady in in the morning to fumigate the place.

Instead, I pour myself a healthy Johnnie Walker over the rocks. You weak motherfucker, you couldn't leave well enough alone, it's bad enough you fucked her, you had to bleed all over her rug, tell her about the firm. Christ, it could be all over town by lunch tomorrow. The second Scotch helps; stop panicking, she's not like that, she'll take your secret to the grave. But what if it slips out inadvertently? It's bound to, she works for Robertson and he's obsessed with it.

She answers on the third ring. "That was quick."

"Yeh." Shit, why the hell did I call?

"Is something wrong?"

"No, no." I kill my drink, lean across the counter for the bottle, pouring myself another, just a couple fingers.

"Will?" She's alarmed.

"Listen, what we talked about earlier . . ."

"Yes?"

"Why don't we just forget it, okay? We never had that conversation."

"Well . . . how could I do that? Why would you want me to?"

"Just don't tell anyone, okay?" Keeping the terror out of my voice, not entirely successful.

There's a pause at the other end.

"Pat?"

"Why would I tell anyone?"

"You wouldn't. It could just slip out, you know." Fuck, if I step on my dick anymore I'll tear it out at the root.

"Not from me it won't," she tells me with certainty. "I think you're projecting what you would do."

"I meant by accident. That's all."

"I'm not you, Will. Your secret's safe with me."

"Hey, I knew that."

It hangs between us over the hum in the line.

"It's late," she reminds me.

"Yeh. Got to kick ass in the morning."

"I'm glad you called. That you felt you could."

"So am I." I mean it.

"Next time try to be more positive, all right?"

I bang the receiver against my forehead.

"All right. I promise."

"Good. Good night Will."

"Good night, Pat."

She hangs up on me. You dumb shit, every time you think you have the world by the balls it turns out to be your own balls you're squeezing. And right now the pain is killing me.

"YOUR HONOR, we'd like to be heard on this issue."

Judge Martinez nods.

This is a hearing on a change-of-venue motion we've filed. The jury's yet to be selected. This could be crucial.

Moseby ambles over from his side. He must've had garlic bread for lunch; his breath reeks, wafting across the front of the bench. Mary Lou wrinkles her nose, brushes her hand across her face. Frank grins at her; pieces of his lunch stick in his teeth. She shakes her head in disgust. The others feign indifference. I've long since quit thinking about him, except as my opponent. The issues are too big to get caught up in personalities.

"Counselor?" Judge Martinez peers down. He's the senior judge on the court, a former D.A., who made sure the case fell on his docket, not so much for the case itself—he's handled dozens of murders, he doesn't need publicity or the aggravation that goes with these—but because if the bikers are found guilty he doesn't want the case reversed on appeal and figures he has a better chance of keeping it clean than any other judge. He's a tough, generally pro-prosecution jurist, but he runs a straight courtroom.

"On what grounds?" Martinez asks.

"On the grounds that our clients can't get a fair and impartial trial in Santa Fe, your honor," Tommy says. "This case has had more pretrial publicity than any case in New Mexico history."

"They have to be tried somewhere," Martinez reminds us.

"We have three volumes of newspaper and magazine clippings, your honor," Paul says. "Six hours of videotapes. It's impossible that anyone who lives in Santa Fe hasn't read or heard about this case."

"I don't know," Martinez says. "That's what jury selection's going to tell us."

"The evidence seems overwhelming, your honor," Tommy argues.

Martinez glares at him. "I'm supposed to be the judge of that, counselor," he rasps.

"No offense, your honor," Tommy replies quickly. Rule number one—don't piss off the judge. "All I meant was there's more of it than any other case our research has found."

Martinez turns to Moseby. "What's the prosecution's view on this?" he asks.

"We want to try it here, your honor," Frank replies, taking care not to breathe on Martinez. "We feel we can impanel as fair and impartial a jury here in Santa Fe as anyplace else in the state. It's a notorious case, Judge Martinez. The prosecution's going to deal with that the best it can. The defense ought to, too."

He's a slob, but he's cunning. Admit the problem and by doing so disarm it. It puts him in the catbird seat: we're bitching and he's making do the best he can.

Martinez ponders while we wait. He knows that Moseby's demurral, while essentially bullshit, has enough truth in it to hang a decision on; and he also knows this could be one of the most important decisions he makes during the entire long, drawn-out affair. If, after going through an entire trial and finding the defendants guilty, an appellate court decides the jury wasn't impartial, the whole shooting match could start again. States don't like spending millions of dollars on retrying cases that could've been done right the first time.

"I'm going to withhold judgment on this," Martinez says finally. I groan inside; I was afraid of this, which is why we delayed asking for the change right away, agonizing for weeks over it, going through a lot of discussion and soul-searching. We could spend a month trying to get a jury and then have Martinez decide we were right and the case has to be moved. Then we'd have to start all over again. It's becoming the fashion to do this here, and it's a royal pain in the ass, not to mention being time-consuming and damned expensive.

We trudge back to the table. Behind us, our clients, cleaned up for their court appearances but still menacing as hell, look to us for signs, good or bad. We try to give them nothing; we'll discuss our feelings in private, we don't want to send any signals publicly that the prosecution might capitalize on. But they know by now that no news is bad news, they've been inside for months, they're taking on the defeatist attitude of the incarcerated. I feel for them, then catch myself in the irony; under normal circumstances I'd be happy to see people like them safely removed from society. Right now all I'm looking at are four more victims of a hopelessly fucked-up system.

"THIS IS the 'NBC Nightly News' with Tom Brokaw."

It's five-thirty. We're sitting in my office, watching the tube: Paul, Tommy, Mary Lou, me. We've made the national news. It's been a slow day, I guess; even so, this is the big time. We savor it with a kind of morbid fascination, like ancient Christians standing on the floor of the Colosseum, looking up and gawking at a hundred thousand bloodthirsty Romans.

We're the lead story after the first commercial break. The NBC correspondent, a blow-dried woman wearing a Gucci scarf artfully tied around her neck, stands at the bottom of the courthouse steps. Behind her, jockeying rudely for position, is the obligatory crowd of attention-seekers, fighting for their two seconds on camera.

"In Santa Fe, Judge Louis Martinez has finally impaneled a jury in New Mexico's most sensational murder trial in several years, in which four members of the outlaw motorcycle gang known as the Scorpions allegedly killed and violently mutilated drifter Richard Bartless. With me is District Attorney John Robertson, whose office is prosecuting this case."

The camera widens out to include Robertson, who looks every inch the proper man of the courtroom (to my less-than-impartial eye he appears unctuous and faintly sweaty) in his three-piece Hickey-Freeman suit.

"Are you glad to be finally going to trial?" the blow-dry queen asks, her face screwed up all-pretty-like, TV's idea of what passes for serious.

Robertson nods. He's serious for real, this is major personal to him. "The people of New Mexico deserve this trial," he says. "This was a vicious, heinous crime and the perpetrators need to be severely dealt with. We don't want it to get caught up in a bunch of legal malarkey," he continues, an unseen dig at the defense, nicely played to the public, you plant as many subconscious hooks as you can, "we have the evidence to prove they're guilty beyond a shadow of a doubt and we want them to pay for their crime."

"You'll be asking for the death penalty?" she asks.

"Anything less would be a gross miscarriage of justice."

"Screw you too, Jack," Mary Lou tells the image on the tube, watching alongside of me. Her hand drops lightly onto my thigh, an unconscious gesture of reassurement. I get a twinge.

The rest of the team catcalls the screen, expressing like sentiments. We're developing our own bunker mentality, us against the world and fuck 'em all but six, the kind of self-support you need to carry you through.

On the screen the camera shifts angles, and suddenly there I am for the whole world to see. I'm looking good, my clothes fit and aren't wrinkled, my hair's in place, my look is bright. An altogether formidable opponent, alert and at ease with myself and my task, not uptight like the impression Robertson made.

The people in the room applaud. I'm thinking about Claudia, that she's watching her daddy with pride. It feels good—I'm on the case.

"With me now is Will Alexander, one of New Mexico's foremost criminal trial lawyers and the lead attorney for the defendants. Tell me," she asks, "are you and your partners satisfied with the progress of the trial so far?"

"No," I answer. I look serious, I don't have to fake it. "The trial hasn't actually started," I properly correct her, "this has all been preliminary, but no, we aren't as satisfied as we'd like to be."

"For what reason?"

"Unlike the prosecutor, we're going to conduct our defense inside the courtroom," I tell her and the world, getting my digs in. "But I will say this: I don't believe the defendants are being judged by a fair and impartial jury. Not as I understand the meaning of the words 'fair' and 'impartial.' More than half the jurors are women, none of them have ever been on a motorcycle, none of them have ever been inside a jail, let alone served time in one. These are some of the reasons we had asked for a change of venue, which was regrettably denied."

"So you contend there is a built-in bias towards the accused," she says.

"What do you think?" I answer. Always take the offense, if they're defending they can't attack. "You read the local papers you'll see our clients have already been convicted, at least by anyone who's heard anything about it, which is practically everyone in this state, certainly in this county."

"And that's why you asked for the change of venue," she presses.

"It was one of the reasons."

"How do you feel about Judge Martinez turning you down?"

"Check with me when it's over," I answer.

I watch as the camera comes off me, moving in close on her for a brief wrap-up before cutting back to Brokaw. What she says is this: no member of any biker gang has ever been executed for committing a crime, particularly the crime of murder. The enormity of that is what's fueling so much interest in us, beyond the case itself. Society wants to burn an outlaw.

Paul turns it off. "Not bad," he says.

"I came across okay," I admit. I don't hide my light under a bushel. "Serious and caring."

Everyone chuckles. Anything to break this damn tension.

"You were good," Tommy adds. "Robertson looked worried."

"Because he has the most to lose," Paul continues, an important point. In the strictest sense that's not true; the bikers have the most to lose. But he's right in the trial sense, lawyer versus lawyer. Everyone figures the prosecution has cards and spades in this one; if they lose and we win they're dogshit. So the conventional wisdom goes. On the other hand, I've won more than my share of cases that didn't look hopeful, at least when they began. So it's not like the betting's going all one way.

The four of us spend a couple more hours together, last-minute practicing for tomorrow's opening statements. I'll go last: I'm the star, the *jefe*. Moseby'll most certainly do his shuck and jive ol' boy shtick, but he won't orate, because if he does I'll level him when it's my turn. You have to be true to yourself in the courtroom, if you can shoot the moon you go for it, otherwise you play your cards conservatively and don't go for the bluff, certainly not at the beginning.

Paul and Tommy take off. Mary Lou stays, banging away at the word processor, last-minute polishing on her remarks. She's never been in this deep before; I know how scary your first murder case can be. I stand at my window, looking out at the dark city. The only lights still on are from bars, where I won't be tonight. I sit down in my chair, my back to Mary Lou and the room, on automatic pilot, playing my opening in my head.

She finishes her changes, prints them out on the laser printer. It's quiet for a moment—she's gone down the hall to Xerox.

I sense her behind me before the actual touch, her hands on my shoulders, massaging them strongly. I tense, then relax. It feels good, comforting, her hands rhythmically stroking.

"You don't know how much I admire you," she tells me, digging deep. "Sometimes I get so enthralled watching you in the courtroom I forget I'm on the job."

"Thanks." The massage feels wonderful. I have an overwhelming impulse to kiss the palm of her hand, tongue it. I manage to resist. I can smell her, her perfume mingled with her faint body odors, we've been on the go for fifteen hours. She's slipped out of her heels, sways on her stockinged feet.

I'm hard. If there was ever a time in my life I didn't want that, this is it. I try to think of multiplication tables, batting averages. She continues kneading, her strong thumbs stretching my neck muscles. I want to melt.

She massages my temples. I close my eyes, breathing with the tempo of her moving hands. As I finally start to relax, feeling an ebb in my desire, a hand slips to the side of my neck, an unmistakable caress. The moan almost passes my lips; I manage to stifle it.

Jesus Christ. *She's* on the make for *me*. Patricia was right; she knew something women know instinctively.

I take the hand from my neck, holding it, standing and turning to her. It's finally out in the open. This will be the greatest sexual coupling in modern times, if I've ever known anything in my life I know this.

"I'm dying to sleep with you, Mary Lou," I tell her. Dying's the operative word here, but not in the way she'd understand.

She breaks into a girlish smile, happy and relieved. "Oh, Jesus. I was afraid I was making a complete fool of myself, but I couldn't help it, so . . ."

Now I know where they got the expression about knees turning to jelly. I feel like I'm actually going to collapse. All this time fantasizing about her, and she's been doing the same thing.

"But I can't do it. Not now."

She stares quizzically at me.

"We can't." I'm starting to get dry, cottonmouth. "We're working together eighteen hours a day," I say, pushing the words out before I weaken, "if we're lovers it clouds the issue. One time with you and I'll be ruined forever, I'll be mooning like a schoolboy. It just isn't professional, Mary Lou."

What a fucking joke. It's never stopped me before. Of all times to grow up.

She looks at me like I just got off the five-ten from Mars.

"What're you talking about?" she says, "it happens all the time."

"It does?" Suddenly I feel like a seventh-grader.

"Of course."

"I didn't know that," I stammer.

"You never have?"

"No."

"But you're a celebrated . . . cocksman," she says.

"Maybe. But not where I eat."

"But it's unavoidable, Will, you work with people around the clock, sooner or later you'll find one that turns you on." She looks right at me, making sure I'm not putting her on, playing a little game. "You're serious, aren't you?"

"I'm afraid so."

"Shit. I've been saving myself for the right one for years, staving off half the senior partners in my firm, and I fall for a virtuous man. Probably the only one left in town; definitely the most unlikely."

"Sorry," I tell her. Man, how I am.

"Unprofessional," she says, as if it's a foreign word, a language she's not accustomed to hearing. "Guess I'm not exposed to that kind of thinking these days."

Jesus, Mary Lou, don't give up so easily.

"Can I have a raincheck?" This is no act, she's serious.

"When this trial is over," I promise her, "if you're still interested," I caution.

"I'll still be interested," she assures me.

Maybe this is a sign. A good woman finds the inner me attractive.

I walk her to her car, which is parked in the lot across the street. She unlocks the door, turns to me.

"A preview," she says, planting a quick one flush on my mouth, "so you won't chicken out about honoring that raincheck."

"Don't worry." Her taste lingers. Virtue doesn't always have its own rewards.

She drives off, winking her lights at me. I watch her disappear. For the first time in my life I've turned down a piece of ass I wanted.

"IN THE CASE OF the State of New Mexico versus Jensen, Paterno, Hicks, and Kowalski, Judge Louis Martinez presiding, all rise."

The butterflies leave my stomach as I stand. We're in Courtroom A, the biggest courtroom in the state. Classic Southwestern adobe architecture: high-ceilinged, dark wood beams, elaborately carved benches. It's what a courtroom's supposed to look like, even more so to me than the neo-Roman and -Greek stuff you find back east. I love participating in trials here; it makes lawyering feel like an elevated profession.

It's crowded. Every seat is taken, people are standing in the back in violation of the fire regs. Reporters hover, sketch artists got here at the crack of dawn, jockeying for decent seats. There are seven lawyers, the four of us and three from the prosecution side, plus staff, all of us wanting to stake out our position, gain the upper hand.

Martinez gives a little speech. All trials are unique, all trials are important, but this one is a little more unique, a little more important. This is a capital offense involving multiple defendants, any or all of whom may wind up being executed by the state. Which means, he's telling everyone, this has to be scrupulously tried. No grandstanding, no media histrionics, no F. Lee Bailey–type playing to the mob via the press, using the John Landis case in L.A. a few years ago as an example. He's not going to impose a gag order on the participants, particularly the lawyers, he says, unless they force him to. That's fine with me, I think to myself as I listen to him, there's going to be press coverage coming out the yin-yang before this is over, most of it not in our favor. Robertson and his minions can't win it on the outside, they'll have to win it right here, with a tightly sequestered jury; they'll have to win it on merit if they can. The newspaper and television pundits, those high-and-mighty arbiters of right and wrong, have already concluded we're stone-cold losers, but that's peripheral shit, titillating on impact, but ultimately not important.

Moseby delivers the prosecution's opening remarks. His suit is pressed, he's clean-shaven, he's had a haircut. Still, he's a rube; a cultivated rube, 'one of us.' Small-town, a husband and parent, God-fearing, a regular churchgoer like you folks. (I have to stifle a sour laugh when he mentions that; still, I know too well that that kind of cheap crap plays.)

"I am a public servant, pure and simple," he tells the jury. "I have no ax to grind. I'm here on behalf of the people of New Mexico for one reason—to see that justice is done."

He talks for over an hour, presenting his case in two basic thrusts: one, he has incontrovertible evidence. An impeccable eye-witness. The indisputable findings of one of the country's foremost forensic pathologists. Physical evidence that clearly ties the victim to the accused. So forth and so on.

The second, more important part of his argument is an attack on the defendants, which, he's saying between the lines, is really what this trial's about. I can't blame him, I'd do the exact same thing with defendants like these. He throws plenty of red meat, but it's nothing compared with what he'll do in final summation. Still, just listening to him, it's damning. They are outlaws, they hold the rules of civilized people in contempt. That is known, a given. They have no morality, no soul. They're psychopathic, he tells the jury: they know the difference between right and wrong but they simply don't give a damn, they have no social or moral obligations, the only thing they care about is their immediate personal gratification. And if that results in suffering or death to some innocent party, too damn bad.

He winds up riding a crest of moral outrage. These four beasts killed in cold blood. They committed murder in a calculated, premeditated way. They caused the victim great suffering, they committed horribly perverted indignities. And they laughed about it.

Moseby concludes by walking to our side of the room and standing in front of our table, close enough to the defendants, Lone Wolf particularly, to touch them.

"We'll see who's laughing when this jury brings in its verdict," he says, staring Lone Wolf right in the eyes, "when this jury of decent, *civilized* men and women bring in the only verdict they can under the evidence: murder in the first degree. Murder punishable by execution."

My hand's on Lone Wolf's wrist under the table, gripping as hard as I can. My heart's pounding; we've warned them over and over that this kind of accusation's going to be thrown at them, they have to keep their cool. One incident, one outburst, and they might as well plead guilty as charged. And still it's almost impossible, they only know one way to go: charge straight ahead.

I look at Lone Wolf. His eyes are cold, there's definitely murder in them. He's *capable* of killing, that I know.

He relaxes his tension, I let go of his wrist. I'm sweating. He turns to me, his look saying: 'I can handle this.'

I exhale silently. One hurdle cleared. I'm proud of him. He's not going to blow it for me.

We go in turn; Tommy, Mary Lou, Paul. Each talking about the specifics of his (or her) own client, each talking about the case, presenting things from different angles, different perspectives. Professional, prepared. Planting little seeds of doubt that hopefully will be full-grown by the time the trial's over. Reasonable doubt, pushing the boundaries of reasonable doubt. Could they have done it? Maybe. Could someone else have done it? Definitely maybe. We'll present our witnesses, too, scores of them, who will show that the accused could not, absolutely could not, have committed this crime under the circumstances. Can't be, ladies and gentlemen of the jury.

It's late afternoon. The sun throws long tendrilly shadows across the room through the floor-to-ceiling south-facing windows. The dust hangs suspended in the serried air, grown thick over the course of the day despite the ubiquitous air-conditioning. It's my turn, the last opening statement. I stand, ready to give 'em hell.

There's a commotion in the back. Someone's opened the door partway. Martinez looks up, annoyed. This isn't allowed, not in this courtroom, especially not this case, the very first day.

"Bailiff," he calls.

A marshal quickly approaches the bench, whispers something in the judge's ear.

I glance over at Moseby. He's sitting back, at ease. Next to him, Robertson smiles. He's been here most of the day, he's going to be spending a lot of time in this courtroom, to let the people know how seriously he takes this case. They're both too smug, they've been let in on the secret, whatever it is. Robertson looks over at me, cocking his head. Fuck *me,* he's saying, fuck *you.*

"All right," Martinez instructs the bailiff, "let her in."

The door swings open. A woman in a wheelchair is being pushed into the courtroom by a deputy sheriff. She's probably fifty or so, but looks at least a decade older. Country to the bone: lank gray hair pulled back in a severe bun, long veinous hands, pocked with liver spots, the fingers callused, nails cracked, grotesquely twisted into themselves. Brutal, painful arthritis. A plain dumb face devoid of makeup. She's dressed in black like an Amish spinster, down to her lace-up orthopedic square-heeled shoes.

The buzz goes up, particularly among the reporters clustered in the rear, as the woman is pushed down the center aisle, all the way to the gate in the rail that separates participants from spectators. The deputy stops, awaiting instructions. The woman laboriously turns in her wheelchair, staring at the defendants. It's painful to watch; even Lone Wolf looks away.

"May we approach the bench, your honor?" Moseby asks.

Martinez nods curtly. I join Moseby in front of the judge. He'd better have a solid reason for this bullshit.

"This is pretty damn unusual, counselor." Martinez admonishes Moseby with more than a touch of annoyance in his voice.

"I know it is, your honor." He turns to me, dripping with contriteness. "I don't mean to step on you, Will, I really mean that, it's just . . ."

"Hold on, ace," I interject vigorously. This is pissing me off royally, momentum is vital, this could completely fuck me up with the jury before I even get started. "Who the hell is this woman and why is she being brought in here just as I'm about to start my opening statement, judge?"

"Her name is Cora Bartless," Moseby says, throwing down a trump. "The victim's mother."

Jesus, Mary and Joseph. Talk about a kick in the balls.

"We expected her here first thing this morning, your honor," Moseby says, turning back to Martinez, "but there was a screw-up on her airplane connection out of Salt Lake City because of the wheelchair. They made her sit in the airport half the day before they figured it out. She put up her own money to fly out here from Arkansas, you can tell by looking at her she doesn't have money to throw around but this is everything to her. She wants to be at this trial, your honor," he says aggressively. "She deserves it."

"You didn't handle this very well, counselor." Martinez is mad and wants Moseby to know it.

"It was the airline's fault," Moseby whines.

"The airline my ass. It was *your* fault. For cutting it so close."

He steeples his fingers. "Well, she's here now. Can't shove that one back in the jar." He turns to me. "Do you want to recess until tomorrow, counselor? If you do just say so."

I look at my team, at the defendants, at the poor unsuspecting woman sitting in the wheelchair, an unknowing pawn in a tawdry game Robertson and Moseby are playing.

"I'd prefer to do it now, your honor," I tell him. "In fact, I insist on it."

"I'm going to call a half-hour recess so we can get her settled somewhere unobtrusive," Martinez tells us. "Then you're on."

During the recess I let the defendants and my colleagues in on Robertson's dirty little scam. My erstwhile friend and Moseby are carefully seating her at the far edge of the front row where the jury can clearly see her.

"Motherfucker's dead," Lone Wolf says in his high whispery voice, looking over at her and them. "Stone fucking cold dead."

I lean towards him, keeping my voice down so no one will hear. "Listen to me, shit-for-brains. I am not going to tell you this again: you are to shut up in this courtroom and anywhere else where you might be overheard, *comprende?* I'm not going to see this case go down the drain because some reporter or court officer hears that kind of garbage from you. You do what I tell you when I tell you and nothing else or we're walking and I mean all four of us."

The other bikers look at him, at me.

"Do what he says, man," Roach whispers.

Lone Wolf wheels on him, as much as he can sitting in his chair.

"It's all of us," Dutchboy adds. For the first time since I've met them, they're asserting themselves as individuals, not just being dummies letting Lone Wolf do not only their talking, but their thinking as well.

"Don't bring us all down 'cause you're pissed at something," he says.

"It's all our lives," Goose pleads. "You know we're all together with you, Wolf, but come on, man. Please."

Lone Wolf is obviously taken aback by these sudden declarations of independence. "It's an expression, for Christsakes." He puts his hand on Goose's shoulder. "Just an expression. You know me better'n that."

"I do know you," Goose answers. I've never seen him stand up to Lone Wolf before. "That's why I'm saying what I'm saying."

"It's just an expression. Anyway . . . how am I going to get to him when I'm locked up tighter than a virgin's ass?"

"You got your ways," Roach says.

"All right," I say. "Let it go. But no more loose talk. From any of you."

"Fine by me." Lone Wolf leans back in his chair.

"What about the aggrieved mother?" Tommy asks. He's worried, he's not experienced at being surprised like this.

"What about her?" I repeat. "She'll watch." I pause. "Like everyone else. Maybe she'll learn something."

Paul and Tommy smile at that. The big gun's ready to fire his first salvo. Mary Lou smiles too. I like it—the knight errant going out to slay the dragon; at least inflict some serious damage. Poor woman; I'm going to be beating her off with a club after I finish my opening. I catch myself: get your cock out of this, man. People's lives are at stake here. Your cock's going to take a holiday.

"Your honor. Ladies and gentlemen of the jury." I pause, look around.

The sun is almost setting, bathing the room in a warm, enveloping magenta light. It's peaceful, almost lulling, until you remember that four men are on trial here for murder. Then the chamber doesn't look so peaceful; more sarcophagus-like.

I face the jury, establishing eye-contact with them, these twelve men and women. They do not know me, yet in some basic way I will know them intimately. I will try to find a way to get them to trust me, so that what I tell them isn't simply a lawyer's language of client-defense but the real thing, the truth of the matter.

"You're here for a reason," I tell them. "A very simple reason. To see that justice is done. That's why I'm here, too. That's why the judge is here, and the prosecutor. We may have different ideas about what justice is in any particular case, but we are all here to serve it. To find it. Even the spectators watching us, the reporters in and out of this courtroom—we're all involved, no one is impartial, because one of the basic tenets of this great country of ours is that we're all in it together, we're all responsible. We're all here to judge innocence and guilt."

I pause, turn and stare at the victim's mother. She looks around until she realizes I've fastened on her, abruptly turns away. Robertson and Moseby look back at me for her. During the break Ellen, one of the paralegals, had done some quick research using one of the phones in the lobby, getting back inside before court resumed with a smile of triumph, pressing a note in my hand.

"That lady over there," I continue, pointing to Mrs. Bartless, fixed in her wheelchair directly in their line of vision, they don't know who she is yet, Moseby was hoping to save that for a delicious moment, "she's here to find justice, too. She has a special interest in finding justice in this case. Because it was her son who was the murder victim."

The expected murmer arises from the crowd. A couple reporters dash out. Robertson and Moseby stare at me, at her, finally at each other, a study in consternation. Judge Martinez looks at me with renewed interest; it's going to be a good contest, he won't have to worry about falling asleep up there under the hot lights.

"She wants to find out who did it," I say, "and when she does she wants the guilty party put away. Not just stuck in a cell for the rest of his life: she wants him exterminated, eliminated, wiped off the face of the earth like her son was."

Another seed goes in the ground. One person, not several. One person did it, I'm saying. Which one, if one of those in the dock? A much harder call than to throw a blanket over the whole gang.

Mrs. Bartless's mouth is open, her eyes darting about nervously, looking to Robertson and Moseby for reassurance. They're preoccupied. She sits, stuck in the wheelchair.

"I can understand her feelings. I'm sure you can, too. They're legitimate feelings, heartfelt feelings, and if anyone deserves to be present here, it is this unfortunate woman." Now I fire a shot across the prosecution's bow. "But what is not legitimate is that this woman is being used!"

"Objection!" Moseby's on his feet, his face florid.

"Over-ruled." Martinez turns to the jury. "You are to disregard that outburst by the prosecution. Opening and closing remarks by their very nature are subjective and not bound by the same rules we adhere to during the body of the trial." He swivels around to the prosecution side, leaning forward. He is one unhappy judge, and he wants everyone to know it, especially the prosecutors. All he needs is to have the trial overturned on some petty legality like that.

"You are out of order," he tells Moseby harshly.

"Yes, sir." Bastard won't even look the judge straight in the eye.

"Another such outburst and I'll hold you in contempt."

"Yes, sir."

Martinez turns back to me. "The court apologizes for the interruption."

"No apology necessary, your honor," I say deferentially. My team, lawyers and defendants, are smiling. A bird's nest on the ground which we'll gladly take.

"Proceed."

Once again I turn and face the jurors. "This woman didn't get here today by accident. She didn't cash in her savings bonds and fly here from her home a thousand miles away so she could see the men the prosecution says killed her son. She didn't even know the trial had started until yesterday, when she was called up and told about it by a member of the District Attorney's staff. Ladies and gentlemen, the prosecution brought this woman here today. They've been looking for her for months and they finally found her and they bought her an airplane ticket and they got her a room in a motel down the street and they're going to pay for that room and her meals and anything else she needs until this trial is over. Even her wheelchair attendants, who cost twenty dollars an hour. They're paying for it; rather, you're paying for it. The taxpayers of the state are paying for it." I pause, letting that sink in.

"And they should. It's the least they can do for her." Immediately I regain the high moral ground. "But what they shouldn't do, what none of us should do, is use her. Life has already used her enough, far too much. The prosecutors don't want Mrs. Bartless here so she can see a trial; they want her here so she can be seen. By you." I'm at the jury rail, practically leaning over inside it, pointing at them, looking at each of them in turn.

I turn back to look at her. Robertson is morose, his head down. Moseby glares at me. Good; maybe he'll fuck up some more.

"The prosecution wants you to feel sorry for this poor woman.

They want you to feel so sorry for her that you'll convict anyone that they tell you killed her son, even if who they tell you didn't do it. Well . . . I guess that's okay. Although this seems to me to be pushing it. It's theatrical and a little underhanded, but they have a job to do."

I walk back to my table, take a sip of water, cross the room so that I'm standing near the prosecutor's bench, able to look at them, Mrs. Bartless, and the jury all at the same time.

"What isn't okay," I tell the jury, "is that they're using her. And worse; they're using you. They're afraid they don't have a real strong case against the defendants here, so they're going to ask you to convict them not on evidence, but because this poor woman in a wheelchair lost a son and someone has to pay.

"The problem is, they're right. They don't have a strong case. So they're going to cloud the issue. But ladies and gentlemen of the jury: this trial is *not* about Richard Bartless's mother. Like him, she too is a victim, and she, too, is being made to suffer." I pause once again. "Let me ask you this—hasn't she suffered enough already?"

The jury looks at her. A few of the women squirm. This is a ticklish situation; I don't want them to feel so sorry for her that they'll eat anything thrown at them, but by the same token I must defuse this issue, get it out in the open and out of the way. I have to get them to stop seeing her.

"We're all on trial here," I tell them. "But in this trial, only these defendants can be found guilty, and they alone can permanently suffer. They can be sent to jail, or even executed, for a crime they *did not* commit. I don't have to prove that; that's the prosecution's burden. As you deliberate during this trial, please remember that. The prosecution must *conclusively* prove guilt, beyond a reasonable doubt.

"There's already been enough suffering over this murder. Let's not put anyone through any more suffering. Not Mrs. Bartless. And not these four innocent men. I'm confident that you will judge this case on the facts presented, and although you'll feel in your hearts, you'll make your decision with your minds. And when you do that, you'll make the only decisions you can. You will find my client and the other defendants not guilty."

IT'S BEEN A fucked weekend. It was inevitable, after the high of my opening statement—there was nowhere to go but down. That evening I was the toast of the town; I'd beaten the state boys at their own game, at least for one day. There isn't a lawyer alive that doesn't want to stick it to the prosecution whenever he can because they have everything going for them. So when they're hoisted by the petard of their own clumsiness it makes all private lawyers feel good. That's always been my personal feeling, anyway.

What I wanted was to be with a woman, and I couldn't. Mary Lou is there but that's out; after my holier-than-thou speech about professionalism I'd be a fool to make a play for her. The only way something like that would work would be if it was true love. I'm not ready for true love again, I don't seem to be very good at it.

Saturday morning. We caucus in my office. Since the prosecution will lead off we're in a holding pattern, kind of. We have an idea of what they're going to do and we prepare as best we can around that.

Mary Lou lingers a moment after the others leave. She looks very young and appealing, in sandals, T-shirt and jeans, hair pulled back, almost no makeup.

"I thought about you last night."

"So did I," I reply.

"I'm attracted to you. Not just the lawyer stuff, the courtroom. You."

"You're seeing me at my best."

"So what?"

"So nothing I guess." What does she want? Straight-forwardness is hard for me to deal with, I prefer deviousness. Maybe that's why Patricia and I fell away from each other. She's straight, too.

"We could see each other," she says. "I don't mean sleep together. Be together."

That's novel.

"I mean, look, Will," she continues, "we're working together on a murder case. We're in lock-step until this is over. Let's not be polarized because we want to make love and can't or won't. That's ridiculous, isn't it? You don't shy away from Paul or Tommy, do you? You wouldn't brush me off if I was two hundred pounds and had warts on my chin. So why stay away from me because we have the hots for each other? That's like some kind of junior high school trip."

She walks to the door, turns back to me. "You know where to find me," she says. "So find me."

A few minutes after she leaves, Andy sticks his head in. No farther. We regard each other silently.

"I heard you breathed fire," he says, breaking the ice.

I kind of nod, shrug.

"Hell, that's what you do, Will. Nobody better."

"Thanks."

"You've got a good team."

"We're good together," I say. "How're you doing?" I have to ask in spite of myself.

"Getting along. A little dry, actually. It's quieter around here. Your leave of absence is costing us but we're okay."

"Good. I mean that you're okay." Fuck it, I'm too concentrated to grind any other axes right now.

"I want to see you win, Will."

"That makes two of us."

"The case and the other stuff."

"Like I said, me too."

He cocks a friendly finger at me, turns away. I feel good; I'm not the only one that's suffered from this.

"CALL RITA GOMEZ."

I watch as the state's case takes the long walk from the back of the room to the stand. She forces herself to keep her gaze straight ahead, wobbling unsteadily in her new, unaccustomed high heels, scrupulously avoiding eye contact with any of the bikers. Lone Wolf is staring at her with a singular intensity, an almost palpable heat radiating from his eyes.

"Keep it locked up," I caution.

He's still as a statue, his eyes boring in at her. Sooner or later she's going to have to look at him; when she does she might explode. The others stare at her, too. She was prey to them before, a defenseless muffball in the company of mean, off-the-wall predators; now she's the prime threat to their lives, the barrier between them and the free world, and they only know one way to react to something that basic: eliminate it. They can't do it physically, not in here; they'll try to do it through force of will. It can happen, I've seen it done.

She's a sad case, a K-Mart window mannequin. Her hair's been done up with so much styling gel it's as stiff as frosting on an Italian wedding cake. They obviously took her shopping for a new wardrobe but they let her pick it out—a bad mistake, even Moseby with his lack of taste must see that, the bright dress a size too small, horizontally-striped in alternating bars of yellow, red and green, stretching tight across her breasts and can, the skirt too short, the pantyhose too dark and shiny, heels too high, she must have plucked this outfit out of the Frederick's of Hollywood catalogue, it makes her look like the whore we're going to show her to be. Whoever put her makeup on (it couldn't have been her) used a trowel; her eyelashes are so coated with mascara they look like a tiny row of rosary beads. Blood-red lipstick, rouge, purple eye-liner, all over so much base that her face has the frozen look of the Joan Crawford dummy at Knott's Berry Farm's Wax Museum, the whole thing'll crack the first time she opens her baby-doll mouth. She's barely twenty-one and they've got her looking like an eighty-year-old grotesque out of a Fellini film. Although better that, I suppose, than the rash of nerve-acne it's only partially able to cover.

Four men might die because they had sex with this pathetic girl. Talk about holding life cheap.

I catch myself; I've awakened to similar, and not so long ago. A harsh reminder of what can happen when you let your cock do the thinking.

Moseby handles her well, the church deacon counseling the vulnerable young thing who's fallen on hard times but only temporarily, she's of good stuff at heart and will see the error of her ways and assume a position as a decent member of the community. Slowly, patiently, he leads her through the day and night of the crime.

She'd gone to the bar with the victim early in the evening, she starts out, it was still plenty of light out, they'd had a few drinks, just a couple, they weren't drunk or nothing, the bikers had cruised on in, made a big macho scene, scared the daylights out of everyone . . .

"This is fucking bullshit," Lone Wolf whispers fiercely.

"Fine," I hush him. "We'll catch her lies on cross-examination."

"The jury's hearing this shit!"

"That's okay," I tell him. "The more she lies and gets caught the better it'll be for us."

"But she's under oath, man," he persists. "How the fuck can she just sit up there and lie like a fucking rug?"

"You been sleeping under a rock or something?" I ask with a degree of incredulity. "What do you think goes on in a trial? You've been around this block before."

"And they put us down," he snorts contemptuously.

"Cool it," I tell him. "It's important I listen closely to this." I push a legal pad in front of him. "Make notes for me."

He starts scribbling furiously. I turn my attention back to the stand.

Richard had ranked on these guys, she's saying, they'd all been out back in the parking lot and he'd realized he was crazy to fuck with; excuse me (she's embarrassed enough to blush, it's almost as if she's been coached to screw up, play the bimbo, then recover, it reminds me of that movie *The Verdict*, where James Mason says to the prominent old anesthesiologist, don't say 'aspirated,' say 'throw up.' Don't say 'messed with,' Moseby would've told her when they were going over her story, say 'fucked with' and then make a show of remembering where you are and correct yourself, it makes you real to the jury, they'll be more likely to believe you), to mess with them, she continues, so he rabbited and ran off and left her, they all went back inside, hung around the rest of the night, so on and so forth. I've got her grand-jury transcript in front of me, I leaf through it as I listen, she's right on the money, virtually word for word.

That's to be expected, of course: she's been coached. All witnesses are, it's S.O.P. It can be a double-edged sword, though, sometimes it can be to the other side's advantage; if they crack, slip up on cross, they can wind up chasing their own tails, and blow everything. It's happened to me more than once.

Rita Gomez continues on, about how when the bar was about to close the bikers asked if anyone wanted a ride home and she said she did because they had scared off her ride so they said they'd take her and instead of dropping her off where she was living they kept on going up into the foothills and raped her.

"Objection." Paul is immediately on his feet. We have a strategy, the four of us working in tandem, in situations like this we want him to make the objections as much as possible, he's got that courtly old gentleman image, the jury won't find him threatening or obnoxious, as they might with a young Hispanic male, a young and obviously aggressive female, or a well-known sharp hired gun. Paul's nice old Gregory Peck. When Gregory Peck plays a lawyer his clients are always innocent.

Martinez, an experienced jurist, immediately excuses the jury; he knows that what Paul's about to state could bring a mistrial if the jury is present.

"Rape has nothing to do with this trial," Paul says to Martinez, once the jury's been removed. "There's been no charge of rape, no medical evidence or representation from the prosecution at any time."

"She's telling us what happened, your honor," Moseby replies.

Martinez shifts his look to Rita. "We're not here to find out whether or not these men raped you. This is to find out if they murdered somebody. If you want to bring rape charges, that's a separate matter."

"But they did," she says, confused. "Rape me."

"We're trying to show a pattern of continuing unlawful behavior on the defendants' part, your honor," Moseby presses, "both in the past and in this specific instance, on that very night. If the murder had resulted because these fellows here had been robbing a bank and killed the guard wouldn't we be able to talk about the robbery as well? We are going to show that this killing didn't take place in some vacuum; these guys do all kinds of bad stuff and the murder was the culmination on that particular night."

"But my client and the others are not on trial for murder *and* rape, your honor," Paul says. "It's not an ancillary charge, it's never even been brought up."

Martinez thinks a moment.

"I'm going to allow this line of questioning to continue," Martinez finally answers. "Be aware that this is not a trial about rape. I'm allowing the prosecutor to introduce it because it might have had or still have an effect on the witness's testimony and behavior at the time. But if the prosecution wants to bring that charge in, they will have to bear the burden of introducing evidence that a rape occurred and that these defendants committed it upon this witness, and that it was germane; by that I mean part of and crucial to the case before you."

Turning to Moseby, he warns him: "If this turns out to be a false lead, I may have to declare a mistrial, and I most emphatically do *not* want one of those in my courtroom."

Paul sits down, upset. We all are. Now it's not just murder, which is trouble enough; now it's a gang-rape on top of that, the appetizer to the main course. I'm not so sure, though, that it's necessarily going to hurt us any more in the long run than we have been already. The fact that she alleges rape doesn't make it so, and if we can eventually prove that she willingly had sex with them (we can't say they didn't fuck her at all, there's too much on the record that says they did), it could taint everything about her.

I motion to Ellen, the paralegal who's also doing some investigating for us, to come over. She's young but capable, I'd like to find a way to sponsor her into law school. I issue instructions briefly to her, in hushed tones out of anyone else's hearing. She makes notes while I talk, and immediately leaves the room.

Rita continues on. As she gets closer to describing the murder her voice, already low and tentative, gets lower, almost a whisper. Martinez asks her to speak up. She does, then drops again. Then Mary Lou asks for more voice, Tommy does too.

The jury is leaning in to hear her. I'm not crazy about that, it means they have to direct all their attention to her. I object, too. Martinez becomes a little more forceful in telling her to speak up, but he's protecting her, she's a scared dumb girl who, if she's telling the truth, was brutally traumatized; even if it's only partly true, it was a shitty, scary experience.

Moseby knows the judge is sympathetic, as is usually the case in a prosecution, plus she's Hispanic like Martinez, there's an unspoken protective coloration here, so he defends her rigorously, knowing he's got the most important ally on his side in this aspect of it: she's scared, they threatened to kill her, she's not the one on trial.

To me, though, she is. All prosecution witnesses are. The burden of proof is on the state, which I've always taken to mean that their witnesses must be credible. They're on trial to be. Often they're not; they lie. For lots of reasons. Sometimes they don't even know they're lying. They have an idea and it becomes their tangible, physical truth.

I'm inside my own head. Rita Gomez is on trial in the courtroom of my inner mind and I'm devising ways to get her to tell the real truth. Because what she's saying now is bullshit, there may be some truth in it, maybe it's mostly true, but the bullshit contaminates it all, it's all spoiled. The rotten apple theory. It's a good theory, it often turns out to be real.

Her narrative has us back up the mountain now, her and the victim and the bikers, now they're stabbing him, now they're cutting off his Johnson and sticking it in his mouth, now Lone Wolf has taken out the pistol and is shooting the corpse. Her description is complete and graphic.

The jury is cringing. Some look from her to the defense table. It's hard to keep a tight asshole at times like these. Yes, the bikers are terrible people, I wouldn't want one of them marrying my daughter, and this is more guilt by past association, but this kind of testimony could convict a saint. And it's stuck in the courtroom's consciousness now, everyone's: judge, jury, defendants, all who have entered here. It sticks to us like fear sweat, you can smell it.

"Is this the murder victim, Richard Bartless?" Moseby asks her, holding up a two-by-three-foot blowup. "As you knew him?"

A touched-up high school graduation picture of a sweet young man. Moseby turns it, so the jury can see it clearly.

"Yes, sir. That's Richard."

The room is hushed. If ever one picture was worth a thousand words, ten thousand; it's one of those moments when you want to bury your head under a metaphorical rock and hope it goes away, while knowing it probably won't.

I glance at my colleagues. We all feel the same—like shit.

The witness is coming down the homestretch with her story now. They brought her back to the motel, laid her one last time ("at least they got one thing right," Lone Wolf confides to me, "and notice she didn't say 'rape' "), swore her to secrecy under penalty of suffering a variation of the victim's fate, and rode off. And she hasn't seen them from that day to this. Until now.

"And those men," Moseby concludes. "Are they presently in this courtroom?"

"Yes."

"Would you point them out for the benefit of the jury?"

She stands, setting herself, poised on the balls of her spike heels. For the first time since she's set foot in the courtroom she looks directly at them. She shakes as she extends her right arm full length, makes a fist, and points an accusing finger. The famous fickle finger, this one a knuckle-chewed digit with a fake inch-long nail painted bright red: the scarlet finger.

"It was them."

11:30 P.M. WE CROSS-EXAMINE Rita Gomez tomorrow. We're going to tear her a new asshole, destroy her credibility: destroy *her*, if we have to. The idea that this little cunt, this whore, cretin, low-life sack of shit might be believable enough to a jury that they will condemn four men to death is an insult, it burns my ass way beyond my normal underdog-lawyer's righteous indignation.

I feel good: I like being angry and outraged. If I find myself walking through a case, not really giving a shit deep down, I know I'm in trouble and so is my client. When I'm roiling, kicking ass inside my head, translating that to action, then it's working.

Earlier this evening I spoke to Claudia on the phone. An unsatisfying conversation: she misses her daddy, her anxiety compounded by the impending move, the separation that will last forever. I've barely seen her in the past few weeks and I'll see even less of her until the trial's over, which could be months. She tells me about school, her friends, her mother, her mother's upcoming new job, none of it with any enthusiasm. She feels cheated, that we're at fault. She's right, of course, certainly by her lights, and there isn't a damn thing we can do about it; I'm still guilt-tripped all the same, it sits sour in my stomach like an ulcerating stone.

We can't talk as long as we want. She extracts a promise from me that we'll have some time together this weekend, even if only a few hours, maybe over Saturday night. I can feel the hurt in her voice as she hangs up; she is my only blood left in the world and we are fading apart. At times like this I wish I'd never gotten the call from the bikers, that I'd actually taken the leave, forced though it may have been. We could have spent so much time together, my daughter and I, time I've never given her. Now I'll never be able to; no matter what happens later these moments will be gone.

Quarter to one. We finally break it up. We've got our shit together, tomorrow's our turn. Mary Lou manages, without arousing suspicion, to be the last one to go, lingering near the exit, a tacit invitation. Not for tonight, the last thing either of us could or would do now is to make love, especially for the first time. More a connective pass, mutual support. It's nice. She's a nice woman; the fear I initially harbored about her, this good-looking aggressive hotshot young female lawyer who wouldn't have the requisite soft emotions (a ballbuster of the imagination, in other words) isn't there anymore. It's amazing how you can come to like someone when they tell you up front they feel that way as well. I always like women better when I'm not afraid they're going to reject me.

I close her car door for her, watch her drive away, her taste lingering on my mouth. It's a warm, dry night, starry, a night full of promise I won't partake of. I stand here, leaning against my own car, wanting to take more out of the world, wanting, in some basic way, new for me, to join with it more. I want some new birthings in my life. I want to be happier than I am.

"YOU ALLEGE THEY raped you?"

"Yes." Fidgeting, squirming. It's hot, muggy in here.

"All of them?"

Peevishly: "Yes. I already said so a thousand times."

"Objection." Moseby is on his feet once again, even as the words are coming out of her mouth.

"On what grounds?" Martinez asks. Maybe for the two hundredth time.

"This topic's been covered, your honor. Every which way but loose."

We're in the third day of cross-examination of Rita Gomez. My partners have all had a whack at her. Now it's my turn.

"How many times are we going to be interrupted by these irrelevant objections, your honor?" I ask. Moseby keeps trying to stop the flow of our arguments, chicken-shit objections. Martinez is tiring of these tactics, too; his look to Moseby is not friendly.

"Fine, it's been examined," I continue, answering Martinez's anticipatory look, "but certainly not from every angle. The prosecution introduced the allegation of rape, not us. We were happy to try the case in front of us, but it's been expanded; okay, fine, we can deal with that. But we have to be able to scrutinize all of it as carefully and fully as we think is necessary because the prosecutor—not us, your honor, the prosecution—is basing his case on a chain of cause and effect. We have to be allowed to follow it, wherever it takes us."

"Agreed. Objection over-ruled. And Mr. Moseby . . ."

"Yes, sir?"

"Let's keep it flowing okay?"

"Yes, your honor. Absolutely."

"Miss Gomez . . ." I turn back to her. She's dressed more demurely now, has been since the first day. I found out that Robertson was livid when he saw her, he sand-blasted Moseby's hide, and then sent his own wife out shopping for her that night. Now she's attired like a Sunday-school teacher: modest little dark-blue dress with a white collar, low white heels, fake pearls. Much less makeup. Younger-looking, more vulnerable.

"It must have been very painful. All of them raping you as you say. All those times."

"It hurt like hell. I was bleeding real bad."

A pencil cracks behind me. Moseby. He exchanges a quick look with Gomez and Sanchez, his investigators who broke the case.

"So you went to the hospital . . . which hospital was that?"

She starts to say something, bites her lip.

"I . . ." she stops cold.

"You say you were bleeding terribly."

"Yeh. It was bad."

"Did you go to a hospital?"

She bites her lip again, searching the courtroom. I intercept the look: Gomez and Sanchez. Staring straight ahead, cigar-store Indian stoic.

"No," under her breath.

"Speak up, please," Martinez tells her.

"No," she says.

I turn to look at the jury. They're paying attention.

"Weren't you afraid? If you were bleeding terribly, didn't you think you should be examined by a doctor?"

"Of course I was scared. You would be too if it happened to you. But I was more scared of going to a doctor than the bleeding."

"Why?"

" 'Cause a doctor would have told the cops and then they'd have found about the bikers and I was scared they'd come back and kill me if I said anything. That's what they told me they'd do. I believed them, I knew they would, I seen what they already done to Richard."

"So you never went to any hospital or had any doctor examine you following this incident?"

"No."

In this particular instance, I believe her. Regardless of whether or not my clients had killed the victim, they had fucked her and fucked her hard. But there's no way the cops would've taken her someplace where they would have kept a public record. One reason, among others, I'm sure, that the prosecution didn't add rape to the murder charge. It's conceivable, of course, that she could have been seen by a private doctor; every lawyer in town knows of doctors who have cozy relationships with the police; but as far as a record goes, there isn't one. These cops may be crazy or venal, but they aren't stupid.

"Not even after the police found you?"

She turns away, to the detectives seated behind the prosecution table, her look imploring 'what should I say?'

"Answer the question, Miss Gomez," Martinez says, more than a touch of annoyance and anger in his voice.

"No." She swallows. "Not then. By then I was . . . getting better."

"These are good policemen, first-rate men. You must have been all better for them not to have taken you to a hospital as a precaution."

"Actually I was, yeh. All better."

"But you did tell them you'd been raped."

"Yeh. At first I didn't want to but finally I did."

"Even though it would bring the wrath of the bikers down on you. You've said that yourself, several times."

"They promised me protection."

And what else, you pathetic little creature?

"And because I'd been thinking about what they'd done," she intones. "To Richard. I just didn't want 'em to go scot-free from that."

I look at the jury. Is the stench reaching them? I can't tell.

"Between the time you were allegedly raped and the time the policemen found you," I continue, "did you have sex with any other man or men?"

"Are you crazy? I could hardly walk."

"I thought you just said you were all better."

"I meant from the bleeding. I was still sore."

Lying little cunt. If my clients hadn't already admitted to having sex with her I'd be doubting whether anything happened at all.

"So they just accepted your statement that you had been raped by these four men."

"It's the truth. Why shouldn't they?"

One way or the other, the prosecution's in trouble. If she wasn't examined, and there's no evidence that she was, then Gomez and Sanchez fucked up royally. And if she was, they're suppressing evidence. They stink to high hell, I'm itching to flush it out.

"Let's go back to the bar where you first met the accused," I say. "You got there what, six, seven o'clock?"

"Around then, yeh. It was still plenty of light out."

"You went with the victim? Richard Bartless?"

Rolling her eyes. "Yeh, I went with Richard."

"In his car?"

"Yeh."

We've established that already. I'm just reconfirming.

"Which one of you drove?"

"Him. My license got suspended."

"Oh? Drunk driving?"

"No." Sassy, practically sticking her tongue out at me. "I didn't pay some parking tickets so it got suspended."

"But you got it back since then . . ."

"Yeh . . ."

"With the help of the police? The same officers you gave your statement to?"

"Objection!" Moseby's on the balls of his Thom McAns.

"Withdrawn, your honor," I say quickly before Martinez can sustain it. Back to her: "He drove?"

"How many times you gonna ask me the same stuff?"

I stare at her, as if something just came to me. I cross to the evidence table, extract a document, walk back to the stand.

"Take a look at this if you would, Miss Gomez," I ask her, handing it to her. "Carefully. Read everything on it."

"Out loud?"

I shake my head. "That's not necessary, unless you want to."

"I don't like to. I'm not so good a reader."

"To yourself is fine. Take your time."

She reads it slowly, her lips moving word by word. The courtroom is quiet, the air hanging on us, another garment. She finishes, holds it out to me. I take it from her, on the move towards the jury box.

"What is it you just looked at, Miss Gomez? What I just showed you?"

"Some kind of bill?" Perplexed, tentative.

"Exactly. Very good." I turn to the jury, exchanging a smile with them, a friendly nonthreatening smile. Then I face her, leaning on the far end of the jury box.

"Know what it's for?" I ask.

"I'm . . . I'm not sure."

"Isn't it for a car?" I ask her, "a car repair?"

"That's what I thought it was, yeh."

"Actually, it's for Richard Bartless's car. A blue Honda," I add, looking at it. Back to her: "Is that what he drove? A blue Honda?"

"Yeh, that's it," she answers fast, eager to show she knows something. "Had a ton of black smoke coming out the exhaust."

"He was stopped because of that, wasn't he? Stopped by officer . . ." here I read: "Dan Kline of the Highway Patrol."

She giggles. "Yeh, he got stopped all right. Pissed him off royally."

"It says here that Officer Kline told Richard he couldn't drive it anymore until he got it fixed. That he had to get it fixed and bring in the paperwork in three days or the car would be impounded."

"What do you think got Richard so pissed off?"

"But he took it in?"

"Yeh, he took it in to some shop near the motel."

"Ricky's Auto," I say, reading it from the paper in my hand.

"I guess. Yeh, I guess that was it."

"And you co-signed for the repair, didn't you? That is your signature next to Richard Bartless's, isn't it?"

"He didn't live in New Mexico and he didn't have no credit cards or anything, so I had to sign. It didn't mean I had to pay or nothing."

I take the document from her, pass it to Martinez.

"At this time we'd like to introduce this into evidence as defendants' exhibit 35, your honor."

Martinez looks at it, nods, hands it to the bailiff, who walks it over to Moseby. Frank glances at it, perfunctorily at first, then studies it carefully, showing it to his deputy, then taking it back and reading it again. He frowns, looking at his witness, then behind him to his investigators. He stares at the piece of paper for a long moment before reluctantly handing it back.

"No objection," he states in a flat voice.

I suppress a smile; I surprised him, you don't like to be surprised by your own witnesses. The bailiff enters it as defendants' evidence number thirty-five. I regain it from him, walk back to the stand.

"You were just helping out," I say to the witness. After a pause: "How long was it in? Couple of days?"

"At least. They had to get some part from Farmington."

"So what'd he do in the meantime? Rent a car?"

She titters.

"You serious, man? He couldn't afford no rental car."

"How did he get around then?"

"Walked. Hitched rides."

"You too? When you were with him?"

"Had to. My license was suspended, you already asked me that."

"Right," I say. "Sorry about that."

Moseby's head is in his hand. He has to hear this, but he doesn't want to see it, like it won't hurt so bad. He's glad Robertson's not in court today.

"Interesting, these dates," I continue, looking at the paper. "They seem to overlap when you and Richard Bartless drove to the bar, and met my clients, and so on."

"Huh?" She doesn't get it.

"You've testified you and Richard drove to the bar together. You've testified to that several times already."

"Yeh?"

"That Richard had a bad encounter with my client and the others, which made him drive off, leaving you stranded. You did say that, didn't you?"

"Yeh." She's squirming, it's hot despite the air-conditioning, she's not used to pantyhose, I have a feeling she's itching in a place you can't scratch in public.

"Well, according to this," I say to her, moving close now, close enough to smell her cheap perfume, "his blue Honda was in the shop that day. In fact he never got it back."

"How could he?" she says, trying to show me and the world she's no fool. "He got dead first."

"That's right," I respond. "He did. But that night, the night you say you drove to the bar with him, he didn't have a car. His was in the shop and by your own admission he didn't rent one."

I'm facing the jury as I finish my sentence. Their look shifts from me to her.

She squirms again. Hoist by her own bullshit petard.

"Damn," she says suddenly. "How could I have forgot?"

"Forgot what?" I ask.

"That Richard's car was in the shop." She moistens her lips, ready to take the plunge. "See, what happened was, we *had* been driving around, but then he got busted like you said, so that night we hitch-hiked."

"Did you?" I ask dryly, turning to the jury. I love it, I just caught the state's number-one witness in a bald-faced lie.

"Yeh. I mean, how else were we supposed to get around? You ever try taking a bus around here?"

Someone in the back of the room titters. Martinez bangs his gavel.

"You hitch-hiked to the Dew Drop Inn," I say.

"Yeh. We did. I remember now."

That would've been a sight. A long-haired freak and a girl who looks like a two-dollar hooker.

"Which means that when you told the court earlier you drove there with him you were lying."

"I forgot is all! Don't you ever forget nothing?" She's sweating through her pancake, her underarms are turning black.

"You're under oath, Miss Gomez," Martinez reminds her. "It's important that you remember as much as you can."

I pick up the beat. "So when you said—when you told us all, myself, the judge here, the jury sitting over there—when you told us you were left without a ride after Richard Bartless was allegedly chased off by my client and his friends that wasn't true, was it? You never had one to begin with." I'm right on top of her. "In fact he left before my clients ever got there, isn't that right?" I yell unexpectedly, my voice echoing.

"No!"

"Objection!"

"They never even saw each other, did they!"

"No!"

"Objection!"

"I mean yes!" she says.

"Over-ruled," Martinez says sharply to Moseby.

"You hitch-hiked there, probably alone, or got dropped off, and didn't feel like hitch-hiking home alone late at night. You'd rather ride on a motorcycle with a good-looking guy who was maybe a little scary, which turned you on. Isn't that what really happened, Rita?" I'm going a mile a minute, she's all wrapped up, no way out.

"OBJECTION!" Moseby's mouth is spewing spittle, his face beet-red. He looks about ready for a coronary.

"Withdrawn, your honor." I smile up at him, an I'm-sorry-if-I-went-a-little-too-far-but-I-had-to-get-to-the-truth smile.

"Keep it in bounds, counselor," Martinez admonishes me softly. A rap on the knuckles with a wet noodle.

"Yes, sir. Sorry."

"Continue, please."

I get a drink of water, walk back to Rita.

"Let's go back to the bar," I say. "The Dew Drop Inn. You drink there often?"

"Depends."

"On who's buying?"

"Something like that. If it's payday. The usual."

"Have you ever gone there alone?"

"Yeh," she admits, "sometimes. But not that night," she adds forcefully. "Me and Richard went together that night."

"Yes, you've made that point. Hitch-hiked there together."

She nods. She won't be so quick to volunteer information from now on.

"You started drinking at seven. That's when you've told us you arrived."

"Around then."

"And you drank until you left."

"On and off. I mean I wasn't chugging 'em or nothing."

"From seven in the evening until two in the morning."

"Yeh but not all the time. I didn't have all that much money. I had to nurse 'em."

"Did Richard buy you a drink? Assuming he was there?"

"He *was* there and yeh, a few."

"Anyone else? Any other fellows?"

"A couple might've . . . yeh, a couple guys did."

"A few drinks each."

"Yeh."

"What were you drinking? Tequila?" An easy guess.

"Some. Some wine coolers."

"Tequila with wine-cooler chasers. Maybe a few beers."

"I don't drink beer much in bars," she shakes her head. "My kidneys can't handle it. Just when I'm home alone is all."

"So you stuck pretty much to the tequila."

She nods. "I don't get hangovers from tequila."

"You must be a hell of a drinker," I say. "Tequila from seven at night until two in the morning. I'd be out cold."

"I can hold it pretty good," she says, patting herself on the back. Like it's an admirable trait. Actually, I've always thought so myself. Maybe I'd better take another look at that.

"Sounds like it," I tell her. "Although with that much tequila in you I can understand why it might've been hard to remember whether you drove there that night or hitch-hiked. That much tequila in me I doubt I could remember my name, let alone anything that happened that night at all."

"I can remember," she says defiantly. "I can remember good enough."

"So you've said," I reply. "Before the night in question," I ask, shifting gears again, "when was the last time you were in the Dew Drop?"

She purses her eyebrows in concentration.

"I think . . . I'm not sure."

"The night before?"

"I don't know. I don't remember everything I ever did every single day."

"It's possible."

"Yeh, I guess."

"If I were to produce witnesses that positively placed you there the night before would that help refresh your memory?"

She licks her lips again. Her lipstick's cracking. The prosecution should request a recess, fix her up. She isn't making a favorable impression on the jury.

"Now that I think about it," she admits, "I'm pretty sure I was there then."

"It's your regular hangout, isn't it."

"More or less," she answers. "I ain't no barfly though if that's what you're getting at."

I shake my head 'no.' "I'm just trying to establish some of your patterns, Miss Gomez. Your social behavior as it were." I lean towards her, then almost recoil. That perfume's hard to take, the daily effect has to be giving Martinez one hell of a headache.

"So you were there the night before," I continue.

She nods. Martinez instructs the jury that's a 'yes.'

"With Richard, another friend, by yourself? What?"

"Just me. I couldn't find nobody to go with me."

"But you found somebody to leave with you, didn't you?"

"Objection! This is completely irrelevant, your honor," Moseby whines.

Martinez looks at her, pondering it. I can tell that the more he sees and hears her, the less he believes.

"Over-ruled," he says. "I think the witness's pattern of behavior is important here," he tells Moseby. I like this; he's using my language, he's hearing me. "I'm going to allow the defense a broad field to play on," Martinez continues. "If it turns out to be a blind alley I'll reel you in, counselor," he informs me.

"Thank you, your honor." I turn back to her.

"You picked up a guy in the Dew Drop Inn the night before this alleged killing and went home with him, right?"

She looks at Moseby: do I have to answer?, she's asking silently. He stares at her. His anger at losing the momentum is apparent.

"Answer the question, Miss Gomez," Martinez instructs her.

Almost a whisper: "Yes."

"Speak up so the jury can hear you," Martinez tells her.

"Yes." Louder, with defiance. "I went home with a guy I met in the bar."

"Someone you knew?" I ask. "A friend?"

"I'd seen him around."

"In the bar."

"Yeh."

"But you didn't know him."

"I'd seen him."

"You picked up someone you'd never met before and went home with him and slept with him, isn't that right?"

She hates my guts now, but she hates Moseby's more. He didn't prepare her for this. Of course, if he had, she might've had second thoughts about coming forward.

Too late now.

"Okay. I did. So what? They . . ." pointing at the defendants, "still did what I said they did. What I did or didn't do some other time don't make any difference about that."

"How much did he pay you for sleeping with him?" I ask, brushing aside her qualifiers.

"OBJECTION!" Moseby is beside himself.

"Over-ruled." Martinez is leaning forward in his chair, he's definitely involved.

"How much?" I ask again. "You went to bed with this fellow you picked up in the Dew Drop Inn," I say. "You had sex and he paid you. How much?"

She looks down at her shoes. "Fifteen," she mumbles.

"Fifteen dollars?" I repeat. Jesus, talk about your low-rent trash.

"He bought me some drinks first," she says lamely, by way of face-saving explanation. "He was a nice dude, I ain't in it for the money," she adds desperately.

The laughter rolls across the room. Jesus, somebody throw the poor bitch a life-rope. If it wasn't my clients' lives on the line I might muster some compassion for her.

Martinez gavels for order.

"Expenses," I say helpfully.

"Yeh," she says. "I lost a couple hours at work."

"Girl's gotta make a living," I throw in flippantly. "Sorry, your honor," I add quickly. Watch yourself, Will, I remind myself silently, you've got Martinez leaning your way, you don't need to irritate him unnecessarily.

"Okay," I sum up. "It's now on the record that you frequent bars alone, you sleep with men you've never met before, and you charge them for it. In this state, Miss Gomez, that's called prostitution." A beat, almost as an afterthought: "have you ever been convicted for prostitution, Miss Gomez? Convicted for it?"

I glance over at the jury; nobody's asleep yet.

She's mute.

"Answer the question, please," Martinez tells her for the umpteenth time.

"Do I have to?" she whines.

"Yes, you have to," he says, not bothering to hide his irritation. "You have to answer all the questions you're asked, not just the ones you want to."

She crosses and recrosses her legs, shifting in the chair, trying to avoid the inevitable; her foot's jiggling out of control, her shoe is in danger of falling off.

"The answer, please," I say.

"Yes." She finally says in a low whisper.

"How many times?"

"I . . . I'm not sure."

I'm already back from the defense table with her record in my hand.

"Isn't it true," I continue, reading from her sheet, "that twice you've been convicted for prostitution? And two other times for soliciting?"

"You're the one reading it," she says.

"I take that for a yes?"

"If that's what it says, then yes," she throws at me in anger. "I said so, okay? You happy now?" Whining like a kid who's willing herself not to cry.

I look down at her sheet again. My look's for show, I know what's on it.

"It says here you've also been convicted for public drunkenness."

"I never was . . ."

The record's in her face, my finger on the appropriate line. Her head jerks back as if I'm holding a blowtorch to her.

"You were never what?"

"It wasn't all that big a deal. Jesus, people get drunk, so what? Big deal. I just mouthed off to the wrong people that's all."

"I know what you mean," I say. "I've done that a few times myself."

That comes out before I realize it. Martinez looks at me quizzically; I shake my head, press on.

"Something else comes to mind, Miss Gomez," I say, almost as an afterthought. "We've established that Richard's car was in the shop on the night in question. It was out of commission. Would you agree?"

"It wasn't running, yeh, okay. I messed up on that, I forgot is all."

"That's okay. But something strikes me then . . ."

I face the jury as I ask the next question.

"How did the defendants get Richard Bartless up on that mountain? They couldn't have gotten up there on a motorcycle. He would have fallen off."

The room goes silent.

"Miss Gomez?" I prompt.

"He . . . uh . . . they . . . uh . . . they stole a car," she blurts out.

"They did *what?*"

"I forgot about that," she says. "They took one of the cars that was in the motel parking lot and they hot-wired it and that's how they did it. Got Richard and me up there."

I look at Martinez, at the jury, at the prosecution table. They're all staring at her in disbelief.

"Miss Gomez." Judge Martinez leans down from his perch. To say he's concerned is the understatement of the month. "How is it that in all your testimony up until now you've never mentioned this?"

" 'Cause I forgot," she whines. "They'd raped me, they had a knife on me, they had Richard all tied up, I thought they were going to kill me, I didn't remember." She's bordering on hysteria. "What difference does it make how they got us up there? They did, ain't that what all's important?"

"And what happened to this quote stolen car unquote?" I ask her. "It flew away or something?"

Moseby's fidgeting like crazy. He blew this one, and he knows it.

"They brought it back," she says. "Left it out back, I guess."

"Just brought it back? Miss Gomez . . . I hope you won't find my saying this the least bit insensitive, but doesn't this sound a little ridiculous to you as you hear yourself say it?"

"I don't much *remember!*" she cries out. "I'd just watched them mutilate and kill a man. I wasn't paying attention to no goddam car!"

Despite that sympathy-grabbing outburst, by the time I've finished my cross and Martinez puts us in recess until the morning, I'm feeling pretty good. She's a shabby piece of work: a public liar, drunk, and whore. Pretty hard to send four men to Death Row on that kind of testimony.

IT'S BEEN A WONDERFUL day, away from all the bullshit. Claudia and I were in the mountains all day, hiking when we felt like it, examining the high desert wildflowers, Claudia exclaiming on each one's unique beauty in reverential tones, as if no one had ever seen that kind of beauty in these scrubby flowers before, the newest eye on the world. We caught our dinner in the river and cooked and ate it there, packing out our garbage, leaving as little trace of our coming and departing as we could. The sun was down by the time we drove home, the sky purple-orange across the mountains far to the west, our faces wind-burnt, sun-burnt. We played the Grateful Dead as we slowly headed down the winding roads leading back to town, "Truckin' " and "Uncle John's Band."

The kind of day you want to bottle and keep forever.

We're reading *The Yearling*. Her small head, the long light-brown hair still wet from washing, rests on my shoulder. As I read I look at her face, her delicate features. My flesh, my blood. I'll die before I let her go. I'll die if I have to let her go. I'm already into the long, slow slide into my dying. Living in this moment, I'm rapturous. If I could only stay here.

I finish the chapter. She cuddles closer, not wanting to go to bed, to be apart from me.

"Can I stay up a little longer?" she pleads. "Just fifteen minutes."

"It's late already, angel. It's been a busy day. All that sun, it pulls the energy out of you and you don't even know it, I really want you to get enough rest." Her mother had cautioned me that she was on the verge of a cold, to make sure she got plenty of sleep.

"Please?"

"Sure."

I tell her a story, a piece of the same story I've been telling her for years, about a little girl who discovers a secret gate into another world and the friendly gatekeeper who is her guide. A magical world, where even when it's dark and scary you know that hope is just around the corner, that it will all turn out right in the end.

She goes to sleep in the second bedroom, her room. She keeps some clothes here, some toys, pictures, books. Not very many; in my former house she had a princess's room. This is more transitory, I don't want to be here much longer. But it'll probably be the last home we have together where it isn't visits on holidays and summers. She's clutching her old Teddy, her lips faintly sucking in a vestigial throwback to when she sucked her thumb. When she was little; an eternity ago.

I drink a light scotch, look over some papers. I'm too antsy to work; my circuits are over-loaded, burnt-out, anyway it'll be at least another week before we present our side. I know who their other witnesses are, I know as much as I can about what they'll testify to.

Claudia's dreaming, beyond my reach. I want some action.

There's a teenage girl across the quad who's baby-sat for me before. Sad little thing, no figure to speak of, bad complexion, with a hang-dog personality. The kind of kid who isn't out bopping with her friends at the mall on Saturday night.

She's available as long as I'm home by midnight. No problem, I just need a change of scenery; I promise myself I won't drink anything stronger than a glass of wine or a beer. Just an hour or two around grown-ups that isn't business-related, eyeballing grown-up ladies with tits and asses and long legs. Nothing more, pure voyeurism, at this point I couldn't handle even a casual overnight nameless fuck. I'll come home alone, masturbate if I can't sleep; close my eyes and think of Mary Lou. It won't be the first time. Fuck, am I down on myself. Outside the courtroom and the all-consuming intensity of the trial I'm a bundle of raw, exposed nerve endings. I'm not centered, not remotely; being with myself isn't the kind of company I want to keep, I have the need to be distracted from my loneliness by casual encounters with acquaintances or (better yet) strangers. Talk about wallowing in self-pity; I'm practically drowning in it. And I'm enjoying it way too much.

THE BAR AT LA FONDA isn't far from my office. They know me there, first-name basis. What with the publicity from the trial I'm a celebrity, my money's no good tonight. I should be taking advantage and knocking back double Chivases, but I stick to my guns and sip the house Chardonnay.

Half the lawyers in town seem to be passing through, they all want to talk, exchange ideas and rumors. I'm a local hero. Stand near me and you might catch lightning in a bottle.

"Hey, bubba." Andy's materialized behind me, quiet as an Indian. Harriet, his wife, who he met at Columbia, is with him.

"Will," she says, offering her cheek. I brush it with my lips. She's good people, a rock. Andy's always made the right decisions.

"Hi, Harriet. Looking good." Tall, aristocratic, good bones. She could be a model out of the Tweeds catalogue.

"Batching it tonight?" Andy asks.

"For an hour. I have Claudia for the weekend."

Nothing I can do about the wine glass in front of me. Andy sees it, discreetly doesn't comment. He knocks back the rest of his own Scotch on the rocks, signals the bartender for another, pointing his finger at mine.

"No thanks," I tell him. "Just one tonight."

"One's permissible," he smiles. "The tension you're under more than one's permissible."

Well, hell. Now the son of a bitch is condescending to me. Poor sad Will, the drunk of the legal profession, he isn't even strong enough to keep a promise to his partner.

"Andy tells me you're doing a wonderful job," Harriet says.

"Too early to tell," I answer modestly.

"He is," Andy says. "If anybody can walk those turkeys it'll be you, pard." He claps me fraternally on the back. He's had a few, he's loose.

"They're innocent, Andy," I say.

"So what?" he counters. "You think anyone gives a shit? I know you're going to dazzle your jury, Will, you're gonna place those bikers in a convent in Burlington, Vermont, at the time of the murder, is it going to matter? Stick a wet finger up in the air, man, can't you tell which way the wind's blowing?"

"I don't need to hear this."

"It's reality talking, son."

"It's Saturday night, Andy. Let's let reality off the hook for a couple hours, okay?"

"Shit yes. Hey listen man, you might do it. I've seen you in action. You're the best." He holds his fresh drink in toast. We clink. White fucking wine.

"Take care," he says.

"You too."

"See you around."

"Yeh, see you."

They leave. He's talking low to her, whispering in her ear. She glances back at me. I smile. It hurts.

One more and I'm out of here. I don't know what I was looking for but this isn't it.

And then Mary Lou comes out of the dining-room. She's with a man. I know him, one of the senior partners in her firm, a married man twice her age. It instinctively bothers me in my gut, even though there's probably nothing to it. It's selfishness is what it is; I can't have her so I don't want anyone else to. Not even platonically, which I've never believed in anyway. If a woman's attractive to you you want her, she could be your wife's best friend, her sister, if you want her you want her. Your cock is always more powerful than your ethics.

They must've had dinner in the restaurant, stopping in the bar for a nightcap. They sit across the room. She's dressed up like a woman, not a lawyer. The light is flattering to her; she looks great, succulent.

I don't want her to see me. I don't like what I'm seeing. It feels demeaning to her. Fuck; I'm jealous.

Of course, she does see me. She stares for a moment, excuses herself from the table, walks over to me.

"What're you doing here?" she asks.

"Didn't know I needed permission." I'm smiling, low-key, but I'm on edge.

"I don't mean that. Why are you alone?"

"They don't serve minors in here." I explain about Claudia, my short break. "In fact," I say, checking the time, "I've got to leave now."

"I'm coming with you." Her hand is on mine; not by accident.

"What?"

"I'll follow you. I've got my car."

"No."

"Why not?" she asks, putting her hand back on mine.

"You're with another man for openers."

"A lawyer, for Godsakes." As if lawyers are eunuchs. "A man in my firm."

"A senior partner. A married senior partner," I add, unable to resist the dig.

She doesn't rise to the bait. "Let's just go, okay? I won't even make a pass, I promise. We'll just talk. I need to talk to you, Will, I really do."

She crosses the room and talks briefly to the man, who glances at me, nods. Business is business. She comes back with her purse and wrap.

"What did you tell him?" I ask.

"That I was going home with you."

"Jesus H. Christ!"

"Joke, Will, joke," she says, calming me. "I told him I needed to run some stuff by you, it couldn't wait. He understands, we've all been there." She realizes I'm not buying this. "It was a friendly dinner, Will, nothing more. His wife's out of town and he's lonely. He's not my type, anyway." She looks me in the eye. "I don't chase after lost causes."

She finishes my drink for me, takes my arm. We promenade out. I don't want this, but I really feel good. Flag that; I want it, but I don't think I'm going to be able to handle it.

We talk for hours. We leave the lights off, sit on the couch in the living room. The windows are open: the hot, dry, late-summer winds blow in the scent of night-blooming flowers. She tells me about herself, her life, her family, I do the same back, all the stuff you do when you're courting someone. The stuff you've saved up until you're with someone you know wants to hear it.

We can't not talk about the case; it's what brought us together, it's all-consuming. She tells me the scuttlebutt that's going around town, the overwhelming sentiment against the bikers on the street, how the legal community's looking at it.

It's all wine and roses for her, a young lawyer, a woman, conducting a major murder defense. My situation's more complex, more precarious. The whisperings about the firm and me are getting louder, more persistent; apparently Fred isn't being very discreet. (I make a mental note to brace him the next time I see him, we have an agreement and I'm going to hold the bastard to it.) In a sense I'm walking on a long highwire. If I win, I'm still major stuff, with or without my firm; if I don't, I could be hurting.

We talk until there's nothing left to say except is she going to stay or leave. I'm stuck, frozen in gear, I can't do anything either way.

It doesn't matter, it's her script and she wrote it long before tonight.

We start out kissing each other for a long time with our clothes on, lying on top of the bed. French kisses, high school make-out kisses, the kind you never outgrow. Then she undresses. I watch her as she strips, not at all self-consciously, unhurried, letting me feast on each part of her body as she reveals it: to me, for me, alone. She has a good body, not quite as slender as it looks in clothes. Better, actually; full, womanly. No soft fat anywhere, she must work out. Ample hips, lovely round ass, smaller breasts than I would have thought for a woman of her size, the skin pale, almost translucent. Long nipples and large round areolas. She doesn't have much bodily hair, curly tendrils around her vagina. She's smooth everywhere else, waxed.

My disrobing is more prosaic, I'm anxious to catch up. I want it to go slow, to stretch it out as long as possible, kiss every inch of her, from her ears to her toes. That all goes out the window as soon as I touch her, she's too hot, we both are. We eat each other, cock and pussy, for less than a minute, and I'm inside her.

She's wet but she's also tight, she's never gone through childbirth. I'm on the verge almost immediately, I have to stop pumping, we lie together, trying to be still. Then we go at it again, long, slow thrusts, she's grabbing me hard by the ass, pulling me deeper into her, kissing me all over my face and neck, digging into my back with her fingers, moaning into my throat.

I smother her mouth with mine; I don't want Claudia to hear. She comes with a series of jolts that lift me into the air, I release behind her, an explosion, everything inside me flowing up and through my cock into her.

We open our eyes at the same time, kiss, nibbly little kisses. I couldn't move now if the house was on fire.

"Will?"

"Yes?"

"Were we unprofessional?"

"I thought we gave a very acceptable accounting of ourselves."

"You mean it's okay?"

"Yeh, it's okay."

"Just okay?"

"No. Better."

"Are you always so effusive after making love?" she asks. She looks happy.

"I'm not used to my lovers using the word 'effusive' after fucking," I say. "But to answer your question, no."

"Oh."

I look at her. She really cares about me.

"I don't want to sleep with anyone else anymore," I tell her.

She caresses my cheek with her fingers in reply. "We'll have to be careful in public," she says. "I don't like to be gossiped about."

"Me neither," I assure her. Christ, that's all I need.

"But I want to be with you as much as I can. Is that being too forward too fast?"

I'm scared suddenly; not because it's too fast, but because I want her.

"I hope not," I say.

"I'm very open to you, Will. You could hurt me without even knowing it."

"I'd know. I won't." At least not intentionally.

"Okay. I think that's enough for now."

She curls into me, ready for sleep, her head resting on my shoulder. It feels like it's rested there for years.

A light goes on in the hallway, spilling under the door. I'm bolt upright immediately, Mary Lou's head falling onto the pillow as her eyes pop open.

"Daddy?" Claudia calls. Her voice is shaking.

"Be right there, sweetheart," I call out. Mary Lou looks at me. Should I . . . ?

I shake my head 'no,' my finger to my lips. I slip into my robe and go into the hall, shutting the door tight behind me.

"What is it, angel?" She's standing in the open doorway of her room, clutching her Teddy.

"I had a bad dream."

I come over, pick her up, hold her to me for a moment. "What was it about?"

"A monster was chasing me. In a cave."

"Have you seen any scary movies lately?" I ask. That triggers it more than anything, I've had friends take their kids to stuff like *Halloween* or *Friday the 13th* because they couldn't find a sitter.

"No. Well, I saw kind of a scary one on TV."

"That was probably it. Anyway it's over now." I carry her back into her room. "It's okay, I'm right here. Go back to sleep."

"I'm too scared."

"No you're not. I'll stay with you for a minute."

"I want to sleep with you in your bed."

"You can't, angel. Not tonight."

"I want to." She starts to cry, half-real tears. "I won't be able to get back to sleep by myself."

"I'll tell you what," I say, "I'll stay here with you 'till you fall asleep."

"I'll wake up again." She snuggles closer. "Please, daddy. I won't toss around."

I sit her on her bed, sit next to her.

"I can't, Claudia. Not tonight."

"Why?" She doesn't understand; why should she? "We did last time."

"Because I've got someone with me."

She stares at me for a second, then jerks away, turning to the wall, crying. I reach out to touch her; she slaps at my hand.

"Claudia . . ."

She wheels on me, enraged.

"This is our weekend together," she yells through her tears. "You promised me."

"It is."

"Alone. Not with some other person." She turns away again, her body racked with sobs.

"Honey, I . . ."

She starts throwing a fit. Major. Slamming her fists against the mattress, kicking, screaming into the pillow. I back off, sitting on the edge of the bed. There's nothing I can do but let it work itself out.

"Will." Mary Lou is whispering from the hallway.

I turn. She's standing in the dark, fully dressed. I get up, walk to her, closing Claudia's door.

"I'm leaving."

Either way I turn, I'm fucked.

"I don't want you to."

"It's all right, Will, I understand. I know exactly how she feels; I want you for myself, too." She touches my cheek. "There'll be other times. Soon."

I walk her down the sidewalk to her car, kiss her goodbye. Then I go back inside, carry Claudia into my room, tuck her in. She isn't asleep, as I thought; she sits up, facing me.

"I don't want to share you, daddy," she says.

"You don't, angel. Not the way it counts."

"I don't want to leave. I don't want to move."

What can I say to that? That I don't want her to either? She knows that; the rest is not for me to decide.

"You're still here. Let's worry about moving when it happens."

That doesn't satisfy either of us.

"I wish you weren't having this stupid trial," she says. "I wish I could come over every day and we could be together every day."

"It'll be over pretty soon," I say. "And you know I'm always with you in my heart."

She likes that; it's something, anyway.

"Daddy?" she asks.

"What, angel?"

"Promise me you won't have anybody over when I'm here anymore."

I take her in my arms. My little baby.

"I promise."

"IS SHE ALL RIGHT?"

"She's fine, yeh."

Mary Lou and I are in the courthouse coffee shop, downstairs. Just the two of us, an hour early. Paul and Tommy haven't shown yet. That's good; we need a private moment.

"What about you?" she asks.

I sigh, looking at her. I didn't sleep well last night, thinking about this.

"I can't see you anymore." I stir the sugar in my coffee that I already stirred when I put it in. "Not until she's moved and this trial's over."

"Will . . ."

I shake my head. "I've got her and I've got this trial. I can't handle more than that now. Shit, Mary Lou, I've got other problems as well, stuff you don't even know about."

"I think I do."

"Yeh?"

"Your partners?"

I look at her, not acknowledging anything one way or the other.

"It's no secret on the street you're thinking maybe you should be moving in another direction. That's why you took the leave, isn't it? To think things out?"

"Partly," I say.

"Anyway," she says, "about us. I don't know what to say. I like you and . . . maybe I shouldn't say any more."

"I like you too, Mary Lou. A lot."

"Funny way of expressing it."

"I'm over-loaded emotionally. I couldn't do us justice; whatever us is."

"This isn't going to be easy," she says.

"For me either. I want you real bad, I didn't expect it, but I do, but we've got to cool it for awhile."

"As long as it's just for awhile."

"It is."

"You're a funny guy, Will," she says. "You definitely don't fit the mold."

"I used to think that was cool," I tell her. I look up; Paul's come in, spotted us. He's ambling over. "Now it's getting old. There's something to be said for being square, you know."

"That isn't you," she laughs. "I could never go for that."

I give her a half-assed grin. She puts a hand on mine for a moment, then withdraws it as Paul looms close.

"I'll be good," she whispers, teasing. "But only until the trial's over."

"I hope so," I tell her. I do. I honestly do.

"CALL DR. MILTON GRADE." Dr. Grade strides down the aisle, through the gate, to the dock. He stands ramrod straight as the oath is administered, carefully crosses one leg over the other as he sits, pulling his pant leg up with forefinger and thumb, making sure the crease stays crisp. Local legend has it he's the only man in New Mexico who has his suits tailored in London. He's pretty old now; the state mandatory retirement age has been waived for him, twice. He looks good, though; full shock of white hair, piercing blue eyes, strong Roman nose. The great American doctor.

There's a life-size blowup on an easel between the stand and the jury box of Bartless as he was received at the morgue. It's black-and-white, and since it's a blowup it's grainy, but it's still ugly as hell. The defendants look at it with curiosity; they don't seem particularly repelled, but more importantly to me, they show no signs of ever having seen him, at least not in this condition.

The photograph casts a powerful spell on everyone in the courtroom, particularly the jury. When Moseby revealed it I first looked to my clients, of course, and second to the jury. There were some sharp intakes of breath, some mutterings, but it wasn't as bad as I'd dreaded;

if one of the women had screamed I'd have moved immediately for a mistrial.

I turn away from the jury and look at the victim's mother. She stares intently at the picture, but to my surprise doesn't make a sound. Either she was prepped by the prosecution, warning her she'd get thrown out of the room if she got out of hand, or it's too alien to her to register.

Moseby leads Grade through his testimony, and how he arrived at his conclusions, particularly the one that the victim didn't die of the gunshots, but of the stabbings. Grade dwells, a bit too long for my taste, on the emasculation, how it was probably performed, and whether or not the victim was dead before he was separated from that particular body part. To his credit, Grade asserts that the victim was 'almost certainly' dead before they cut his pecker off.

Grade is a good, professional witness. Direct, precise, his testimony specific and factual. He makes few assumptions, and those he does make are hard to challenge; he's been doing this a long time, he's an expert at not letting himself get tripped up. He's testified in virtually every state in the country over the last thirty-five years, and there's never been a conviction overturned on appeal because of something he said. Defense lawyers can have a hard time dealing with him, because juries cotton to him; his credentials are first-rate and proven, not a common commodity in a small state like this. And he's likable, he smiles on the stand, no pomposity; a patrician who doesn't act superior to people, talks like a regular guy.

The prosecution takes all morning, they want to cover the bases. They conclude just before the lunch recess.

When we resume, Paul takes up our case. He asks various questions about the way Grade arrived at his conclusions regarding how Bartless was killed; he's trying, we all will as we cross-examine, to find a chink in the armor that would make it, if not impossible for our boys to have done it—we have no expectations of pulling a rabbit out of the hat with this witness—to at least cast some doubt on what happened up there, so that we can cast our seeds of ambiguity.

"Regarding the stab wounds . . . forty-seven in all . . . that you claim are the specific cause of death, Dr. Grade," Paul asks.

"Yes?"

"Why didn't the victim bleed more? You stated in your autopsy report that there was hardly any loss of blood."

"That's correct, yes."

"Shouldn't there be, sir? With all those stab wounds?"

"Under normal circumstances, of course," Grade answers easily. He shifts his position slightly, leaning forward. "But these were not normal circumstances."

A faint buzzing starts inside my head. What was it that Rita Gomez had said? Something about the way they had stabbed the victim with the knife? It was something out of the ordinary. Since our claim is that they weren't there in the first place, none of her specifics resonated. I'm going to want to review that section of her testimony during a break.

I look at Paul. He's sensed something's not quite kosher as well.

"Let's move on to time of death," he says, deftly changing gears. "There would seem to be cause for a conflict of opinion as to the exactness of that, wouldn't you agree, due to the deterioration of the body?"

Grade answers professionally. I'm only half-listening—that beat in Grade's earlier reply is lying uneasily in my stomach.

Tommy handles the rest of the questioning of Grade. Nothing new—he's a buttoned-down expert. We didn't expect much; our case will be made in a different direction, irrespective of medical expertise.

We wrap up shortly before four-thirty. Judge Martinez is checking his watch; he's ready to call it a day.

"If we are finished with this witness . . ." he begins.

Moseby's on his feet. I've never seen him so nimble.

"I have a couple of questions to ask on redirect, your honor."

"Fine. We'll start in tomorrow."

"With the court's permission, I'd rather ask them now. They won't take long, and I want to pursue something that was brought up earlier."

Martinez cocks his head in our direction.

"If it won't take long, we have no objection, your honor," Mary Lou states for the defense.

"Let's proceed, then," Martinez says. "If it appears to me that we're going to get embroiled in detail, I'll adjourn until tomorrow."

"I'll try to ensure that we don't," Moseby assures him.

He turns to Grade.

"You've previously stated that the victim died of the forty-seven knife wounds, not the gunshots to the head."

"That is correct."

"And you've also stated that there was an abnormally small amount of bleeding," Moseby says.

"Yes, I also made that statement."

"Shouldn't he have bled a lot? I mean, forty-seven stab wounds. You'd think a man would be practically drained from that many stab wounds."

"Under normal circumstances, yes," Grade says. "But as I stated earlier, these were not normal circumstances."

"How is that?"

"The victim was stabbed with a knife or knives that were hot. The heat would have sealed the wounds and prevented any substantial bleeding from occurring."

"That's an interesting theory, doctor. Rather unique. What made you think of it?"

"I had come across a comparable case in a medical journal," Grade says, "not too long before I examined this corpse. The similarities were too close to ignore."

The hair on the back of my neck stands up. Rita Gomez had testified that the bikers held their knife over a fire before they stabbed Bartless. We'd assumed that was a bunch of crap, like everything else she was saying. Now here's Grade with a theory that confirms her, almost perfectly.

"Excuse me, your honor." I'm on my feet, glancing at my partners. They look at me; they're as confused as I am. "I've read everything in Dr. Grade's autopsy report and the subsequent reports he's made pertaining to this case. I've never seen anything in there about hot knives." I look at Moseby. The fucker's standing there like the cat that ate the canary. "If the prosecution has withheld material from us, your honor, material pertinent to our case, we'd like to know. Now."

'So I can file for a mistrial' is what I leave unsaid. Martinez hears my unspoken remark loud and clear. He leans forward, looking at Moseby.

"Counselor?" he queries.

"We haven't withheld anything, your honor," Moseby says, seemingly without guile. "And anyway, we didn't raise this issue. Defense did, in their cross-examination less than two hours ago. They 'opened the door,' and if Dr. Grade came across some interesting material in a journal, as he's now informing us—material that while it would not necessarily be linked to the direct cause of Richard Bartless's death, might help explain a certain incongruity in the way the corpse was presented, I think we're entitled to hear about it. It might strengthen the connection of the defendants to the murder," he adds.

Paul's first on his feet. It was his question that gave Moseby this opportunity. "We need some time, your honor."

"Granted. We'll adjourn until tomorrow morning." Martinez bangs the gavel and exits immediately.

Grade leaves the stand. Moseby strolls over to his side of the room. Something's wrong here; he spent the whole trial setting this trap for us, and we walked right into it.

We huddle; nobody's heard anything about this, or knows about it. Hot knives? Some kind of ritual, what? We'd discounted what Rita Gomez had said, she's an obvious liar and freak. But to have a pathologist as prominent as Grade confirm it in virtually the same language scares the shit out of me.

We send Ellen out to start cross-checking it in the medical and legal journals, then question our clients. The bikers don't know what Grade's talking about. How could they?; they were never there to begin with. The whole story of hot knives means nothing to them; just more legal bullshit to try and railroad them.

"WHAT DID HE SAY?"

Mary Lou hangs up the phone.

"The same thing all the others said: no."

"Fuck!" I scream at the ceiling.

"You betchum, Red Ryder."

It's almost midnight. We're in my office. For the last several hours we've been manning the phones like a PBS telethon, trying to locate a reputable pathologist who would be willing to rebut Grade's testimony; or at least, cast some doubt on it. We can't even find one who will examine the case and give us some advice; certainly not on notice this short, when the doctor concerned is someone with Grade's bona fides.

"The hardest thing in the world is to get a doctor to say another doctor is wrong," Mary Lou says. "I can't tell you how many malpractice cases our firm defends every year for the insurance companies, legitimate stuff, not ambulance chasing, where the physician is clearly incompetent, and you can't even get his hospital to deny him privileges, let alone become a party to a decertification proceeding."

"They're worse than lawyers," Paul notes with his usual dry wit.

The humor falls on deaf ears. We fidget, looking at each other, at the walls.

"It's too late to call anyone else now," Paul observes, checking his watch, "even on the west coast. We'll have to start in tomorrow."

"We're in court tomorrow," I reply, testy. I hate being caught up short. I say it: "I hate being hung out to dry like this. I feel like a rank amateur."

"That's not fair," Mary Lou protests. "To yourself or the rest of us."

I know that, but so what? We got caught with our pants down today, and all the world was watching.

"And it wasn't in any of the discovery," she adds. "We don't have a crystal ball to tell us what *might* jump out."

"We're *supposed* to know what'll jump out," I rant. "That's what a good lawyer does. That's what we get paid for." I'm illogical, I hear it in myself even as I speak, but I can't help it. I'm freaked.

"Maybe we should've checked into Rita Gomez's story more carefully," Tommy ventures cautiously.

"Like how?" I snap.

"She had mentioned heating up knives. Maybe we should've checked to see if there was a fire up near where the body was found, for instance."

"Rita Gomez's story is a piece of shit from beginning to end is why we didn't check out stuff like that," I answer. "We've proven that in open court."

"The jury's still out, counselor," Paul gently chides me.

"Meaning?" I challenge. I'm a bitch tonight, I'd probably take my own child's head off if she looked at me sideways.

"The fact that you don't believe her doesn't mean the rest of the world automatically doesn't, too," he replies evenly. Paul's not a fighter like me; he doesn't like a fire burning in his guts, but in his quiet, unassuming way he stands up for what he thinks. It's one of the qualities I prize in him; normally.

"Are you saying you think there might be some truth to what she says?" I fire back.

"Will . . ." Mary Lou tries to deflate the tension.

"I think they raped her, yes," Paul answers calmly.

"They're not charged with rape," I flash back at him.

"You asked if I believed any of her story."

"Okay. Let's say they did rape her. What does that have to do with murder?"

"They say they didn't."

"It's a moot point," I tell him.

"No," he says. "It isn't."

"Guys. Stop this bickering. We have work to do." Mary Lou steps between us. Tommy's to the side; he wants no part of this.

"If she's telling the truth about that, which I tend to believe," Paul continues, "and they're lying, which I also believe, then maybe other parts of her story are true, and maybe other parts of theirs aren't. It's not a moot point, Will."

I exhale slowly.

"You think they're guilty, don't you?"

"I didn't say that."

"But you do."

"I don't know," he says. "But I do know that they're guilty of something; something connected to this case."

"They didn't kill this guy." I'm churning inside, I'm a dervish spinning out of control. "Don't you know that? By now don't you at least know that?"

"I'm not as convinced as you, no."

We stare hard at each other. It's a déjà vu moment—we happen to be in the conference room, the same room I was in when Fred and Andy lowered the boom, and as was the case in that incident, we're on opposite sides of the table.

"Then why the fuck did you take the case?" I demand.

"Because I needed it," he answers honestly. "And they needed me."

"They needed somebody to fight for them, tooth and nail," I tell him. I'm yelling.

"I am," he answers. He's still calm, at least outwardly.

"Opening the door on the goddam hot knives shit, that was really fighting for them," I throw at him without thinking. As soon as I say it I wish I hadn't.

"Will! You're out of line!" Mary Lou is in my face.

"I know I am, I know I am," I answer as fast as I can. "I'm sorry, I can't help it. I'm sorry, Paul," I tell him.

"You didn't mean it," he says. "We're all testy tonight."

I slump against the wall.

"Moseby set us up, the bastard. He set us up and we walked right into it. Right over the goddam cliff, like lemmings. I thought I had the slimy bastard's number and he outfoxed me like I was a first-year law student."

"It's one point, Will," Mary Lou says. "It's not the case. We have a good case."

"We shouldn't have let it happen that way," I reply. "We can't afford mistakes."

"We'll be okay," she says. "Once we start presenting our witnesses that testimony will be all washed away."

This is the woman talking, not the lawyer. She's trying to help me, soothe me. I wish I could let her.

"Hey, listen," Tommy kicks in. "If it hadn't been introduced this way, they'd have found another way to get it in. Paul just happened to be in the line of fire. It could've been any of us. They want to win this case and they're not going to play by the rules unless the court forces them to."

He's right. I can feel the anger ebbing out of me. It isn't Paul's fault. He's doing the best he can. And if in his gut he doesn't believe in their innocence, completely or even partially, so what? A lawyer can defend a guilty client as well as he can defend an innocent one. If all your clients had to be innocent, most of them wouldn't have lawyers. It's one of the best parts of the system.

As we're breaking up, Paul puts a fatherly arm around my shoulder. "You okay?" he asks.

"I will be. I just hate surprises."

"We all do." He smiles at me. "I had an ulcer once, because I got pissed off one time too many. Like you're doing. You do the best you can, Will, but you can't let it kill you."

The problem is, it's the fire that sustains me. If it ever goes out inside, I won't be worth a shit as a lawyer; and right now, that's all there is to me that is worth a shit.

"YOUR HONOR. We would move at this time for a continuance of sufficient time in which to analyze this portion of Dr. Grade's testimony and to procure an expert of our own."

We're in Martinez's chambers. Us and Moseby.

"We object, your honor," Moseby says.

"I figured you would," Martinez says. He leans forward in his chair. "I can't do it," he tells us. "I *won't* do it. That testimony yesterday resulted from your actions, not the prosecution's. I've got a jury impaneled here. I can't stop this trial now, not for this."

He glances at Moseby, back at us.

"Here's what I'll do for you, though. You can supplement your witness list. I shouldn't allow it, but I want to give you every opportunity. We'll be in trial another week or so. If you're going to find an expert, that should give you enough time."

I'd like to thank you for your help, judge, but I can't. The possibility of finding a credible expert, acquainting him with the case, and convincing him to testify against a fellow doctor, are somewhere below the proverbial slim or none.

"IT'S A SIMPLE PROCEDURE," Grade says. It's an hour later, we've reconvened.

He's talking to Moseby but looking at the jury, patiently leading them. "Not at all complicated. Something struck me when I first viewed the corpse. Granted, it had been decomposing for a few days, and was certainly not in good shape, but something about it seemed out of the ordinary."

"Which was?" Moseby asks.

"That there was, as has been noted, hardly any bleeding. Forty-seven knife stabs, some of them rather deep, there should have been bleeding."

"Why wasn't there, then?" Moseby continues his questioning. "Why wasn't there more blood?"

"Because," Grade says, and now he leans forward, he's going to say something important and he wants the room to know it, and they do, judge and jury are leaning forward with him, "the wounds were cauterized as they were being made." He stands, picks up the pointer lying next to the easel. "May I?"

Martinez nods. Grade steps down from the stand, comes around to the easel. He points to one of the wounds in the photograph.

"As you can see, there's darkness around these edges. Like a crust." He moves the pointer around the wound.

I can see the dark contours around the wounds; I thought they came from the traumatic impact the knife had on the body, that's the way it had been explained to me. I don't see any crust, but it's only a photograph.

"You can see this dark crust around almost every wound on the body," Grade says, pointing to various knife wounds in the picture. "I came to the conclusion that they were formed by heat. The heat cauterized the wounds and stopped the bleeding. It's common in medicine."

"Are you saying, then, Dr. Grade," Moseby asks slowly, dramatically, "that these wounds were caused by . . ."

"Hot knives. Yes." Grade finishes for him.

"That each time before the victim was stabbed," Moseby continues, "forty-seven times in all, the people who stabbed him heated the knife and then stuck it in?"

Grotesque bastard. The jury hears that, they're lapping it up, it's drawing them in like moths to a flame.

"That is exactly what I am saying." Grade puts the pointer down, resumes the dock, but remains standing, towering over everyone but Martinez.

"That's an interesting conclusion, Dr. Grade," Moseby says, "but not very common. In fact I'd never heard of it until you mentioned it to me."

No shit, I think. Neither had anyone else. Except the state's star witness.

"I agree," Grade answers. "And if I hadn't come across this theory only a short time before I examined this corpse, it would have slipped by me completely."

"In a medical journal?" Moseby asks.

Grade nods. "I don't recall exactly which one—I read so many. You have to, to stay current. As I remember, the doctor who wrote it was an expert on homosexuality and in particular homosexual murders."

I can feel the heat rising from Lone Wolf. Jesus, we don't need this. This guy's liable to freak right here if he's wrapped into a gay killing. I lean towards him.

"You better control yourself, man," I warn him.

"If that motherfucker calls me a faggot I'm going to tear his fucking heart out," he growls.

"You do," I hiss at him, "and you're sealing your verdict."

He scowls at me.

"I mean it," I say.

He sits back, seething. Just get us through this, Lord, without it blowing up in our faces, that's all I'm asking.

"It's your opinion, then, doctor, that this murder has homosexual overtones?" Moseby asks.

I grip Lone Wolf's wrist, hard. His teeth are grinding so tightly he could fracture his jaw.

Grade refers to a folder. "Rectal smears taken from the victim's anus revealed sperm," he says. "That's in the report."

"I know that, doctor," Moseby states. "I just wanted to make sure it was part of the trial record."

Asshole. A straight-forward lawyer would've presented that in an honest way. This is more bullshit playing to the crowd.

Grade puts the folder aside. "If I could add something . . ."

Moseby smiles at him. "Of course, doctor. You're the expert."

"Even if there had been no sperm present I would have drawn the same conclusion."

"That it was a gay murder."

"The man's penis was cut off," Grade says with a show of disgust, almost as if he has to spit to cleanse his mouth. "It was a heinous and brutal and disgusting act. Whoever did that is sick."

A rumble moves through the courtroom. The jury sits tight-lipped. Several look over at my clients.

"I must add," Grade continues, "that whoever did do it has to have some sexual problems. Some conflicts about his . . ." he pauses; then pointedly, "or *their* sexuality."

"Objection!" I shout.

"Sustained. Witness will refrain from supposition of that nature," Martinez tells Grade.

"I'm sorry, your honor."

"Strike that last sentence," Martinez instructs the court reporter.

Big fucking deal.

"About this homosexual killing . . . excuse me, this possible homosexual killing . . ."

"Objection!" Mary Lou's on her feet. "There's been no introduction of homosexuality or any sexual conduct regarding this killing," she says. "The mere fact that the victim's anus contained sperm does not mean that anal intercourse and the murder occurred at or around the same time. They're two entirely separate issues."

"Over-ruled. This murder is sexual on the face of it. They cut off his penis." Martinez turns to Moseby. "Continue, counselor."

Shit. We've lost him, for now at least.

"We have a possible homosexual killing," Moseby says. "How does that tie into a motorcycle gang?"

I object again. "Since when is Dr. Grade an expert on motorcycle organizations, your honor?"

Grade smiles at Martinez. "Let me assure you that I'm not." He adds almost disdainfully: "In the slightest. But there is extensive literature in many psychiatric and psychological publications that talks about the male bonding in motorcycle gangs, particularly those characterized as outlaw gangs, and homosexuality. It's common knowledge."

"In other words, doctor, this murder had definite homosexual overtones, and the makeup of motorcycle gangs, the psychiatric profiles as it were, also show homosexual components, in psychiatric and medical terms," Moseby says.

"Without any doubt."

"You're dead, motherfucker! You hear me? You're fucking dead!"

Lone Wolf has jumped up as if he's about to leap the table and attack Dr. Grade with his bare hands.

"You're dead, man! I'm gonna tear out your fucking heart and I'm gonna fucking eat it!"

It's bedlam. Martinez yells, "Bailiffs!" I'm holding onto Lone Wolf in a bear hug. The others are shying away. The jury is half-standing, ready to bolt.

I look at Grade. He's standing, staring us right in the eye. He's not afraid, the only one in the courtroom who isn't.

They cuff Lone Wolf, slap on leg irons, hustle him out of the room. Martinez hammers his gavel.

"Thirty minute recess," he barks. "I want attorneys in chambers."

"You would-be Oliviers are not going to get away with this, do you hear me?"

We're all in there, us and the prosecution. Martinez is scorching the walls.

"First you pull this crap with the mother," he says, pointing an accusatory finger at Moseby, "then you," aiming it at me, "can't even control his goddam client!"

"It took us by surprise, your honor," I say, "it won't happen again."

"It better not, goddam it." Martinez is spitting mad. "I don't want to chain and gag him for the rest of the trial, it doesn't look good, but if it's the only way to restrain him, I will. These are dangerous men, counselor, I won't put officers of the court or the jury in jeopardy."

"I'll do the best I can."

"It better be good enough." He expels some air. "This is a bitch, boys and girls. Don't turn it into a damn circus. I expect professionalism in my courtroom."

Everyone agrees to try and maintain professionalism. I glance at Mary Lou when Martinez says that word. She doesn't look at me.

We cross-examine Grade after lunch, continuing for the remainder of the afternoon. Ellen returns late in the day; she's been unable to find any literature about homosexual gang killings and hot knives. We're treading water.

Grade is forceful and straight, but he's their witness. You have to be careful with a witness like him, if you lean on him too hard you risk alienating the jury. On the other hand, if you're only lobbing him slow pitches down the middle you aren't doing your job.

We dance around until near sundown, bag it for the day. I reserve the right to bring Grade back for further cross.

It's been a shitty day for us.

None of us gets any sleep tonight; we're in the office until dawn, trying to find a reference to Grade's 'hot knives' theory. We go through volumes of case law, pull up every computer program we can access: American Bar, *Supreme Court Reporter, New York Times,* Library of Congress, *New England Journal of Medicine*—any psychiatric or psychological journal we can find in the files. Nothing.

"What if this article doesn't exist?" Tommy theorizes. It's dawn, we have an hour to go home, shower, change and be back in court.

"You mean Grade might've made it up?" Mary Lou asks. "I can't believe that."

"He's no spring chicken," Paul says. "He could've mixed it up with something else."

I look at them sourly. My mouth tastes like shit, my armpits stink, I'm tired, frustrated, and pissed off. "Which one of you wants to bring that accusation?" I ask. "Against one of this country's foremost forensic authorities, if he does say so himself."

No one volunteers.

"And then he miraculously remembers where he read it, quotes chapter and verse," I continue. "Really makes us look good. We're doing our homework, aren't we. Jury'd really love that." I expel a sigh. "It's a set-up and we're stuck. We're going to have to accept it on face value, try to shoot it down with our own stuff."

I pick up my briefcase, stuff some papers in. "Last one to leave locks up." I trudge out, slamming the door behind me. Alexander, Hite, and Portillo. Somehow it doesn't feel like home anymore.

"WERE YOU AT THE MOTEL when the policemen arrived?"

"Yes, sir." Low, barely audible. Scared to death.

"And were you still there when Rita Gomez left with them?"

"Yes."

Her name is Ellen Sage. She's the other motel maid, the one I encountered when I was a day late and a dollar short in my own quest for the lovely Rita.

Tommy's questioning her. He's establishing that Gomez and Sanchez were in fact the officers who discovered her, took her away, and eventually produced the statement from her that got this show on the road.

"How long after you first saw her in the condition you described did the police come?" Tommy asks.

"I don't know." Whining, squirming, twisting her skirt in her hands. No fancy new clothes for her; an unvarnished little twit.

"Try to recall, please, it's important."

"Couple days. Three. I don't know exactly."

"And when she left with them," Tommy continues, "you saw them leave? Actually saw her get into a car with them and drive away?"

She nods. "I was cleaning number six. It's right out front. You can see everything."

"The door was open?"

"Yeh. They make you do that . . . the management."

"You've identified the officers she left with as detectives Gomez and Sanchez, that is also correct?"

"Yeh. Them." She points to them, sitting in the first row behind the prosecutor's table.

"Okay," he says. "Now . . . when she left with them, was she better? Had she recovered from the way she had been the morning you found her?"

"Objection," Moseby says, lumbering to his feet. "This witness hardly qualifies as a medical expert."

"Sustained."

"Let me put it another way, Miss Sage. Did she look better to you?"

"Hell, no," the girl says. "She could hardly walk. I'd gone out just that morning and got her two boxes of Super Kotex. She had half a box stuffed up under her panties when she walked out that morning." She stifles a giggle. "She could hardly walk she was so stuffed up."

"Was she still bleeding when she left with them?" he asks.

"She was an hour before," Ellen says, " 'cause I helped her change. She was a damn mess. I was glad when they came 'cause I figured that was the only way she'd ever go to a doctor. She needed it but she wouldn't 'cause of her being scared and all."

"Did the officers say anything to you about seeing that she would be taken care of? Medically?"

"They said they'd make sure she was okay," Ellen replies. "I never thought they wouldn't," she continues. "That girl was bleeding like a stuck pig."

SANCHEZ AND GOMEZ (no relation to the lovely Rita, one in ten surnames up here is Gomez) testify. How through exhaustive police work they'd found her, convinced her that they would protect her from the bikers, finally got her to talk, and of course advised her of all her rights, including offering her an attorney (which she declined, I'd like to know how vigorously they pursued that). There had been no deals cut, she wasn't guilty of anything except being scared to death. She had volunteered her testimony freely and without threats or coercion.

"She had been raped? That is your testimony?" Mary Lou asks Sanchez. She paces back and forth in front of him, her heels clicking on the tile floor.

"She said she was." His eyelids are naturally heavy, it gives the impression he's about to fall asleep. Maybe he is.

"But you didn't have her examined? You didn't take her to a hospital?"

"No." Laconic, very Southwestern. He's not going to say anything more than the required minimum.

"Why not?"

"She wouldn't go."

"Did she say why?"

"She was afraid if it became public news they'd find her and kill her."

"But she did anyway. Go public."

"That was later."

"When?"

"After we talked to her."

"How much later? From the time you found her until the time she agreed to talk?"

"Five days."

"So for five days you and your partner were holed up with this girl somewhere . . ."

"Objection!"

"Sustained."

"For five days you and your partner interrogated this girl until she agreed to testify for the prosecution."

"Yeh."

"During which time she was recovering from being raped."

"That's what she said."

"And you believed her."

"No reason not to."

"But even after she agreed to testify for you, and was promised protection from the men she claims assaulted her and killed her companion, you still didn't take her to the hospital. Is that correct?"

"Yeh."

"Weren't you concerned for her? A woman who had been raped as many times as she said she was, a woman who said she witnessed a murder, who claimed her own life was in jeopardy. How could a responsible police officer not have had that woman examined?"

"She didn't want it. I'm not her father, lady. We offered. She refused."

"Isn't it your sworn duty to see to it that she was medically examined if she claimed she was raped regardless of whether or not she wanted to be? Particularly in the state she was in? Her friend testified she was bleeding 'like a stuck pig,' I believe that was the way she described your witness."

"She told us she was okay. I wasn't about to look under her skirt."

The audience titters. That's just what you would have liked to do,

I think. I wonder how many hookers got instant justice from him in the back of a squad car.

"That's very professional, detective," Mary Lou counters. She pauses.

"Of course," she says, thinking out loud, "you might've taken her to a private doctor. A friend. Someone who's helped you out before."

"No, lady. That isn't SOP."

"A private doctor," she continues, "who wouldn't ask questions. Who wouldn't even keep a record of it so your witness wouldn't have to give a statement right then and there . . ."

"Objection!" Moseby yells, this time with urgency.

". . . so you and your partner could work on that story of hers until you got it the way you wanted it," Mary Lou says, pressing on. "In private."

"Sustained."

". . . so it would be exactly the way you wanted it to be," she finishes, "not just whatever happened to come out of her mouth the first time she was publicly presented."

"Objection!"

"Sustained!" Martinez glares at her. "Are you deaf, counselor?"

"Sorry, your honor," she says ever so contritely.

"You will completely disregard that last line of questioning," Martinez instructs the jury. "Strike all that," he directs the stenographer.

"Do that again," he warns Mary Lou, "and I'll hold you in contempt."

"Yes, sir. Sorry."

"All right, then. Proceed."

She looks back at our table for a second before moving on. I nod imperceptibly to her; it may have been stricken from the record, but not from the jury's minds. The possibility exists that the state's star witness and arresting officers are all part of one package of lies.

"While you were questioning her was there a matron present?" Mary Lou asks now. "A policewoman?"

"No."

"Isn't it standard procedure to have a female officer present when a woman is being questioned? Particularly for as long as she was?"

"There wasn't one available."

"In the entire county? Not one available policewoman or matron?"

"Guess not. We requested one. Didn't get one."

"Isn't that a violation of your rules?"

"We made the request. The rest you'll have to talk to someone else about."

"While you and your partner were sequestered with the witness what did you talk about?"

"The case."

"The facts of the case?"

"The facts she was telling us, yes."

"What else?"

"Nothing else."

"You didn't tell her anything you knew? Like maybe something out of the autopsy report?"

"Objection!" Moseby leaps up for that one.

"Sustained." Martinez admonishes Mary Lou: "Don't push it."

"Yes, your honor."

It feels like a setup. It's such a neat fucking bundle.

"You only discussed the case according to what she knew," Mary Lou says.

"That's right. By the book."

"By the book? A woman who claims she was the victim of multiple rape, was allegedly forced to witness a grisly murder, this woman is interrogated without another woman present and is never examined by a doctor and you call what you did going by the book? What book are you referring to, detective Sanchez, the Book of the Dead? Because a woman in the condition she described herself to be in could have dropped dead while in your custody, officer."

She stomps away from him. "No further questions," she tosses over her shoulder as Moseby objects again.

"But she didn't," Sanchez says flatly.

Essentially, that's the prosecution's case. There's additional evidence: bloodstains were found on Roach's pants legs which matched the victim's type, AB negative. Not many people, only about five percent of the population, have that type. By itself that isn't much, we can introduce evidence that a fellow biker who'd gone down in an accident in Albuquerque had the same type and that Roach had helped carry him, which would account for blood on his pants. Under normal circumstances the two facts would neutralize each other, but these aren't normal circumstances.

The bikers' knives were tested for blood. The results were inconclusive. The knives could have made the stab wounds, but none of them are very good fits. But the fact remains that the bikers all carried knives.

I watch the jury as our clients' records are read: if they had to reach a verdict this very moment, we couldn't get a bet down in Vegas in our favor.

BUT THAT WAS YESTERDAY and today's a clean slate. I cannot feign false modesty: we are conducting a brilliant defense. We're dazzling them with footwork, dancing all over that courtroom. We're witty, charming, we have our facts at our fingertips, we're playing our witnesses like they're priceless Stradivarii. We dovetail beautifully, each following up on the others' presentations like a Marine Corps drill team. We have dozens of witnesses, we make sure each one's testimony is thoroughly covered in our offices and utilized to maximum advantage in the courtroom.

We're following the bikers' comings and goings from the time they first hit Santa Fe until the time they left, and beyond, when the body was discovered. Almost every hour is accounted for, in many cases down to the minute.

The night in question, and the morning after, is the critical time. Several witnesses, each independent of the others, including the bartender and the manager, testify that was the only night the bikers were in the bar. The witnesses are certain; you don't forget characters like these four. They left at closing time, two o'clock in the morning; they closed the place. Rita Gomez went with them. There is absolutely no doubt, the witnesses tell the court, that they could have left earlier. Absolutely none.

One entire side of the front of the courtroom is filled with large flowcharts and blown-up maps on easels. They show time, place, distance from one area where the bikers were, or allegedly were, to another. We parade our witnesses, from the time the bikers left town, one after the other, a stack of alibis so thick you could strain your back lifting them: the kid that sold them the gasoline, Maggie from route 14, the bikers they partied with in Albuquerque. Scores of people who saw them, if only fleetingly. We introduce the receipts that tell where they were at any given time from the minute they rode out of Santa Fe. Every witness, every scrap of evidence that is useful is presented. We've covered this legal waterfront like a San Francisco fog.

Our defense goes into its second week. My co-defenders and I are the toast of the legal community. In the bars, clubs, and restaurants where lawyers congregate after hours we're the main topic of conversation: how well we're conducting our case. I'm on a high, floating, I'm electric, alive. I *am* the toughest motherfucker in the valley, my erstwhile partners are going to be crawling on their hands and knees to get me back in the firm when this trial's over.

In my more reflective moments I know the feeling for what it is; ego gratification on a pretty shallow level. Yes, it's nice to be admired and respected, but that can zip by quicker than a Nolan Ryan fastball. And what goes around comes around, all the trite and true sayings. I want to get back in the firm; I think. I want to see if there's really something there with Mary Lou, away from the glamour of an important trial. I want to be loved and respected and rich. But what I really want is for my daughter not to be taken away from me, and for my clients to be found not guilty. And those are the two things I'm the least secure about.

THE CLERK OF THE COURT has a high, reedy voice that seems inadequate for the size of the courtroom, dissipating into the air before it can reverberate against the walls and ceiling. You feel such a voice should bounce, echo, resonate with authority. The voice of the law. I'm probably the only one that notices stuff like that. I like to hear my own voice resonate.

"Call Steven Jensen," the clerk says.

Lone Wolf stands. He turns for a moment and stares at the jury; not a threat, a look—this is me, make sure you know who I am. He has undeniable presence. He walks to the dock, places his hand on the Bible, takes the oath in a firm, clear voice. He's dressed in a suit and tie. It won't fool anyone; he's a wolf in sheep's clothing for sure.

The outcome of the trial could hinge on what happens while Lone Wolf is on the stand. It's a calculated risk, putting him on. We've debated it endlessly. In the end, we decided we had to. We won't call the others to testify. They're too nervous, unpredictable. Lone Wolf is unpredictable, too, he could blow things sky-high, but we have to put him on, we have to confront the jury head-on with him, especially after his outburst at Grade.

I learned a long time ago that constitutional rights to the contrary, a defendant's silence, his refusal to testify in his behalf, is too often construed as a tacit admission of guilt; the jury wants to hear the accused say he didn't do it. And there's another reason, particularly in cases like this one where the accused are thought of as being beyond the pale. We want the jury to see that they are people, human beings. That they can speak, that they are not animals, but men; men who perhaps live by a different code, but men. They have limits, like all men, limits that they have personally defined, marked off, won't go beyond. In this instance their boundaries exclude sodomy and murder, not as a package, and this is critical, because this crime is specific. Maybe under other circumstances they would kill. Maybe I would, too, or anyone else. But under these specific circumstances, they would not. That is what his presence is going to say; what he is going to say.

The danger, of course, is that once I put Lone Wolf on the stand, his prior record, and by inference the records of his partners, will be brought out by the prosecution on cross-examination. It will hurt us, we know that for sure, we discussed it with our clients at length, but in the end we all decided that to not go on the stand at all would be even worse.

I lead him through their story. Yes, they all had sex with Rita up in the mountains, but it was okay with her. That's how she earns her living, she's already copped to that, he says. He's lying there about it being okay, we both know it. I can't help that. I'm paid to defend him, not to justify his every action. If the goddam cops had done their job right he'd have had to tell the truth about it. Tough shit. I'm not going to do their job for them.

It goes well. He's a good witness, articulate, funny, with charm.

His public voice is louder than I'm used to, there's a whiskey drawl in it. A voice that women would find attractive. I can see some of the women in the courtroom looking at him; he's turning them on. I'm a man who does things he shouldn't, but that's the way men are, he's saying. That's what real men are. Maybe not faggots, but that's something else. He wouldn't know about that. He has no interest or desire in fucking a man, not even as some kind of sick punishment. Real men don't fuck guys in the ass.

By the time I finish my direct it's the end of the day. We recess until tomorrow, when Moseby'll cross-examine. My colleagues and I regroup to my office, order in sandwiches and coffee. It's been a good day. Lone Wolf did well; he told his story and he was civilized. I think he dissipated some of the ill will built up by his verbal attack on Dr. Grade.

We finish our homework and split up. I kiss Mary Lou goodnight outside her car. I'd like to be going home with her; that's for another time, I'm going to keep my vow of abstinence with her. It's a head-game I play with myself, if I do A then B will happen. If I don't get involved with her or with any woman for a while, then Claudia will stay in Santa Fe. It's a dream, a wish. It's all I have to go on.

LONE WOLF LOOKS DOWN at Moseby, who is pacing back and forth in front of him.

"I can't help how you feel, man, that's how it was," he drawls in response to a question. Low-key and cool.

It's been a long morning. For the first half-hour of cross-examination I had terrible butterflies in my stomach for fear that Lone Wolf was going to do something stupid, crazy, fuck up all the good he'd built up yesterday. As the questions and answers droned on, I became less tense, to the point where I'm relaxed now. Alert, but at ease. Moseby's been looking for an angle all morning, some edge to pry the lid off Lone Wolf's composure. He hasn't done it. Lone Wolf's in command.

"Let's go back up on the mountain again," Moseby says now. "The first time."

"There was only one time, ace," Lone Wolf says.

Moseby picks at his teeth. "The time the four of you were up there with the girl. That time."

"That's the time, man. The one and only."

They've been sparring like this all morning. I wonder how long Moseby's going to keep it up; he isn't looking good. He's not stupid, he knows when he's not looking good.

"One more time," he says. "You say Rita Gomez freely and of her own volition had sexual intercourse with you. Without coercion or threats. You didn't even have to pay her."

"I know a sad sack like you finds that hard to believe, but yes, she did. Ladies like outlaws and outlaws like ladies, friend, don't you know that? Don't you listen to country music? I thought ever'body out west here listened to country music."

Smiles and laughter from the spectators. The jury, too. This man is a good witness, a real con artist. That he sounds like John Wayne doesn't hurt his cause either.

"I'm a fan of the classics myself," Moseby smiles self-deprecatingly, his stock in trade. That's good, he'll make points like that. "Anyway . . . you had sex with Miss Gomez but not with Richard Bartless."

"He wasn't there so how could I?"

"But even if he had been there you wouldn't have, because you don't have sex with men."

"You got that right, ace."

"How do you feel about sex with men? Abstractly, in general."

"It makes me want to puke," Lone Wolf says. He grimaces.

"Just the idea of it."

"Goddam right."

"How do you feel about homosexuality in general, Mr. Jensen?" Moseby continues.

"Objection," I state. "This is not a trial about homosexuality." I know in part it is but I want to ward it off as much as possible, this is where Lone Wolf's fuse is shortest.

"Over-ruled," Martinez snaps. "The victim was anally penetrated. Homosexuality is part and parcel of this. Answer the question," he directs Lone Wolf.

"It's sick," Lone Wolf says.

"You feel homosexuals are sick," Moseby says. "Do you feel sorry for them, then?"

"You crazy, man?"

"The answer is no?"

"Damn straight it's no." He leans toward Moseby. "If I was ever going to kill somebody—and I never have—it wouldn't be a queer. Killing queers ain't my style. It's beneath me, you know what I mean?"

"In other words," Moseby sums up, "you have nothing to do with homosexuality or homosexuals."

"In those exact words," Lone Wolf replies.

Moseby starts back towards the prosecution table as if to get something. Suddenly he turns back to the bench.

"No further questions, your honor." He sits down, slumping low in his chair.

Martinez looks at him. He's surprised. So am I. It's almost like Moseby's working with me, not against me.

Martinez shrugs. "The witness is excused."

Lone Wolf steps down, comes back to our table, takes his seat. He winks at me, out of sight of the jury.

They didn't lay a glove on him.

I stand up. "The defense rests, your honor."

Martinez nods. "Closing arguments will commence Monday unless there are rebuttal witnesses." He looks at Moseby. Moseby looks sick to his stomach.

"We're trying to locate one, your honor. We're not having much luck."

"After Monday morning it'll be too late. If you have anyone else he had better be an important factor or I'm not going to allow his testimony. This has been a long trial. It's time to finish it up. I'd like to be charging this jury by the end of business Tuesday."

"Yes, sir," Moseby says. "If this witness turns up, you're going to want to hear him."

IT ALWAYS STARTS OUT the same way. It's late, you've been working your brains out seven days a week, eighteen-hour days. You finally go home to a place you can't stand—either you can't stand the people you're living with, like my situation with Holly, the woman to whom I was married and now am about not to be—the final decree's coming down any day now, just another deadly thorn in my side—or you hate the physical place itself, like this fleabag condo. It's one of the reasons, maybe the biggest one, that you put in those hours. You don't admit that to yourself; your posture is that you love your work, you're a workaholic because of your love for it. That's bullshit, elementary denial. You damn well may love your work, but don't pretend it's the only thing that keeps you away.

Anyway. You're wired, being in trial is like eating raw volts of electricity, you don't turn it on and off like a spigot. You have to wind down. The problem is in a few hours you're due back in court again, and you have to be sharp. People's lives are in your hands. You need your beauty sleep, baby, you have to get your rest. You're going to strip down, maybe take a shower or a hot bath, watch the late news on CNN. And to ensure that you will mellow out, at least enough to sleep, you'll have a glass of wine. One, that's all, it's late, you're going to sleep soon, you'll sleep better. Red wine, that's more suitable late at night, a nice Zinfandel or maybe a Merlot, you still have some of the '82 Newton stashed away you bought for some special occasion. What was that occasion anyway? Doesn't matter, it's nice, good body, good legs, if you can't have the woman of your dreams tonight a nice glass of Merlot will substitute just fine.

It tastes good, you'd forgotten how good, you don't as a rule open a bottle at home when you're alone and you haven't had anyone over that would have appreciated this (except Mary Lou, and the circumstances didn't call for it), you'll top up your glass, maybe lie in bed with it and watch something else for awhile, "Saturday Night Live," and it's a good show, a rerun but you haven't seen this one, and you sip your wine and you're finally, finally after the strain of the work-week, relaxing. Savor it, tomorrow afternoon you're rehearsing your closing arguments, it's showtime again. You have to be double-sharp for that, you won't even allow yourself two cups of coffee.

You watch and sip and chill out until you fall asleep.

One of these days maybe I'll wise up and learn something. It's morning, the bottle is empty, the TV is blasting Jimmy fucking Swaggart, and my mouth feels like the elephant's graveyard. I'm not hung over, nothing near that, one bottle of wine doesn't come close to bringing on a hang over for a drinker of my stature and experience, but I feel bad. I feel slow, unfocused, my head's stuffed with cotton. I have to prepare my final summation today, run it by my colleagues, listen to and critique theirs, and incidentally try to save the lives of four men I strongly feel are innocent of the crime of which they're accused.

Most important, I've violated a trust: my own, to me. I don't mean the promise I made under coercion to Andy and Fred, I'd have promised my right testicle there and then; or the implicit promises I've been making to Patricia for years when she's mentioned how Claudia talked about my drinking; none of that. I mean the promise about taking care of my life. I don't care so much about the drinking, it's the inner lying that's eating me up. If you can't be straight to yourself who are you ever going to be straight to? Quit bullshitting yourself, Alexander. Have the goddam drink and don't be a martyr to it, tell your partners how you feel. Stop making excuses, stop asking the people who care the most about you to make excuses for you. You wake up one day and look around and they aren't there to do it anymore. You got rid of them all. More bullshit: they dumped you. No more family, no more kid, no more law partnership.

The most important things in your life: gone.

I OWN THREE MAJOR SUITS, all Oxxfords: a charcoal-gray, a navy, a medium-gray with a muted pinstripe. I'll wear them for the next three days. By then, except for the deliberations, it should be over. In New Mexico the judge charges the jury before closing summations, so Martinez is going to take part of the morning, at least an hour, then Moseby will give his first closing. He goes first and last: the burden of proof is on the state, they have rebuttal. Then, probably after lunch, it'll be our turn.

Today it's standing-room-only in the courtroom, the fire marshals were turning people away before eight. I've been here early, the first lawyer to arrive. I love days like this, it's what I live for. The slender wall between a defendant and annihilation. An awesome responsibility.

The others join me. Everyone's nervous; we'd be crazy if we weren't. A few minutes before nine Moseby and his team walk in, looking harried, preoccupied. I can't believe he isn't ready; but something out of the ordinary is going to happen, I make my living reading body language, his is not the language of a prosecutor about to try to send four men to their deaths.

The prisoners are brought in, seated. We wait. A couple minutes after nine the clerk calls for order, and Martinez comes from his chambers in the rear. He's wearing a scowl.

"If there are no rebuttal witnesses," he says, glaring at Moseby, "I'm ready to begin charging the jury. Any objections or additional witnesses?"

I stand for the defense.

"No objections, your honor. No further witnesses."

Moseby rises.

"Your honor, the prosecution wants to present a rebuttal witness."

"Objection!" I hear myself, Paul, and Mary Lou overlapping one another.

"Approach the bench," Martinez barks.

I look at Moseby as we cross to the front. Bastard has something up his sleeve, that's the reason for the way he presented himself this morning, and for the scowl on Martinez's face. He must've been notified minutes before, in his chambers. No wonder Moseby was late.

"The defense was not informed of any rebuttal witnesses," I say hotly. "He can't pull this, your honor," I add, pointing my thumb at the bastard's gut, "it's against the rules, plain and simple."

Martinez turns to Moseby. Explain this, he's saying silently, and you'd better do it well.

"Like I said on Friday, your honor," Moseby says, "we've been looking for this witness for weeks without any success. That's why we didn't notify anyone. We just found him late last night. We had to charter a plane to get him here on time."

"Hey, fuck this . . ." I start.

"Counselor," Martinez admonishes me.

"I don't care, your honor." I'm disgusted, I don't give a shit about decorum. "I'm not going to let this low-life pull this twice."

"Listen . . ." Moseby says, his face turning pink.

I brush him off. "He already did this with the victim's mother. It's a circus, it's unethical, we don't have to jump through these hoops. It's wrong, I don't care who his witness is, I don't believe he couldn't be found and we couldn't be notified. It's a cheap trick, beneath the dignity of your court and the trial you've been conducting."

Martinez steeples his fingers.

"Mr. Prosecutor," he says, "your conduct is less than wholly honest in this matter."

Inwardly I groan. He's going to let Moseby present his witness.

"But," he continues, "in the interest and compelling need for a thoroughly complete trial, I'm going to let him testify." He turns to us. "Sorry, counselors. I can't say 'no' on this one. It's potentially too important."

We sit down, determined not to let it bug us. Brace up, man, I inwardly pep-talk myself, just one more witness, you can handle it, you've handled all the others so far. Moseby hands the clerk a sheet of paper.

"Call James Angelus," he reads.

Lone Wolf reacts like somebody just stuck a cattle-prod up his ass.

"What the fuck . . ." he says, loud enough to be heard by the jury.

"What is it?" I ask. "Who is he?"

"Nobody," Lone Wolf shuts me off. "Just one dead motherfucker."

I look at him closely. I've never seen him shaken like this before.

A man enters from the back of the courtroom. Maybe thirty, slender, his clothes slightly flamboyant for this neighborhood: definitely not from New Mexico, unless he's one of the new breed who've moved here in the past decade from New York or Los Angeles.

"He looks alive enough to me," I observe.

"He's dead to me. Okay?" He's got an involuntary twitch going now above his eye, and he's gripping the table so tightly the blood's left his knuckles.

It takes me a moment to figure out what it is about the witness that seems a bit off; he's gay. He's not swish, there's no mince in his walk, no limp wrist. But he's gay, to anyone who knows.

I look closely at Angelus as he takes the stand and is administered the oath, then at Lone Wolf, sitting next to me, still, like an owl watching a mouse crossing a field of snow, the little creature not knowing that in a few silent seconds he'll be dinner; then back to the surprise witness.

"State your name."

"James Anthony Angelus."

He's scared shitless. For one brief moment he and Lone Wolf lock eyes, then he turns away, shaking, the color draining from his face. My mind's racing, is there something these bastards never told me, did they in fact have a connection with the victim? A homosexual murder, an eleventh-hour surprise homosexual witness, Lone Wolf's reaction. If our clients withheld important evidence from us, that's all she wrote.

"Thank you for joining us today, Mr. Angelus," Moseby says.

The witness is mute.

"For the record," Moseby continues, "are you related to any of the defendants in this case?"

"Yes," Angelus answers before I can rise.

"Objection!" I shout it out. "This is completely immaterial and irrelevant."

Martinez looks at me. He knows what's coming.

"Over-ruled."

"Which one?" Moseby asks.

"Steven Jensen. The one who calls himself Lone Wolf."

"What is your relationship to him?" Moseby says.

"I'm his brother."

It's a story of love, and anguish, and fear, and ultimately utter rejection. Two brothers, abandoned early by alcoholic parents, drifting from one county home to another. Always managing to stay together. The older fiercely protecting the younger; the older a big boy for his age, a natural warrior, the little one smaller, more vulnerable, more overtly needy. Their love is both real and desperate; without the one, the other has nothing of flesh and blood, ceases to exist outside of paperwork.

One day, when they're fifteen and twelve, a troublemaker comes up to the older brother and says the little one's a faggot, he got caught touching another kid's weenie in the shower room. The older brother thanks the troublemaker for this information by punching his lights out, inflicting permanent neurological damage. He gets sixty days in the county detention home. Before he's taken away he confronts his little brother: did you do that sick shit? The little one swears on a stack of Bibles he didn't. The older one believes him. He goes and does his time, the first of many.

He comes back to the home, to his little brother. Technically he's old enough to bail out, he's almost sixteen, they don't even want him here anymore, but he won't abandon his brother, so they let him stay. He gets a job, makes money, comes back to the home at night. His little brother is doing well in school, he has a shot at a future. The older brother will do everything he can to make sure he gets that shot.

Then it happens again, only this time the little one can't duck it. He sucked off a kid. The older brother is beside himself with rage, shame, fear and love for his little brother. You got to stop this shit, he tells him, it's sick, disgusting, you can't do this to yourself. To me. The little one cries, he doesn't want to, he can't help it.

He's lying, of course. It's true he can't help it, but he does want it, he wants it more than anything. It's who he is, when he's with a man sexually, even at this tender age of by-now thirteen, it's the only time he feels alive, that he isn't hiding. But he lies to his brother, there's no girls around, he was confused. From now on he'll just jerk off until he can get to meet some girls and have sex with them, the right kind.

That's what the older one wants to hear, and he's going to make it happen. Get rid of any taint of faggot sickness. That weekend he takes his younger brother out on the town. He has money, good money, he even has a car he's bought, don't tell them at the home, he warns his little brother, they'll kick me out for good and then you'll be alone. The little one doesn't want to be alone, he won't say anything to anyone.

They go to a whorehouse. It's just a cheap apartment with some teenage runaway girls living in it, selling their pussies for ten bucks a throw, including sixty-nine, around the world, the works. The older one picks out the cutest and youngest one, gives her twenty dollars, tells her to show his brother a great time, make a man out of him, don't come out of the bedroom until the deed is done, until you both have to crawl out. He frogs his little brother on the arm, go get her, Jimmy, he's seen his brother in the shower room, for thirteen years old he's got a good set, he'll do great. Start a stud farm.

Twenty minutes later she comes back out alone, hands the older brother his twenty bucks. Save your dough, she tells him with contempt, the kind of contempt only a fifteen-year-old whore can have, his equipment don't work, her jaw's sore from trying to get him hard. Take him to the Greyhound station, find him a sailor.

He goes into the filthy bedroom, the come-stained sheets. His little brother is sitting on the edge of the bed. His eyes are red but he isn't crying. I can't help it, he tells his older brother, it's who I am. If you don't want to be my brother anymore it's okay, he says, I don't blame you. But don't try to change me anymore, I can't do it. I can't be something I'm not.

But he's still a kid, barely a teenager, he needs. He starts to cry again and turns to his older brother, the one who was always there for him, the only one. He hugs him. His older brother starts to cry, too. Then he pushes his little brother away. You're a faggot, he says through his own tears, a goddam queer, I hate faggots. I hate you.

His little brother tries to hold on to him. He's dying, his older brother is his lifeline. The older brother pushes him away again and this time it's hard, he pushes the little one against the wall, and then he hits him, hard across the mouth, and then he hits him again.

The little brother is in the hospital for a month. He almost dies. When he gets out the older one is brought to trial, assault and battery. The little one refuses to testify against his older brother but they convict him anyway. They give him a year in the state reform school. (This is where he met Gene, the president of the Albuquerque chapter of the Scorpions.) After he's sentenced and the marshal is escorting him out the little brother calls to him, 'I love you,' he says, 'you're my brother, I'll always love you no matter what.' The older brother turns to him. 'You're not my brother anymore, faggot,' he says.

It's the last time they ever see each other. Until today.

MOSEBY EXAMINES JAMES ANGELUS.

"Why do you think your brother is so frightened of homosexuals?" he asks in a soothing tone, like an uncle would use on a favorite nephew.

"Objection! Leading the witness."

"Sustained."

This would be laughable if it wasn't so pathetic. Moseby's a redneck, he's been a public queer-baiter for years. Now he's Mr. sweetness and understanding.

"Do you think your brother is afraid of homosexuals?"

"Yes."

"Why?"

"Objection, your honor! This line of questioning is leading the witness and is intentionally inflammatory."

"Over-ruled."

Shit.

"Please answer the question," Martinez instructs Angelus.

"Because I'm one and he's afraid it's in our blood and maybe part of him is, too."

I turn to look at Lone Wolf. His head's buried in his arms.

"Do you think he's so afraid of that," Moseby asks, "that he would kill a homosexual if it brought his submerged feelings too close to the surface?"

"Objection."

"Sustained."

It doesn't matter. Everyone on the jury heard it, and it went straight to their guts.

"Why did you change your name?" I ask.

"I didn't like it. It wasn't of my choosing. I didn't want the same name as him."

I don't know what the fuck to do. Try to discredit him. How? He doesn't have a record, not even as a male hustler or anything similarly tawdry, we ran a National Crime Information Center check through the computer, he came back clean in a matter of minutes. He's a software programmer in Silicon Valley. Just your average guy who happens to be gay and hates his brother because he's not allowed to love him.

"Do you love your brother?" I ask. I'm fishing, I don't know what for. The lawyer's nightmare.

"I wish I could say no, but I guess I still do. But we're not brothers anymore. Only biologically."

"After today you'll never see each other again?"

"I hope not." He pauses. "I know he wouldn't want to. He doesn't want to now," he adds emphatically.

I take a shot in the dark.

"How much did they pay you to come here and testify?" I ask.

"Objection!" Moseby's almost apoplectic.

Martinez thinks about this one. "Over-ruled," he decides. "Answer the question."

A break. Why didn't you help me out earlier?

"I . . . I don't know what you mean," he stammers. He's actually blushing.

Jesus Christ. A wild swing with my eyes closed and it's a home run.

"How much money," I say slowly, enunciating clearly, "did the prosecution pay you to fly here and testify against your brother Steven Jensen?"

His head drops.

"Ten thousand," he whispers forlornly.

"How much? Speak up man!" I lean in so close to him I can smell his breath mints.

"Ten thousand dollars."

"They paid you ten thousand dollars to fly out here and testify against your own brother, the only flesh and blood you have in this world."

"I'd've done it for nothing."

"I don't doubt it," I say. "I've seen a lot of hate in my life, Mr. Angelus, or whatever name it is you want to call yourself, what did you do, appropriate it from a lover . . ."

"Objection!" cries Moseby.

". . . but never this much wrapped up in one person," I rush on, even as Martinez is sustaining Moseby. "You must really hate yourself." I throw my Sunday punch. "And what you are."

"OBJECTION!"

"Withdrawn." I walk back to my seat. A small victory, but a victory nevertheless. At least it's another hook to hang an appeal on; and the moment that thought comes to me I stop because I realize where my thinking's really at: that we're already in the appeal process.

I can't think that way—it would be a mortal blow to my defense. They're innocent, I've been convinced of that from the start, it's too late for doubts.

My eyes engage those of Paul, Mary Lou, Tommy. We're all thinking the same thing.

"No further questions," I tell the court.

"The prosecution rests, your honor."

"I DIDN'T KILL HIM, man. You've got to believe me."

Lone Wolf and I are sitting across the table from each other in the holding room located in the basement of the courthouse. The harsh overhead lights give Lone Wolf's face a sinister cast, the shadows deep under his eyes which are almost lost in the darkness. A cadaver's face. He still looks frightening now, but the bitter consequences of this morning's appearance by his brother have him scared stiff. It's the first time I've ever seen fear in him that he hasn't been able to camouflage.

"I don't have to believe you," I say, shaking my head negatively. "Twelve people on the jury have to believe you."

"Goddam man, I didn't." He hesitates. "You still believe that, don't you?"

I think for a moment. I've got to be clear about that, I have to be honest with him.

"It doesn't matter. I'm your lawyer. You're getting the best defense I can give you." I shake my head, like I'm trying to wake myself from a nightmare. "But for what it's worth, yeh, I believe you. Right now I wish I didn't, though."

"Why? I mean I'm glad you still believe it but . . ."

"Because it's going to make it harder to take if we don't pull this off."

"What are the odds?"

"Off the facts, eighty, maybe ninety percent. Off emotion . . . not as much."

"Fifty-fifty?"

"Not right now." I stand up. "I've got to get back to work. I've got to overhaul my summation."

The guard comes in, cuffs him. He turns to me as he's led out.

"I didn't kill him."

"Yes; but you also told me that your brother was dead."

"He was." He looks away. "To me."

"LADIES AND GENTLEMEN OF THE JURY . . ."

All the world's a stage. This one's mine. The vaulted room, the judge seated up there in his black robes that go back to antiquity, the prosecution's team waiting their turn, my partners in this case seated at our table, the defendants. Watching me, listening to me. Real life-and-death theatre. I'm pumped. The adrenaline's flowing. There are lawyers that do this and dread it. Other lawyers won't do it at all; they can't handle the stress. And for some it's mother's milk, they thrive on it, it's their life's blood. The kings and queens of the courtroom, the cream.

"Somewhere in all the testimony you've heard, in all the evidence that's been presented, there's a small, pure kernel of truth. It's like a vein of gold, you know it's there but sometimes it's hard to recognize, and harder to get to, to extract. You have to separate it from the stuff that looks like gold but isn't, the stuff that can mislead you, send you down the wrong path, keep you from what it is you're after. You are after the truth. You are not after vindication, you are not after payback, you are not after solving a problem for society. You are after the truth and you have to find it and be true to those findings, you can't let how you feel or how society's supposed to feel or what you think 'should be' get in the way of finding out the truth. You have to find out whether or not my client, Steven Jensen, this man sitting before you, killed another man."

I'm the last defender to make summation. Tommy went first—we wanted to start with someone the jury would instinctively like, and his client, Goose, is the easiest to defend. Then Paul with the kid, the reversal of Tommy. Then Mary Lou.

I'm going last because it's my case. I brought the others into this, I'm the one who has to make the final incision, free the umbilical. And I'm the star, the one the crowd comes to see, the one who'll be on television. There's ego involved, I don't deny that, so what? I've earned it, it's reality.

My argument will be based on the timetable established by the state's witnesses, principally Rita Gomez and Dr. Milton Grade, and the credibility of those witnesses, particularly Rita Gomez and, to a lesser extent, James Angelus, the turncoat brother.

Two big charts have been set up so they can be seen clearly from the jury box and the bench. One is a blowup of a map of the area, including the bar—the Dew Drop Inn—where the bikers picked Rita up, the area in the mountains where they took her (and where the body was later found), the motel where she worked and from which (according to her) they abducted Bartless and took him back to the mountains, and the road from Santa Fe to Albuquerque, route 14, where they filled their tanks and ate breakfast. The other chart is a timetable, from 2:00 A.M. until noon. It's broken down into half-hour increments, with a blank drawn next to each time: 2:00——, 2:30——, etc. Between the two charts is a large mockup of a clock, with movable hands.

Slowly, carefully, I lead the jury through the chain of events as Rita Gomez told them; she's the case. If we can show that what she said happened was impossible, within the timetable she herself established, we have an honest chance for acquittal.

"They left the bar at two o'clock," I say. "Several witnesses, including Miss Gomez, have testified to that. So we can take that as a given."

I go to the chart. Next to 2:00 I write 'leave bar.' I position the hands of the clock to 2:00.

"They drove up to here," I continue, tracing the road that leads to the mountains, to the spot where she said they parked, where the body was later found. "The distance, according to this map which was prepared and authenticated by the state of New Mexico department of highways, is twenty-seven miles. It's a windy road, you can't drive it too fast. The speed limit is forty miles an hour. But let's say they went faster. Let's say they got up there in half an hour." Next to 2:30, I write 'arrive at alleged crime site.'

"By her own admission she had intercourse with each of them two times. Even with a minimum of foreplay; and I don't think, ladies and gentlemen, that a fifteen-dollar-a-pop hooker engages in much foreplay," I tell them, pausing for a minute, letting that dig at her character sink in, "even if it was straight, fast, dirty sex she had with them, that had to take at least another half an hour." I pause again. "Now I'm really cutting against my client's interest here, folks, by tightening up this timetable as I am, but I want to give her testimony every benefit of the doubt. So okay, half an hour for sex."

I fill in the 3:00 blank, move the hands of the clock.

We work together, the jury and I, through that night, according to the testimony of the state's star witness. How long it took them to get back to the motel. How long the sex and beer-drinking she said happened there took. How long Bartless was with them, arguing and fighting. How long it took to subdue him, to throw him and her in the car.

"The phantom car," I state. "The car that never existed in any statements anyone made. The car that was never reported stolen or damaged. That was ever-so-conveniently there so the accused could use it to transport Richard Bartless up to the killing site."

I pause.

"The nonexistent car. The car that never was. It was never there, ladies and gentlemen. You know that and I know that. It's just another thread in the fabric of lies this witness has been weaving."

The hands on the clock keep moving. The timetable on the chart is filled in. It's dawn and we're still back up on that mountain with Bartless, Rita, and the bikers.

"After the victim was violated," I say, not dodging that, "after he was sexually assaulted, and we don't dispute he was, the evidence says it and we agree to that: after that he was murdered. He was stabbed forty-seven times according to the coroner's report. We don't dispute that, either, that there were forty-seven stab wounds. And according to Rita Gomez, every couple of times the victim was stabbed, the knife that did it was heated until it was red-hot." I shake my head at that. "They're killing the guy but they want to cauterize the wounds. I don't know about you, folks, but ritual or not it sounds like horse manure to me. But, the state's star witness says it happened, so hypothetically we go along with it. Just hypothetically, because we don't really believe it for a minute. Then they emasculate him. And then they hang around for awhile. According to Miss Gomez, at least fifteen or twenty minutes. And then they shoot him."

I turn to my charts. "According to these diagrams, ladies and gentlemen, and my very conservative estimates, it's between seven and seven-thirty in the morning and my client and Miss Gomez are still up on that mountain." I fill in more blanks, move the clock hands. "By her own story it's probably later, more like eight-thirty or nine, but I want this to be air-tight, I want her to have the benefit of every doubt. So okay, seven-thirty, no, make that seven. Still up here," I say, pointing on the map, "up here in the Sangre de Cristos."

We finish exploring the odyssey of Rita Gomez. They dump the body off the road, then they take her home, and then they threaten her, and two of them (including my client) have sex with her again. Then, finally, they leave.

I look at the chart. It's nine o'clock.

"According to the state's star witness's own sworn testimony, they left her at nine in the morning. At the earliest. One could rationally say it was more like ten or eleven, following the chain of events we've just documented here. But we're willing to accept nine. We won't take even fifteen minutes of slack."

I cross to the defense table, drink some water. My thirst is real. I gather a file, walk back to the jury box.

"There's only one problem with this story. It didn't happen. By the state's star witness's own testimony, it *couldn't* have happened. According to her, at the same time that she, my client and the other motorcyclists, and Richard Bartless were all up here," I'm pointing again to the murder site, using a yardstick, "physical evidence *proves* they were way down here." I trace the yardstick along the black highway line on the map, down to Cerrillos. "Fifty miles away. An hour's ride."

I pause to let that sink in, glancing at Martinez. He's looking at me with keen interest. It's important that if I can't get him on my side, so to speak, I at least guarantee his neutrality.

"Now just like the state's," I continue, "there are our witnesses. Witnesses who have sworn that my client and the others were with them at the time the state's witness says the murder took place. Well okay, they have witnesses, we have witnesses, we throw it in your lap and let you decide which ones are telling the truth and which ones are lying. We could do that; that's what the state is going to do."

I tap the file of evidence on the jury-box bannister.

"But that's not enough. I know what's going on here, ladies and gentlemen, and so do you. I know that won't be enough in this case, given the people who stand accused before you, given the ridiculous, terrible, and prejudicial coverage in the media, given the fast and loose way the state's witnesses have played with the facts, have misrepresented the truth. So I've got real evidence here to prove what I'm saying."

I pause for a moment.

"But before I produce that evidence," I interject, "I must say one other thing. It's not my job, or that of my co-counsel, to find out who *did* commit this crime. I'm not Perry Mason; I'm not going to pull the real criminal out of my hat. That's not why I'm here. I'm here to show you that my client is not guilty beyond a reasonable doubt. Please keep that in the front of your minds at all times."

I open the evidence file, take out the gasoline credit-card receipt. I hold it in front of them for a moment, then hand it to the foreman.

"I'd like each of you to take a good look at this and then pass it on. Take an especially good look at the day and date that's imprinted on it. It's not handwritten; it came out of a machine which, I'm sure you'll recall, we had calibrated by two independent testing agencies, both of whom attested to its accuracy. We all know the date. Now look at the time. Look at it carefully. It says five-fifty-seven A.M. Think about that, ladies and gentlemen. Five-fifty-seven in the morning—the morning in question."

I wait for the receipt to go full circle back to the foreman, who hands it to me. I put it back in the file.

"That's not conjecture," I say. "That's a *fact*. There are other *facts* as well. You're going to take these *facts* into that jury room with you tomorrow when you start deliberating. You'll look at them, examine them closely. I know for a *fact*," I continue, hammering the word home, "that you will, because you're conscientious men and women."

I put the file on the evidence table.

"The state's entire case hinges on one thing and one thing only," I say. "Rita Gomez. She's their whole case. I don't know . . . maybe everything did happen up there the way she said it did, but then again maybe it didn't. Dozens of witnesses say the defendants weren't there when she says they were. Dozens of witnesses say my client and the others never even laid eyes on the victim, but she says they did. Dozens of witnesses have testified, under oath, that Rita Gomez is a public drunk, that she was drunk the night in question. She herself has testified that she is a prostitute, that she engages in sex for money. And she has admitted that she's lied. So the prosecution's case rests solely on the testimony of a drunken prostitute who is also an admitted liar. A whore, a drunk, a liar. All wrapped up in one package.

"Now let's talk about some of the other things she said. She claims to have been raped, but she never went to the hospital. Even after the police found her, and she told them about what she claims happened, they didn't take her to the hospital. Maybe there was a reason for that, people. Maybe the charge of rape was a lie, to further incriminate these men. And maybe they knew it was a lie, she and the officers who found her, and they knew that if she was examined the doctor wouldn't find any evidence of rape and the rest of her story wouldn't wash then, either, so they all decided she'd claim rape but they'd shy away from testing her. They would have to because the truth wouldn't back it up. Or maybe," I go on, "there was some sexual misconduct. And they didn't want that coming out prematurely, because they wanted to make sure they had time to help her get her story straight; straight the way *they* wanted it. They couldn't take the chance that she might say the wrong thing, talk to someone in authority too soon, like a doctor. All we know is that she, and they, were out of contact for several days. Highly unusual behavior."

I pause for just a second to catch my breath, then press on. I'm on a roll and I want to sustain it.

"Rita Gomez, the state's only eye-witness, claims to have seen a murder take place. But she didn't tell anyone; she kept it completely to herself. She says she was scared for her life. Then the police come upon her and bang, she spills her guts. What happened to that fear? Yes, I know they promised her protection, but what does that mean? Do you honestly believe, any one of you, that someone so scared, as she claimed to be, would talk that fast and that freely? She wouldn't; maybe eventually, if they worked on her, really put the screws to her. But according to both her and them they didn't have to. She started singing as soon as they walked in the door."

I shake my head. "It doesn't wash. Put yourself in her shoes. They don't know that you know anything. It's pure circumstance that you had a passing acquaintance with Richard Bartless, and these men. You could say you don't know how he got there, and they'd believe you. They'd have no reason not to. Under those circumstances, as fearful for your life as she says she was, would you talk?" I take one dramatic beat. "We both know the answer. The answer is no."

I take a moment to let everything I've said sink in.

"It's simple, ladies and gentlemen. Depressing and insulting to our system of justice, but nonetheless simple. She either made her story up, or she was coerced into saying it. In either case, it's a lie. It didn't happen; not the way she said."

I look at the jury, individual faces. Some are looking at me. A few at the defendants. Some at the prosecution table, and a couple are looking past the prosecution table to the detectives who broke the case, Sanchez and Gomez.

I turn and look at them, the detectives. They look back at me. They don't like me. Good. Maybe the jury will pick up on that and make the connection that what I'm saying has weight, some honesty.

"Think about this," I say, turning again to the jury. "Those detectives had her in hiding for several days. No one knew where she was, not even a police matron. Now ask yourselves this: why do you hide someone unless they have something to hide, unless you're helping them hide it? Unless your story doesn't wash, unless you have to embellish it. Think about that, ladies and gentlemen. Policemen are supposed to protect and serve. How were they serving her by not allowing her to be examined for rape? How were they serving her by hiding her out, away from anyone who could comfort her? They weren't protecting and serving her, folks. They weren't protecting and serving justice, either. They were protecting and serving the prosecution's case. In fact, they were probably making it."

I look back at the prosecution's side again. This is personal now; these guys are going to be out to get me. So be it. They've tampered with the truth, I know it; as I've said the words, the certainty of this has rung out clear as a bell.

"And what about the coroner's report?" I go on. "He gave clear times about when the death occurred. Yet they contradict the timetable the state's star witness drew for you that we've followed here today," I say, pointing to my charts. "Are we supposed to infer that one of the country's most eminent criminal pathologists miscalculated? Because if we believe Rita Gomez's testimony, the state's only eyewitness, we have to. We have to say he goofed. Or we have to believe him and discredit her. The testimony of Rita Gomez and the testimony of Dr. Milton Grade directly contradict each other. We can't believe them both.

"There is one thing in both of their testimonies, however, that I do have to question. The so-called 'hot knives' theory. You've all seen the horrendous photos of the victim when he was taken to the morgue and examined by Dr. Grade. His body was in awful shape. Yet Dr. Grade testified that he was killed with a hot knife, which, by the way, has never turned up. It's a very bizarre theory, the prosecution hasn't brought forth any witnesses to corroborate it, except Rita Gomez, who we've proven to be a liar. And I have to say, with all due respect to Dr. Grade, that it's mighty coincidental that he and she allegedly arrived at this 'hot knives' story independently of each other. Too coincidental for me to believe. For you, too, I think.

"And then there's Steven Jensen's brother. My heart goes out to him. He's lived in torment his entire life. His brother abandoned him, and his personal sexual lifestyle is abhorrent to him. So he comes here and tells you that Steven Jensen so hates gays that he'll kill one, practically on sight.

"Well," I say to the jury. "If that really is the case, then why hasn't Steven Jensen laid waste to hundreds of homosexuals over the years? I'm sure he's encountered some, we all have. So what? It's completely irrelevant, as irrelevant as James Angelus's testimony. He didn't come here to tell you his brother has homicidal feelings towards homosexuals." My voice is starting to rise, I'm mad and indignant and I want them to know it, I want them to know I'm calling the prosecution on this bullshit. "He came here because the state paid him. Ten thousand dollars. And on top of that, they tried to hide it, because they knew it was dirty and underhanded. It was sleazy, like the rest of their case. James Angelus came here because they're trying to buy the case, just like the way they brought in the victim's mother. They must be pretty desperate to resort to such shoddy tactics."

I take a breath.

"Let me tell you the real truth here. The real truth is my client didn't commit this murder. Neither did his friends. There was a killing, all right. But they didn't do it. No one knows who did it. And that's the problem, because the state has to pin this on someone. They have to throw some red meat to the lions. So they pick on four men who, I will be the first to admit, are not choirboys. And they were with this girl on the night the victim died. And from that the prosecution decided that they did it, and came up with a story to fit the crime."

I walk in front of the jury now, slowly, looking each one in the eye.

"The state has one witness—a witness who has perjured herself on the stand, right here in front of you. They have no physical evidence, because that knife was never found. Neither was the gun that shot him. On the other hand the defense has presented dozens of witnesses, every one more credible than Rita Gomez, who I must remind you again is not only a convicted prostitute and public drunk, but also a demonstrated liar.

"There's yet another thing that has to be said about these defendants. Would whoever did in fact kill the victim have been so stupid as to leave a witness behind? After he had already committed a murder he could be executed for? Of course not. He'd already murdered one person. It's not going to help him to spare another life; on the contrary, it would be ludicrous to leave a witness behind. And that's precisely why these men *couldn't* have done what they've been accused of. They may be mean, folks, they may be tough, but they're not stupid. The real killer wouldn't be taking any prisoners. The simple reason these men didn't kill Rita Gomez is because they hadn't killed Richard Bartless.

"So . . . why are we here today? To judge the innocence or guilt of my client and the others. The defense doesn't have to prove their innocence, yet we have. We have presented you with concrete physical evidence that proves these men couldn't have done it. The prosecution by law has to prove their guilt, but they have not; not at all, not one iota.

"It's a heavy burden to be a jury in a murder case. You're going to decide whether someone is guilty or not, and if they might live or die. And if you're going to decide that they're guilty, you have to really know it. You have to know it in your heart and your gut, and you have to know it from the evidence, the facts. You have to know it beyond a reasonable doubt.

"Ladies and gentlemen of the jury. Do not judge my client on who he is or what he's done in his past. That's not the issue here. You must judge him solely on this case, the *facts* of this case. And when you do you will arrive at one and only one conclusion: that he is not guilty, and that he should walk out of this courtroom a free man."

"GOOD MORNING, ladies and gentlemen. My name is John Robertson. I am the District Attorney for Santa Fe County."

He stands at the edge of the prosecution's table in his number-one three-piece suit, his Phi Beta Kappa key dangling prominently. He smiles at the jury, a confident, friendly smile. The smile of the righteous, the man with the goods on his side.

It's a calculated risk, his closing for the prosecution. I'm sure he weighed the pros and cons and decided that at worst it was a toss-up. On the down side there's lack of familiarity: the jury's gotten to know Moseby, he's comfortable with them as an old shoe, there might be unconscious resentment against Robertson for coming in at the eleventh hour and stealing his thunder. On the other hand, Robertson has been in and out, they all know who he is. And he's the boss, it's his ultimate responsibility, the buck stops with him. What he's trying to tell the jury is this case is so important I have to do this last scene myself, I can't leave this most essential part of it to anyone else, not even my most trusted and competent associate. I was elected to this job and I have to give you our best. Please forgive any aspersions this may cast on brother Moseby here; there are none intended. But I, and only I, am accountable here.

He does say this, in a less obvious and self-serving fashion. Of course, what the egotistical bastard's really saying is I'm a politician, I'm on a career ladder and this is an important rung, this is the most important and visible case we're going to have in New Mexico this year, certainly in my jurisdiction, and I'll be damned if I'm going to let some civil-service underling steal the thunder; senate seats and governorships are built on summations like the one I'm about to give. I want the television coverage. I'm the cherry on the sundae.

"What you have before you is simple," Robertson says. He's standing in front of the jury, solid as a rock. I admire his delivery. If I'm Jack Nicholson, he's Charlton Heston, a little square maybe, a touch behind the times, but you know where he stands, he'll never scare you.

"You have to make a choice," he continues. "You have to decide who to believe, the state's witnesses or those of the defense. On one hand you have an eye-witness who both sides, prosecution and defense, have already agreed was at the site of this murder, with the accused, on the night it happened; and the expert testimony of one of this country's foremost forensic pathologists, both of whom told the same story about how the victim, Richard Bartless, died, completely independently of each other. Neither of these people, nor any of the other witnesses we have brought forth, have anything to gain by their testimony. On the contrary, they have a lot to lose. Rita Gomez could lose her life. These men on trial before you are not, to use the defense's own terminology, a bunch of choirboys. They're part of a nation-wide ring of self-styled outlaws and criminals. Their friends both in their own gang of motorcycle outlaws and in other, similar gangs, have sworn revenge on anyone who testifies against them. Rita Gomez is going to be a marked woman the rest of her life, whether these four men are found guilty or not. Rita Gomez was, and still is, a very frightened young woman. But she could not remain silent in the face of such a heinous act.

"Dr. Milton Grade's qualifications don't have to be elaborated on here by me; you all know how expert and unbiased he is. He told you unequivocally what happened that night up on that mountain. He arrived at his conclusions from knowledge and experience, years of it. And it completely matched the story Rita Gomez told the police and the grand jury and you. Neither one of them knows the other, neither one of them has to this day met the other. And yet they both are telling you the same thing: that Richard Bartless was abducted by the four men on trial here, kidnapped against his will, taken up to the mountains north of here, brutally sexually assaulted, and murdered. Without remorse.

"Let's talk for a moment about the defense you've seen put on for your benefit for the past weeks in here. I have to admire it; it's a great escape act, a Houdini defense. An act of magic, of derring-do and sleight-of-hand. But like any act of magic it's based on a *perception* of reality . . . let me emphasize that, ladies and gentlemen of the jury, *perception* of reality, not reality itself. They don't really have a defense, so they try to fake you out. And if you're not careful, if you're not diligent in examining the facts of this case, if you're blinded by the light they're shining in your eyes, you're going to mistake the perception for the reality. It's like that ad that was on television a few years back, about how you can't tell Imperial margarine from butter, you remember that?"

Some of the jurors smile; they remember, or think they do.

" 'You can't tell the fake from the real thing,' is what the ad said," Robertson tells them, smiling himself. "Well, maybe you couldn't," he continues, "maybe some people can't tell margarine from butter, and anyway to most people it probably doesn't matter much, unless you've got a cholesterol problem, and then it could matter a lot. In fact, it could be a matter of life and death. Well, in this case, if you can't tell the fake from the real, the lies from the truth, it will definitely be a matter of life and death. It will mean Richard Bartless's murderers and sodomizers will go free, or they will pay for their crimes."

He pauses. He's doing well, I have to give the bastard credit.

"Here's how the defense's shell game works, ladies and gentlemen. They don't deny that the defendants and Rita Gomez left the bar together. They can't, because dozens of their own witnesses testified that they did. So what they're saying is she was too drunk to be credible. But there's been no evidence produced to that. Yes, she drank that evening. But she was sober enough to speak to them when they were ready to go, to tell them what she wanted, clearly and without hesitation. None of the witnesses said she wasn't.

"And she was with them at the murder site on the night of the murder. Again, no one questions that. And they had sex with her. She says she was raped. They said she did it willingly. And to back that claim of theirs up, that of her own free will and without any pressure or threats whatsoever she had sex with all of them, two and three times each, they say she is a prostitute.

"You know what that is, ladies and gentlemen, that kind of argument? That a prostitute can't be a victim of rape? It's a crummy argument is what it is, beneath the dignity of a civilized society. Make no mistake, ladies and gentlemen of the jury, Rita Gomez was brutalized by these men, terrorized by them, threatened with her life if she ever told what happened up there. Please do not, for one second, think otherwise. Do not make the victim the victimizer. Rita Gomez is not on trial here."

He turns and points to the accused sitting at our table.

"They are."

He walks over to the evidence table, picks up a folder, the one with the gasoline receipts. He holds the receipt up in front of the jury.

"Here's the defense's case," he says with unconcealed derision. "A piece of paper with a date stamped on it." He shakes his head in mock sorrow, then becomes scornful. "If that isn't the most pathetic defense I've ever seen in my life. I mean come on now, ladies and gentlemen. They must think you've all been lobotomized. A piece of paper that anyone could have tampered with from a machine in a remote filling station. Who knows how accurate that machine is? For all we know it could have been broken, or the receipt forged, or any number of things. Unless you think machines are infallible. Unless you've never had a problem with a gas bill or a water bill or an electric bill."

The members of the jury nod and smile, looking at him and each other. I get the message from them that machines are not infallible.

"And that witness," Robertson continues. "A kid with stars in his eyes, whose ambition in life is to own a motorcycle and ride with the likes of these." Dismissing the bikers with a backhanded wave.

"Then there's their other key witness," he says. "A seventy-eight-year-old woman who remembers what Elvis Presley ate for breakfast in her diner thirty years ago. And the exact day and the exact time the accused showed up at her doorstep. And the exact orders each of them ate, and the exact amount it all cost. Well, I don't know about you, but I can't remember all that detail so exactly, and I don't know if I trust someone who does. Especially if they're getting on in years, I don't mean that as a knock at age, someday if I'm lucky I'll reach that age and I won't like it if people doubt my every word, but the doctors do tell us memory starts to slide when you get up in years, it becomes selective. And when you've lived alone for a long time, as that witness has, you live inside of yourself more, by the nature of things you create a world inside your head, or the loneliness would become unbearable. And maybe you'll tell someone what they want to hear even if it isn't exactly the truth, as long as they'll stay and have another cup of coffee with you.

"This murder had strong homosexual overtones," Robertson is telling the jury now. "The defense would have you believe that's not part of this case. They're trying to tell you that the hatred and loathing one of the defendants had towards his brother, his only blood kin in the world, because of his homosexuality, is meaningless. That's an insult: not only to your intelligence, but more importantly to the memory of Richard Bartless, who suffered and died because of one of the defendant's, the acknowledged ringleader's, hate and fear of homosexuality.

"Not only is homosexuality a part of this case," Robertson says, "it's the linch-pin. For years Steven Jensen has hated his brother. For years he's lived with the fear that maybe he, too, is tainted, that maybe it's in their blood, in their genes. He does everything he can to be as macho as possible. He sleeps with scores of women. He joins a tough motorcycle gang, becomes a leader. He thinks he's above it, that it can't touch him. But he's wrong. Any psychologist will tell you that there's a lot of latent homosexual feeling in these motorcycle gangs, with their allegiance to their buddies and their utter contempt for women.

"Do you know what happens to a woman whose boyfriend or husband joins one of these self-styled outlaw motorcycle gangs?" he asks, his voice ringing with fury. "She has to have intercourse with every member of the gang, and when they're finished with her they urinate on her. I guess to some people that's macho, that's manly. Personally, it turns my stomach. It makes me sick."

He looks at us with contempt. We've got our hands full keeping the bikers from freaking, especially Lone Wolf.

"If you blow this now," I remind him for the hundredth time, "it's automatic Death Row." My colleagues are saying the same thing to their own clients.

He's under control, meaning he isn't going to go over the table and attack Robertson.

"I'll deal with it later," is all he says. I don't care to pursue that right now.

"In any crime, especially a violent crime such as this," Robertson says, "you have to have motive and opportunity, unless you're dealing with psychopaths. Well, we may be dealing with psychopaths here, although believe me they know right from wrong and can act on the difference, but we definitely have motive and opportunity. Richard Bartless heard these men trying to hurt Rita Gomez, and he came to help her. It was a brave decision. But to men like these, that doesn't go. It's an affront to their so-called masculinity. They're not going to put up with it. For cold-blooded killers like these, that's motive enough. Plus they'd had sexual intercourse with her against her will, that could be a felony. They thought they could scare Rita Gomez into silence, but they knew that wouldn't work with a man, with Richard Bartless. They had to shut him up. That is motive aplenty.

"And they had the opportunity. It was the dead of night, they could take him up to that mountain without anyone seeing them. And they did.

"Once they got him up there, all the repressed fear about their masculinity came to the surface. Maybe he did something that pushed a button, maybe he called them out on their so-called machismo. And they went crazy, they were going to show him. They were going to show him they were so manly they could have a woman and a man, too. And they did. They had intercourse with him, too.

"After that they had to kill him, because he was a living testament to their shame. So they performed an exorcism on him, they couldn't just put him out of his misery with a simple gunshot, they had to stab him forty-seven times with a hot knife and they had to cut off his penis, his own manhood, so that even in death he couldn't threaten them. And then, as an afterthought, to try and throw the police off their trail, they shot him.

"You have a choice to make," Robertson says, his voice dropping, almost to a whisper. "You can disregard all the real evidence, the hard evidence, the expert testimony of one of this country's foremost forensic pathologists, and the testimony of the only eyewitness to this crime, and let this scum sitting before you walk out of here free men. Or you can examine the evidence carefully and truthfully. And when you do, you will arrive at one and only one conclusion. That they are guilty of murder, and they should be put to death for that. Anything less would be a miscarriage of justice, and a stain on all of humanity. I know that you are going to make the only choice; the only right choice. You are going to find them guilty of murder in the first degree."

IT'S AXIOMATIC in a capital case that the longer the jury stays out, the better it is for the defense. The jury has been out three days now. The first day we were all sweating bullets: if the jury had come back then we'd have known all our guys were going to fry.

They didn't; nor did they on the second day. When we trooped back into court at the end of day two and Martinez told us to go home, it wasn't going to happen, not until tomorrow at least, our collective sigh of relief would've floated a hot-air balloon clear to Taos.

Robertson is outwardly stoic; whatever he feels is buried. Moseby sweats visibly, wears his emotions on his sleeve. There's been dissension in their office. Our spies (secretaries who talk to my ever-loyal Susan) tell us there was a postmortem donnybrook over Robertson's giving the rebuttal for the state. For the first time in memory Moseby stood up to his boss, calling him a grandstander, a politician who won't leave a track when he's gone. For his part Robertson attacked Moseby and his investigators, Gomez and Sanchez, for botching the rape section of their case, to the point where it may have tainted the entire investigation in the eyes of the jury.

Might be the jury's picking up their vibe. Juries can do that, they sometimes develop this extra-sensory perception that tells them which side feels better. It can translate into a decision in favor of the confident side. I've seen it happen. That's why no matter how bleak I feel in my gut about a case, I always show a strong front.

Day three ends the same way. By now several things could be happening in the jury room, none of them comforting to the prosecution, who wants to hang all four of the bikers. It could be the jury's arguing a lesser verdict, maybe murder two or manslaughter, or they could be thinking a couple guys did it and the others didn't (for me personally this wouldn't be good, if one burns it'll be mine), or in the best-case scenario one or more of the jurors just don't think the state presented a strong enough case. My dream is all twelve have enough reasonable doubt that they'll acquit, but you don't live on dreams in here. All we want is one holdout, not guilty is the optimum but a hung jury works, too.

MARTINEZ SENDS A MESSAGE to the jury. It's four o'clock in the afternoon, Thursday, day four. How are you doing, the message reads, are you progressing towards a verdict? We're coming up on a weekend, if it looks like a deadlock let us know now.

Our fingers are crossed so tightly the flow of blood is practically stopped. If the foreman replies that they aren't getting anywhere, Martinez is going to have to declare a hung jury. There won't be enough champagne in Santa Fe to accommodate our celebration.

The message comes back that they're not sure, there are problems, but they're not ready to give up. They need more time, at least another half-day.

I want something more definitive than that by lunch break tomorrow, Martinez messages back. Do your best. You have a sworn duty to arrive at a verdict if that is at all possible.

He'd rather have his nails pulled out than try this case again. So would Robertson. If there's a second trial the victim's mother doesn't happen; Lone Wolf's brother is probably a memory, too. And they know we'll hammer the shoddiness of their investigation.

On her way home Mary Lou stops in a church and lights candles. She isn't even Catholic.

"HAVE YOU REACHED a verdict?"

"We have, your honor."

It's five-fifteen in the afternoon, past normal closing hours. Just before lunch the jury had sent out word that they were finally arriving at a conclusion.

We were back in the courtroom by then; the lawyers, not the defendants. We took it as a positive sign; if they were thinking of coupling the murder with the rape they now were told conclusively not to. If they did, in fact, it could mean a mistrial. Martinez told them that strongly. That's all he needs; at the last minute, the jury fucks up on the instructions and the whole shebang goes in the toilet.

The note came out at ten to five: they're ready.

The defendants are brought up from the holding cells. They sit at the table with us. Robertson, Moseby, the prosecution sits at their table. Behind them, the victim's mother and the cops, Sanchez and Gomez. Lone Wolf's brother is not among us. Neither, of course, is Rita Gomez, or any of the other witnesses.

It's packed in here. A crush of media, overflowing into the corridors outside. I can barely breathe; that's true for everyone at our table.

I glance over at Robertson. He feels my look, turns with one of his own. Four lives and my partnership are on the line here for me; a chance to grab the gold ring for him.

"Would you please pass the verdicts up," Martinez instructs the foreman.

The jury foreman passes the verdict sheets to the bailiff, who carries them to the bench. Martinez looks at each of them slowly. He looks at the defendants. I can't get a read. He studies them again, nods, hands them back to the bailiff who takes them to the clerk of the court.

"The clerk will read the verdicts," Martinez announces, his eyes on us.

The clerk rises.

"In the case of the state versus Steven Jensen," he says solemnly, "we find the defendant guilty of murder in the first degree."

A roar goes up. Robertson and Moseby hug. Martinez gavels for quiet.

"Silence!" he yells. He's pissing into the wind.

Lone Wolf slumps. I put a comforting arm around his shoulder.

"I didn't do it, man."

"I know," I say. It's hollow reassurance.

"In the case of the state versus Richard Paterno, we find the defendant guilty of murder in the first degree."

Now it's Roach's turn to collapse. I can't believe what I'm hearing, it's like an explosion in my ears.

"In the case of the state versus Roy Hicks, we find the defendant guilty of murder in the first degree."

Dutchboy. Twenty-two years old. He looks at the others, bewildered. How did I get here, is this real or am I dreaming?

And finally Goose, the old graybeard. Guilty. He breaks down, the only one with even a hint of tears.

"Oh man. This ain't happening."

I'm numb. The jury believed that fucking bimbo. Four men that I know, that I *know,* are innocent, have just been sentenced to die.

THE JURY RECONVENES a week later for the death-penalty phase, which is a formality. I knew that going in—if I didn't get them off clean, they'd fry. The jury wastes no time. There is nothing redeeming about these men. They are not in any way part of civilized society, and have to be removed from it in the most extreme way possible. They are to be incarcerated until such time as they will be put to death by lethal injection.

The bikers are cuffed, placed in leg irons, led out. I've already told them we'll appeal; it's automatic in a death-penalty case. If it goes all the way to the Supreme Court they'll be on Death Row for seven years, maybe longer.

"No hard feelings, I hope," Robertson says. He's come over, extended his hand.

I don't take it.

"They're innocent, goddam it." This is heart-breaking.

He doesn't see it that way; he's quietly elated.

"The jury said otherwise. That's how it works."

"They were framed."

"You're pissing against the wind, Will."

"Someday I'm going to prove it," I argue hotly. Fuck civility.

"They were guilty, Will," he says calmly. He's won; he can afford to be civil. "They were guilty before they ever stepped into the courtroom. And everybody knew it except you."

"The old 'we're gonna give 'em a fair trial and then we're gonna hang 'em.' " It tastes bitter in my mouth; and true. "You neglected to tell me that part when you called me into this; kind of an important oversight, wouldn't you say?"

He won't rise to the bait.

"I thought frontier justice was history, John."

"Sometimes it's the only way," he says, as he turns his back to me and walks out.

The courtroom empties. I don't want to leave; there's nothing good out there for me. There's nothing good in here, either. I'm paralyzed in my own emotions.

Finally, only Mary Lou and I remain. She half-hugs, half-leans against me.

"We did our best."

"That's small consolation," I say.

"Come on. It's time to go."

She takes my hand.

"Not yet," I tell her. "I need space. Please."

She nods, slowly. "Are you going to handle the appeal?"

"Yes."

"By yourself?"

"I guess. It's automatic anyway, at least this part."

"Do you want help?"

I shrug. I'm lost.

She straightens up, picks up her briefcase.

"You know how to reach me if you want to," she says.

I nod.

She starts to say something more, thinks better of it, turns and walks out, her high heels echoing in the empty chamber.

It's dark when I finally go outside. There's no one around; to the victor goes the coverage. I get in my car and start home. Tonight is no time for celebration; more for mourning. Either way I'm going to get blasted until I don't remember why.

PART THREE

I'M SITTING IN THE BAR of the Albuquerque Airport, waiting for my flight. In the background the radio's playing a medley of my favorite Christmas hits: "Grandma Got Run Over by a Reindeer," Cheech and Chong's "Santa Claus and His Old Lady," "Jingle Bell Rock." In half an hour I board a plane for Seattle, bearing gifts. Christmas in a strange town, with my daughter in her new digs.

It'll be my first time there. I could've had her for the holidays—that's part of the agreement Patricia and I made—but it doesn't seem right, Claudia's traveling back and forth right out of the box, like a yo-yo. Let her be with both of us, get accustomed to her new surroundings. It's got to be hard.

I catch the bartender's eye, cock my finger. *Una más.* José Cuervo, you are a friend of mine. Actually, it's Johnnie Walker. Same difference.

It's been a shitty couple of months, to put it mildly. The Monday after the verdict came in I received the final divorce papers. Holly cleaned me out; the house, all the furniture, her car, most of the joint account, the works. What's yours is mine and what's mine is mine. Fuck it, I didn't care, truth be known it's a relief. The slate wiped clean, no reminders.

I didn't give her alimony; she works, art gallery management, good money. We didn't have kids; she was 'never ready.' Thank God in retrospect, sharing one is tough enough. She took her own name back, plans on selling the house and moving to Taos. Fine with me—if I never see her again it'll be too soon.

A week after that, Andy and Fred lowered the boom. They'd decided a long time ago, probably the day they made me take the leave of absence. If I'd won the trial they might've reconsidered.

But I lost.

For the record it's an amicable parting, conflicting directions philosophically about where each of us wanted to go with the practice. It cost them $200,000, but it's spread out over four years, which won't do much more than cover my office expenses.

Some of my clients came with me. Fred made vague noises about restricting the exodus, but it was strictly the clients' choices, I kept my mouth shut. Secretly, of course, I was pleased. Susan came with me, too.

I won't starve to death, and I'll have enough work to keep my mind from turning inward, where the self-pitying sleeps.

At least I suckered Holly. Not the way I wanted, but when you're on a losing streak any victory tastes sweet, even if you have to eat a ton of shit to taste it. She won't get a penny of the buyout; if they'd made their move two weeks earlier she'd have an extra hundred thousand in her account. She'll feel cheated and put-upon when she hears about it. Isn't that too fucking bad. Like I said, I'll take a victory any way I can get it.

Fred wanted to trip the door, knowing my timetable on the divorce. Andy wouldn't let him. Someday I'll have to thank him for that, once I get over hating their chickenshit guts.

Actually, I am already over it. It was finished months ago, the first day they called me out, cut me adrift. This merely formalized it. I don't wish them ill; we had a lot of good times together, on the way up.

Mary Lou called me when she heard the news. She was distraught, genuinely upset. It's a terrible injustice, she'd said, kicking you like that when you're down. Like it doesn't happen all the time. If you're not down they can't kick you, right?

We got together for a drink so she could see first-hand I was all right. What she wanted was to take me home and take care of me. As politely and gently as possible, I turned her down.

Simple reason: if I'd gone home with her I wouldn't have been able to leave. It would've been all lovey-dovey and I'd have wound up moving out of my shitbox and in with her. We'd eat breakfast together and dinner together, terrific meals she'd just whip up after a hard day at the office, or romantic twosomes in quiet little restaurants.

We'd fall in love, for real. And I can't do that. I'm too damn low to get into any new entanglements. I need space; not that I want it, but I need the discipline. I feel like everybody's looking at me, feeling sorry for me, which I'm sure they are. I don't want to bring that into a new relationship. And there's a sublimated pool of feeling, a small attic in the back of my brain where I keep my bad feelings wrapped up like bundles of old newspapers, that's down on all women now because of Holly and what she cost me; I loved her once, too. Mary Lou shouldn't have to carry that burden. When it's gone, and it will be in time, then I'll think about a relationship.

Maybe.

If it was just fucking, that would be all right. But it couldn't be just fucking with her. I tried to explain that. She fought it, said if that's all it can be now, fine.

Neither of us believed it. That's why we went home separately.

Since then I haven't called her. When I get up the guts, she'll be with someone else.

Shakespeare says "when sorrows come they come not single spies but in battalions." No shit. The worst came last. Patricia moved a month ago, the weekend after Thanksgiving. They left on a Saturday morning, in her car.

Claudia had spent the last few days with me, our own private Thanksgiving. We shopped together for an organic turkey, which I cooked with the trimmings. She made a pumpkin pie, all by herself, I didn't have to help her a bit. We hiked in the mountains, fished, played catch with her Dan Marino–autographed football. Everything but talk about her leave-taking.

We saved that for Friday night, sitting on her bed surrounded by her old stuffed toys. Beyond the 'I'll miss you's' and 'I'll call you's' and 'we'll see lots of each other' stuff we didn't really know what to say. It's uncharted territory, we've been separated almost from her birth but we've never been separated for real.

I stood outside Patricia's house and watched as they drove away. Claudia climbed over into the back seat on top of the books and records and pressed her face against the rear window, watching me recede in the distance. I waved to her. It was cold out; we'd had an early snowfall the week before and there were still scattered patchy remnants of ice and snow. I could feel my face stinging from the wind as it blew against my wet cheeks.

The Johnnie Walker tastes good, even better than usual. I'll nurse it, make it last until I board the plane. "Blue Christmas" by Elvis comes over the radio. Talk about timing; in the movies they'd say it was too on-the-nose. That's the problem with life sometimes; it doesn't come out like the movies.

EVEN THOUGH PATRICIA had told me where they were moving, her new apartment still comes as a surprise. It's in a high-rise, on the twenty-second floor, practically a penthouse, with great views overlooking Puget Sound. You can almost see to Canada it's so high. All the furniture is new out-of-the-wrapper, of course, and tastefully understated, as befitting a freshly-successful attorney.

"A decorator did it," she confesses, a proprietary hand caressing the linen shade of an Anne Taylor table lamp. "I didn't have the time. It was all done and waiting for me . . . us . . . when we got here."

"*Très chic,*" I say. A blind man could tell that a decorator had done it; maybe that's because it's basically unlived-in. No cigarette burns or wine stains. Except for a few Nancy Drew mysteries scattered about the floor, nothing of Claudia either. I wander around, looking out at the views. It's early evening, Patricia just got back from her office (also newly-decorated, I later discover). She kicks off her pumps, tosses her coat onto an over-stuffed chair. Her clothes are new, too. Tasteful and expensive, a power outfit. Her tits are about the oldest thing she's got now. I wonder when the face-lift is coming.

"I had to buy a whole new wardrobe," she explains, noticing my look. "It's a more formal town for business." She pauses. "And I'm not buried in the stacks anymore."

She doesn't quite pull off throwing the last sentence away. There's the touch of the defensive in it, the need to justify.

"That's good," I answer.

"Anyway," she says, flitting around the new furniture like a lost hummingbird, "about dinner, why don't I order in? I would've cooked but I didn't know what your plans were, when you were arriving . . ." she tails off awkwardly. Suddenly we're strangers in a way we never were before.

"If it's okay with you I'd like to take Claudia out," I say. "The two of us."

"Oh." She hesitates. "It's a school night . . ." She catches herself. "Sure, of course, Will, whatever you want."

"So anyway where is she?" I ask. I'm uncomfortable as hell here, it's not that I feel like an intruder (although I do): I flat-out don't belong. They've been here a month and it's so settled in its antisepticness, so grown-up. The home of a well-to-do, middle-aged career woman.

"Downstairs with her friend Lily. They're in the same school together so they come home after school and play. Same grade even. Lily's mother doesn't work. I'm so lucky, there're two girls right here in the building her age. Her two new best friends."

She's nervous around me, she can't stand still. I'd called her office when I landed and she'd arranged to take the rest of the day off and meet me at her place. I came straight over without checking into my hotel, which she'd gotten for me, two blocks away. 'I don't think it would be a good idea for you to stay here, Will,' she'd said, like she'd been thinking about it. I wasn't sure then: a stirring in my pants, brought on by hearing her low voice over the phone, reminded me of our last encounter, not an unpleasant memory. But seeing her now, I whole-heartedly agree; I have no eyes to stay with the woman standing before me. The new clothes, the new pad, new everything, it's all great, I'm glad for her, for real I am, but it feels wrong, like a kid playing grown-up in her mother's oversized shoes. It isn't her; the Pat I know. Whatever sex appeal she'd had for me is gone, up in smoke somewhere with the T-shirts and running shorts.

She calls down, tells Lily's mother to send Claudia up right away. "Would you like a drink?" she asks. "I don't remember; do you drink martinis?"

Martinis? The last time I saw her she was guilt-tripping herself over a beer.

"I've been known to," I say.

"I'll join you." She walks into the kitchen, pulls out the gin—Bombay, I admire her taste—the vermouth, pitcher, ice cubes.

"Super dry?" she asks.

"The drier the better." I watch as she mixes the drinks with a practiced hand. She's done this before.

"I didn't know you drank," I say. "I mean you don't drink do you?"

"Oh, you know," she laughs: too loudly, forced. "When everyone else is . . . actually, I don't hardly. Once in a while, to unwind." She hands me my martini, with two olives in it, the same as hers. "Cheers."

"Cheers." We both sip. I don't like this. In one month she's moved into a decorated high-rise, done in her absence and with none of her own particular taste, changed her mode of dress to that of every other upwardly-mobile career woman, and started drinking serious whiskey.

She makes a face at her drink, pops an olive in her mouth.

"It's an acquired taste," I say.

"I don't plan on it becoming much of a habit," she tells me. "Not enough to acquire a taste; a real taste."

Like you, is the unspoken inference. I don't care; if my drinking stops her from taking it seriously, I've done my bit for mankind. And my child.

"Probably a good idea," I say. I can see she's a bundle of nerves, I'm the link with the past she's putting behind her, she doesn't want anything, me especially, fucking things up.

The door flies open behind me and by the time I've turned Claudia's in my arms. I lift her, holding her close.

"Oh daddy-do," she exclaims in her child/grown-up way, "I didn't know you were here."

"Just got here, pumpkin," I say. "I haven't even been to my hotel yet." I put her down. She's a big girl; I'd forgotten. One month.

"Come on." She grabs my hand. "I'll show you my room. It's really neat."

As she drags me away I look back to Patricia, standing on the unsoiled shag carpet in the middle of the living room, an unconscious, apprehensive smile frozen on her lips. Without even realizing it, she's drained her glass.

It's amazing how quickly a couple of weeks can go by. Not to a kid; to a kid time drags, a week can go on forever. But for an adult who's trying to hoard precious hours, even minutes, to have them in the bank against weeks or months of separation, time flies like a rocketship. It's hard to be in the moment when you're afraid of what the future may not hold.

School is out—Christmas vacation, why I'm up here. Patricia's working extra-hard, even during the holiday lull. "I have five years of catching up to do," she tells me later that first night I'm there, "they work their butts off." Welcome to the private sector, I felt like telling her. But I didn't, because her former job wasn't her fault, and she's happy working hard. She doesn't say it but she's also happy I'm taking Claudia off her hands for a little bit, giving her the chance to dig in without guilt-tripping herself.

So Claudia and I are constantly together. After the first few days of picking her up in the morning and taking her home at night I move her into the hotel with me: books, clothes, teddy bear. We roam the streets, the art museums and coffee shops, a man and his girl on the town. Her maturity amazes me, Santa Fe is a wonderful little jewel but Seattle is a real city, big, lots of variety. She takes to it like a duck to water, the endless choice of movies, places to eat lunch, places to shop. We buy belated Christmas gifts for some of her friends back home; she's wistful about them, many of them friends from the cradle, but the new friends are swell, they're just like anyone else.

She's adapting beautifully. Part of me, the selfish part (most of me), is sorry. Somewhere in the back of my mind I've filed a scenario about a tearful child begging her daddy to take her home, to where it's really home, where everything is good and comfortable. In other words, where I live. But the better part of me, and I'm discovering there is one, albeit small, is happy, genuinely so, because the move hasn't been as traumatic as I feared, and she seems to be at peace with it. Of course, it's all new still. Maybe when reality sets in she'll feel differently. I hope not; mostly.

"Are you going to let me stay up 'till midnight so I can see the ball come down?" Claudia asks.

"Sure," I tell her. "How will you know it's a new year otherwise?"

"From the calendar, silly," she giggles. There's a bit of coquettishness in her laugh. She's growing up, my little girl.

We'd spent a few days skiing, returning to Seattle New Year's Eve day. It was great fun, by the end of each day we were exhausted, eager to climb into bed early. Now we're back in my hotel room eating a room-service dinner; her choice, I gave her the option, we could've gone out. I'm glad she chose this; I don't want to share her. Besides, I know dinner in a hotel room is her idea of supreme luxury. Shrimp cocktails, cheeseburgers, ginger ale and chocolate cake à la mode. All the good stuff. Out of deference to her (in my head, but still . . .) I'm not drinking tonight; it actually feels good, not merely penance.

We talk: about her new school and friends, her mother, me. Her mother's new job is disturbing to her. It takes more of Patricia's time than the old one, much more. She can't visit the new office after school like she used to, either. It's too far away, Patricia doesn't want her taking city busses by herself, and the atmosphere isn't conducive to children lying on the floor reading and drawing. The clients wouldn't understand, she was told. Something about confidentiality, a new word she's learned. Her mom's much more uptight now.

She's also not there as much. The hours are longer, and she's dating. No particular man, as far as Claudia knows. That one gives me a jolt, that she's dating, I don't want her anymore, I truly don't, but the idea that other men do is disturbing. Your basic garden-variety primitive masculine jealousy: other men sleeping with the mother of my child. It's an ugly thought; the jealousy. I didn't realize I was still so chauvinistic.

"Have you met any of the guys she's going out with?" I ask.

"One."

"What's he like?"

"He's bald."

"Besides that," I laugh. "Anyway, what's wrong with being bald?"

"Nothing, I guess. You aren't."

"Wouldn't you love me as much if I was?"

"Yeh. But you're not."

"Did you like him?"

"I guess." A shrug saying I don't really want to talk about this. "I just met him for a minute when he came to pick mom up."

Patricia's gain is Claudia's loss. It's inevitable, in the long run it may even be healthy, but it bothers the hell out of me. A new kid in a new city spending too much of her time with other kids' mothers and sitters. I know it's none of my business but I'm going to talk to Pat about it. She won't like it, but that's tough titty. Claudia's my child, too.

Dick Clark does the New Year's bit with the ball now. We watch on television as thousands of nuts scamper about Times Square, drinking and yelling, some of them stripped to the waist even though it's below freezing out, like you see at football games in Pittsburgh or Cleveland. I realize with the time delay those ant-like figures up on the screen are all asleep or crashed out somewhere by now, but the manicness comes through, different from when I was Claudia's age watching with my grandparents. Halloween for real, with real stabbings and real blood. I was always happy my kid was growing up in a small city instead of a big one; now she's going to be part of that thundering herd.

A disquieting thought. I put it out of my mind. She's here now, having fallen asleep minutes after the magic hour, still in her party dress. For too brief a moment, as I watch her lying there, her mouth slightly open in child sleep, she metamorphoses in my fanciful imaginings back into the child of old, daddy's little girl, barely out of diapers and still sucking her thumb.

But that's not her, not really. She's a couple of years from teenagehood. Changing and growing, finding her true self, the one she'll live with the rest of her life. Like I'm doing. The way I feel right now, she'll get there before me.

THE NEW MEXICO state penitentiary is less than a half-hour's drive south of Santa Fe, down the same back road the bikers took when they were leaving town (they thought for good) seven months ago. It's cold out, bitter. February's the coldest month of the year, this year even more than usual, cold as hell and dry. We've had northern winds for a month, they've blown everything away, even the color, nothing bright outside, the sky itself pale, pale washed-out blue, almost clear, like the blue of mountain creek water during a false-spring runoff. Overhead an occasional streak of cirrus clouds, the sun faint yellow, half-transparent, skirting the mountains. Not a picture-pretty winter's day; going outside is labor.

I drive down to see the bikers, my once-a-month visit. Visit number four. Before all this is over there'll be hundreds once we start going into court on formal appeals.

I'm their only human contact with the outside world. I think about that a lot. It's a funny thing, or maybe not so funny, but I've become extremely ambivalent about them in hindsight, about the case. Not the way it turned out, but my involvement. The feeling blindsided me, I thought I'd be completely engrossed in the appeal, because of the obvious injustice of what happened to them. That part still holds true: they were screwed and I hate that, I hate the way the system lets that shit happen, to them and to others like them, all the time. And I'm going to fight like hell to overturn that decision. I am, it's not just an idle promise I make to myself to assuage my conscience. I am going to see this through to the end.

But there is a part of me that wishes I'd never gotten involved. For openers, I lost. I don't lose that many, and to lose a big case doesn't feel good, it's not part of my agenda, particularly when I'm taking such an ass-whipping in my personal life. It certainly helped push the dissolution of my partnership over the edge. Granted, I wouldn't have wanted to stay there, it would've been an impossible marriage, but I would have liked to have left on *my* terms, not theirs. No one likes getting canned, whatever the language says it was. And to be going out on your own with a defeat as your most recent decision is not as good, simply put, as going out with a win. I have business, but I'd probably have more if the decision had gone the other way. Winners attract, losers repel.

But that's not the main issue. We all lose, I'll rebound. What eats at me, constantly, like a rat gnawing in my gut, is the time with Claudia that I lost, time I will never recapture. I thought I knew at the time I was losing it but in a certain sense I didn't, because until she and Patricia actually, physically left, and I was without her, it wasn't real for me. I didn't gut-believe it. I'd still be missing her as much as I do now, but I would've put in the time. There would have been no recriminations, like there are now. Bottom line, these guys cost me part of my life. Sometimes, I'm realizing, that's more important than the black-and-white pursuit of justice.

Too late now for excuses, second guesses, might-have-beens. It's like what getting drunk's gotten to be: feels good while you're doing it, but the payoff changes your mind about is it worth it. It's for losers, all that stuff. I can't help that I lost a case, a partnership, a child, most of my life's savings. I am not a loser. I've got to get my act together and live by the Mickey Rivers school of life (one of my favorite baseball sages, up there with Casey Stengel and Satchel Paige): 'I'm not going to worry about the things I can't control, because if I can't control them there's no point in worrying about them; and I'm not going to worry about the things I can control, because if I can control them there's no point in worrying about them.'

"Hey, there, hoss, how's it hanging?"

"Long and low," I say.

"Beats the shit out of short and low," Lone Wolf replies, his lip curling off his canines in a half-assed smile, the teeth stained almost-black from the plug of Red Man tucked in his cheek. A man can acquire some nasty habits in prison, when he's sitting around with nothing to do while waiting for the hammer to drop.

We're in the attorney-client meeting room on Death Row, not a pleasant place to be. Sterile, overlit, unremittingly cheerless. Meetings in here feel like oral surgery without novocaine. In the old days, before the prison was rebuilt, it had a kind of funkiness about it. It was, albeit under the grimmest of circumstances, a place where human beings could relate to each other, which is important here, because everything about doing time on Death Row is terrible, utterly demeaning and depressing, a mixture of boredom, futility, and certainty.

We sit facing each other on hard plastic chairs at a long Formica table that runs the length of the room. A floor-to-ceiling Plexiglas barrier separates us. It's two inches thick, bullet-proof. We talk on telephone receivers that connect across the barrier. We're the only ones in the room. Everything we say and do is privileged: once a month the room is swept for bugs, for the state's protection as well as the prisoners'. One illegal eavesdrop on a lawyer-client discussion and it could be a major lawsuit, even an overturn of a death sentence. The state doesn't want shit like that—they play it by the book in here, willingly. They can afford to; it's all so stacked in their favor they'd be stupid to cheat.

"What's the good news?" Lone Wolf asks.

I shake my head: there is none. He asks the same question each time I see him, not because he thinks there might be some good news—he knows I'd be telling him if there was some the minute I heard myself—but as part of a ritual, our own Kabuki. Another habit to be cultivated to keep the days going, like doing a certain number of pushups or flossing your teeth at certain self-regulated times.

"Same old same old," he says.

I nod. I wish I wasn't here. Lone Wolf doesn't say so, but I suspect he wishes the same. There's nothing I can say or do. The appeals process in a death-penalty case is a long proceeding, tedious and nit-picking in the extreme (unless it's you sitting there, about fresh out of options) with lots of checkpoints along the way. It pretty much takes care of itself as far as the technicalities of the law are concerned. It's a hoary cliché but nonetheless still a true one that no judge or legal system, no matter how harsh, including those in Texas, Louisiana, Florida, the places where they actually kill people in quantity in the name of justice and the American way, wants to see a man put to death by the state until he's exhausted all his appeals. Since we're the only democracy left in the world that still executes its citizens, we have to be careful about it, or at least make a show that we are.

The problem with this case, the appeals side of it, is we conducted it too good, my colleagues and I. The way you get to retry a murder case, or any capital case, is to find a mistake. A big one, that would've (or at least could've) changed the outcome if it hadn't been made. More convictions are overturned because the defense fucked up than any other reason. In hindsight, these boys would have been better off with a shitty defense, because that might have been grounds for retrial.

No such luck here. Every lawyer in New Mexico, from the penthousers to the ham-and-eggers, knows we did the best job that could've been done, given the lynch-mob attitude in the community. (Aside from the opening we blundered into on the coroner's report, which in hindsight was inevitable. They would've snuck it in one way or the other.) So what we're looking for is something the judge said or did, or something the prosecution did (or didn't do) that would warrant a new trial, or at least a reopening of this case.

So far, I've drawn a blank. Judge Martinez did a first-rate job. We couldn't have asked for a fairer judge. Some of the time you catch them on the instructions to the jury, about how to weigh the evidence or what can't be used. None of that here. Everything was proper, as kosher as a Jerusalem rabbi. In the years ahead I'm going to be filing reams of motions revolving around Martinez's decisions, but I won't win a one. All I'll do is buy some time.

If I ever pull this off, if I ever get this nest of vipers reversed, it'll be through a hole the state's provided for me. Robertson and Moseby. Some fuckup of theirs, something royal. I don't know what that is yet; I don't even know if it exists; but I do know that for these four men doing their time on Death Row it's the only avenue out.

Anyway. Lone Wolf knows all this. He knows the odds of pulling a Perry Mason, of finding new evidence the court will accept, or turning a witness, that kind of theatrical stuff, is a one in a thousand chance. He and the others fight to accept that, because they have to live in dual worlds: the real one, life in prison, and the one they want, the free world.

Knowing all this, he still asks anyway.

"Nothing?" he asks again. "Shit, man, there's got to be something."

"I'm looking," I tell him. "I can't invent what isn't there."

"Why not?" he says. He's still got a sense of humor, a macabre one. It's keeping him alive.

"Because if they caught me I'd be in here with you," I say. "Then where would we be?"

We make small talk for awhile. I bring him news of his friends. Other than me, he isn't allowed visitors except for immediate family, and since he isn't married and his only family is his brother, who helped put him in here, he doesn't see anyone else. Especially the other three. They're here on this floor with him but the segregation is complete, none of them have laid eyes on any of the others for one second since they've been inside.

"What about the cunt?" he asks. "You find head or tail of that lying bitch?"

"No."

Rita Gomez. The state's star songbird. Star liar. We shaked her but we didn't break her. What I realized in hindsight, going over things, was that she was smart enough to spin a convincing yarn but too dumb to break. It didn't matter what was asked, she had her answer and she stuck to it. Catching her in lies didn't do any good, she merely incorporated them, swallowed them up, made them another appendage to the story. Even at the end, when she had more barnacles on her than Moby Dick, she didn't succumb. Too goddam stupid.

Or . . . too scared. She was coached well, very well. That's fine, everyone coaches their witnesses, but with her it felt almost beyond that, that she was telling their story for them. It's something you want to believe but you can't, because if you do, there's no safety net. If the state sends men to their death on perjured testimony we're back to fighting with sticks and rocks.

I looked for her after the trial, but she was gone. Vanished, without leaving a trace. It wouldn't have mattered, once a trial is over you can't open it up again and put a witness back on the stand, unless, of course, they've flat-out lied, and we know that wasn't the case here, she was with them, and they did rape her, and she did know the victim, and all that jazz. But there were things missing, I knew it, we all did. I wanted to put them to rest. And maybe find some technical grounds in the way the cops coached her that would've given me a fingerhold.

I checked, hard, but the trail was cold. Rita Gomez no longer resides in the state of New Mexico. The odds we'll see her again are about as long as my guys finding a way out. The best we can hope for right now is that they keep their noses so clean that the governor, whoever it is when their number finally comes up, commutes them to life.

I don't tell them that, of course. It's too cruel, hope has to spring eternal in the human breast. So we talk, we bullshit for the allotted hour.

Time to go. We stand, placing our hands on the Plexiglas, palms to palms, fingers to fingers, the closest to another human touch this poor bastard will feel for a long, long time.

MY NEW OFFICE ISN'T physically very far from my old office, only a couple blocks, but it's light years away in prestige. It's an old run-down adobe, once a mansion, now converted to little rabbit warrens, where fringe type lawyers like me, who can't afford the normal goodies—law libraries, secretaries, and copying machines—hang their shingles. It's got a half-time receptionist, a woefully inadequate library, a copier that's usually out of order, and a coffee machine. Period. Two-room front office–back office suites, the secretary in front, the principal in back. Probably no less personal than a big New York firm, where the senior partners don't even know half the lawyers in their office, but a far cry from where I used to put up my boots.

These first couple months have been tough: I'd been following the same routine for a dozen years. Even when they forced the leave of absence on me, I'd used my old office. I was like an old dog there, I could have navigated the place blind. What with the separations and divorces I've gone through, my office was more of a home to me than most of the places I've called home.

You can get used to anything, though, and I'm slowly getting comfortable here. I've always been a kind of solo bird anyway. The other habitués are a good lot by and large, a mixed bag. There are some young turks recently removed from law school who can't stomach the bureaucracy of government work, defense or prosecution, and unable as yet to connect with the bigger, prestigious firms. (Like Alexander, Hite, and Portillo, now doing business as Hite and Portillo. The week after they booted me out they took a quarter-page ad in the Santa Fe *New Mexican* to make sure everyone knew. Big men, my old partners. It was strange seeing it, but surprisingly it didn't hurt. Maybe by then I was numb.)

The rest of the building is two- and three-person firms, several of them women, and older singles, not like me, I'm still a force in this town, men more like Paul, my associate from the trial. Lawyers who need a place to hang their hat, get out of the house, even if there are days, maybe most days, where nobody crosses the threshold. A place to be professional.

Speaking of Paul, I haven't seen him since the trial ended. We wrapped things up, promised to keep in touch, and promptly fell off each other's phone list. It's inevitable; we all have our own dreams to chase. I doubt that he'd go out of his way to meet up with me; my jumping him on the 'hot knives' incident drove a wedge between us that's too basic to paper over. And I'm sure that deep down that hurts him, that he was the one to do it.

Tommy I see with regularity. He approached me after I was shown the door, asked if I was looking for someone to partner with. It was tempting; he's going to be a force to contend with down the line. But I turned him down, although I left the door open for possibly later, if we both wanted to. My relationship with him is a variation on the theme I played out with Mary Lou: a part of my past I have to put some distance between for now. And like her, when I want to get together again he won't be available.

He's a good soul, Tommy, he goes down to the pen to see Goose every month without fail. He isn't Goose's lawyer anymore, we all agreed as there was no conflict in their cases I'd take on the appeal for all of them, it was mine at the start and it'll be mine until the bitter end. Even so, Tommy's there for the old biker, like a dutiful son. It means everything to Goose, it probably keeps him alive. Unlike the others, who are younger and might see a light at the end of the tunnel years from now, Goose is resigned that if he isn't executed he's going to die in prison. It would make some men homicidal; with him it's probably more likely to be suicide. Either way, the state'll get its pound of flesh.

In brief, my life is getting back to some sort of normalcy. I get up, I go to the office, I meet with clients, file briefs, go to court, the usual stuff. I joined a gym, go three days a week after work. Nautilus, aerobics, swim. I'm getting into shape. I'm not drinking as much; it isn't as attractive right now, as necessary. A scotch or a glass of wine seems to satisfy me. Maybe it's the reflection Patricia held up to me.

Aside from my monthly visits to the pen, the most constant reminders I have of my clients are the crank confessions that still come into the office, periodically floating to the surface like dead carp. Anytime there's a sensational crime the nuts come out of the woodwork, looking for their moment in the spotlight. Either they did it, and can prove they did it, or they know who did it and can prove that. It's a sick psychological phenomenon we have to put up with in the legal profession. Even though you know they're phonies you have to check them out, which is time out of your job and money out of your client's pocket. After a while, when the case has been over as long as this one, you do as little as possible to verify that it's a fake; but you have to do it. The one time in a million you don't will be the one time it's the genuine article.

So far, seventeen of these claims have come to us. All bogus, as they always are. Within the next few months they should finally stop, only to revive when the next sensational case comes along.

The biggest change in my life is that I haven't been laid since I got back from Seattle. The odd chance drifts by, but it doesn't connect. I haven't jacked off this much since high school. I think about Mary Lou, wonder how she's doing, but except for a Happy New Year's call we haven't spoken. Sometimes I fuck her in my less-than-sweet dreams.

Most of the time, except when I'm doing business, I keep to myself. I went out for lunch one day, about a month ago, and saw Andy sitting in the restaurant. The sight of him froze me; I didn't want him to see me, my ego wasn't strong enough. It hit me like a thunderbolt, I didn't know that feeling was there until the moment it happened. I actually felt myself shaking.

His back was to me. I turned to my companion, a young lawyer from the office next door, and made some feeble excuse about having to get back, I forgot an important phone call was coming in.

Out on the street I broke into a sweat. I started walking back to the office, trying not to run.

"Hey, Will."

Andy had spotted me after all. Slowly, I'd turned and walked back towards him.

"Hello, Andy," I said, forcing a casualness I most certainly didn't feel.

He looked at me.

"How are you?" he said. The tone of his voice was not throwaway conversational.

"Getting by," I replied.

He looked me over more carefully.

"What's that on your shirt?" he asked, pointing to a stain my tie couldn't cover.

"I spilled some coffee this morning," I answered defensively. "Normally I'd have changed but I don't have any appointments this afternoon . . ." I heard my wimpishness even as I found myself unable to stop explaining. Why did I feel I needed to justify myself to this man?

He ran a thumb and forefinger down the placket.

"Doing your own laundry these days?" he asked, half-joshing.

"The occasional shirt," I admitted sheepishly.

"If you're going to do your own washing you'd better learn how to iron," he said. "That shirt looks like you slept in it."

"I don't sleep in my clothes," I said, "and what difference is it to you what I look like? I'm not with the firm anymore, I can't embarrass you."

"You're an embarrassment to yourself, Will," he said bluntly.

"So go to hell yourself." I started away. He put his hand on my shoulder, stopping me.

"You're still fucking up, Will," he said. "Worse than ever."

"Like hell I am," I told him. He had me on the run and I didn't like it. "And anyway what's it to you?"

"You're a friend, that's what. And I still give a shit about you, even if you don't give one about yourself."

"Save the sermons for the courtroom."

He looked at me with a combination of pity and disgust.

"You're falling off the edge, Will," he said. "And you're closer than you think."

He turned and walked away, leaving me shaking.

Since then I've had Susan bring me in a sandwich from the deli, or I go to places I know he and Fred don't frequent.

That incident scared me; it showed me that under all my jive independence I do care about how others see me, and how they do see me isn't very pretty. I've got to work on it, either stop being a victim of my ego, or stop giving a shit about how others see me, or both. The funny thing is, I thought I was that person. I was working with a safety net then; when the net's taken away you're not as brave as you thought.

It's disquieting, feeling vulnerable. It's a feeling I've never known. Scratch that, it isn't true; what's true is it's not a feeling I've ever *admitted to*.

I'm doing penance for all the years I've been bullshitting myself. I hope there's a payoff to it.

"HELLO, STRANGER."

"Hello your own self."

I didn't know she was behind me.

"You look good, Will. Fit. Trim." She punches my bicep. She packs a good, strong punch.

"I've lost a few pounds," I tell her, flexing my arm. I didn't know she was so strong. "About ten, actually. Been working out."

"It looks good on you. Not that there was anything wrong with the old look," she adds.

"You look good, too, Mary Lou."

"Thank you, kind sir. So where are you headed?"

"Denver. I've got a deposition," I say. Goddam, does she look good. All dressed up in her power-lawyer's clothes. Unlike Patricia, on her it looks natural. Probably just a case of different expectations. She smells good, too; she's right on top of me, it's a crowded line, I can't help it, the combination of perfume and her own bodily essence is unmistakable even though it's early in the morning and she showered a couple hours ago.

"What about you?" I ask.

We're in the United ticket line at the Albuquerque airport. Besides her briefcase she has a small suitcase and a carry-on garment bag.

"Same place," she says.

"Denver too? What for?" Shit.

"Mini-seminar. Products liability. Today and tomorrow."

"That's right, I forgot about that," I say. "I was going to attend," I add, "but I'm not doing much of that these days so I passed." I can't help myself; I've got to let her know I'm current. That it's still business as usual.

"Lucky you," she says. "It'll probably bore my tits off."

"Hope not," I say, glancing down reflexively.

"You could check it out this evening," she says provocatively, laughing. "Only kidding, Will," she adds quickly. My face must look very silly right now. She changes the subject.

"Where are you staying?" she asks.

"I'm not. I'll be done by three. Just a quick in and out."

She smiles at the inference but doesn't comment. In the old days with the firm I might have stayed over, had a good meal, spent the evening entertaining a potential client. Now that it's all my own money I'm more frugal. It's not a comfortable feeling, it reminds me of when I was a kid going out on a rare occasion to a restaurant with my parents and only being allowed to order the cheapest entrees on the menu, hamburger steak or spaghetti and meatballs when I really wanted the fried chicken or breaded veal cutlet that cost an extra quarter. I've never forgotten that feeling.

"I'm at the Brown Palace," she says. "There's a cocktail party this afternoon. Why don't you come over after you're done? I'm sure you'll know most of the people there."

I'm sure I will, too: that's the problem.

"Yeh, okay, maybe I will." It's an obvious lie, she has to know it.

"I'll be disappointed if you don't." She looks me square in the eye. She's persistent, I give her that.

We buy our tickets, drift over to the boarding area. I pour myself a complimentary cup of coffee, glance at the headlines in *The Wall Street Journal*.

"So are you dating anyone these days?" she asks abruptly.

"Actually, I'm celibate these days."

She arches an eyebrow.

"It's true," I say. "Honestly. I haven't had a date in . . . I guess a couple months now." I hadn't realized it was that long.

"That'll be the day," she says.

I sip the coffee. It's bitter, undrinkable. "What about you?"

"Here and there."

I shrug; I hope it looks like it's casual. "Anyone in particular?"

"Would you be jealous if I was?" she asks.

Fucking aye I'd be jealous. "Curious," I say. "Forget I asked. It's none of my business." My palms are sweating, I feel my face getting red.

"Too bad," she says. "I was hoping you would be. Even a little bit."

She's being straight with me; it stops me cold. I owe her that much in return.

"I would be," I confess. "At least a little bit."

Her fingers touch mine. I want to kiss her, badly.

"Stay over tonight."

"I didn't bring a change," I say.

"I'll buy you one."

I REALIZE NOW THAT Patricia has set me free. An unconscious act, definitely not premeditated, in fact had she known on a conscious level, she might have approached everything differently, because of her jealousy of Mary Lou, not only of Mary Lou's participation in our highly-publicized murder case and the career advancement that came with it, but of Mary Lou's proximity to me, professional and personal. Mary Lou not only got to work with me (something Patricia had been burning to do for years, both as an acknowledgment from me that she was legitimate, that she belonged, that she was as good as the others, something she'd never believed while she lived in Santa Fe, and as an avenue to the big leagues, at least what goes for the bigs in these parts . . . stop putting yourself down, man, those days are over, remember?, that was a big league case for sure and you were a star, even in a losing cause), she became my lover as well, only for the one night then, yes, but in my heart and gut for a longer duration, as I look back now she was never not there from that first time we touched in the office late at night. Patricia didn't want me, I know that, we've both known it for a long time, there are real, fundamental reasons we didn't make it, but like me, she didn't want someone else to have what she didn't have, even if she didn't want it, couldn't have it.

Or maybe it's all my own shit, transposing myself onto her.

Either way, the move to Seattle, physically taking Claudia away from me, and her own change into the new her, the her I didn't know and am not comfortable with, don't desire anymore, makes it possible for me to make love to Mary Lou now in a way that's different from the way I've made love with any woman I've been with for the past ten years: since Patricia, when it was still the real thing.

Mary Lou comes out of the bathroom naked, her clothes folded neatly across her arms, lays them down on one of the Queen Anne chairs, slides under the covers next to me. In the bathroom, besides putting in her diaphragm, she'd stripped her face of makeup, brushed her hair back. Her skin glows, musky and flushed.

"Do you take your diaphragm wherever you go?" I had asked peevishly, jealously, when she'd told me she needed a minute to get ready.

"Jesus Christ. Why are you so insecure?"

"It strikes me as being a bit . . ."

"Unprofessional?" she laughed.

"You know what I mean." You're ready for a fuck if somebody comes along that turns you on. What happened to true love?

"Do you remember that phone call I made from the plane? I had a friend go over to my apartment and same-day Fed Express it up. It got here an hour ago. Stop being jealous, Will, you're too much an open book, I only make love with men I'm crazy about, so I haven't since we did it."

There's a book by a writer named James Crumley called *The Last Good Kiss*. I read it years ago, and I don't remember what it's about. That doesn't matter; the expression has stuck with me, but until this moment I hadn't realized what it means.

It's what we're doing now. The long, slow ride towards heaven on earth, the sheer egolessness of giving and receiving pleasure. There is nothing else, nothing, no pinpricks of the world outside the two of us: job, children, past, future, none of that exists. She fascinates and fulfills me completely, all delight.

It's at least an hour before I enter her. It matters, but it almost doesn't, because I want to be with this forever.

This is what making love is supposed to be all about. It's different when you're forty from when you're twenty—you don't have that pure, limitless animal energy and stamina—but the absoluteness of sensuality and pleasure is so much stronger, so consciously *there*. The first time we fucked, back during the trial, was that: a first-time fuck. Fortunately, it was good; they aren't always, even us noted cocksmen know that to be so; but good or bad, first-time sex is its own experience.

This is different. I'm not religious but this goes beyond any strict interpretation of evolution. People fall in love this way.

"Are you hungry?" I ask.

"Famished."

"Ahhh, don't, I'm too sensitive down there now! No! Let's rest for awhile." She grabs me by the hair, pulls me back up so we're face to face again.

"You're beautiful."

"You're wonderful."

"Not beautiful?"

"Handsome."

More kissing, more touching. We lie on our backs, fingers intertwined, worn out.

"Actually, I am hungry," I say.

"Actually?"

"Actually."

"Actually, I am, too. For your cock. And maybe a club sandwich and a Heineken's."

"And some cherry pie. À la mode. Butter pecan."

"You sound like you're stoned."

"I am. Eating you's like taking a mini–acid trip."

"Shit, Will. I mean is that poetic or what?"

I stagger into the bathroom for a glass of water. I can barely crawl, let alone walk.

"I'll call room service," she says.

"Good idea. I don't feel like getting dressed."

"They wouldn't let you into the dining room, anyway," she tells me.

"Why not?"

"Look in the mirror," she giggles. "Your face is a dead giveaway."

"Giveaway what? What face?"

"The face of an obsessed pussy-eater. They don't allow pussy-eaters in the public rooms of the Brown Palace Hotel."

There's no feeling in the world that can compare to the beginning of a love affair. Of falling in love, of the feeling of falling in love, the wanting, the desire of it. The eagerness to please, to have, to take, to give. The hidden delicious fear of is this the real thing, finally? All this is in and out of my thoughts as we make love all night long almost, almost until dawn, finally I'm able to shut the goddam brain down, to just be with this emotionally, so that I hold nothing back, there's none of the spectator at the match, the watching of the doing while the doing is happening, the self-censoring man. It all goes to her, it all comes back to me from her, through her.

She's a wonderful lover, skillful yes, I knew that from the first time, but that's only the surface, she flows constantly, heart and sex together. To please me, to give me love. We're a great fit, the way our bodies come together physically, the distance between her breasts and pussy the right match for my chest and cock, our mouths together effortlessly, our legs wrapped together. She smells erotic, not just between her legs but everywhere, her underarms, legs, under her breasts, her neck, her feet, her palms, fingers, toes. Eat, kiss, suck, fuck, rest, body against body, then touch, stroke, kiss, bite, suck, fuck again.

No fantasy has ever been this good. Life, better than imagination.

At three o'clock we order up a bottle of Dom Pérignon from room service. $175.00. She signs for it, leaving the kid night-bellman not only a lavish tip but a hard-on, he doesn't even try to conceal the bulge in his pants as she sits cross-legged on the bed signing the check, a blanket loosely draped around her, covering virtually nothing, her laughing after he leaves backing out (his eyes glued to her all the while) at what the reaction will be when it shows up on her expense account. We drink it from the bottle, watching part of a movie on TV—*Wuthering Heights*. I mean shit, come on, somebody in heaven has to have had an eye on us. It has to have been ordained, this evening, this day, this night.

We fuck once more, then collapse into sleep, her hand resting delicately across my cock and balls.

"Wake up, Will," she sings. "Time to smell the coffee."

"No way."

I grab at her blindly, my eyes still closed. How the hell can anyone sound so cheerful on two hours sleep? She sidesteps my hand, pulls the sheets off me.

"Come on back to bed, Mary Lou. We haven't made love yet this morning." I hear my voice; I sound like the kid who wants two chocolate doughnuts, who won't be satisfied with the one that was offered. I want it all, the whole candy store.

"Aren't you the greedy little bugger. We made love at four o'clock," she reminds me, as if I'd forgotten.

"It was still dark out so it was technically night. Anyway who cares?"

"Me because I have a meeting this morning. Early this morning."

"Bag it."

"Would that I could."

I open my eyes, prop myself up on my elbows. She's dressed for business, serious business.

"You're beautiful. Even in clothes."

"Thanks. So're you. Even not." She sits on the edge of the bed. "But you've got to get up."

"Can't."

"Why not?"

"Got a problem." Pointing.

She lightly brushes the pulsing head with her blood-red fingernails.

"Not fair," I groan.

She casually strokes me for a moment, semi-consciously; then she goes down on me, gorging on me, taking it all. I come almost immediately, flopping back on the sheets like a spent fish.

"I'll start your shower," she says, wiping her mouth delicately with a corner of the sheet.

"I've got a better idea," I tell her. "I'll wait here for you. You do whatever it is you have to do and then come back. To my waiting arms."

"No can do. I've got meetings all morning, a symposium over lunch, then I've got to fly home and brief my senior partner on this stuff before we close shop for the day." She yanks the covers down. "Chop, chop, big boy. Up and at 'em. You're taking me to breakfast and we have to move quick. Come on now."

She drags me out of bed, shoves me into the bathroom. As I'm adjusting the hot water I hear her on the phone. She sounds impatient. "As soon as possible, okay? Just hang onto your britches." The power-lawyer talking to a recalcitrant client.

I luxuriate in the shower less than I'd like; she's got an agenda and I have to meet it, at least until after breakfast. I put on the new clothes she bought me yesterday at Neiman's, and we ride the elevator down to meet the day.

"What's wrong with the hotel dining room?"

"This'll be better."

We're driving through downtown Denver. She's at the wheel, in a rented Taurus.

"You know your way around."

"I interned here for two summers."

She drives with purpose; back erect, hands firmly on the wheel.

"This place we're going for breakfast. What is it? *Where* is it?" I'm looking out the window. This is not a quality neighborhood.

"You'll see." A Mona Lisa smile. "Trust me. You'll like it. I promise."

We're in the heart of the barrio now. I haven't seen a sign in English for at least a dozen blocks.

"I thought you had a packed schedule."

"I know what I'm doing," she answers, a mite testy. "So just sit back and enjoy the ride, will you?"

"Wherever it is you're taking me they must make a hell of a breakfast burrito."

Again, that infuriating Mona Lisa smile. She places a reassuring hand on my thigh. "This will be the most satisfying breakfast you'll ever have in your life, or double your money back."

She parks in the middle of the block, in front of a small faded-pink stucco house, trimmed in peeling turquoise. This is a quiet residential street—there isn't a restaurant or commercial building on the entire block.

"Okay. What gives?"

"An old friend wanted to cook you breakfast."

"An old friend? Come on, Mary Lou, what's going on here?"

She gets out of the car without answering. I reluctantly follow her lead; she's pulling some kind of number on me and I don't have a clue as to what it is and that pisses me off; I don't like surprises. I'm beginning to wonder if this whole incident, beginning with our chance meeting at the airport, was a setup.

The door to the house opens. A man comes out. He's short, compact, Hispanic. Dapper comes to mind. He looks like a well-bred horseplayer, his shoes shined to a high gloss, the crease in his trousers razor-sharp. His steel-gray slicked-back hair is the only giveaway that he's in his mid-fifties, not a decade and a half younger. He walks to us, formally shakes Mary Lou's hand.

"You got here fast." His voice is accentless, deep for a small man. Authoritative.

He's a cop. He looks vaguely familiar, but I can't place him.

"Victor Mercado, Will Alexander," Mary Lou says, making the introduction.

"I hear you're a hell of a cook," I say, not bothering to mask the sarcasm.

His face creases in a wry smile. "I've got something good cooked up for you. Please come inside."

The living room is tiny, but immaculate. A large black-velvet painting of Elvis hangs over the sofa. I glance over at Mary Lou. She's tense. What the hell is all this?

Mercado opens a bedroom door off the hallway.

"Come in, please," he says.

A moment passes; then a trembling Rita Gomez shuffles into the room. She looks at me for a brief moment, then averts her eyes.

I don't know who's shaking more, her or me.

"Sit down," Mercado instructs her, indicating the sofa.

She sits. Her hands are balled up in tight fists. I turn to Mary Lou, who's grinning broadly.

"Victor used to run the FBI office in San Antonio," she informs me. "Now he runs the best P.I. firm in the southwest. We met a couple of years ago on an investigation," she continues, "he's been helpful to me from time to time . . . not only in Texas but Santa Fe and just about all over."

"I got tired of the bureaucratic bullshit," Mercado explains. "And the money's a hell of a lot better."

I must have seen him in Santa Fe once or twice; that's why he looked familiar. I look from him to Mary Lou; could she have slept with him? Immediately, I check that thought. She doesn't do that—I do, it's my inadequacy I'm projecting. He's helping her for the right reasons. Jesus I'm lame sometimes.

Mary Lou glances at her watch.

"I've really got to run." She gives me a quick peck on the cheek. "Call me when you get back." She smiles. "Now maybe you'll believe me."

She's out the door before I can ask what or how or why. She's given me this incredible gift and she won't even stay for a proper thank-you.

I turn to Mercado.

"How . . . ?"

"I figured she'd have to talk to someone in Santa Fe," he explains, glancing at Rita, who's sitting forlornly on the edge of the sofa. "Loneliness, desperation. Whatever. Fear. I came up to your neck of the woods, checked out the situation, and took the liberty of shall we say intercepting a few phone lines that seemed likely. The routine kind of stuff you learn in the bureau."

"Isn't that . . . irregular?" I ask.

"Mary Lou's a good person," he says straight-forwardly. "It was important to her. Sometimes you have to cut a few corners."

She did this all for me. Mary Lou.

"I'll wait outside, " Mercado says circumspectly.

He closes the door behind him, leaving the two of us alone.

I stand there, waiting. Finally Rita Gomez looks up at me.

"They said I wouldn't have to see nobody. Ever again. That's what they told me. They promised me to my face." Her voice is low, barely a whisper, like she's talking to herself, remembering what they told her, as if in saying the words it would make them so.

"Who?" I prod. "Who told you that?"

"You know who."

"No, I don't." I think I do, I'm pretty sure, but I want her to say.

"They said I wouldn't see nobody connected with any of this once it was over. That I'd never have to say nothing about it ever again. They promised," she whimpers, almost crying.

"The police."

She nods, her head barely moving.

"Gomez. And the other one. What's-his-name. Sanchez."

She nods again.

"And the other one," she says.

"Which other one?" I'm confused; as far as I ever knew, they were the only cops who ever dealt with her.

"The one with the food all over his shirt and tie. The one picks his teeth right in front of you. Who did the talking in the courtroom."

Moseby.

"The D.A.," I say. "The assistant D.A."

"Yeh. Him."

"What about Robertson?" I ask. "The regular D.A."

"Who?"

"The other man in the courtroom who did the talking. Besides the judge."

"Him. No."

"So it was just the three of them . . . who made you these promises. Nobody else."

"Yeh." She nods her head, almost as if bowing in prayer.

"The ones who got your confession."

She looks at me as if to ask 'what could I do?'

"It was me or them, they said. They said they already had plenty of proof and if I didn't admit it was them bikers it would be me up there being tried for the murder with them. As an accessory to the murder. Of Richard."

They took her to a cabin up in the mountains. It was the only cabin anywhere around, you couldn't see anything from it. It was a long drive, several hours, she asked how come we're going up here, what's wrong with questioning me in Santa Fe, they said so nobody will bother you, upset you.

She was still feeling kind of weak from the bleeding and she was hungry so she told them she wanted something to eat and then she wanted to sleep for awhile so one of them went out and got her some chili and Cokes and they all ate chili and she drank a couple Cokes and they had beer and she had to go to the bathroom and she was embarrassed to tell them for some reason, maybe because of the bleeding, so she held on until she couldn't anymore so finally she asked could she go? And they said sure so they let her go to the bathroom and they told her to take a shower while she was in there, so she took a shower and later on, a couple days later, she discovered a peephole into the bathroom where they'd been watching her shower. By then there was so much other stuff going on it didn't matter, they saw her tits, her swollen pussy, so what? They must be pretty hard up if that turned them on.

So she came out of the shower that first time and they had a bunch of pictures spread out on the table, what passed for the kitchen table, and they told her to look at them carefully. It was a bunch of pictures of Richard, all fucked up. Real sick shit, they tried to make her look at them but she couldn't, the pictures made her want to puke, she ran into the bathroom and puked, they were so disgusting. So then after she came out they told her what had happened to Richard, all the stuff that she talked about at the grand jury and then at the trial, was in these pictures. That was how she found out what had happened to Richard, the first time, for real. Because she hadn't seen it happen. She said she did, at the grand jury and later at the trial, but she didn't.

So after she puked up all the chili and Coke and washed her mouth out, they were nice to her, the cops, wasn't that awful about poor Richard, all that kind of dialogue, then they said to her how did it happen? So she said what do you mean? So they said to her up there in the mountains, when you were up there with Richard and the bikers, how did it happen, what happened first, what happened second, who raped you first, who raped you second, who raped Richard first, who raped him second, and so on, who actually knifed him first, who cut his dick off. Everything that happened.

"I don't know what you're talking about," she told them. Like her rape, she told them about that, everything she could remember, which as she talked about it was just about everything, then how they dumped her off finally and raped her a couple more times and then took off. It scared her to talk about it but she did, and the more she talked about it the more she hated the bikers, she'd been able to not think about it, like it didn't happen, but talking about it made it for real, that it did happen, she knew it did, she couldn't say it didn't. But anything about Richard, she couldn't say about that, because it didn't happen.

So then they looked at her kind of funny, like maybe they didn't believe her or something, so they said you were up there with them when they killed Richard and cut his dick off and stuck it in his mouth, and she told them she wasn't, she just wasn't.

So then they said again she was, and she said again she wasn't, and they looked at her funny again, and they told her to go to bed, to get some sleep, she was tired from what had happened to her, the rape and the hospital and all, and they would talk to her again in the morning. It was true, she was tired from all that, she went into one of the bedrooms (there were two) and fell asleep without even getting out of her clothes that's how tired she was. Later she found out they had a peephole into that bedroom, too, so they were probably watching her get dressed and undressed. She didn't care; plenty of men had watched her get undressed, it was no big deal to her. She heard them talking and getting beers out of the fridge and the next thing she knew it was the next morning and her mouth tasted like shit from puking the night before and they gave her coffee and sweet rolls and a new toothbrush and toothpaste and toilet articles they'd bought for her. Nice things, like a lady'd picked them out.

Then they showed her the pictures again and made her look at them for a long time, real good. They told her how it happened, how they figured it had happened, the same story she told the grand jury later, and she kept telling them it didn't happen that way, she didn't know how it happened because she wasn't there. So then they said okay let's start back at the beginning. Did you know the victim Richard Bartless? Yes, she told them. She knew him, she'd already said that she knew him, she wasn't arguing that. Okay, so did you ever go to the bar with him? Yes, again. No problem so far. Did you meet the bikers there that night? Yes. And did they take you up to the mountains and rape you? Yes. And bring you back to the motel? Yes. Where Richard was also living at the time, next door to you? Yes. By now she could see where it was going. And Richard came into your room and tried to stop them from hurting you? No, she'd told them, that's where it stops being true, being what I know, what happened to me. They just kept going on: and they tied him up and took both of you back to the mountains. No. And they fucked him up the ass, going on questioning her like she was saying 'yes' instead of 'no.' And they took this knife and got it hot in the fire and stabbed him dozens of times. No. Just keeping on asking, like it's 'yes.' And cut off his dick and stuck it in his mouth. No. And shot him in the head. No. And threw the body over the edge and took you back to the motel and talked about killing you or not and finally not killing you. No part and yes part. And leaving, riding away, leaving you there, swearing you to secrecy. Yes.

So they did that and had some coffee (she had a Coke) and then they started over again, the same thing, from the beginning. The same questions, the same answers. She had to go to the bathroom again and she asked 'Could I' and they said no, not yet. She was ready to burst and she told them, she had to go, she couldn't hold it no longer, she was going to pee on the floor, which would have embarrassed her worse than any of the other stuff, being raped or anything, she didn't know why but she didn't want to pee on the floor in front of these cops. So finally one of them, the nicer one, Gomez, says you can go, but listen, he tells her, when you come back we're gonna ask you these questions again, and we want you to start telling the truth.

After lunch a third man joined them. Moseby. He told her who he was, how sorry he was for what had happened to her, that he was going to help her. That made her feel good until he started talking to her about what the detectives had been talking to her about, the murder and how she'd been up there and had seen it. So she told him the same thing she'd told them, that maybe it happened the way they said it did but she didn't know because she wasn't there, she didn't see it.

That got him mad. He called her a liar, a whore, a slut, told her if she kept on lying like this he wouldn't have no choice but to arrest her and charge her with covering up the crime, being an accessory to it. That scared the shit out of her but what could she do? She'd always been told not to lie about something to the police and here were the police telling her to lie.

They talked to her all afternoon and night, she was bone-tired, being raped and bleeding had sapped her strength, she had to go to sleep, but they wouldn't let her. They talked to her all night long, in shifts, the cops and Moseby taking naps, spelling each other, keeping her awake, prodding her when she started to nod off, making her drink coffee, which she didn't like, and Cokes, not letting her go to the bathroom until she practically peed in her pants, taunting her about that, keeping her up all night long and the next day, until her brain was fried, she couldn't hardly talk, didn't know what she was saying. They kept asking her the same questions, over and over. Finally she passed out from exhaustion.

That was in the afternoon and when she woke up it was dark again. She was lying in bed, naked. Someone had undressed her. Fucked her for all she knew, there was fresh Kotex covering her pussy, fresh blood. It could have been from being so tired, but the bleeding had pretty much stopped, so she figured someone had been doing something to her while she was passed out. It didn't matter; all she wanted was for it to be over. But she was still afraid to lie; she thought they might be tricking her, that if she did say 'yes' to the questions she'd been saying 'no' to they'd arrest her for lying, that it was all a trick to get her to lie so they could arrest her for something. So she didn't know what to do.

They came into her room and told her to get dressed again, it was the same clothes she'd been wearing, the only clothes she had up there, they were getting rank, she didn't want to put them back on but she did, she didn't have any choice. She came back into the living room and there was another man there, a fourth man, and there was a machine on the kitchen table. They told her to sit down at the table next to the machine and they put a strap on her arm from the machine, which was a lie-detector machine, they told her. They told her they were going to ask her the questions again, and the machine would tell if she was lying or not.

She felt good about that: because she wasn't lying, she was telling the truth, and the machine would tell them she was telling the truth, and they'd let her go, they'd believe her finally. So they asked the questions again, all the same questions, and the fourth man was looking at the machine kind of funny, writing stuff down on the paper as it came out of the machine, looking up at Moseby kind of funny-like. Moseby looking at her funny, like he was angry, like what the machine was telling them wasn't what they wanted to hear. She couldn't help that; she was telling the truth.

They started talking among themselves, the four men. 'This is serious,' they were saying, 'this is pretty serious.' So then Sanchez came over and sat down next to her, facing her, and suddenly slapped her across the face, real hard, he slapped her so hard he practically knocked her off her chair, it stunned her, she was scared shitless, from the hurt of the slap and the surprise.

"You're a lying sack of shit!" he'd screamed at her. "The lie-detector just proved it. It says you're lying." He started to slap her again but Gomez stopped him, told him that wasn't solving nothing.

So then she was really scared, because she'd been telling the truth and the lie-detector had said she wasn't. So then they started asking questions again, about what happened when the bikers brought her back to the motel after they'd had her up in the mountains the first time, and she told them, she told them what happened, how they'd ridden off finally and she'd collapsed into sleep.

Then Gomez, the nice one, said 'Let me talk to her privately,' and Moseby said 'No fucking way, she's a goddam liar and I'm taking her back to Santa Fe and booking her as an accessory to murder, I'll fry her ass along with the goddam bikers, she's covering for them, she's as guilty as they are, lying little cunt,' and Gomez said 'Hang on man, just let me talk to her private for a little while,' so Moseby said 'Okay, but just for a little while, then I'm calling off this charade and we're taking her back to Santa Fe and booking her as an accessory to murder, you try to help someone and they don't want it, fuck 'em,' and Gomez said 'Just for a little while.'

They went outside and he offered her a cigarette and lit it for her, real gentleman-like, looking at her nice like she wasn't some sack of shit, some fuck-hole for any man to stick his dick into who felt like it, even passed out and bleeding.

"Now we know that they raped you and scared you to death," he'd said, real calm. "You told us they did that." She'd said 'Yes, that was true.' So then he said "And when they brought you back to the motel you were practically passed out and you hardly remember them leaving, you were probably passed out by then," and she'd answered that this was true, also. "And somebody did knock on the wall while this was happening, back at the motel," he'd said. Again, yes. "Could it have been Richard?" She thinks; it could have been, his room was next door, she was so fucked up by then she couldn't say. But it could have been.

"Okay," he'd said. He moved his chair closer to hers, lit her another cigarette. He had sad eyes, nice eyes, dark brown like hers, looking at her like he really cared about her, that he wanted her to be all right, and not get booked for murder, which she didn't do, which she knew he knew she didn't do.

"Okay. You don't remember anything else until you woke up, much later." He looked at her when he said that, like he was totally sincere. And she'd looked back at him and said 'yes,' that was true. At that point she had passed out and didn't remember anything else until she woke up several hours later.

So then he took one of her hands in both of his, they were big hands, they covered her hand completely, but they were gentle hands, they felt good holding her hand, he held her hand softly, like a man holds a woman's hand when he likes her, as a person and a woman, not just something to fuck, but as a real person, and he said "So it's possible that you were so strung out, so tired, so scared, that they did take you back up to the mountains with them, with them and Richard Bartless, and that those things did happen, killing Richard and the rest, and you were so tired, so strung out, so scared, that you don't remember. That your brain isn't letting you remember."

She had felt her heart stop for a minute. He was holding her hand in his hands and looking right into her eyes and she said 'Yes, it could have happened that way,' even though she was pretty sure it hadn't, but it could have, anything's possible. And he'd said 'That's how the brain works sometimes, when something's so bad it doesn't want to remember, it shuts down, like it's a storehouse and that stuff is locked away in a file somewhere so you don't have to know it's there, except it is, but you put it somewhere

where you don't have to look at it, because it's too ugly to look at. It's how the brain protects us from ourselves.'

So she'd looked at him and nodded, like she understood what he was saying. She did understand; she understood what he was saying, and what was expected from her.

They had another cigarette together, and split a Coke, and he told her everything was going to be all right, that he would take care of her, protect her. That nobody would hit her again, if anyone did, Moseby or anyone, he didn't care if it was his boss (which Moseby was, technically), he'd punch their lights out, he wasn't going to let her get hurt anymore, she'd been hurt too much already. Then he'd held her hand again in his, like he really liked her, as a person and as a woman.

They had stayed there three more days, her and the detectives and Moseby. They bought her new clothes, treated her nicely. They went over and over what happened that night, over and over again, until she really did start to believe it was the way Gomez had said it was, that it had happened like what they had said and her brain had blocked it out, the part with Richard, because it was too awful to think about. And after a while she did believe it, or she thought she did, it was easier that way, to really think she did, and they went over it with her, again and again, looking at the pictures, going over what happened, who did what, when. Until finally she really did believe it, at least she did then, later she started not to believe it but she did then, and she could tell them the story better than they could, because she did believe it so she could tell it better than anyone because she'd been there, she'd seen it, it had happened to her. For real, so she believed then.

They brought her back down to Santa Fe and she dictated her statement to a court stenographer, with a witness, that everything she said was true, that she was giving her statement without any coercion or pressure, that it was her own statement that she was giving without anyone telling her what to say. And she'd told it to the grand jury and later at the trial.

I don't know whether to shit or go blind. She's looking at me, waiting for my reaction. I have one; several. Right now, what I want more than anything is a drink: I realize I'm shaking like a leaf. Then something kicks in, maybe there is a better part of me, maybe last night was the real start of something better. Fuck the drink, man, that's the last thing you need. What you need is clarity.

"But you know now in your heart that it was all a lie," I tell her. "For real."

She nods, mute.

"There was no storehouse in your brain where you were hiding the truth, the awful truth."

She nods again.

"It was all a lie," I continue. "All bullshit lies." I'm outraged, I'm fucking outraged; but I have to maintain my cool, this sad excuse for a girl is so fragile one wrong word or move could send her around the bend. "Everything you said at the trial, from the time they brought you back to the motel. Everything about Richard Bartless. All lies."

"But not the other stuff," she says. "They did kidnap me. And rape me."

"Yes," I answer.

"They ought to be punished for that, shouldn't they?"

"Absolutely. But for that, for *that*, not for a murder they didn't do."

"Yeh. I guess that's right," she says.

I know what I have to do. One more question.

"Why did you leave Santa Fe? Why did you leave New Mexico?"

"They told me to. They told me I'd never have to see or hear about any of this again. I didn't want to," she says.

"Did they give you money? To relocate?"

She nods. "Five hundred dollars."

"We have to go somewhere," I tell her. "Someplace where I can get this recorded; what you've told me."

I can see the fear in her eyes.

"They'll throw me in jail. They told me they would," she says, pleadingly.

"No." I shake my head. "They won't; I'll make sure of that, that's a promise. Anyway, we're not going to the police. Not after this. I'm going to get your statement, then I'm going to hide you someplace. I'll pay for it myself. Someplace where they won't be able to find you."

"What about the bikers?" she asks.

"They're in jail, lady," I tell her. "You put them in there, remember?"

"But what about their friends?" she asks. "They're going to come after me, too."

"No, they won't. I promise."

She looks at me; she doesn't believe that for a second. I can't blame her. Why should she? Every time someone's told her to believe them it's exploded in her face.

DON STRICKLAND'S a member of a Denver law-firm who I've worked with before. Everything's all set up when Mercado and I arrive at his office with Rita—court stenographer, witnesses (Don and his secretary), videotape. She gives her statement, soup to nuts, she's resigned to telling the truth at last. I show her the tape, we make the necessary corrections, she signs an affidavit attesting to what she's seen.

"This is going to blow someone's little red caboose sky-high," Don says.

"Tell me about it." Robertson's caboose is what it's going to blow. At least he's clean, for now anyway. A dupe. I don't know what's worse: to be the ring-leader, or to not even know what the troops are doing behind your back. Bad scenario either way.

Moseby'll be disbarred. There'll be some heavy toasting to that around the choice watering holes. Sanchez and Gomez'll probably get a slap on the wrist and be pensioned off. Cops take care of their own.

I don't care. I want to see my four walk out of prison—period. Society can take care of itself; I'll be satisfied with my singular victory.

Don's secretary sets me up with a furnished apartment for Rita, one of those corporate deals you rent by the month. A phone comes with it; I make sure it's unlisted. We're settled in by late afternoon; I give them a two-month's deposit. And I arrange through Mercado to have a local detective agency check up on her at random intervals, so that she knows she's being watched but doesn't know precisely when. I want her staying put.

I'd thought about bringing her back with me, but nixed that fast. If the wrong people spotted her back in Santa Fe, before I took her deposition to court and it was public knowledge, the odds are she'd be dead in a day. If they played this rough before, they certainly wouldn't back off now.

Rita looks around, pleased with her new digs. Probably the nicest place she's ever lived; beats the shit out of my current place. That's good; I want her to be comfortable, I want her to stay put, not get antsy. We've been grocery shopping, enough to last a couple weeks. She's got her staples, some beer, a few girl-things, color TV with cable, a couple new changes of clothes: what more could she want?

"It's nice," she says, running her hand along the fabric of the curtains. "I like it's got a swimming pool."

"Make sure you don't make any friends out by that pool," I tell her. "Nobody."

"All right already. You done told me that ten times."

"I want to make sure it sinks in. We've got to be super-careful until we get back into court. If those cops found out about this . . ." I leave the rest unsaid.

She nods solemnly. She's already on enough shit-lists.

"I'll try to call you every day," I say. "And you can call me if you have to. You have my numbers."

She holds out the paper with my office and home numbers on it.

"Okay." I take a last look around. "This'll all be over soon."

"I sure hope so. I been cooped-up enough over all this shit. I don't like it."

"Beats the alternative," I tell her.

"What?" She doesn't have an extensive vocabulary.

"What it could be instead," I explain. Like sleeping in a pine box, or worse, buried under a thousand tons of trash in a landfill somewhere.

"Oh. Yeh." She gets it now. "I'll be careful. Don't worry."

"Lock the door when I'm gone. Both locks."

Easy to say: don't worry. While you're asleep, Rita, will you be calm? Will all your dreams be peaceful, the dreams of babies? No outlaw motorcycle gangs with knives for dicks, tearing you apart rape by rape, no venal cops threatening you with life in jail, or worse? Will you be able to live, day after day until this stink is over, without ever worrying, without once feeling those cold tentacles of fear? Because once you let them in, let them touch you, get hold of you, the worrying never stops. Is that possible for you, Rita? Maybe you can live on blind faith. I sure hope so.

I can't; I'm already worried. For her, for the bikers, for all of us dancing to this fucked-up dirge.

"YOU SHITTING ME or what? I mean is this the fucking truth? Tell me, goddam it!" Lone Wolf thunders, leaning forward towards me, his body raised on his knuckles which are white with tension, his breath clouding the glass between us as he gets as close to me as he can. "Tell me for real, motherfucker!"

"It's true," I tell him. "Now sit down before they throw your ass into solitary."

He sits back, breathing heavily, sweating, his shirt is suddenly wet down the front, under the arms. He's shut all his feelings down for months, now he has to deal with them again.

"I don't fucking believe it. I do not believe this."

"Believe it."

We look at each other. All of a sudden he breaks into a huge smile.

"Glory hallelujah. Maybe there is a God."

Maybe there is, although I don't think that matters one way or the other in this case.

"So now what? How soon do we get out of here?"

"You don't. Not for a while."

"But she turned her story. She's their whole case," he says, uncomprehendingly. "Fair's fair . . . isn't it?"

"Fair doesn't count. You ought to know that by now."

"But still . . ."

He's scared again, already. A minute of euphoria; less. Then what it is.

I explain how it's going to work. (Later today, I'll go through this same exercise with the other three. I'd asked to be allowed to see them all at once, that this was a special one-time situation, but my request was summarily vetoed, especially since I didn't give the warden particulars, which I have to save for the court.) I'll take Rita Gomez's video to the Supreme Court and petition for a motion for a new trial, based on this recanted testimony, which was suppressed during the original trial. Once they've granted it, assuming they do, I'll move that the charges against the bikers be dropped because her stuff won't be usable anymore, without it the state doesn't have a case, and anyway the whole original trial was riddled with perjury and coercion. I feel pretty confident that's the way it'll go; Robertson wanted to burn these puppies, but he's not an idiot.

"So how long?" he asks.

"Count on six months," I answer. "It could be less but the wheels of justice grind slowly, especially when the state's got egg all over its face."

"Yeh."

He can do six months standing on his head. They all can. He doesn't like it, none of them will, but at least they can see the end coming.

I look at him.

"How are you?"

He looks back at me; the look I remember from before, when we first met.

"Innocent, man. Like I always was."

IN THE SUPREME COURT for the State of New Mexico. Order: Upon motion by the defendants in the State vs. Jensen et al., the Court hereby remands this matter for a hearing on defendants' motion for a new trial.

SIMPLE ENOUGH STATEMENT. Of course, it took two months to get to it. I couldn't get hold of Paul, that first night back, but Tommy and Mary Lou and I celebrated, the three of us far into the night, then she and I the remainder. She has a nice place, the new girl of my dreams, just north of town, an adobe house with a stellar city view, new but authentic, exposed piñon vegas running the length inside. I stayed that night; the first time I slept at a woman's place since Holly left me (which technically was my place, too, although she claimed otherwise). The first of many, hopefully.

So it's the next morning, I'm in Robertson's office, he kept me waiting forty-five minutes, what else is new, old friendships may die hard but they do die. I'm sitting across from him, trying not to look like the cat that ate the canary, he's impatient, 'I've got a full schedule today, this better be important.' Wordlessly, I hand him the affidavit.

He starts to skim it, stops short, looks at me with alarm, reads it slowly. I'm watching him, sipping my coffee. He reads with concentration, a couple times flipping back to check something he's already read. It's a longish document, twenty-odd pages, he takes his sweet time. I'm in no hurry; he can take all morning if he desires, I want this to sink in.

He finishes it. It falls from his fingers to the desk. I reach over, deftly pick it up, put it back in my briefcase. He steeples his fingers, looking at the far wall, the ceiling. Getting his thoughts together as best he can. I'm patient; I can sit him out this time.

"Can I have a copy of that?" he asks.

"At the appropriate time."

"When are you going to file it?"

"This afternoon if I can. Otherwise tomorrow."

He nods.

"I wouldn't if I were you," he says finally.

"It's a good thing for my clients you're not me," I answer. "Why not?"

"Because it's a pack of lies. A complete and utter fabrication. It stinks to high hell, Will, and it could ruin your career." He picks up a pencil, nervously twirls it between his fingers like a drum majorette.

"I disagree."

We stare at each other, a Mexican face-off. The psychic wall between us at this moment is thicker and more impenetrable than the real glass one that separates me from the bikers in prison.

"I'm a liar," he says flatly. "A perjurer. A fabricator of false evidence. A criminal."

"No one's saying that," I reply. Cautious, boy, don't get into a spitting match with him.

"It says so." He points to my briefcase. "That rag in there."

"The two cops. Moseby. Not you."

He shakes his head. "The buck stops here," he intones, finger stabbing hard on his desk, "my department, my men." Long exhale of breath. "My life."

"You were duped."

"Screw you, Will."

"I'm serious, John. Your own people sandbagged you. Can't you see that? For Godsakes, can't you see that now? Finally?"

His face is turning red, the veins bulging in his forehead. If he wasn't such a physical specimen I'd be scared for him. I'm already scared for me.

"I'm supposed to take the word of some goddam whore, some chippy greaser who can't add two and two, I'm supposed to now believe that everything she said was a lie, that now she's telling the truth, that my number one deputy and two of the best men in this county's sheriff's office, who between them have forty or more years of experience, with a couple hundred commendations, not a blemish on either one's record, I'm supposed to believe they concocted the whole thing?"

"I do," I answer as calmly as I can. I'm very calm; I know I'm right, I know he knows it, or at least is harboring strong doubts about everything in this case. About his own judgment.

"Funny," I muse, pressing my luck a tad. Sometimes I just can't help myself. "When she was your witness she was a paradigm of truth. Now she's a chippy liar."

"Shit." He waves that off. "Don't confuse the issue." He looks at me like I just stepped in a pile of dogshit and tracked it into his office.

"Where is she?" he asks.

"In a safe place."

"Where?" he demands.

"Someplace where your people can't get to her," I fire back. "Like they did last time."

"You'd better hope so."

I bristle. "Is that a threat, John? Are you threatening my witness?" Son of a bitch, we are really playing hardball now.

"Take it any way you want," he answers darkly. "I don't break the law, I uphold it, remember?"

"It's hard to sometimes, when I hear that kind of shit."

"Fuck it all." He leans forward on his desk, getting in my face. I don't back off.

"If my boys're lying," he says, "then so is Doc Grade. Merely one of this country's most eminent and respected forensic pathologists. He's lying, too, isn't he, Will?"

I'd thought about that. "Not necessarily," I say.

"Oh, yes, necessarily," John says. "They support each other. Without his testimony, hers is suspect. They go hand-in-glove."

"Not if your boys knew about his theory before they found her," I throw back at him. "Not if they took it and incorporated it into the stuff they fed her."

Robertson snaps his pencil in half. "You're smoking some powerful weed, Will. What else? Maybe she didn't even know them? How about that? Maybe that was a lie, too."

"We know she did," I say. "A hundred people testified to that."

"What if they're all lying, too?" he asks.

I stand. This is going nowhere but bad.

"See you in court, John."

"I'll be there." He looks at me with the conviction of the true believer. "I almost buried you before, Will. This time I'll finish the job."

Or you'll dig your own grave, asshole, I think but don't say as I walk out on him, feeling his eyes on my back even after I close the door behind me.

"RITA. IT'S ME. Will Alexander. Open the door."

I knock again. No answer. It's almost ten at night, she should be here.

"Rita?"

Fuck. Why isn't she here? I talked to her just yesterday, told her I was coming up, to make sure she was there, waiting. Our motion for a new trial is next week, I want to go over everything with her again.

It's been four months since I took her statement, four months since I first broke the news to the boys in the slam, four months since I braced John Robertson in his office. Four nut-cutting months. I've had over two dozen meetings with Robertson. Moseby was in on some of them, although Robertson was careful not to do anything that could prejudice him later: his *número uno* lieutenant could be on the other side someday, a defendant in a perjury and obstruction-of-justice trial, if it ever came to that.

Appeals are automatic at the death-penalty level, the higher courts get involved in all of them, no big deal. Once Robertson calmed down and saw this was legitimate, that I wasn't grandstanding, self-promoting myself into a media-circus dog-and-pony show, he and I agreed to keep it quiet, let it be judged in the courts, not the press.

It'll be a bombshell when it hits, though. The closer we come to the hearing date the less sleep I've gotten; I'm not alone there, I'm sure Robertson, my fellow lawyers, his people, the bikers, everyone connected who knows it's coming down has done his or her share of eyeballing the ceiling at 3:00 A.M.

"Come on, Rita, open up." I knock again, harder.

From behind doors up and down the corridor I hear muffled televisions, stereos, the usual evening noises. Behind her door, though, it's silent.

"Rita!"

I pound. Nothing.

She isn't there. After I told her when I was coming, made her repeat my instructions back to me. Goddam it, why the fuck aren't you here, you scuzzy bitch? Why does nine-tenths of my life revolve around this cretin, this piece of flotsam?

She's fucking somebody: that's it. She's with a man behind this door that I'm at this point practically knocking down; my knuckles'll start bleeding soon if I keep pounding this hard. She picked up some sailor (sailor? not in Denver; some cowboy), is even now spreading her legs for him, her practiced juicy snatch awaiting his pleasure. Or maybe it's one of the detectives we're paying to keep tabs on her. Let's face it, the profession isn't what it was when Sam Spade was prowling the mean streets.

Talk about your primal love-hate relationship; I need her desperately and hate her passionately at one and the same time.

Too bad. I hate to break up a love-tryst but business before pleasure. I have a key to the place; I made sure of that. I take it out, unlock the door.

"Honey, I'm home." I push the door open, like Ricky Ricardo used to do, wondering what Lucy was cooking up this time. Play it cool, ace, she's everything to you.

Like the song says, the light's on, but there's no one home. Shit scattered around: a couple days' dishes in the sink, food in the fridge, the closets half-empty, ditto the drawers, some of her toilet-articles are still in the bathroom. She threw together what she could grab fast. Not a leisurely exit; she took off running scared.

Flown the coop. Gone.

Mary Lou flies up the next morning. We scour the town: bars, hotels, motels, YWCAs, restaurants, anyplace someone on the run could be hiding out. Greyhound, Amtrak, the airlines. Nothing, which is no more than I expected. I don't know her friends, if she has any, how much money she had, how big a jump she got on me. If she bailed right after our last conversation she could be anywhere now, including out of the country.

We spend two days looking. It's like trying to find a needle in a haystack, worse; because we don't know where the haystack is, if there is one.

She could be dead.

I try to put that thought out of my mind, but I can't help it. She could've been gotten to. I warned her, over and over, don't make friends, don't give anyone your phone number, don't bring anyone home. Above all, don't go to the cops for any reason. They are *not* your friends. They'd like to see you out of the way worse than anyone, because you're a potential cop-killer, destroyer of their deepest, closest bonds.

And they knew she was up here; they'd sent her. They've had four months, four months is plenty of time for the police to find someone when they want to. The Denver cops would've helped them, if not actively, at least by getting out of the way.

That's a chilling thought. Robertson wouldn't countenance that, ever. I know Moseby doesn't have the balls to do something that desperate, but Gomez and Sanchez; who knows? A long shot; but long shots happen sometimes.

More likely, the reality, the terrifying prospect of having to go back to Santa Fe, go to court, face the men who'd set her up, was too much for her to handle. It wasn't her fault that she got raped, that she knew some shitheel who got himself killed by the same bunch of bad guys who'd raped her, threatened her life. She was a victim, that's all. She doesn't want to be a victim anymore.

I can understand it. For the first time, I feel for her.

"Now what?" Mary Lou asks.

"I don't know. You got any ideas?"

We're in a lounge at Stapleton Airport, waiting for our flight to Albuquerque. We've been here less than a half-hour and I'm three Johnnie Blacks to the good. Every time I try to cut down on my drinking this kind of shit happens.

"I've never been to Hawaii," she says.

"Did you pack a bathing suit?"

"I brought my American Express Gold Card. Same difference."

We look at each other in despair. I signal the waitress for another round.

"Will . . ." A cautioning.

"What the fuck's the difference?" I feel so bad I want to cry. "I'm entitled. I'm drinking for five."

"They wouldn't want you to. I don't either."

"They pay me for my advice, not the other way around," I say, wallowing in my angry self-pity.

"I don't."

"Aw babe," I wail, "come on, lighten up, please? I don't deserve to be lectured at. Not tonight."

"All right." She shrugs, washing her hands of it.

Shit. I hate it when someone gives in that way. Victory through guilt-tripping.

The waitress comes over to take our order. I put my hand over my glass.

"Changed my mind," I smile wanly. She walks away. I glare at Mary Lou. "Happy?"

"Yes," she says. "So . . ."

"I don't know." I drain my glass, licking the last drop of Scotch off the ice-cubes.

"We'd better find her," she says. "We can."

She takes my hand across the table, kisses the palm.

"We can do it," she says. "We will. We have to."

"MISS GOMEZ HAS THE FLU, your honor. She's running a temperature and she's unable to get out of bed. I have a note from her doctor."

I hand it up. Martinez glances at it. It's not a forgery; a real doctor in Boulder wrote and signed it. There just wasn't a real patient, but the doctor was a friend of a friend.

"How long a postponement would you like, counselor?" he asks politely.

I look over my shoulder. Robertson and Moseby glare at me; they're not liking this, they know I'm vamping. Robertson doesn't know the real skinny, he thinks I'm milking this for maximum effect, but he doesn't suspect the truth. Moseby I check out extra hard; if he's in on her disappearance he's doing a better job of covering than I give him credit for.

"I'm sure a week'll be sufficient, your honor. We want to make sure she's well enough to travel and hold up under the strain of the hearing."

"Objection?" Martinez asks.

Robertson could bitch and moan, but he knows the judge'll give me this one.

"No, your honor. Not if it's one week."

"A week from Tuesday," Judge Martinez says, consulting his calendar. "That's a week and a half, Mr. Alexander."

"Thank you, your honor. We'll be here."

"Are you ready, Mr. Alexander?"

"We have a problem, your honor."

"Are you telling the court you're not ready, counselor?" he asks, harshly.

"My witness is missing."

"Excuse me?"

Behind me, Robertson and his contingent are talking rapidly among themselves.

"We are unable to locate Rita Gomez at the present time. She has . . . uh . . . she's vanished from sight, or at least from our best efforts to find her," I tell him, lamely.

At this particular moment, if the earth were to open up and swallow me whole, it would be a blessing.

I've never worked as hard in my life as I did in this last week and a half. I flew back to Denver right after I got the postponement. Mary Lou came with me. She's been incredible; everything you want in a partner and a woman. She took all her vacation time to do it. When, if, this is ever over, I'll owe her a bunch, which I'll gladly pay.

To their credit, the detective agency pitched in mightily. Three men, two hundred a day each plus expenses, all of which they waived. We'd had words when first Rita had disappeared, but as they logically stated, they couldn't have been responsible for her every waking moment unless we'd hired a live-in, and we hadn't; we didn't think it was necessary, and we couldn't have afforded it anyway. Everyone we knew in Denver, every lawyer, old friend, acquaintance, everyone we could enlist to help find her, we called on. Thousands of phone calls. Every bar, restaurant, flophouse. The hospitals and morgues. Everything in a hundred-mile radius was covered like a blanket. And she didn't turn up; not a trace, not a faint odor to track.

"She could be anywhere," Mary Lou said one night, late, when we'd collapsed in our hotel room. "It's two weeks."

"I don't think she's left town," I answered, stubbornly. "At least not the general area." I believed it; I don't know why, but I did. "I think she's gone to ground. She's with a friend, slipped through a crack somewhere." I'm convinced of that; that she was too scared to form a plan, that all she could do was bolt mindlessly for the nearest safe hole, like the rabbit she is, and hope that if she's still enough, the hunters won't find her.

"You want to believe that, Will."

"That's right."

"So do I. But we've got to face what happens if we don't find her."

I know already. It's not faceable.

The head of the detective agency was embarrassed.

"I've never run up against one this cold," he told me.

"You did your best."

"We'll keep looking informally. No charge."

I thanked him, went outside. Mary Lou was waiting for me in the cab. We rode to the airport and flew home.

Mary Lou checked in with Mercado. Dead-end there as well. Rita had wised up—no electronic trail this time. It was our last dying-gasp hope.

That was yesterday.

Martinez looks down at me from his perch on high.

"Do you have any idea where Miss Gomez is at the present time, Mr. Alexander?"

"No, sir. Not precisely."

"In general? Anything?"

"No."

"Are you asking for another postponement?" he says.

"Under these special circumstances, I would like one, your honor, yes."

"Objection, your honor!" Robertson cries out, jumping up. "There's no basis at all for another postponement. The first one was dubious but this would be completely uncalled for."

The judge looks at him, at me.

"If I were to grant you another postponement could you give the court any reassurances whatsoever that you could find this witness? That there is a reasonable chance that she could be brought into this courtroom in a reasonable time?"

"No, your honor. I can't make such reassurances."

"Then we'll have to proceed without her," he so informs me.

Martinez has looked at Rita's video.

"Do you have anything further to add?" he asks. "Any other witnesses or anything in corroboration, in addition?"

"No, your honor," I say. "The deposition stands on its own."

Robertson tears it to shreds. His job isn't difficult; any reasonably competent first-year law student could do it. She claims she was lying then and telling the truth now; why not the opposite? One statement's as acceptable as the other.

He puts Gomez on the stand.

"Did you do any of this stuff that she says you did?"

"No."

Sanchez: "No. A pack of lies from beginning to end."

Moseby turns to Martinez, to me, to Robertson. He's wearing a clean, pressed shirt. A first.

"Not only didn't I do any of these things," he says, "I bent over backwards to make sure that what she was telling us then was true, because of the kind of person she is. I checked and double-checked every aspect of her story. I have never treated a witness this way; I have never broken the law this way, or bent it even a little. I feel like *I'm* on trial here," he says, very aggrieved, "and I'm not. And I resent Mr. Alexander here bringing these kind of trumped-up charges against me and these policemen. You try to do your job for the community and this is the thanks you get."

I stand in front of the bench.

"If it may please the court: I move for a new trial, based on the new evidence presented in this motion and the video statement," I say.

"I am against a new trial," Robertson tells them. "Vehemently against one. We should nail this case shut, right here, right now. This is nothing but a desperate attempt at overturning a fair and just trial. A pitiable, desperate attempt that anyone can see right through. It's beneath the dignity of this court to even consider such a mockery of justice, of our system of laws."

He piles it on nice and thick, in case Martinez doesn't get it.

Without elaboration, Martinez denies our motion. He spends less than twenty minutes deliberating; he had nothing to deliberate.

Slam fucking dunk.

I'VE NEVER FELT SO SHITTY and impotent in my life as I do at this moment, and I've been practically making a career of feeling that way the last couple of years. Even when Holly left me, or when Andy and Fred gave me the boot, or when Patricia moved; even at the end of the trial, when the ground collapsed under us. These men have put their lives in my hands and I've failed them, utterly failed them again, and worse than that, I raised their hopes and now I have to bury them.

The warden, a decent man, does me a big favor; he lets me meet with all four of them at the same time. Technically, it's against the rules, but it's his prison, he can run it pretty much the way he sees fit, as long as things are cool, which they are.

It's the first time the four of them have laid eyes on each other since they were put away, almost a year ago. There's an impulse to grab each other and hug, squeeze as hard as they can, but they know better: touching is strictly verboten, one high-five could stop this meeting before it starts, buy them additional penalties besides the standard ones they're already enduring; complete lockdowns or worse. So they hug psychically, their eyes bright with love.

These four men, the four toughest, scariest human beings I've ever known, are desperate for love; the way they are here, now, in front of me, is proof that the meanest animal can be tamed if he's in prison long enough. I am a cynical man, I have always been a cynic, with good reason, but a moment like this reinforces the belief that there is such a thing as rehabilitation, that even the blackest sinner can turn to the light. (I sound like one of those jive-ass TV evangelists, Jim Bakker or one of those scuzzballs, but it is true.)

We're in one large room; no Plexiglas separating us this time. They'd heard the news, even before I called and told them, a jailhouse grapevine's faster than AT&T, but they don't know what it really means. So she didn't show; sooner or later she'll have to, and then we can press ahead again. She's the state's key witness, if she's turned they have to grant a new trial, isn't that the way it is? It's a matter of time; isn't it?

"So you mean even if she shows," Roach asks, "it won't matter?"

"Probably not."

"Why the fuck not?" Dutchboy; he doesn't get it at all.

Lone Wolf says nothing; his eyes are flat, fixed on me.

"Because . . ." I am getting a migraine the size of Rhode Island. "Because you can only go to the well so often; they don't let you keep coming back whenever you feel like it. We could've been denied the first time, our original petition. We were lucky to get back in. They don't give you a second chance in this game; not usually," I conclude miserably.

"But she admitted she lied," the kid says.

"Doesn't matter." We all turn to Lone Wolf. It's the first time he's opened his mouth. "Does it?" he asks me.

"No."

"Why?" Dutchboy persists.

He doesn't understand, this twenty-two-year-old man-child. Doesn't want to; to understand, understand and thus acknowledge, is to be resigned to never leaving this place, outside of being carried out in a coffin.

"There's a procedure," I explain. I want them all to understand; everything I know. "There are rules laid out for an appeal. You can't keep going back to the courts every time you think you have something new, especially if you've already gone to them with a specific, like we did with this perjured testimony. Otherwise people would spend their whole lives doing it, and the state could never kill anyone or bury them alive in joints like this forever, and the state doesn't like that. The state wants its pound of flesh."

"So even if the whole case is built on a lie," Goose asks, "it doesn't matter if they can slide by on a technicality."

"That's right." He knows; he's always known.

"I can't believe this," Roach says. He's shaking, his leg tap-dancing under the table. He's the most volatile of them, he could go right now.

"It's like that movie," Dutchboy says. "About that guy in Texas. You know."

"*The Thin Blue Line*," Goose prompts.

"Yeh. That guy'd still be in there. 'Cause some punk lied and the cops wanted to believe him. Like us. Shit, I'll bet this kind of shit happens all the time," he marvels.

"No," I tell him. "Thank God it doesn't. But it does sometimes, and each time is too much."

"Especially when it's you," Roach says.

"So even if she shows," Goose repeats; he wants to be absolutely sure he knows what's going on; "even if she shows and swears on a stack of Bibles, it won't matter now."

"I can't say. But the odds are against us," I tell them. "Not only because she didn't show this time," I elaborate, "but because she's a liar, she's saying 'I lied then but I'm telling the truth now.' One cancels the other. Who's to say she's telling the truth now, that she wasn't telling the truth then, and is lying now? It's happened before."

The silence fills the room.

"So now what?" Roach finally asks. "What do we do now, just fucking lie down and wait to die?"

"No," I say, "we keep going. There's other avenues. I'm certainly going to try to find her and force another hearing, but even if that doesn't happen there are other avenues. Years of them."

"Technicalities," Lone Wolf says flatly.

"Mostly," I concede. "But they have worked before."

"Yeh," he sneers. "To keep 'em from dropping the load on you. A lifetime inside instead of the death penalty. Whoopee," he adds without mirth.

I tell them straight: right now it's all we have.

We talk a little longer. Human contact of any kind is gold to them. Then there's nothing more to say. They're led out, handcuffed and manacled, taken back to their cells, not to see each other again for God knows how long.

Lone Wolf's the last to go. As he's shuffling out, the heavy chains hanging from him like shrouds, he fixes me with a look.

"What's the point?" he asks.

"You're still alive, man." I make my point as forcefully as I can. "Anything's possible as long as you're still alive."

"Depends," he says. "On what side you're standing on."

They take him away.

I'm scared. It's dangerous to hold out hope to a desperate man and then yank it away. It makes him crazy. It would make me crazy.

Crazy people do crazy things. Fuck the consequences.

IT'S AFTER MIDNIGHT. I sit in my dark office and look out over the town, what I can see of it from here, the dark adobes, in the distance the state offices, all dark now. I'm alone.

I feel that I'm at a crossroads in my life. I have felt that before, it seems to be a continuing motif in my life, feeling that I'm at a crossroads and thinking about being at that crossroads, wherever it happens to be at the time. I've always had a strongly melodramatic side to my personality; it's served me well in the courtrooms but has, I'm afraid, now that I'm finally looking at it, hurt the rest of me. It has cost me dear relationships. It has forced me to imagine slights where none were present, or were small. I have had the need to build my molehills of annoyance into mountains of pain, until the pain became real and I lashed out at the causes of it, not at myself, the core cause, but at the reasons I'd built up in my mind. I am one of those people who would cut off his nose to spite his face. I have never gotten past that childish pose. There is something in me that wants to hurt me. A psychologist would probably say I don't feel worthy of good things, so I make sure I don't get them. That may be. But it is costing me the most important things in my life, the things that, when I'm not reveling in my self-pity, make me feel good, feel alive. I'm full of bile towards Andy and Fred, but I liked them once, there was a lot of strong feeling between us, we created something important together that had some lasting power; it outlasted me. And I fucked it up. It wasn't them; it was me. It's been so long since Patricia and I split up that I don't remember the specifics anymore, but I'm sure there was much of the same behavior; the preening, the need to be on-stage all the time, to be top dog, to bully and control. I concede that it undoubtedly would have ended the same way, ultimately, but I know that the reason I feel unresolved about it is because of who I am and how I was. Not a man; not a real man.

I'm afraid I'm going to be that way with Mary Lou, and I don't want to be. I'm beginning to fear that part of my destiny in life is to fuck up the things that mean the most to me. That scares me.

All this started hitting me as I drove back from prison this afternoon, finished the day, said good night to Susan, diddled around, pretending to work. I didn't want to leave tonight; I don't know why. Maybe I don't want to stop thinking about this stuff; going home, going to bed, will end it, this episode, and who knows what the morning will bring?

What happened was, I was thinking about the bikers on the drive back into town. About the raw deal they were getting, how it was cutting their lives short, how hard it was on them, them more than most, because they were outlaws, outlaws in the romantic sense of the word, whose very essence is to run wild and free like mustangs, and how being caged up was for them more than being in a physical box, it was shutting down their souls, their core beings. And without really realizing it I was empathizing with them, being an imaginary one of them, an outlaw lawyer and his outlaw biker clients; and I was liking the connection: the Hunter Thompson of lawyers. Conjuring about riding on a motorcycle across the mountains and valleys, a biker chick behind me, hugging my manly back, drinking and whoring and all that good shit. Of course, it would not be a vocation like theirs, but an occasional fantasy, one I could dip in and out of at will. It would be neat, like being a rock star would be neat, hanging out with Mick Jagger and the boys. An outlaw celebrity.

And then the absurdity of it hit me. The bullshit absurdity of it. These men aren't romantic heroes; they're criminals. They rape and pillage and hurt people, and take delight in doing so. I'm forty years old and that's what I aspire to? How immature am I, not even deep down but right up front? Would I want my wife (if I ever have one again) or my girl-friend, or for that matter any lady-friend of mine, or worst of all, God forbid, my daughter, to be with one of those men for one second? Fuck, what is wrong with me that this kind of silly, shallow, chicken-shit imagery is attractive to me? What's missing in me that feels the need to emulate or admire one shred of their beings?

So that's why I'm sitting here. Because I feel the need to think about these things.

I want to grow up, is what I think it is. I'm tired of this life I've been living, this eternal provoking, chasing demons that don't exist, making them up so they then do exist, and letting them push me around. Tired of fucking up my life in the noble cause of teenage romanticism. Part of me has never gotten past that kind of shit and it's got to end. James Dean is dead; or something.

I drink, therefore I am. I play at being the badass, I bail out, I want never to have responsibilities; real ones, that hurt but can't be helped. I wear a tie but deep down think of myself as a road warrior. The eternal kid.

But shit happens. Life goes on. I am not a romantic outlaw, and those men in jail, much as I want to help them and will do everything I can for them, are not me. Not the slightest bit.

We will go on, still tied in a sense, but separate.

"HAPPY BIRTHDAY TO YOU, happy birthday to you, happy birthday dear Claudia, happy birthday to you . . ." A cappella yet. Her friends sing her birthday to her, still pre-teens and so hip, they own the world.

Eleven years old. My child who is no longer a child, who is changing before my very eyes. Since I don't see her every week like I used to (a month can go by, more, although I try religiously to be with her one week-end a month, my frequent-flyer miles'll buy me a trip around the world pretty soon) each new time we get together is a shock, because the change is startlingly visible, she's at a time in her life where things move fast, like the stop-action photography they use in nature documentaries, watching the flower grow and unfold in thirty seconds, the clouds move across the sky from dawn to dusk in an eyeblink. On her last visit here she confided in me that one of her friends, who's just a couple months older than Claudia, had started her period. I winced, visibly. Now there's three of them, as if once it gets started it becomes an avalanche. Biologically capable of having babies? And they want bras, period or not, tits or not. Training bras in the fifth grade; I took her out to the mall one Saturday afternoon, she ran across some of her friends, after the giggling and gossiping and catching up they gravitated to the lingerie section, checking out the starter bras, snickering to beat the band, looking around to see if the parents were watching. Claudia seems less into that stuff than most of them, fortunately; at least what I know from what I see and what she tells me, but I'm not sure if she tells me everything anymore, like she used to. Each time we see each other now there's that period of adjustment between us; an hour or less, but it's palpable, it hangs over us, I'm not part of the routine, I'm not there for her, whether I want to be or not. She's still an innocent, I can tell from her conversation, even when she's trying to be grown-up. Her mother was a late bloomer, it could be two or three more years before she has to worry about Tampax and the rest. Still, when your own mother has silicone tits, you know the score. I read recently (I notice stuff like this that I never noticed before) that there's an epidemic of early maturation which has to do with the stress that kids are under these days, that they're being forced to grow up faster. I don't know, I think kids have always led desperate lives; I do know I want to hold onto her childhood as long as I can.

It's a warm day. The party's north of town, at my friend Lucas's ranch (the erstwhile hippie developer), the fellow whose streams Claudia and I were fishing when the body of Richard Bartless was found and everything started. It's a beautiful spread, besides the stables and houses there's a tennis court, a swimming pool, and a Jacuzzi. Lucas not only remained my client and friend when I broke off from the firm, he steers business to me, often at the direct expense of Fred and Andy. Lucas gets a kick out of that. He thinks they're puritans, too quick to condemn. That's 'cause I drink with him and they don't; I like to read a valuable lesson in this.

He and Dorothy don't have kids of their own, they're way too hedonistic to let anyone else into their lives, but they've always loved Claudia, they lavish presents on her at any opportunity, and today's no exception: they've given her a $500 Kachina, and a squash-blossom necklace. She's old enough now to appreciate such things, and she ooohs and aaahs over them appropriately.

I should, but don't, protest such lavishness from them. I wouldn't let anyone else spoil her this way, but I figure one set of rich god-parents is permissible. You have to get along with all kinds in this world, she might as well get used to it properly.

The party is half a dozen of Claudia's best friends, all girls. All so happy to be with each other. Seattle's okay, but this is home.

The ranch is all decked out, rodeo-style. Each girl has been assigned a horse of her own for the day. We spend the morning riding up into the foothills to the east, seven little girls in jeans and riding helmets, guiding their horses up the trails. I bring up the rear, video camera on my shoulder, trying to keep the image steady as I chronicle everything about the day for posterity, for her to look at when she's grown, for her kids; for myself when she's grown and much farther away than a two-hour plane ride.

"My dad's cutting the cake," she tells everyone. "Save me the piece with the rose, daddy."

The girls are in their bathing suits. It's late afternoon, hot. The party's winding down, we'll eat our cake and ice-cream and head on home. Without meaning to, I notice the shapes of some of her friends.

They have curves, some of these children. Budding little breasts and hips. They don't seem to be aware of any sexuality, but maybe they are; I don't know. I do remember kissing girls in fifth grade, and making out in sixth. And I lived in the country.

"Delicious cake," Ellie Godswiling says. We're sitting on lounge chairs at the edge of the pool. Her daughter is one of the guests. Ellie's come to help schlepp some of the girls home.

The girls are sprawled out on the grass nearby. They're talking freely, laughing, unselfconscious. I'd asked Claudia if she wanted any boys. 'Boys would be a drag,' she'd told me. 'It would all be posing. I want to be the center of attention.'

"Is it home-made?" Ellie asks.

"Sure," I say. "From scratch."

"I didn't mean you," she says, blushing slightly. "I thought maybe your girl-friend baked it."

"Girl-friend?"

"Claudia told Maria you had a steady. Someone from work," she says, half questioningly.

I look up at her, squinting against the afternoon light. Is she coming on to me? She's my age, divorced, zaftig in a nice way.

"Not really," I lie lazily. Nothing's going to come of this, I just feel like playing, to see where it might go.

"Oh," she says.

"It's store-bought. From Lukavitch," I say.

"No wonder," she exclaims. "Theirs is better than home-made. My home-made anyway," she says, smiling tentatively. I think she is on the make but doesn't know how to go about it; probably isn't dating much, maybe not at all. She leans forward slightly as she delicately forks some cake into her mouth, showing me a glimpse of cleavage. Big, soft breasts, lightly freckled on top. She'd be a loving, sloppy fuck, not to be attempted in total sobriety.

I could do that. I could work it out so we were thrown together tonight. A generous offer on daddy's part: we'll continue the party at my place, Claudia can have them all over for pizza, I know she misses her friends and wants to see as much of them in the limited time she's here as she can, she's told me so. I get jealous sometimes, wanting her all to myself, but there's time for me. She makes sure of that, too.

The girls are old enough to be left alone for a little while in the evening, and I'd make book that Ellie would find a way to show up, she'd have some excuse, like she was afraid I didn't have enough cups or plates or Cokes. We could leave the girls and go to a nearby bar for a quick drink, to escape the commotion. One drink would lead to three, she'd be too high to drive, I'd offer to give her a lift home, it's not far. And then of course walking her to her door, since I'm a gentleman, and then a friendly goodnight kiss, which would turn to passion and groping and all the rest. I could do that, but it would be cruel. Even so, I could. Sitting here looking at her freckled breasts and soft, heavy body, the prospect is mildly exciting. Mildly.

What would be truly exciting would be to jump Mary Lou's bones and go for one of our marathon fucks. We had agreed to stay apart for the weekend. She didn't want to horn in on Claudia's time with me. A noble gesture, more noble, as I sit here pondering it, in the thinking than the actual doing. Claudia's becoming more comfortable with Mary Lou, but when I'm with both of them my attention's divided. Claudia deserves me to herself on her birthday. If I get desperate I can swing by Mary Lou's Sunday evening after I put Claudia on the airplane.

I put the thought of fucking Ellie out of my mind. If she were to rape me I couldn't resist, but the new me wants to be good. I'd like to believe that I'm strong enough to pull that kind of behavior off; I never have been before.

"Did you have fun, dad?"

"Yes. Did you?"

"It was the greatest party I've ever had," she tells me.

"I'm glad. You sure did okay with the loot."

"I love my new doll."

The Kachina's sitting in the place of honor on her shelf, right next to Teddy and Penguin, her oldest and favorite dolls, the ones she takes to bed with her at night.

"And the necklace," she says. "Lucas and Dorothy are nice."

"They love you. You're practically a daughter to them."

"I only have one daddy," she says, snuggling up to me. "And he's the greatest."

"Thank you, my angel." Jesus, that I might have given up this evening for a sloppy piece of ass. Or even a good piece of ass, you never can tell. It doesn't matter; this is better, the difference isn't even measurable.

"I only have one daughter, and she's the greatest," I add.

"We're a family of greatests," she says.

"That we are."

"Mommy, too. She's great."

"Yes, she is."

We're momentarily quiet; that bears reflection.

"Mom misses you."

"She does?" She does?; where is this coming from?

She nods. "A lot."

"I don't think so," I say. I don't like where this conversation's going all of a sudden; I want to change directions before it becomes significant.

"She's fond of me," I say, groping along, "we've always been friends even though we haven't lived together for a long time, and she might miss something about that. I miss her too, but that's because she's always been here and I've always seen her because of you. That's probably how she feels about me, too. That's all. She's got a whole new life, it's real full, her new job's much more challenging than the old one was, it probably gets to her sometimes, she probably says something like 'it was so much easier in Santa Fe,' something like that."

I look at her; am I making sense?

"That's true," she says, "it was much easier. A lot easier for me; a lot better, too. I could see you whenever I wanted, not just once a month."

"It's almost summer vacation," I remind her. "You'll be with me all summer."

"It's not the same."

How could it be?

"But it's nice up there in Seattle," I tell her. "You have some nice new friends, the ones I've met. You told me that yourself, that you liked the kids up there."

"Yeh but they're not my *friends* like here. Real friends."

"They will be. It takes time."

She doesn't believe that. I'm hearing the words out of my mouth and I'm not believing it, and she's got a bullshit detector more sensitive than radar.

"I want to move back," she says.

"I don't think that's possible, honey. Not now."

"Why not?"

"Because."

"Because why?"

"Because mom's your mother and a young girl needs to be with her mother. Most of the time."

"What if I was a boy?"

"I don't think it would matter. Anyway, you're not."

"You always said it didn't matter if I was a girl or a boy."

"It doesn't."

"Then why should it matter if I'm a girl and I want to live with you?"

"I didn't mean it that way. Kids usually need to be with their mothers."

"But not always," she says. "You and I get along perfectly well, don't we?"

"Of course we do."

"Then why should it matter?"

Jesus. I'm supposed to be one of the best lawyers in town, a behemoth of argument, and she's kicking my ass.

"I guess that part wouldn't."

She smiles up at me: see?

"But that's not the only reason," I say.

"I know what you're going to say," she tells me.

"What?"

"That I'm getting to be a young lady, and a young lady needs her mother's guidance." She makes her voice sound like an adult's; like Patricia's.

"Well . . . that's true."

"Mary Lou could help me with that stuff," she says.

"Mary Lou?"

"Isn't she your girl-friend?"

"Sort of." I feel like I'm on the witness stand, being grilled.

"So she could."

"That's not her role. That's your mother's role."

"Mom doesn't have time for that stuff these days. She's working her buns off," she says.

Ah so.

"So do I," I venture cautiously.

"You're supposed to."

"What does that mean?"

"Fathers are supposed to work like that. She's a mother."

"Mary Lou works that hard," I say.

"She wouldn't if she had a kid," she retorts.

"I can't answer that because she doesn't have a kid, and it doesn't matter anyway because Patricia's your mother and Mary Lou isn't. They're different."

"I hardly see mom," she says with anger. This has obviously been building, and now it's erupting. "Sometimes I go to bed before she gets home. I'm sick of it!" she exclaims with real vehemence.

Shit. How in the world did it ever come to this? Why should she be the one that has to bear the brunt of our ambitions? She's a kid, she deserves a parent who's there. I wonder if Patricia truly knows what's going on.

"Mom has a new job," I say, trying to be patient, to fairly present her side. "Sometimes it can't be helped. It'll change soon."

"What if it doesn't?"

"Look. School's out in a month, you'll be with me all summer, we'll play it by ear okay?"

"I don't have any choice, do I?"

That's a good question.

"I don't," she says.

"Don't you think your mom's feelings would be hurt?" I ask.

"I don't know. Maybe. I don't know."

"You've been her whole life practically. I think it would hurt her a lot."

"I'm not anymore. Her whole life." She leans on her elbow, looking at me. "What about you? Aren't I important to you, too?"

"The most important thing in the world."

"So then?"

"I've had things she hasn't," I say. "I'm more successful, I've made more money . . ."

"She makes a lot of money now. More than you I'll bet."

"Maybe." Shit, that's all I need. Claudia sitting there calculating which parent is making more money.

"And I was married again, which she wasn't . . ."

"You hated it. It was worse than not being married. You told me so yourself," she says. She's got me cards and spades.

"And I'm in a great relationship now," I say.

"With Mary Lou."

"Yes."

"How come she didn't come today?"

"She didn't want to horn in on your parade."

"You wouldn't have let her, would you?"

"No."

"She should've come. She would've had fun."

"I'll tell her that. She'll be glad to hear it," I say.

"She sounds like I'd like her," Claudia tells me.

"She'd like you, too," I say.

"That's important," she says. "In case you marry her."

Damn, but she's fast. "We don't even talk about that, Claudia."

"Someday you might. I just wanted to let you know that I like her. In case you were interested."

"Thanks."

My mind is racing. Children are notoriously prescient; is she divining something I'm not aware of?

"That's what mom needs," she continues.

"To get married? I don't think she has the time to think about it with this new job, do you?"

"She does anyway."

"How do you know? Does she tell you?"

"She doesn't tell me anything anymore," she says. "She *orders* me."

"Are you sure you aren't exaggerating?"

"No. Everything she says is an order. She's always mad at me."

"Claudia . . ."

"She is. She's always losing her temper now. No matter what I do she doesn't like it."

"It's the new job," I say. "It must be really hard on her, much more work than she's used to. She isn't used to it, and she's feeling guilty about not spending more time with you, so she acts like that. You know she loves you."

"Yeh," she answers with no enthusiasm.

Our hot chocolate's gone cold. I put it back in the saucepan to heat it up. She pads into the kitchen after me. She's in her nightgown, ready for bed. It's after ten, past her bed-time. I thought we were going to have some cocoa and a quick, easy talk.

"She's dating, isn't she?" I ask. "She told me she was seeing some nice fellows."

"Creeps."

"Not all of them, I'm sure."

"All of them. I'm sure. Mom hardly dates the same guy more than once."

"She has high standards."

"They're all creeps. I wouldn't let any of them near me."

"She'll find someone," I say. "Now that she's prosperous and confident it's just a matter of time."

"I don't care. Sometimes I think she's afraid to."

Out of the mouths of babes . . .

The phone rings as I'm pouring the hot chocolate back into our cups. Claudia answers, listens a moment, hands it to me.

"Are you watching TV?"

"What?"

It's Mary Lou. "Turn on your TV." She sounds really wound up.

"What channel?"

"Any of them. All of them."

"What'm I looking for?"

"Just turn it on! I'm coming over." She hangs up abruptly.

I hand Claudia her chocolate, walk into the living room, flick the television set on. There's a queasiness in my stomach that seems to be growing.

"As soon as you've finished your chocolate," I tell her, "it's teeth and bed. *Comprende?*"

"On my birthday?"

"It's almost ten-thirty. Drink and go . . ." I stop short as the picture on my television screen comes into focus.

The state penitentiary is on the screen. Searchlights illuminate the sky, moving back and forth behind the wire fences where the cameras are positioned, outside the main gates. There are no lights coming from inside; the only lights to be seen are the fires, several of them, coming from different buildings. The images are all in long shot; it's a couple hundred yards away from where the cameras are to any of the buildings behind the fences.

Dozens of policemen, state troopers, and firemen are milling around the front. Police cars and fire trucks, television camera trucks, other vehicles are jammed into the parking lot and the dirt areas around it. It's all confusion, milling around, men can be heard yelling offscreen, voices yelling on top of each other. It's chaos.

An announcer steps in front of the camera. Behind him, from inside the walls, there's a sudden explosion. The announcer instinctively cowers, covering his head. Then another explosion; a fireball flares into the sky from one of the prison building roofs.

The announcer composes himself, turns to the camera. He's jittery; this place could explode, for all he knows, eight hundred prisoners, armed to the teeth, could come rushing out any minute.

"The best information authorities out here can get," he says in a shaky voice, "is that what apparently started as a spontaneous argument over allegedly rancid food served at dinner has erupted into a full-scale riot inside the prison. Prisoners in building four, a medium-security building that allows free movement within its walls, overwhelmed their guards, took the guards as hostages, stormed the other buildings and shut the prison down from the inside. They forced guards and prison authorities to open all the cells in all the buildings, including the maximum-security unit, where men are kept in individual cells under twenty-four-hour lockup."

Death Row. My guys are out now: animals released from their cages, prowling the halls. Doing God knows what.

Claudia looks at me.

"Daddy . . ." she says, her voice shaking. She knows about the prisoners, about my involvement.

"Go to bed, honey."

"Dad . . ."

"Go to bed. Now. I don't want you watching this."

"All right." She's unusually docile. She doesn't want to see any of this, either.

I give her a hug and a quick peck on the cheek. She leaves the room. I squat on my haunches in front of the screen, watching.

The warden materializes on camera. He's disheveled, his face black with smoke and grease, his hair and clothes awry. He's calm, though, at least outwardly; this is what they pay him for. He wants to show the public that they're getting their money's worth, and he wants to hang onto his job.

"Could you give us an update on what the situation inside the prison is at the present moment, Warden Gates?" the announcer asks.

"I don't know what it is," the warden answers bluntly. "Nobody knows right now. We don't have any communication with anyone in the cellblocks. They've cut all the lines."

"What do you plan to do?"

"Try to get some kind of communication going," the warden snaps. "That's the first thing. We've got to find out what's going on, what the situation is, what they want."

"How many hostages have they taken?" the announcer asks.

"Don't know that either." A couple straight-forward questions and the warden's turning testy; he's lost control of his prison, the worst thing that could happen to him. "At least half a dozen guards, probably more. And several prisoners, trusties."

"Have there been any killings?"

The warden looks back at the buildings. Flames are shooting out of some of the windows, especially in one area, the number one maximum-security unit.

"Yes."

The warden is abruptly pulled away by some of his people. The announcer continues.

"At this moment," he says, "there is utter confusion here. No one outside, including the prison officials, knows what is going on inside." He turns around to look at someone behind him. It's the warden again, coming to the microphone with a piece of paper in his hand.

"I have a statement to make," the warden says. "We have some more information; although it isn't completely substantiated, it comes from a reliable source who was inside when the rioting started, and seems to make sense." His face is set in a grim mask; he's angrier than he was earlier. He's getting more frightened by the minute as well; I can almost smell the fear coming off the screen.

"It is now believed that the riot was not a spontaneous action," he reads, "but was something that had been planned for months. This past week half-a-dozen men, hard-core prisoners who had previously been living in one of our maximum-security units, were transferred to the medium-security building where the riot started, to alleviate over-crowding in the maximum-security unit, a move mandated by court order." He shakes his head in disgust. "I didn't like that order and I told the court so, that it could be dangerous, but they said they didn't have a choice, we don't have enough facilities to house our prisoners and these men had to be moved. So I moved them. It is now my understanding," he says, his voice practically choking with angry emotion, "that these men had planned this incident while in the maximum-security facility, knowing they were to be transferred out."

That makes sense; that makes a whole lot of sense. Prisoners don't take over an entire prison spontaneously. They've probably been thinking and planning this for months, maybe years.

Mary Lou lets herself in. She's in a T-shirt and jeans, no makeup. She comes over, gives my hand a quick, reassuring squeeze, flops down next to me.

"Did you hear?" I ask.

"What the warden just said? Yes, I was listening in the car."

"This could be bad," I say.

"Our boys?"

"They could be dead," I say.

"Do you think so?" She shivers involuntarily; she hadn't thought of that.

"No, but they could be." I've gone into the kitchen, grabbed a couple beers from the fridge, popped the tops. I hand her one.

"More likely," I say, "if there was any killing done, they were part of it."

"God. I hope not. Oh God I hope not."

So do I; but why shouldn't they? They were all geared up for a new trial, a new chance, and the system kicked them in the balls. They've got nothing to lose now; might as well go out in a blaze of glory.

We watch for a couple more hours. It's close to midnight. The coverage is fragmented; lots happening but no real news.

I pick up the phone, start dialing.

"Who are you calling?" she asks.

"Robertson. Maybe he knows something."

"That's a good idea," she says.

"If he'll talk to me," I add.

"He'll talk to you. Why wouldn't he?"

"Because I crossed some bullshit line he drew and he doesn't forget. He's got the memory of an elephant. And the finesse of a pit-bull."

The line is busy. I fidget around for a few minutes, try again. It's still busy. He's in the hot-box; I'll have to wait to find out what's really going on.

We make love. It feels strange, disjointed, in weird juxtaposition with what's going on outside my bedroom walls, but we hunger for each other. It should exhaust me, help me sleep (a good rationale, as if I need one, I still can't stop guilt-tripping myself), but it doesn't. Neither of us can sleep.

So we stay up, almost until dawn, talking. About where we've come from, the disappearance of Rita Gomez, the feeling, felt by both of us, that there's a conspiracy going on inside Robertson's office, a cancer he's unaware of perhaps, but a cancer nonetheless. I feel like John Dean trying to explain Haldeman and Erlichman to Nixon, before Tricky Dick got personally involved; he won't hear, he can't hear, it's too gut-level personal, it would cut at the heart of everything he stands for, everything he is.

Mary Lou and I make love again and finally fall asleep sprawled across each other.

The food had been getting steadily worse. Some days it was inedible, a leper in Calcutta would've rejected it. Then the air-conditioning went down in three of the five cellblocks, and it was an oven inside for a week. Worst hit were the maximum-security units, where the men are confined to their cells twenty hours a day anyway. The warden wanted to bend the rules, let the men go outside during the day, in the yard, he knew he was buying trouble cooping them up under such conditions, but he was vetoed from above, from the state Department of Corrections. Later it was learned the Director of Corrections never even knew about it. Some functionary made the call; as is always the case no one could ever find out who it was.

With all the new mandatory sentencing laws that had been legislated over the past few years the over-crowding had gotten progressively worse; one-man cells had gone to two-man, and then to three men. Three men in a ten-by-twelve-foot space twenty hours a day. With the third bunk in there, there wasn't even room to fart. There had been a dramatic increase in fights; that was inevitable. Within the past year three inmates had been killed by other inmates.

And while the air-conditioning was down the prison kitchen, which was notorious for cutting corners, served some bad meat that was clearly rotten, you could tell just by looking at it. Over two hundred men came down with severe food poisoning. The prison infirmary couldn't handle that number of patients, so the sick men had to be treated in their cells. The whole place stank of vomit for days.

It was a boxcar of powder waiting for a match.

Three weeks ago the long-awaited prison renovation got underway. A new cellblock was going to be built, three hundred new cells added. It wouldn't solve the problem completely, but it would buy some time, a few years. A few years is a lifetime for the bureaucracy, that's all the far down the road they can see. They thought they were solving the problem forever. The prison officials knew that to be false, that as soon as there were three hundred new cells there would be six hundred new prisoners for those cells. But it was a start. They hoped it would help things out.

Before they started building the new cellblock they first rebuilt the control center in the main cellblock, the nerve center for the entire prison. That was their first priority—they wanted better security, especially if six hundred new cons were coming in. This control center is the place where one guard could automatically lock down the whole prison, or conversely, open it all up. The workmen, from a well-known San Francisco multinational construction company that had successfully (and cost-efficiently, only much later did it come out that the materials were substandard) built many prisons both in the U.S. and abroad, replaced the old, antiquated bars that surrounded it with state-of-the-art safety glass, glass certified to be ten times stronger than metal, that would even withstand an 8.5 earthquake. With this glass in place the guards would have a much better view of the cellblock, the main maximum-security block. There had been blind spots with the bars, a few times in the past prisoners had used those blind spots to start riots. That opportunity would be gone.

The workmen doing the job, who were heavily guarded at all times, were initially very careful about cleaning up at the end of each day's work. Not a washer was left behind. As time progressed, however, a certain amount of complacency set in, and they started leaving stuff out, materials and tools they knew they'd be using the next day. The guards didn't police the workmen's actions, because that wasn't their job. Their job was to ensure that the workmen were protected from the inmates, and that's what they did.

The week before the riot started, six inmates were temporarily transferred from maximum to medium security. This was necessitated, as the warden would explain later, by court order. A prisoner had petitioned the State Supreme Court about over-crowding in the prison, and the Supreme Court had granted a temporary injunction. There was more room in medium security, so some men were transferred in there.

Unfortunately, due to a messup in the paperwork, which happens in any organization, some more than others, a few of the names got mixed up. Some men got transferred who shouldn't have been. They were men who, by the nature of their crimes and their violent, psychotic personalities, had to be locked up all the time. These men were the ones who got together in the medium-security yard, right away, their first day there, and planned it. It was one of those accidents that occasionally happens when a system is understaffed. The men hadn't thought it out before. They couldn't have; they had been living in segregation from the general prison community, even within their own cellblocks. But when they got thrown together with all that freedom of movement it came together.

That's the way it was: a series of accidents that all came together at the same time. The wrong men were given too much freedom. The prison was being remodeled, so there were tools left around. And the new glass-walled control center had just been finished, but hadn't been tested for security.

The prisoners who had easily broken out of the medium-security cellblock stormed the main building, the maximum-security cellblock. The guards, meanwhile, had retreated to the control center and immediately locked down the entire block from their nucleus inside, while at the same time locking themselves safely in. They were in control of the only power to open the cell doors in the entire building (which included the cells on Death Row), and the riotous inmates were outside the center, with no way in.

It was a standoff. The guards would hold firm, the troops would come in, and the riot would be put down.

Except that isn't what happened.

On their way to the maximum-security unit the inmates who were rioting had broken into the medium-security weapons depot. Someone had failed to lock it down properly, and they were able to bust their way in. They outfitted themselves with an assortment of rifles and shotguns, the most powerful weapons they could get their hands on. So that when they stormed the maximum-security building, they were armed.

The tools that the workmen had been using when they went home that afternoon had been left outside. The prisoners found them also, and brought them into the maximum-security building as well. High-powered acetylene torches, jackhammers, pneumatic drills. Shit that can cut through or break down anything.

As mentioned, the new state-of-the-art safety-glass walls that protected the main control center, where all the guards had barricaded themselves, and where all the electronic systems that opened and closed the cell doors were, had not been tested. Certainly not under fire. The pneumatic drills and jackhammers cracked them in under five minutes. The eight guards inside were overpowered and disarmed. And with the flick of a few switches, all the cell doors in the entire prison were thrown open.

The inmates who had been confined went on a rampage of their own. They started tearing the place apart, ripping out plumbing, setting fires, doing anything destructive they could think of. They raided the pharmacy, took everything, every psychotropic and other kind of drug they could put their hands on. Within an hour most of the population was stoned, and with that, paranoid to the gills. For protection they made shanks, crude home-made knives that could rip a throat with the flick of a wrist.

Most of the guards and all the administration personnel had managed to escape; with one exception. Three women, clerical/receptionist types, had been taking an illegal nap. They had sneaked off after lunch and were literally sleeping on the job, in one of the empty recreation rooms where inmates met with their families on weekends, but which sat unused during the week. (It was well-known that occasional sexual encounters took place in these rooms as well, between staff members.) The women had been disoriented when the first alarms went off, and by the time they realized what was happening, it was too late to get back to their office. The first wave of prisoners had spotted them, and nabbed them. Although the initial inclination of most of the men was to rape them all, the leaders cooled it, not out of any sympathy for the women, who in their opinions deserved it, as all women do, but because it would slow them down, and might jeopardize their success. They had to take over the prison first, then they could all fuck their brains out.

They showed their compassion instead by locking the women up in a windowless room that had almost no ventilation.

All the cell doors had been opened from the control center with one exception: those in the protective custody wing. In that wing were the cells that housed men who had to be totally segregated from the rest of the prison population, for their own safety. Men who were detested by everyone, whose lives were worthless in the open.

A few of these men were child molesters, generally considered by inmates to be the lowest kind of sexual degenerate. Primarily, however, these special-custody prisoners were snitches: prisoners who had informed on other prisoners, either within the prison itself or earlier, at trials or probation hearings.

Their cells could be opened only by a system of triple-locks. And the keys weren't inside the prison proper, they were outside, in the administration areas, and other areas that no prisoner could get to. It was the only way to ensure the protection and safety of those men, because they were marked for certain death otherwise.

When it first happened, Lone Wolf ran out of his cell, like everyone else. The first thing he wanted was to rendezvous with his three brothers, the second thing was to arm himself as heavily as he could. The third thing, if the first two were successful, was to get the hell out of the way and stay there.

The four bikers found each other without difficulty. They were in the same unit, although kept as far apart from each other as the boundaries would allow. They joined the rush down to the weapons depot, which was already being over-run. Although very few weapons are kept inside a prison, because of the possibility of something exactly like this, there were a few weapons for emergencies, and as Death Row inmates and one-percenters, they had a certain status within the population's pecking order, so they were able to cherry-pick from the small selection. They each took a shotgun, and Lone Wolf scored two pistols, because he fancied how he looked wearing them.

They also took as many rounds of ammunition as were available. They wanted to make sure they had enough protection. Mostly from their jailers, but from their confederates inside as well. Prison riots can wind up like the French Revolution: the inmates, crazy to begin with, crazier with the power they've suddenly gotten and the drugs they're taking, can turn on one another like a snake eating its own tail, and wipe themselves out. Once you start killing, any swinging dick is fair game.

Thus armed, the bikers retreated to Lone Wolf's cell. There was never a question of whether or not they were going to break out into the free world; no one was going to do that. It was whether you survived or not. The trick to survive was you had to protect your ass.

So they put their collective asses against the wall of Lone Wolf's cell and watched the passing parade.

THE PHONE RINGS me out of a dream. I knock over the alarm clock and the telephone before getting the receiver to my mouth.

"What?" I manage groggily.

"Are you awake?" It's Robertson.

"I am now," I tell him, annoyed.

"How soon can you come down to my office?" There's a tone of urgency in his voice. He's been riding a tiger by the tail all night long.

"What for?"

Mary Lou props herself up on an elbow, looks at me.

"Who is it?" she asks.

"Is someone with you?" Robertson asks from the other end of the line.

"None of your fucking business," I tell him, cupping the receiver and saying his name to her.

"What does he want?" she demands.

"I don't know yet." Still cupping the receiver.

"You don't owe him anything," she says fiercely. "It's the other way around."

"I'll remind him of that when I see him," I reassure her.

"When are you seeing him?" Now she's alarmed; at least concerned. Robertson's been nothing but bad news for us for a long time now.

"Now, he says."

I uncup the receiver.

"Why don't you just tell me over the telephone?" I ask him.

"Because it's too damn complicated," he says. "And there's other people involved. It's an emergency, Will. You've got an interest in it. We all do."

The urgency in his voice is getting shriller. "The governor requested you. Personally."

"An hour," I tell him. "This better be good."

"Have you been watching TV?"

"Last night."

"It's as bad as Attica was," he says. "Maybe worse."

"An hour," I say. "I'll be there." An afterthought comes to me. "One thing."

"What's that?" he asks suspiciously.

"Don't have Moseby around. I don't want to see his lying face."

I can feel his reaction over the line, but he maintains his cool. "Your call, Will. If that's what you want, fine by me. He isn't germane anyway."

Mary Lou makes a grab at my ass as I climb out of bed.

"Keep it warm for me," I say.

"That's never a problem," she says. "How long are you going to be?"

"I don't know. Sounds like they're picking brains. It's my daughter's vacation with me," I remind her. "Only two more days. Nothing's going to mess that up."

I GO UP TO Robertson's office the back way, dodging the reporters who have congregated on the front steps. The media circus is always the worst part of these things; they won't let situations work themselves out, they have to fan the flames until it's a major conflagration so they'll be able to fill thirty minutes of airtime.

Robertson's waiting for me in his office, alone. I'm surprised; I thought it would be jammed.

"Thanks for coming," he offers. "I really appreciate it. Others will, too."

"Ask not what your country can do for you, et cetera," I tell him modestly.

"Let's let bygones be bygones. Is that possible?"

"Are you shitting me?" Where does he get the *cojones* to even put that to me? For that I'm missing much-needed sleep, entwined in the bosom of my amour? "That's too easy, Johnnie. It implies it's over and it isn't; not for me, not for them." Pissant son of a bitch—now that his back's up against the wall he wants to be buddy-buddy with me again, like nothing's happened. He can't have his cake and eat it, too. Not with this puppy.

He slumps in his chair. "Can't anyone give me a break?" he asks.

"You're talking to the wrong person," I tell him. "You ought to know that."

"I thought I'd give it a try." He throws it up lamely, waiting for me to block it back in his face.

"Give it a rest is what you ought to give it."

"Yeh. Okay. What the hey, I had to take the shot."

He looks like shit. No sleep, no shave, no shower. He pours coffee for both of us. I've been down that road, using Taster's Choice in lieu of amphetamines; he'll have need of those, too, before this is over.

His secretary buzzes him on the squawk box.

"Warden Gates is on his way up, sir."

"Send him in as soon as he arrives."

"And the governor telephoned from his car. He'll be here in less than five minutes."

That gets my attention. I sit up, sip my java. At least I look presentable, although I don't feel it. I stood under the cold shower for five minutes and I'm still tired. Mary Lou took a sick day, she'll take Claudia to the park, until I can catch up with them. It's the first time my two women'll be together alone. I hope it works.

Robertson freshens his coffee, scarfs half a Winchell's jelly-filled in one bite. Bad stuff—if you've got to eat that crap you should stick to the plains or powders.

I feel like I've been set up. This is no accident, the governor and the warden coming while I'm here. The three of them have some load to drop on me. It makes me nervous.

"Why don't I come back after you and the brass have finished your business?" I suggest, rising out of my chair. "I'll take a walk around the block."

"Better you should stick around," Robertson says. "We might have something of interest to you."

Like what? My guys are dead, killed in the first wave of casualties, he wants to see my reaction face-to-face? Or conversely: they're the ringleaders, when this is over (and it will be over, one way or the other) they'll be summarily executed?

Why have I been singled out for this appearance before the royal court? There are eight hundred men inside that lockup, where are their lawyers? Why do I have to be signally honored for this bullshit?

I cram a jelly-filled into my mouth, refill my cup.

Robertson's secretary ushers Gates in without announcing him. "No one else except the governor," Robertson instructs her.

The warden pours himself some coffee without asking. He's beat, but he's taken the time to clean up. He wants to look presentable, show the world he's not a gorilla. He's going to be facing reporters for days; the national papers and networks have already sent out correspondents and film crews. Those that aren't hanging out by the statehouse steps are camped out in front of the prison. I watched the start of the "Today" show this morning, the riot was the first news item out of the box.

" 'Morning, Mr. Alexander," the warden says, cordially enough, considering the circumstances, "thanks for coming." He extends his hand. We shake. His hand is dry; he's under control. That's comforting to know.

"What's the deal?" I ask Robertson, irritated. "If you're cooking something up I'd like to know. I don't feed at the public trough, I am not compelled to be here."

"We might have need of your special skills," Robertson says. "Nothing devious, believe me."

A premonition envelops me. I sink back in my chair. Whenever someone says 'believe me' or 'trust me' I immediately look over my shoulder, although I can't see what harm can come from talking to them. Yet.

The door opens. The governor comes in, accompanied by one aide, a blonde-on-blonde woman, severe in look and dress, but attractive. You never see a politician with an unattractive woman unless it's his wife. Although I'm sure he's been up all night like the others, he appears to be completely fresh. He's dressed in a polo shirt, khakis, and the requisite cowboy boots, for all the world looking like he's on his way to his son's soccer game.

We've known each other over the years. I even campaigned for him once, in a no-sweat half-assed way. As politicians go, he's not a bad guy.

The aide fades into the corner. Her eyes never leave his excellency.

"Thank you for coming on such short notice, Mr. Alexander."

"It wasn't presented to me on a voluntary basis, sir."

"Thanks anyway." He looks at Robertson and Gates. "Have you been filled in at all?"

"All I know is what I read in the papers," I tell him.

"We were waiting for you," Robertson tells the governor.

The governor nods, as if that was the right course. A show of not dodging the buck.

"We've been talking all night," he says. "Would you pour me a cup, Elaine?" he digresses momentarily to ask his aide. "Extra sugar this morning," he smiles. Always on; you never know when a photographer might pop out of the ficus. "I need the energy." He turns back to me.

"Excuse me. We were talking—my colleagues here and others, anyone who's affected. All the way to Washington. Which is a lot of people. It's the warden's prison, he's in charge, but this whole thing's gotten crazy now." He turns to the warden.

"It's out of my control," Gates finishes for him. He's up-front about it, but it's got to be killing him. The man's in his fifties, with a lifetime spent in the prison system, coming up from the ranks to the number-one job, and he's lost control; the one absolute no-no. He's out of a job, no matter how this is resolved he'll be gone before the year's out.

"The prison's completely sealed," the governor says, picking it up—we don't have all day for chit-chat, he has to get to the point: the point of what I'm doing here talking with him while the prison burns. "Anyone that could get out, has. The rest are trapped inside."

I nod, sip my coffee. I'm keeping my own counsel, it's their show.

"They took eleven hostages," he continues. "Eight guards, all male, and three female clerical workers." He pauses, knowing what I'm thinking, what anyone would be thinking. "We think they're all right, that they haven't been harmed . . . or molested. We're not sure, we're not sure of anything, but to the best of our knowledge we don't think so. Of course, that's old information."

In situations like this, any information older than fifteen minutes is old information. While we're talking here, eating greasy doughnuts and drinking coffee, a dozen people could be getting whacked.

"I gathered as much," I say, cautiously. "From watching the news this morning. And the radio driving in."

"It's already a full-blown disaster," he exclaims, for the first time showing some honest feeling. "I've been thinking about those women. They're clerks, for Godsakes, they're not trained to handle this. At least if it was lady guards . . . these women, they've got to be hysterical. And you know where that can lead."

To panic, chaos, and destruction. Like the baby crying in church—you'll do anything to shut it up.

"Anyway," he goes on, "there's a new development now. Their leadership, we don't know who it is, they've set up a council, they contacted me through the warden here about—what?—an hour and a half, two hours ago."

Gates nods confirmation.

"They're prepared to talk," the governor tells me. "They want to start a negotiation."

"That's a step," I say. That's good; as long as people are talking, they usually aren't killing.

"The thing is, they don't want to negotiate with anyone officially connected," he says. "They don't trust the system, which, let's face it, given who they are and where they are, I can't blame them."

He looks over at Gates, at Robertson, back to me.

"The governor and I talked about this," Robertson tells me, picking up the ball. "Earlier this morning. He's signed off on it—with my disagreement, I must add." He stares hard at me. "My strong disagreement. But it's his decision to make and under the circumstances we don't have much of a choice."

The governor looks at me like I'm supposed to know what Robertson's talking about. I look at Robertson. I don't know exactly what's coming, but this was a set-up from the get-go.

"The inmates have asked that you represent us," the governor says coolly. "They want you to negotiate for . . . well, us. The authorities. We agree . . ." here he stares at Robertson, a look stating 'we're all on the same page here, boyo, and don't you forget it,' "that you're the right man for the job. Basically, Mr. Alexander, we're authorizing you to negotiate a settlement; we're asking you to take charge. To run the prison until this is over. Because we can't." He throws up his hands in frustration and surrender. "We've lost control. You're the only one they've agreed to talk to."

"Why me?" The words are out of my mouth before I even realize it.

"They figure you as a stand-up guy," Robertson says. The way he puts it, it isn't a compliment. "They think they can trust you." He pauses. "So do we," he adds grudgingly, looking at the governor.

"Do I have to?" I ask.

The governor takes a breath.

"We're not going to force you."

I swish my coffee in my cup. It tastes like graphite.

"What's the alternative?" I ask. "If I pass?"

"We haven't thought beyond this," Robertson says. "We don't . . . hell, Will, we're playing everything by ear here."

"What guarantees do I have?" I ask. I'm thinking as fast as I can.

"About your safety? Honest answer? None that we can give you. They're running the show," he says.

I shake my head.

"From you," I say.

"Whatever," he says, looking to the governor, who nods. "You're the boss."

"The boss." Uh huh. "In other words," I say, "I negotiate, you'll endorse, right? Officially, on paper?"

John and his eminence look at each other.

"Well . . ." the governor says. He doesn't want to play all his hole cards. Unfortunately for him, he has to.

"Yes," he says. "That's correct. The terms will have to be run by me for approval, but yes."

I look at him. "I've got to think about this," I say.

"For how long?" he asks, a bit more anxiously than he'd like to.

"I don't know. But I've got to think about it."

"WHY DOES IT HAVE TO BE YOU?"

"I was requested. Kind of like when the queen wants to see you. You can turn it down but it's considered bad form."

She doesn't see the humor.

"But why you? You're a civilian."

"That's the point. They—the guys inside—don't trust anyone in authority . . . which is one area, at least, in which we are kindred spirits."

"This is a little more serious than a bumper sticker, Will."

We're in a coffee shop across the street, Mary Lou and I. Claudia's been dumped at a friend's, so far none the wiser. Mary Lou's upset, more than I am. She's got a much stronger grasp on reality than I do.

"You're fodder," she says.

"Maybe. But what am I supposed to do?"

"Tell them you won't do it. It's their dirty work—let them clean up their own mess."

"They would prefer to," I tell her. "Asking me to do this was not something that went down easy, I can assure you."

"You *want* to do this," she says.

"No."

"Come on, Will, this is no time to play games. It's a macho ego trip, admit it."

"Well . . ." Come on, man, this is the woman you love. Be straight.

"There's ego involved, yes."

"Ego gets people killed."

"I'm not going to get killed." Keep saying that, pal, it sounds good.

"Do you have a guarantee?" she asks. "Something in writing? You're a lawyer, you know it has to be on paper."

"Sure," I say. "I'll show it to the inmates. 'You can't kill me, I have a letter from my mother.' "

"You're going to do it, aren't you?"

"I don't have a choice, Mary Lou."

"I guess you don't," she says. She's fighting to keep the tears back. "Anyone else would; but you don't."

Outside, she gives me a hug.

"I'll be watching for you on the news," she says.

"I'll be the one wearing the carnation in my lapel," I say.

"Be careful, sweetheart," she implores. "And come back."

"HERE'S THE PROGRAM," I tell them, staring the governor square in his puss. "I'm not going to be your stooge. You're not going to send me in there to do what you can't and then cut my legs from under me once you're back in control again. If I do this—and I emphasize *if*—we establish how far I can go, right now in this room, and the rest is at my discretion. And I want it in writing—from you."

"Will . . ." Robertson moves in quickly.

"Sayonara, baby. Thanks for breakfast."

In less than an hour, the paperwork, duly signed by the governor and witnessed by two of their secretaries and Susan, is safely reposing in the locked safe of my office.

THEY MEET ME at the front gate. Four of them, wearing various styles of masks. They look like Middle Eastern terrorists: the only facial features that show are their eyes, which are sunk back into their skulls with fatigue, fear, and rage.

I'm alone with them in no-man's land, between the two sets of gates. One of them frisks me thoroughly. I steel myself to be as calm and still as possible; two hundred people are watching this live, and millions will be seeing it on the nightly news. The teaser runs through my head: 'Gonzo lawyer stripped and searched; film at eleven.' Hyperbole—I'm fully clothed, and my gonzo days, if there ever were any, are behind me. At least in my own mind.

It's late in the day. To the west the sun is dying behind the hills. After I left Robertson's office I went home to pack a small overnight bag, and to tell Claudia what was happening. She was worried, of course, but she had that wonderful faith kids have in their parents, that they're invincible, especially when they're doing the right thing.

We said our goodbyes. Mary Lou drove her to the airport, in Albuquerque. She was much more upset; she didn't want me to do it. If it was the other way around, I put it to her, wouldn't you? We both knew that answer. I gave them both big hugs and kisses, watched the car until it was out of sight, went back to town and joined the war party.

I'm not scared; not for myself. There's a protocol for this, long established. I'll do the best I can, and either it'll work or it won't. They don't shoot the messenger in situations like this, this isn't Lebanon.

I just have to go on faith that these men are sane enough to remember the rules. Martyrdom isn't much of a turn-on for me; I have no desire to become a home-grown Terry Waite.

What I am scared of, rationally, is not being able to make it work. That no matter what I do, say, or promise, it won't be enough, or worse, that what's already happened has become such a mountain, is so far gone, that there is no solution except siege. I can't promise them the moon; I can't give them their freedom.

They finish searching me. One of them takes my bag, as if he's my porter. We pass through the inner set of gates, which, from somewhere inside, are automatically locked behind us. We walk the fifty yards across the lawn. The prisoner-guards accompanying me (who are comporting themselves very seriously, almost military-style) flank me front and back, side and side. We fast-walk up the steps to the administration building and inside, and the free world disappears behind me at the same moment that the sun drops out of sight in the sky.

THE WORLD IS DARK, and it's on fire. The darkness is not merely lack of light; it's a real, viscous darkness, thick and heavy, darkness caused not by loss of light but by the forceful removal of light, of light violently sucked out of the air and replaced with oppression. You can almost reach out and touch it, as if it were a wall, it feels so thick, so real. Hanging heavy, suffocating, an accumulation of enormous weight. To live in darkness like this would be to go crazy eventually.

The density of the smoke assaults my mouth and nasal passages as soon as I pass into the old maximum-security section. One of my escorts leads me to a sink, where I dip my hands in tepid water, splash my hands and face. Then he hands me a water-soaked towel, helps me tie it around my face and neck.

"It's worst here," he tells me. He's black, he talks with a thick southern drawl. There aren't many blacks in here; seventy-five percent of the inmate population is Chicano, the oppressed minority of choice in these parts. "In case they try to storm us," he informs me, a cautioning, "we got it rigged with oil-drums, we can explode this whole fuckin' place in a fireball, it comes down to that. The fumes're fierce though, ain't they?"

They are; it's hot as hell, the place has been shut down for over twenty-four hours, so the air-conditioning is off. Except for water, which is a self-contained unit of wells and cisterns inside the prison walls, all the utilities are off. If this goes more than a week they'll run out of food, unless they negotiate for it. If it goes more than a week, people much heavier than me will be doing the negotiating, and it'll be at gunpoint. If it comes to that, the hostages will be dead.

I'd given the authorities three days. If I haven't pulled it off by then, or, at the least, have gotten damn close to a settlement, I'm walking out. Then they can do it the hard way.

Everyone inside the walls has been brought to this unit, A unit. It's the original prison building, constructed the old way, barred cells in tiers. All the new buildings are compartmentalized; no unit in any of them houses more than two dozen prisoners. It's a better system because it keeps large groups of the population from gathering together.

When the rioting started, the warden could have shut down the one building where it was happening in D unit; he could have stopped it from spreading prison-wide. Only about two hundred men would have been affected, then. The other six hundred–odd would have been prevented from getting in on the action. The down side would have been that the hostages, at least those who were taken in the first wave, would've been assured of being killed; if not at once, definitely before it all ended. Some wardens would have done that; they would have sacrificed their troops. By the book, you're allowed to do that. Trade lives for the greater good.

To his credit, Gates didn't. He swapped keeping the hostages alive for control of his prison. I'd bet the farm that most prison officials think he's a pussy, that he should've detonated the place, and made the sacrifices.

But most prison officials never have to face this choice, although they spend their lives in dread of it. I have no doubt Gates did the right thing, and I suspect he still feels the same, even though it's costing him.

If I can pull it off, bring the hostages out alive, I might save his bacon. But his bacon, or any other part of his anatomy, is not the problem. The problem is the over eight hundred men who have been locked up like animals in these cages. That they deserve to be locked up, that they have to be, is not in question. There's no other way to handle many of these men. The question is, how do you get madmen, psychotics, losers with nothing more to lose, to agree to docilely go back into their cages?

It's very quiet. Normally a prison is loud. People talking and yelling all the time. There are men in prison who scream every second they're awake. Now there is none of that. It's frightening, the quiet is so intense.

We are in the small holding area outside the main section. Normally, to get in, you go through two sets of thick, lead-covered doors that lock independently of each other, and you wait in between for one set to lock before the other set opens. It's to keep some chump from trying to make a break. Now, all the doors are open. People can go in and out at will; but they don't, because they have nowhere to go.

"Put these on, man." One of my escorts hands me a couple of Baggies, the kind you stick your garbage in. I look down; I notice they're all wearing them over their shoes.

"What for?" I ask.

"The floors are wet inside," he answers dryly. "You don't want to fuck up your new Nikes."

I wrap the garbage bags around my shoes, secure them with plastic ties.

"Follow me," the leader, the black convict, tells me. "Keep up. Don't go sight-seeing on me, you hear? Time for that shit later, maybe.

Right now we got to get you together with the council. Follow up close now."

We press forward, towards the body of the prison. I'm right up against them, asshole to elbow. We round the bend, and as I walk into the cellblock proper I'm assaulted by the unbelievable, overwhelming smell, it hits me before anything visual registers, almost like shock waves of a nuclear explosion, it's that strong and immediate, before anything I see makes an imprint: the most powerful, intense, horrible odor I've ever encountered, the smell of a thousand septic tanks bursting, ten thousand toilets overflowing. I gag violently, my lunch is in my mouth, my hand is up covering it through the towel. I'm not going to vomit in front of these men, not when I've barely set a foot inside the door.

We start forward.

"Watch your step," my escort warns. The floor is very slippery. Linoleum. Easy to keep clean. I realize that it's wet, that there's a virtual river underneath my feet, several inches deep. And immediately I realize, a realization that brings fresh revulsion, that all the toilets *are* stopped up, I hear them flushing, over and over, they've been jammed-up to keep doing it, so that they've overflowed out onto the floor and I am walking through a river not only of foul water, but of piss, shit, and vomit. And blood. I can't help but look down and even though it's dark in here I can see the blood, it flows in clots, almost fluorescent, silvery-red, the water pale yellow, turds and clumps of vomit carried with it. It moves slowly, from one wall to another, seeking an outlet, a release, but there is none so it's a stagnant tidal pool, a swamp of human waste.

I force myself to walk, to keep pace with my guides.

We slide our way across the floor, heading (hopefully) for higher ground.

The carnage is unbelievable. The prison is literally on fire. I can see now all the way down to the other end, a couple hundred yards, and up the tiers, three stories. Fires everywhere, countless fires. Everything is on fire: mattresses, trash, any piece of wood the men have been able to get their hands on. Huge oil drums are all over the place, they must have been brought in from the farm area outside, where they're stored to fuel the equipment. In hindsight you wonder why in the world would a prison keep so much flammable shit around?

It's like handing a loaded machine-gun to a three-year-old. The drums are all spewing fire, small fires mostly, the kind you see on Chicago street corners in winter. But it's almost summer now, outside the heat is in the eighties, in here they are burning fires.

I'm immediately drenched in sweat. It feels like a sauna from hell. It must be a hundred and fifteen in here. The fumes roiling to the ceiling, the oil-smoke thick and harsh to the lungs. I press the wet towel to my face as we march onwards.

Every man in the prison is in this building, it seems, and every one of them is out in these corridors. They stand there, in the corridors and in the cells, watching me as I pass them. They are all masked, like my guides. Bandannas around their faces, burnooses fashioned from towels, from pieces of torn-up sheet. Anything to hide behind. Eyes looking out, intense, ready to explode.

To a man, they're armed. A few; the elite, the appointed leaders, the ones controlling the action, have guns. Shotguns, rifles, pistols. Tear-gas guns, whatever they could get their hands on that can fire a load.

The others, the majority, have their own weapons, made up of what they could find or fashion. Knives, axes, lengths of metal, bedframes torn from the walls, smashed into crude sharp-pointed spears. Others carry bludgeons, pieces of wood, lengths of pipe, bricks, chains wrapped around forearms and wrists. Anything that can kill.

I understand, seeing this, that the weapons, and more important, the masks, are not only for protection from the outside, but are there to cover up from the others in here. It's an uprising, yes, all banding together for one cause, but it's also anarchy, every man for himself. The first rule inside: cover your ass. No one can tell who anyone is, with a few exceptions like the blacks. You've got to cover your ass, hide your face, because you don't know when an enemy might use this chaos as an excuse to settle an old score. You learn super-fast on the inside that almost all deaths in prison riots are revenge killings, inmates killing inmates, usually over very petty shit.

"All right, now, watch your step here. Don't want you falling and breaking your neck, boss," the lead escort tells me, almost jocularly. "You 'bout the onliest hope we got to settle this thing up without no more bloodshed."

Without no more bloodshed. That starts my stomach going again.

Have there been killings? Who were they? Hostages we don't know about, prisoners, what?

He leads me up a set of metal stairs in the center of the complex that winds around the tower housing the control centers where the guards are normally bastioned. From this core area, which extends a hundred feet up and has at its center one secure safety-glass-walled control unit for each floor, a single guard can see three hundred and sixty degrees; he can spot trouble in the making and seal himself off until help arrives, if it's necessary. The uprising couldn't have taken place here, because the population in this unit doesn't have the freedom of movement they give the less-restricted areas. With more freedom of movement comes more responsibility and liberty, and with more liberty and responsibility came anarchy. An irony that will be pondered deeply in days to come.

We're in the middle tier now. I follow my escorts down a long row of cells. The row is crowded with men, moving about aimlessly, holding onto their weapons. They all watch me as we pass. A few throw out choice epithets, such as 'jive-ass white-bread motherfucker,' a few spit on the ground as I pass, but for the most part they watch me silently, hundreds of sets of eyes behind masks boring into me front and back. A gauntlet of fury and rage.

I'm ushered into a large, open room at the end of the cellblock that's normally used as a dayroom for inmates who've earned points for good behavior; trusties and the like. The two televisions have been smashed, as has the Ping-Pong table. The couches have been ripped up for the wire, which is now in use as weapons and defense barriers throughout the building; I passed crude wire barriers on my way through the corridors. Chairs and tables have been brought in; bottles of water, cartons of canned food are stacked in corners.

"Hey there, ace." From across the room comes the familiar voice.

Alone among the prisoners, Lone Wolf is unmasked. He sits at a long table in the center of the inmate council. His place at the table, the fact that he alone is without a mask, and his overall regal demeanor tell me that he's the leader. They are all working in concert, of course, but he's the *jefe*, he's running the show.

It's been six weeks since we last sat face to face. He's let his beard grow longer than he'd been keeping it; for some reason I flash on Che Guevara, on the pictures of Che that used to adorn walls in college dorm rooms back in the radical sixties and early seventies, including my own. Che and Huey and Mao, the unholy trinity to the white kids who were so desperate for a cause, so eager to get in on the action instead of living vicariously on the sidelines like their parents had; looking back on it now, Vietnam was a blessing in disguise, especially to those who didn't go, because it was something to be passionate for, especially after the blacks kicked the white kids out of the civil-rights movement. (So we thought about Nam—we were never going to cop-out, become middle class. Shit, what drugged-out dreamers we turned out to be.)

Three black-and-white posters on the wall, three heroes of my generation, dead and mostly discredited now, or even worse, irrelevant. The permanency of impermanence.

Fuck, man. I have to remind myself: you're in prison, there's no ideology here, just the quick and the dead. Don't romanticize this, not for a second.

Flanking Lone Wolf are several other inmates. I immediately pick out Goose, seated directly to Lone Wolf's left. He smiles at me, peeling off his bandanna, leaning across the table to shake my hand.

There are nine of them, seated in a row on one side of the table, waiting for me. The prison council, the men in charge, the ones I'll be negotiating with.

It's marginally cleaner in here, the air is less foul. They've kept the ugliest part of it away from this area, because this is where the bargaining will take place and they don't want me to be constantly reminded of what's happened. It's a smart move, the conditions in this place couldn't help but color my judgment, no matter how impartial I want to be. I am a lawyer for men such as these, yes, but I'm also part of the establishment, I'm on the other side of the fence, the other side of this table, I make no bones about that. I am not their buddy: we're not in this together except inasmuch as we have a common problem to solve.

Even so, I'm glad to see Lone Wolf and Goose. I'm glad they're alive. I wasn't sure.

"We got us a situation here," Lone Wolf says.

"I can see that," I answer. He's cool; I can be cooler.

We look at each other. I can't help it, I smile. Relief, someone I know I can talk to. Then I turn and look at all of them across from me, each in turn. We take each other's measure in deliberate doses.

How they perceive me, how straight they think I'll be with them, will in large part determine how successful I can be. How successful this will work, without it becoming a war.

Lone Wolf looks up and down the table at his confederates.

"We've prepared a list of grievances," he says, shoving a sheaf of ined papers across the table towards me.

I let it lie there.

"Certain things come first," I continue, "before any of this."

"Like what?" one of the men on the other side asks.

"The condition of the hostages," I tell him.

"They're okay," Lone Wolf says.

"I want to see them."

"That can happen."

"Privately," I say.

He shrugs as if to say 'I knew that.'

"Yeh, we can do that. Something I want you to see first, though. 'll take you myself."

He strides around the table, heads for the door. I follow closely. My black escort accompanies us. Everyone else waits. Something hey're good at.

We're down in the old hole, the solitary unit. It isn't so wet down ere, the courts decreed this area off-limits a few years ago, too cruel nd unusual, so there weren't men down here to stop the toilets up. The smell is just as bad, though, it's a different smell, not rank and our like human shit, but sweeter somehow, more pungent. It's hot s hell, even hotter down here than up in the cellblock. We're all ripping sweat now, it's coming off us in buckets.

The doors along this corridor are solid. One small opening in the ottom to push the food-trays in and get them back.

"Prepare yourself," Lone Wolf cautions me. He pushes open a door.

Armed to the teeth, and now in possession of high-tech ools, tools strong enough to knock over the so-called impregnable walls of the control center in less than five minutes, a core group of rioters made their way to the protective custody wing.

There was one group of prisoners that lived in dread of a successful prison uprising. When they heard that the revolt had succeeded they collectively started saying their prayers. They knew an assault on their wing was coming but they didn't know when; all they could do was wait, and hope that the bars which kept them locked in would safeguard them against those who would want them out from behind those bars. They didn't know who would be coming—the faces—but they knew of the inevitability of it. It was a chance they'd all taken when they'd agreed to turn on their fellow inmates. It seemed like a reasonable risk, because the prison system had a strong vested interest in the safety and welfare of these men. They would be protected against almost everything.

The inmates taking over the asylum was one of the few things they couldn't be protected against.

When the men inside these cells saw who was coming they started screaming for real, a high-pitched hysterical wail, like women or castrati. This was their worst nightmare come true. That the guards despised them, they knew. Everyone despised them, it came with the territory, as did the up-side, which was having their own sentences knocked down dramatically, which in some cases in the past had been as dramatic as a life-without-parole magically turning into time-served and *adiós, amigo.*

They also knew, these bottom-feeders of the system, these lowest of the low, that no matter how much they were hated, despised, and reviled, by prisoners and authorities alike, not even the guards could touch them, because of their special status. They were hated and needed at the same time Without them, some of the men in here wouldn't be: they'd be out on the streets, free. Most of those men were guilty, yes, but they couldn't have been convicted without the testimony of the snitches. A select few (not the bikers specifically, but men like them, in here under different circumstances) were actually innocent of their particular crime. They had been framed by the testimony of one or more of the men in this wing.

The men that the snitches had turned were among the leaders of the takeover. Now these same men were facing their accusers, their reasons for being in this hole, and now they were armed with their shanks and other home-brewed weapons, as well as the blowtorches and high-tech tools. The only things separating them now were locked prison bars and doors; big fucking deal at this point.

The rioters could have killed the snitches right away. They could have set the cells on fire and let them burn to death. But that wouldn't satisfy the blood need, the rage that had been festering for years. These men wanted their accusers' deaths to be slow deaths, as slow and as painful as possible.

So instead of putting the stoolies out of their misery in a fast and (relatively) humane fashion, they did it the long way. The long, slow, psychologically torturous way, building an appetite with the taste of sweet revenge.

What they did was cut through the bars of the snitches' cages with their newly-liberated high-tech acetylene torches and metal-cutters. It was long, hard work, but they didn't mind. On the contrary—they relished it.

As they cut they taunted the men on the other side of the bars, telling them all the slow, horrifically painful ways they were going to use to kill them.

You could hear the screams all over the prison. Even the bikers, isolated on Death Row, could hear them. The cellblock was a natural amplifier, the screams carried all over, echoing off the walls.

"Poor bastards," Goose commiserated.

"They really deserve our tears, don't they? You forgetting it was bastards like them put us in here?" Lone Wolf reminded him, pitiless. "You gonna live that life you got to be ready to die it."

They made no move to intervene. No one did. It was something that had to be done.

The rioters finally cut through the snitches' cages. They dragged them out, kicking and screaming, onto the corridor floor. They were in one section of the top floor.

The first two were killed the most mercifully; they were tossed off the tier to the floor a hundred feet below, shattering against the concrete, their blood splashing all over the walls.

"One, two, three, heave!" The rioters laughed uproariously as they tossed them like sacks of potatoes.

After that, they got more creative. One rioter pulled a snitch out of his cell—it took some doing, the snitch had torn up his mattress and tied himself to the bars with batting and wire, literally wired himself to his cell. He'd done such a good job that his tormentor had to cut him loose with bolt-cutters; it pissed him off royally, 'have the balls one time to die like a man,' his tormentor said. He was disgusted at the lack of heart in the snitch. Heart was important, if it was your time to check out you should check out like a man, with dignity. The snitch didn't give a shit about dignity, he cried like a baby.

It didn't matter. He got to play, now he was going to have to pay. Using the same blowtorch with which he had painstakingly cut the bars of the snitch's cell, his liberator now used it to burn flesh. The snitch's screams were unlike any sound a human had ever screamed, the flame from the blowtorch dancing over his body, paying particular attention to his private parts. Burnt that lying jailhouse sack of shit to a crisp.

His fellow rioters cheered him on. Then they tossed what was left over the side to join the remains of his companions.

That killing liberated their blood-hunger. It became butcher's theater. Several men held each snitch down in turn while one of them would cut off his testicles as slowly and as painfully as possible, talking to him all the while, 'How does it feel to get fucked instead of doing it, you ain't gonna have nothing to fuck with no more, turkey.' Then a shotgun blast to the face, a rifle bullet in the back, or in one case, a steel bar driven through the temple.

They did each snitch one at a time. It took a long time. After it went on for a few hours the men who were doing it, who had been dreaming of such a day for years, even they got sick of it, but they had to finish the job. The luckiest ones were the last few; by then no one had much stomach for it, so those fortunates were executed gangland-style, a bullet behind the ear, and then their equipment hacked off.

After that it got quiet for awhile; everyone, even the most crazed, needed breathing room. But there was an undercurrent of rumble, of electric rumble, that an experienced man could detect, like animals know an earthquake's coming before it does. Lone Wolf was a man experienced in that.

He got up and walked out the door of his cell to the railing and looked out. He could see virtually the whole cellblock from here. There were men everywhere. Some were starting the fires, others were starting the flood. Soon, he knew, it would be total chaos, unless he did something about it. Anarchy, every man for himself and none for all, half the men could be dead if they didn't create something of order.

"Where're you going?" Roach asked.

"Check the lay of the land," Lone Wolf said. "Let's go together. Ain't nobody gonna fuck with the four of us together."

By now enough time had passed so that men were getting scared. First the snitches; then who? Everyone has a grudge in the joint, everyone has someone they'd like to off if given the chance. Now everyone had the chance.

The masks went on. A few men got the idea, they ripped up their sheets and covered their faces with them and ventured out into the corridors, brandishing their weapons as shields, and the others saw it and picked up on the idea, soon everybody was masked from everybody else. By this time the fires were going good, the oil-drums had been brought in earlier, the air was so thick with smoke you couldn't see five feet in front of you. Someone would suddenly appear out of the smoke and your scrotum would get tight, because you didn't know who he was, he could be the cat who sounded you in the yard last week, the one who accused you of hogging the weights, who vowed payback. Or someone who had a grudge against you you didn't even know about. The cat you thought was your best asshole buddy and pal secretly hated you for a million imagined slights.

Lone Wolf knew this was in their minds, that paranoia feeds on itself like a tapeworm. And he knew that his only chance to ever walk out of here alive was to get some order going, so that it could end. Otherwise, when the authorities finally did get back in, the inmates would have done the job for them. There would be nothing left but the burials.

They went first to where the women hostages had been sequestered. Lone Wolf had his suspicions that stuff might go down there first, and he was right. Now that the snitch-killers had had a meal of blood they were ready for the next course, which was pussy. Half a dozen of them had ripped the clothes off one of the women when Lone Wolf and the other bikers stuck their heads into the door.

"Come for sloppy seconds?" the head rioter snickered. "I hear y'all are boss studs." He was ready for action, so hard was his member in anticipation of his first piece of female ass in ten years that the veins were pulsating.

The women were screaming like banshees.

"Don't be doing her that way," Lone Wolf said softly to the man. It was a line he liked to use, from his favorite movie, *One-Eyed Jacks.* Marlon Brando had used it on Ben Johnson's sidekick in a Mexican cantina before he blew him in half for coming on to a barmaid the wrong way.

"What the fuck you saying, dick-brain?" the man queried, turning back to the business at hand.

Lone Wolf cold-cocked him twice with his shotgun butt, the first time in his balls, doubling him over in unexpected pain, then across his jaw, smashing it. The others stared at him, stunned.

"Anyone else?" Lone Wolf had asked. The victim of his attack lay writhing on the floor. The others looked from him to the other bikers, who formed a phalanx around their leader.

"It ain't gonna happen this way," Lone Wolf told them. "You did what you did and that's how it had to be. But this ain't. Now get the fuck out of here."

After the predators left, dragging their unconscious mate with them, and the woman had dressed and they had been calmed down, he left Dutchboy there to guard them. Then they went out into the population.

Within three hours the prisoners had formed a council. Lone Wolf assumed the head; there was no argument. They started acting responsibly, for them. The women and guards were put off-limits. They drew up their list of grievances, and started debating about who among the authorities they'd be willing to talk to.

THE BODIES ARE STACKED the length of the floor, piled haphazardly, arms and torsos of some on top of legs and feet of others. Heads on top of asses, vice versa. They are all naked, and the decomposition is something fierce to see. Unbelievable: I could never imagine something this horrible, let alone the idea that I'd actually be looking at it. This is where they brought them, so they'd be out of sight. They're bloated beyond recognition. A couple of the more advanced cases have exploded, there's flesh and cartilage and shards of bone splattered on the walls.

I blow my lunch; everything comes up.

"I had to show you," Lone Wolf says. " 'Cause you're gonna have to tell them about it."

I force myself to look. There are seventeen of them. They are, were, all prisoners. White, Hispanic, black, young, middle-aged. The victims, the snitches. Seventeen mouths stuffed with seventeen cocks. Even the charred ones.

"I had to show you," Lone Wolf says.

"I guess."

We go outside, shutting the door behind us. The smell permeates everything. It'll keep me focused on the business at hand.

We head back down the hallway to the main area.

"Who did it?" I ask. I have to.

Lone Wolf shakes his head.

"It'll never come out."

"It may have to," I tell him. "You can't kill seventeen men like that and pretend it didn't happen, pull the rug over it. Even if they were snitches."

"I don't know," he says. "They were dead and done before the rest of us were able to do anything."

"Truth?" I ask. "Be straight with me, man. This is no time for bullshit."

"Truth," he says. "Listen, man, you think I'd of perpetrated something that stupid? After what my trial was about?"

"Okay," I say. "I believe you." Whether I do or not it doesn't matter, because I'll find out eventually. Maybe not who the ones were that did it, but whether or not my guys were in on it. That's all I really care about. I want to end this as soon as possible, and I want my four to come out as clean as possible.

The three women have soaked through their clothes with their sweat. The room they're being held in is small, windowless, no air circulation. They're sprawled out on chairs, drugged with the heat, their shoes kicked off, the soles of their stockinged feet grimy and slick. One, slightly younger and more attractive than the other two (the one Lone Wolf stopped from being raped), has taken off her pantyhose in a futile attempt at relief. Rivers of perspiration run down their bodies from their underarms, along their ribs to below their rippled bellies. The tops of all their skirts are black with sweat—if you took their clothes off and wrung them out you'd get five pounds of salt water.

I turn to the two inmates guarding them; overt queens, the next-best thing to a eunuch for the job. Lone Wolf is taking care of business.

"Wait outside," I instruct the guards. My escort goes out with them, allowing the women and me some privacy.

"My name is Will Alexander," I inform the women. I speak softly, conversationally. "I've been appointed by the governor to try and mediate in here, between the government and the prisoners."

"You're the lawyer for those guys on Death Row, aren't you?" the one who was almost raped asks.

"That's right." I recognize her now, she's a receptionist in the medical unit. Martha something.

"Why are you doing this?" she asks. "Why isn't the governor in here?"

"Because they won't talk to him, that's why." She's getting on my nerves real fast.

"Figures." She slumps back, her legs splayed out in front of her. I'll bet she doesn't do that in front of any of the straight prisoners; not now, anyway. I wonder what kind of cock-tease she was before; a woman in jail, any woman, has tremendous power. Some of them abuse it. Some of them have paid for that: during the Oklahoma state prison riot a few years back one of the female guards, who used to flaunt it, tight jeans and push-up bras and the rest, was gang-raped 167 times.

"How long are we going to be in here?" one of the other women asks. Her voice shakes.

"I don't know. Until we reach a settlement."

"God, I don't know how much longer I can endure this," she moans. "I don't know, I'm about to flip out."

"Look," I say, moving over next to her, "that's the worst thing you could do."

"I know that," she wails. "I've been indoctrinated, same as everyone else works here. But I can't help it, I'm scared to death."

"I'll do the best I can, as fast as I can," I say. "We're all in this together." I pat her on the shoulder. "Hang on, okay? It's going to work out."

I move away. I don't want to get close to them, they could latch onto me like drowning men to a life-raft.

"How are they treating you?" I ask. "Do you have enough food and water?"

"Who can eat in this heat?" the third one volunteers. "We have water, though."

"Are they behaving?"

"They were going to rape us at the beginning," Martha says.

"Were you? Sexually assaulted?"

"No," she says. "One of them was about to, they had my clothes off and he had his penis out. But they stopped him. Your men."

"Well," I say, "if that's the worst thing that's happened to you, I think you got off pretty lucky. You could've had eight hundred men raping you. Some of them have AIDS."

They gulp, their mouths round like goldfishes.

"You're not in any danger now," I assure them. "Your guards are homosexual, which means the prisoners want to make sure nothing happens to you." I get up. "I've got to go up there now and get to work. I'll come down when I can to see if you're all right."

"He saved my life," Martha says. "All our lives."

"That's good to know," I tell her. "I'm glad for you."

And for them. My four. Truthfully, more for them.

The guards are more emphatic.

"We sat there listening to them killing off the snitches," the senior in service tells me, "and we knew we were next. And we could tell from all the screaming and how long it was taking that it wouldn't be easy. They'd have done us as bad as they did them, we knew it."

We're in the cellblock cafeteria, where they'd been parked from the time they were pulled out of the demolished control center.

"Those bikers saved our hides," he continues. "No doubt in my mind about it."

"We owe them," chimes in another.

Talk about the worm turning; no wonder the prisoners selected me to be the mediator. If I hadn't taken the job, this prison would have turned into the Alamo.

During a break in the negotiations I ask Lone Wolf why he did it: why he took on the responsibility for trying to put things in order and for saving the hostages' lives.

" 'Cause I didn't want to get killed myself," he says flatly. "Something like this gets started you don't know how it's gonna end up. Gets to be the third, fourth day, you're all climbing the walls, some cat thinks you looked the wrong way at him and offs you. Shit, man, most of these cats're nuts anyway.

"Anyway," he says, "I believe in organization. My organization's got rules, we all live by 'em, we get along fine. People start breaking the rules, it all turns to shit. The thing is with most of these dipshits they ain't never lived by any rules, which is why their sorry asses are in here and always will be. What it is, Mr. lawyer ol' buddy, nobody else was gonna do it. They didn't have a plan, know what I mean? You got to have a plan in life. Mine is to get out of here alive. So I did what I had to do."

IT'S THE USUAL repetitive list of grievances. After five thousand years of trying to figure it out—whether it's Alcatraz or Devil's Island or the Gulag, taking men out of society without dehumanizing them still escapes us.

"They have got to stop feeding us this shit."

Food.

"It will flat-out kill you, you eat this shit year in, year fucking out. We got to get served food decent for human beings." Maggots had been found (more than once) in some meat that was about to be cooked: somebody in the supply chain's making money.

"These cells're built too small for *one* person. Doubling up's too crowded and three's fucking impossible." The number of rapes and fights among cell-mates had gone up fifty percent in the past year.

"The library's a joke. They don't even have state lawbooks in it, let alone federal."

"You could be dead and you still won't get in to see a doctor." AIDS among the general population had skyrocketed; to the point where an AIDS ward was going to be necessary. That was one of the main grievances—keep the fucking AIDS inmates away from everyone else. In the meantime the poor bastards who tested positive were treated worse than lepers. They were completely segregated and shunned.

(At least the epidemic had the effect of cutting needle use to virtually zero. The junkies were kicking rather than risking unsterile needles.)

"They expect us to obey their fucking rules. They got rules, too. They gotta go by the rules like we do." Such as a guard's not allowed to beat a prisoner senseless because the prisoner wears a Rastaman 'do that the guard personally finds obnoxious.

They have a list of eighty-two grievances. Two thirds of them are petty, the annoyances that bureaucracies build up over the years to fuck with people's heads. I sign off on those right away. The others are more fundamental: better food, alleviation of over-crowding, better redress of grievances, stopping favoritism from guards and staff. Most important, to *not* be punished without reason because somebody with a little authority got in a fight with his wife or kids that morning.

The bottom line: they want some dignity. They want to be treated like men, not animals. Even though they have to live in cages, they still want to be treated like men.

Every time a prison explodes, that's the bottom line.

What I'd give for a cold Michelob right now. We've been going at it for fourteen, sixteen hours. Despite the attitude I'd copped with the governor, I don't have a free hand. I don't want one. It's their prison, they have to live with it long after my graceful exit from the scene. Besides, I can't approve things, material or jurisdictional, that can't be delivered.

I have an open line to the governor. He answers halfway through the first ring. We talk.

"The food's not a problem," he assures me. "On the contrary. I'm going to use it as an issue to highlight corruption in the supply chain."

What a sweetheart—anything for his fellow man, especially if he can make brownie points with it.

The over-crowding's stickier.

"The good citizens of this impoverished state vote for mandatory sentencing," he says, his words dripping with sarcasm, "then they turn down a bond issue to build another prison to house all the criminals they want to put away."

It's weird with these politicians, they can be real people but as soon as they assume public office they start talking like they're on television, even if it's a private conversation. It must come with the franchise. I can picture him in bed with his old lady: "I've been reviewing the options, darling, and examining the situation pro and con, it's my considered opinion that we should fuck tonight."

"If it was designed as a one-man cell," I tell him, "they want one man in it. Period. It's gonna be a deal-breaker. Especially with the AIDS problem."

"The county jails are already filled to overflowing," he bitches. "Given that most of them aren't suited to handling hard-core criminals in the first place."

There's a pregnant pause from his end; I can feel the decision coming over the wire.

"So be it, then," he exclaims. I detect a certain glee in his voice. Fuck the taxpayers, they want to have their cake and eat it, too? Well, they can't.

"It's the law, so we'll obey it. We'll take over that abandoned Army depot west of Gallup from the Feds and use those barracks." The bastard's slick, I give him credit: he's had that card up his sleeve for months, now he's going to get to play it and look good, too. "Washington'll be tickled, and we can put some people to work cleaning it up and staffing it. It's going to cost money we don't have, but *c'est la vie*. Even so, we'll wind up throwing a lot of bad people back out onto the streets, but that's tough titty. Maybe this'll wake up the populace to voting another prison."

If Robertson's in the room with the governor, which he undoubtedly is, he's wincing, hearing that. Dumb bastard busts his chops putting the bad guys away, one phone call from me and coveys of them are flying the coop.

"What else?" the governor asks.

"Amnesty."

"There are men dead in there."

"Yes," I affirm, "there are."

"Who were murdered by other prisoners."

"Correct."

"They can't walk that."

"That's what I've told them. They know it. They're trying to cut the best deal they can. Like us."

"Do you know who the perps are?" he asks.

"No," I answer truthfully, "but they do."

"They'll have to face the music. We'd burn the place down first before we granted a blanket amnesty."

For what it's worth, I agree with him, but it's not my place to say. Anyway, I don't want him to forget that I'm an independent agent.

"When are you going to start back up again?" he asks.

"In the morning. We're beat to shit."

"Good luck. I'm here for you, Alexander."

"That's reassuring." I hang up before he has a chance to think about whether that's sarcasm or flattery.

It's night. I don't know what time, I didn't bring anything valuable in with me. The heat is stultifying, it's so hot and dense with smoke I can hardly breathe. I'm sticky, wet, my clothes are a mess, my armpits and balls itch like I've got a terminal case of crabs. All around me, eight hundred men feel the same way.

Normally I would leave at the end of each day and report to the governor. Tonight we've decided I should stay over, because it's close to now or never; we make a deal soon or they lay siege.

But I can't sleep. Too hot, too tense. I'm lying on a bunk in a cell they gave me that's on the top floor, way off in a corner, as far from the action as you can get and still be in the building. It's supposed to catch some breeze, they wanted me to have a little comfort, if such a thing is possible.

There isn't any breeze. The air hangs lifeless, like the mutilated corpses sleeping permanently four floors below.

Outside the cells, silently prowling the tiers, inmate-guards take turns protecting me. Every few minutes, someone looks in on me. I don't know who they are, they're all still masked, they'll remain so until this is over and everyone's disarmed.

It's been very quiet for the past hour; a collective wind of sleep has drifted through the prison, an invisible film that's putting things to rest, for a time. I could feel it earlier, a fog in motion, what the drugged sleep that comes to the addict must feel like. Exhaustion, physical and emotional, has set in, enveloped all in one; all the men in here are part of one chaotic organism. One string is cut and the whole thing collapses.

One of the smart things the prisoner council did was to establish a night-time curfew. Everyone but guards in their cells at night. The prisoners were happy to accept it; it gives them a chance to replenish their energy, to try and sleep. You can't sleep with one eye open, listening and waiting for some hyped-up crazo to slip into your space and cut out your heart.

Somewhere in this prison someone might be sleeping, but I doubt it, unless it's the sleep of sheer exhaustion. A man who could sleep under these circumstances would have to have no conscience, no blood in his veins. Almost everyone, I'm sure, is like me; awake, alert, trying to be calm. It's the best you can do under these conditions.

It's too still; I can't hear the footfalls of my guards.

Cautiously, as quietly as possible, I push up from my bunk. I'm fully dressed, I'd rather stay in these encrusted clothes than take them off and then have to put them back on. I pad silently to the open door of my cell and peer out.

No one's on the floor. My guards have disappeared. I can't see very far, the smoke's too thick, but I know the floor is deserted.

The hair on the back of my neck stands up, electric.

It's a set-up. Something out there is coming for me.

I strain to look down the corridor, both ways. It's impossible to see clearly more than ten yards in either direction. The omnipresent smoke fills the building, backlit by fires near and far.

I have to get out of here. I have to find Lone Wolf.

I slide out of my cell, my back pressed against the concrete corridor wall. I'm scared shitless. This wasn't part of the bargain. As quietly as possible I start shuffling down the corridor in the direction of the command center, where Lone Wolf and the other heavies are bivouacked.

The floor is still wet, and by now it's become sticky as well, encrusted God-knows-what forming a gel under the flow. It feels like walking on rotted jellyfish that have been lying in the sun, viscid and squishy at the same time.

I'm at the complete opposite end from the control center, and on the other side to boot. To get there I'm going to have to traverse the entire building, and drop down two floors.

I stop. Despite the intense heat, my skin has gone dry, clammy. My lips are suddenly chapped; maybe I'm more aware of everything right now, particularly anything tactile—I'm feeling parts of my body that I never feel, like I'm living inside a foreign, hostile country.

Ahead of me, in my corridor, I sense a figure coming in my direction. I can't see him, and I don't think he sees me; but I feel him, feel his silent footsteps on the hard floor. My senses are more highly attuned than I'd thought possible; I feel as tuned in as an Indian scout on patrol. The floor is moving under my feet and I can feel it.

It should be one of Lone Wolf's emissaries, coming to check on me. It should be; everyone else is mandated to be bunkered down for the night in his own little space. Only the appointed guards are supposed to be walking the smoky, dark corridors.

Go back to your cell, man. Go back to your cell and wait, like they told you to. Everything is under control.

The footsteps are steadily coming closer. I can hear them now. Probably twenty, thirty yards away. Slow and measured, carefully. With the floor being as wet and slimy as it is one mis-step and you could fall and break a bone, or even buy the farm completely, over the railing a hundred feet to concrete.

Go back to your cell, lawyer. This is not your element. Do what they told you.

From the opposite direction, a second set of footsteps, also coming in my direction. Coming the same way I've been coming, passing by my cell. I hear the footsteps stop; then they start my way again.

I don't know why it is, the thought I'm thinking this instance; but whatever is happening is wrong. These are not the men Lone Wolf and the convict council have set up for my protection. I don't know why I feel this, but I know it with absolute certainty.

"That you?" one of them calls. The second one.

"Yeh."

"He ain't there. In the cell they gave him."

"Shit."

They've both stopped, where they are. Fifteen yards on either side of me. No one can see anyone else. Five more yards, though, and I'm exposed.

Whoever they are, they want to kill me. Whoever they are; the ones who have the most to lose, the ones who started it, that's who it has to be, the ones who burned down the snitches' cells, tortured and killed them.

"He ain't in the meeting room. I checked, all the way 'round. He'd of had to come by me," *número uno* calls out.

"He must've got by my side before I started," the second one calls back. "So fuckin' thick in here he could've practically walked past me I wouldn't've seen him."

"He's in here somewheres."

I look on both sides of me. Solid wall, no cells to duck into and hide.

The first one calls out. "You stay there. I'll come to you."

You cocksucker Robertson, governor asshole, warden dipshit. This is not the way it was supposed to be.

The first one starts walking towards his comrade; towards me. I hear his footsteps clearly now, carefully navigating the wet concrete.

He emerges from a cloud of black smoke like an emissary from Hell; he sees me, I see him. He stops dead in his tracks, almost frozen in mid-step. For the briefest of flashes we stare at each other. I have one advantage—I knew he was coming.

He has all the other advantages.

"What the . . . Hey!" he yells.

I take off, boring as hard as I can right at him, he's not expecting that, I'm going to try to run right through him, knock him off balance, escape into the darkness.

My soles slip on the wet floor.

I fall forward, catching myself at the last instant on my palms, pushing up. He's come out of his shock, starts at me, swinging his weapon, a sawed-off twelve-gauge shotgun.

"Hey," he yells again. The shotgun swings up towards my face.

He slips.

I'm up, sliding by him, my shoulder dropped low like my coach taught me years ago in tenth-grade J.V. football, smashing into his gut under the shotgun, knocking him back against the railing. His legs shoot out from under him and he goes down hard on his back. As he lands his weapon discharges into the air: it's unbelievably loud, like a bomb going off right in my ear, the explosion is deafening in the silence, echoing like a roll of thunderclaps against the hard concrete walls.

I'm running, my hand on the railing for guidance.

I hear the second man coming and there's another shot in my direction, this time from a rifle; the bullet ricochets off the wall a few feet ahead of me.

I'm running as fast as I can but I don't know if it's fast enough, I can't out-run a bullet, they're probably in much better shape than me, all they have to do all day is work out if they're fitness freaks like so many are inside.

Men are out of their cells now, yelling, it's all confusion, bedlam, I'm half-running half-sliding through patches of smoke, past men who see me appearing suddenly out of the blackness, their instincts drive them, they dive out of my way, they have no idea what's happening except people are trying to kill each other.

Behind me the footsteps, running at me, there seem to be more than two pair now, I can't breathe, the smoke and heat are sapping all my strength, what little I have left after being in it all day and half the night, my legs are turning to spaghetti, I slip on the wet floor again, getting a face-full of the scummy mess, slide, pushing myself up, crawling on my hands and knees, I'm wet with this shit from head to toe, running again, my pursuers closing on me, I hear them behind me.

Through the smoke the four-floor-deep open staircase looms up in front of me. Uselessly anchoring it is the multi-level, blasted-out guard cage, a twisted mass of scorched metal and safety glass, like the hull of a rotting sunken ship, the controls obliterated, the wiring ripped out. I dive for the stairs that spiral around it, taking them three at a time, falling ass over teakettle, my shoulder's hurting like hell now, a wrenching, burning sensation, it feels like I've torn my arm out of the socket, I'm pushing as hard as I can down. Voices yelling incoherently from somewhere off in the distance.

My pursuers are virtually on top of me now, I hear them right behind me, they know this place and I don't. I can't outrun them, I'm not going to make it all the way to safe harbor. There is no safe harbor in this place.

A shotgun blast detonates next to me, it's so close it's almost inside my head, louder even than the previous blast. I hear the pellets hitting flesh and muscle and a man screams. It's all happening right on top of me, fast and furious.

Then two more blasts.

The echoes bounce off the walls, almost as loud as the discharge. They roll down the corridors, throughout the entire building, in deafening waves.

The echoes roll on and on, growing fainter, then at last the noise stops, and it's quiet.

I can't move. I'm curled up into a ball, my head smothered in my arms.

Footsteps walking down the stairs. Feet stop at my buried face.

"You all right?"

The bikers are staring down at me.

"Yeh, you're all right," Lone Wolf decides, looking closer. "You just smell bad. But you ain't dead . . . are you?"

"Dumb luck I'm not," I answer, my voice a hoarse whisper.

"They offed your guards," he informs me. "That's why you were out there on your own."

I nod, numbly. Slowly, I get up, holding the railing for support.

"Sorry about that," he says, flashing me his thin smile, "guess not everybody in here loves you like we do."

Amnesty is no longer an issue. The men who had tried to kill me were the ones who had started the riot and been the ringleaders in the torture-killings of the snitches. They're going to pay, and pay heavily. I'll see to that personally. I get no argument from the prisoner council.

By the end of the day, it's a done deal. All the prisoners' grievances will be addressed. Just as importantly, there will be no unit punishment for what's gone on. Only the perpetrators of the uprising, and those who actually participated in the killings, will face charges. The prisoner council has ID'd and secured them.

We formalize the agreement in the warden's office. Martha the hostage writes it up long-hand—there's no electricity for the typewriters or copying machines. I sign for the state; Lone Wolf and two other prison-leaders sign for them.

It's over.

I STAND TALL, next to the governor, in front of the television cameras. It's a very big deal. His eminence talks about me like I'm the second coming, the saviour of the masses.

Privately, I made sure he knew, in detail, the role the bikers had played. They're entitled to consideration now. He doesn't disagree, but he makes no formal commitment.

"You gave away the store," Robertson accuses me as we move to the side, giving the governor center-stage.

"Next time you do it," I throw back at him. This is not the time to be pushing my buttons. "I risked my life for you and your buddies," I remind him. "My clients saved eleven of your people and probably a hundred or more inmates. You owe them, John. Personally and professionally. The state owes them. If you had any balls at all, any guts, you'd let them out. On an IOU if for no other reason."

"My ass," he mutters. He's sorry he spoke, he wishes this entire episode would go away.

"It will be," I tell him. "Those men shouldn't be in there, John. It was your people that put them in, and they're dirty. If I didn't know it before I know it for sure now, I know it like I know my own heart-beat. And I'm going to nail them. To the fucking cross. They'll be able to drive an eighteen-wheeler up their assholes by the time they get out of where I'm going to send them."

"Keep your voice down, man," Robertson hisses. "Remember where you are."

"I know where I am," I say. "Do *you?*"

He starts to walk away from me. I grab his shoulder, stop him. He's got to hear this.

"They're dirty, John. They're poisoning you. I'm telling you this as a friend, damn it. If you had any brains, any integrity, you'd cop to it and cut your losses."

He braces. He's a mean fighter when he's aroused.

"You can't put it back in the bottle," he tells me. "I'm clean and so are my men and all the bullshit in the world won't change that."

"It isn't bullshit and you fucking well know it," I throw at him.

"I'm betting my career that it is," he says. "And I only bet sure things."

"There's no such thing as a sure thing, ace."

He starts to walk away. Then he turns back.

"Don't think this entitles you to special treatment," he says. "You were performing a public service. No one forced you."

I laugh in his face. After all that's gone down he's got the sanctimoniousness to say that out loud.

"I'll remember that the next time you call me," I tell him.

When I go home I burn my clothes and bury the ashes. Then I take a six-pack into the shower, where I scrub my skin raw for an hour and wash my hair half a dozen times.

"Come to papa."

I'm lying on my back, in my own bed in my own house. Earlier, I had a wonderful home-cooked meal: beef Stroganoff over wild rice, fresh green beans, salad, home-made apple pie à la mode. (And wine—a bottle of Mondavi Cabernet '85 Private Reserve which I'd saved for a special occasion. I consider getting out of jail alive a special occasion.) All lovingly cooked by my honey's own two hands, even the pie.

She comes, her fingers grabbing hard at my hair, her body twisting and tensing with orgasm, 'shit' she whispers, 'oh fuck,' all the creative things you say when your head is coming off from sex, I pull her closer, pushing my mouth against her wet sticky hair, tonguing her, nibbling her clitoris, she comes again, how nice it is to give pleasure, without any inner warning I start thinking of the men inside that prison who will never taste between a woman's legs for the rest of their lives and I start to shake, I'm shaking like I've got fever, Mary Lou's next to me, holding me, 'it's okay, baby,' she says, 'you're safe now' she assures me, her body against mine, holding me, making me safe.

The fear goes away and we make love, tenderly, like in the Song of Solomon, she anoints me with her love.

"I was scared," she says. We're watching David Letterman, finishing the second bottle of wine. "I couldn't let you know because it would've messed up your head, but I was terrified. I was so happy when I saw you walk out of there in one piece."

I turn to her; she's crying, silently, big soft tears running down her face.

"I was so scared," she whispers.

I pull her close. The telephone rings.

"Is this Mr. Alexander?"

I sit up, suddenly short of breath.

"Yes."

"It's Rita Gomez."

"Yes, I know. I recognize your voice."

"I saw you tonight. On TV. That was good what you did."

"Where are you?"

Mary Lou sits up, looks at me, reading my mind. I nod that she's right.

"In Greeley. That's in Colorado."

"I know where it is. Who knows you're there?"

"Nobody. I'm hiding."

"Where have you been?" I ask. "What happened to you?"

"I got a phone call . . ." She's tentative, scared people get that way, women especially. "The day before I was supposed to come down."

"Who called you?"

"I . . . I don't know."

I'll let that pass.

"How did anyone know how to find you?"

"I don't know," she says again. "I didn't tell nobody. I swear."

Five hundred miles away, the walls still have ears.

"Are you mad at me?" she asks, her voice fearful. "For running away?"

"No," I answer. That's a lie; how could I not be mad, she's ruined lives. But that was then; now, I don't know. In light of everything, what happened with her seems to have been inevitable, preordained.

"What did they say?" I ask. "Whoever it was who called you."

"That I'd never make it back to testify. That if I tried I'd get killed." She's scared out of her mind, I can hear it in her voice, clearly, how can I be mad at her, this call takes a kind of guts I've never known.

"You wouldn't have been," I reassure her, as best I can. "I promised you that."

"I was scared."

"Where you are now—is it safe?"

"I think so. I hope."

"Okay, look. Do you remember that lawyer friend of mine? The one whose office you gave your statement in, in Denver?"

"Yes?"

"He's going to come pick you up. He's going to take you to Denver and he's going to stay with you until I get there. Do you understand?"

"Yes."

"You'll be completely safe."

"I don't want to run no more."

"Good. That's good. You shouldn't have to."

"I didn't do nothing wrong. Except what they made me." She's starting to cry.

"You didn't. That's right. You're going to be safe. You don't have to run anymore."

"When will you get here?"

"As soon as I can. By morning."

She gives me her address, a motel, and the phone number. She was smart for once; she registered under an alias.

"My friend will be there in a couple hours," I assure her, "and I'll be there, too."

"I'm not running anymore," she reiterates, as if repeating it gives her strength. "When I saw you on the television and they said what you'd done, you know, I said to myself, 'Rita, if he can help them, he can help you.' "

Son of a bitch. It was worth it; it was really worth it.

"That's right," I tell her. "Now just hang on, okay? I'll be there real soon."

"Listen," she says, stopping me before I hang up on her, "who called me? I think I know . . . who it was."

She'd get there. I knew she would, sooner or later.

"The cop," she answers. "The nice one."

"Gomez." It's always the nice one who fucks you.

"I know his voice."

"WE'RE READY, YOUR HONOR."

"Call Rita Gomez to the stand."

Five months ago I walked out of the state prison, and got the telephone call from my star witness. Today, we're finally back in the District Court again with our petition to be allowed to reopen the trial. The wheels of justice may not be frozen, but they do grind glacially slow.

I didn't know if Martinez would even let me back in; I'd blown it once, you usually don't get a second chance. I'm sure it was the overwhelming, positive publicity from my handling of the prison situation that swayed him in my favor. It's all politics in the end; they don't want the press trumpeting about a miscarriage of justice for these hardened killers who saw the light and saved some innocent lives, and their lawyer who selflessly and heroically brought about a bloodless (only convicts were killed and they don't count) resolution.

Anyway, this is only a hearing, a first step. At best what I get from Judge Martinez is the chance to present fresh evidence showing that the original trial was tainted, and that he should grant a new one. Even if we win here, the odds are long that Martinez will ultimately reverse his decision. But the beginning of the process starts here, and it's vital, because if we strike out this time, it's curtains.

Robertson fought me tooth and nail; he was bitter when the judge ruled he'd hear the appeal, based solely on testimony from a self-admitted perjurer.

"Last time I was a gentleman," he told me. "This time I'm not taking any prisoners."

"Not by the hair of my chinny-chin-chin," was my flip-the-bird reply.

Privately, I'm legitimately outraged that he'd take such a hard line. This enmity between him and me has gotten too bitter for my taste. We're lawyers, can't he remember that? Can't he remember that the bikers saved his ass, the governor's, everyone's, just a few months ago? He's taken such a stand on this, on a principle floating on quicksand, that if it doesn't go his way it could do something terrible to him.

We glare at each other as Rita swears to tell nothing but the truth and takes her seat.

There are only a few people in the courtroom. Mary Lou and Tommy are at my table with me; on the other side, Robertson sits next to Moseby, with Gomez and Sanchez in the first row behind them.

I lead her through the deposition that she gave in Denver. She's scared, but speaks calmly, directly. Occasionally Martinez asks her a question, mostly for clarification. Otherwise, it's low-key.

Robertson takes over after lunch. He strolls up to her, strikes his aw-shucks pose.

"Have you ever read a book called *Alice in Wonderland?*" he asks her.

"No, sir."

"You've heard of it though, haven't you?"

"Yes, sir. Didn't they make a movie?"

"Probably," he says dryly, "they've made movies about everything. So you know generally what it's about."

"Sort of," she answers tentatively, as if she's afraid he's going to quiz her on it and she won't have the answers.

"Do you know what I think?" Robertson continues, kind of smiling at her, almost in a friendly fashion. "I think that you have read *Alice in Wonderland*, Miss Gomez."

"No sir. I never have."

"I think you read *Alice in Wonderland* and thought to yourself 'doggone this sure is neat, the way everything gets twisted all around in here 'till nobody knows what the truth is, if there is any truth to begin with.' That's what you thought to yourself after you read *Alice in Wonderland*, isn't it?"

"No. I told you. I never read it."

"What is it they say in that book?" he asks rhetorically. "About black being white and everything's turned upside down until you can't tell what's what . . . curiouser and curiouser is one of the phrases, do you remember that, Miss Gomez?"

"How could I if I never read it?" she asks, bewildered.

"And you thought, boy, it sure was fun in that book the way truth got stood on its head. More fun than I've ever had. I'll bet it'd be neat to do something like that . . . to turn the truth on its head."

"No!"

"Objection!" I say. "He's badgering her. Furthermore, this line of questioning is ludicrous."

"Is it?" Robertson roars, turning to me. He turns back, faces the judge. "Is it any more ludicrous than this complete fabrication that this witness has come in here with today? She makes Alice look like Diogenes, your honor."

"Make your point, counselor," Martinez chides him.

"My point, sir, is that everything this witness has said here today is a pack of vicious lies, a pack of frightened, evil lies of a paranoid, confused woman. This woman was on the stand for a week at the trial, your honor. She was grilled mercilessly by not one but four separate and distinguished lawyers for the defense. Nonc of this bilge was ever remotely alluded to. And now, more than a year later, she mysteriously materializes and recants everything. On the face of it, it's impossible to believe what she's saying."

Rita Gomez is out of it now; it's between Robertson and the judge. I watch his face as Robertson illustrates how bogus her entire new story must be.

"If this witness is telling the truth now," he says passionately, "then the entire District Attorney's office, and the entire Santa Fe police force, are corrupt from top to bottom. If she's telling the truth now, I'm corrupt."

He's looking up at him, daring Martinez to call his bluff. Martinez has no intention of doing anything of the kind; John's a fair-haired boy in these parts and an acknowledged straight-shooter.

"Let's look at what she's said today," he continues. "She was told by an assistant District Attorney that if she didn't lie on the stand she would be arraigned as an accessory to murder. If that statement is true, that man, who is my top trial assistant, who has conducted hundreds of trials, is corrupt.

"If what this admitted perjurer says is true," he presses on, "if what is true now was false then, they fed her information. They made the case for her. If that's true, those men are guilty of obstructing justice in a murder case. They could go to jail until hell freezes over if that is true."

I'm watching the judge; he's paying close attention to what Robertson says.

"How much coincidence are we willing to believe?" Robertson asks him. "How is it that this admitted perjurer, who knew the men that were subsequently convicted by an impartial jury and are now awaiting the properly and soberly arrived-at carrying out of their sentence on Death Row for this heinous crime, how is it that she knew them, she was with them on that night, she was with the victim on that night, the convicted murderers knew the victim and were seen with him on that night, she was raped by them, on that night, the victim was murdered by them in the same location where they raped her, on that night, all of this is indisputable, it isn't being called into question here today, how is it with all that coincidence, somehow they didn't kill him? It's impossible to believe that. As I stand here and recount it for you now it's impossible to even consider. Listen to what she's saying."

He turns and looks at her.

"According to her, someone got to her. She says, now, not then, but now, more than a year later, that it was the police, the prosecutor's office. Well, she's lying."

He leans in to her. She jerks back in her chair.

"Maybe she's telling the truth," he says. "Partially. Maybe someone did get to her. But I warrant it wasn't the police or my deputy. I'll stake my reputation on that. I'll put my career on the line. If someone did get to her," he says, "it was someone from the Scorpions, the outlaw bikers who committed that murder. They found her and they threatened her and they scared her to death. They're a hell of a lot scarier than Mr. Moseby, I guarantee you that."

"They did not!" she yells.

Martinez pounds his gavel.

"Please restrain yourself, Miss Gomez," he admonishes her. "This is not a trial, but a hearing."

"Objection, your honor," I say.

"On what grounds?" he asks me.

"This is a summation, your honor, and a damn fanciful one at that."

"And this is a hearing, Mr. Alexander. Not a trial."

Having put me in my place, he nods to Robertson to continue.

"Isn't it much more logical to conclude, your honor, that what I'm saying now has the ring of truth, and that this witness's testimony today is a frightened attempt to save her skin? Isn't that where she's coming from, if you look at this with any objectivity at all?"

He walks back to his table, leans up against it, calm now, in control (not that he always wasn't).

"The point of this hearing today is to decide whether there is a compelling reason to grant a new trial. I repeat, a *compelling* reason. And there isn't. You know it and I know it. All we're being presented with here today is one solitary witness who's saying one thing now and another thing at another time. That's over, if it may please this court. That's what the trial was about. Whether her testimony, and that of dozens of other people, was truthful or not. The jury made its decision. It's over now. It's history. This petition must be denied or we will all be party to a terrible miscarriage, not only of justice, but of our entire legal system."

Martinez takes a half-hour break. He asks Robertson and me to join him in his chambers.

"Your argument's great, John," he tells Robertson. "But if she really was lying then, four innocent guys are going to die. Do any of us want that on our conscience?"

He turns to me. "Do you have any other witnesses, any other evidence, anything to present, that will bolster your position?"

Read between the lines, he's saying. You're a hero, you helped the state, but you have to give me something else if I'm to help you now; if this is all you have it's thin gruel, he can't go against the District Attorney after he's put forth such a compelling argument.

Before I can answer, the phone rings. Martinez picks it up, listens a moment.

"Yes, I am," he replies to whatever question's been put to him.

He cups the receiver, peers over it at us.

"The governer," he says quietly.

He listens again.

"Yes, I know," he says at length. "I'm fully aware that these men saved eleven lives. I agree with you—they deserve consideration." He listens again for a moment, shakes his head. "No. I won't go so far as to say I think they're innocent, not even to you in private. They probably aren't, the case against them was strong and compelling. But I tend to agree with you that if there's any possibility, any shadow of a doubt that this witness could have perjured herself earlier, then they deserve to be given another chance."

He listens for another moment.

"I will, and thank you."

He hangs up, looks at us.

"The governor thinks they deserve the benefit of the doubt."

"If there was one," Robertson replies, hanging tough. "The governor's entitled to his opinion, but the law's the law."

Stubborn bastard. You've got to hand it to him.

Martinez looks at him coolly. "I'm aware of the law," he responds without emotion.

There's a letter of commendation from the warden. Also a strong plea from the eight guards and the three women. The bikers, especially Lone Wolf, saved their lives.

"While in chambers, I received a telephone call from the governor," Martinez states. We're back in open court. "He asked that I give whatever consideration I can to the plight of these men who helped avert what could have been a major tragedy." He pauses, looks off above our heads. Then he's back to business. "I thanked him for his advice and support, but I reminded him that I have to base my decision on the law. And nothing else. He understood." He bends down to our brief, looks up again.

"Please understand that I am casting no aspersions whatsoever on you or anyone in your department or on the police," Judge Martinez now says, staring intently at Robertson.

"In fact, in looking at the present evidence, I believe that a second jury, in a second trial, will come to the same conclusion that the first jury came to. But under the circumstances, I feel it is proper, and will serve the cause of justice, that these men be allowed the chance to have another trial, because even if there is only a one percent chance that there was perjured testimony at the first trial, fairness compels us to examine the case once again.

"Therefore, we are granting defendants' motion for an evidentiary hearing for retrial on the original charges."

Robertson accosts me in the hallway.

"I guess you're feeling pretty good," he says. He's surprisingly calm for having lost one he wanted so badly.

"Better," I reply.

"This was politics," he says, his voice under control. "Pure and simple. You were a hero, you helped the state out of a mess, we threw you a bone. Now we're even. They're still guilty and they're still going to pay for what they did, Will. And I'm going to personally escort that little old lady in the wheelchair to the execution when it happens."

I watch him walk away, ramrod-straight. It isn't a case with him anymore; it's a cause, a vendetta.

Let him rain on our parade. We won today. We're alive.

PART FOUR

PATRICIA WAS FIRED. She calls, naturally, while I'm in a closed-door meeting. An important meeting, with an important client and his wife. A client who, if I do my job right and well, is going to make me a lot of money.

Susan tip-toes in, apologizing profusely for disturbing us, of course she wouldn't have if Patricia hadn't told her it was urgent. She whispers this message in my ear, that my former wife needs my counsel immediately; then quickly, before my blood-pressure starts elevating dangerously, she assures me that Patricia wanted me to know it isn't about Claudia, Claudia isn't hurt or anything like that. It isn't about her at all. Just so I don't panic.

"If it isn't about Claudia, then whatever else it is doesn't matter," I quietly tell Susan. I turn, smile reassuringly at the clients. "My daughter lives with her mother, in Seattle. My former wife . . . the first one," I add, needlessly modifying. Shut up already, man, they don't want to know your entire history. They've got their own problems.

They smile back understandingly; they have children of their own. They smile back because they want me to like them. Because they need me, or think they do.

"I'll have to call Patricia back. Don't bother us again," I instruct her, "unless it's the Supreme Court or the governor. On the murder appeal."

Susan apologizes to my clients and leaves. They smile back understandingly; smiling's about all these unfortunate people have right now.

This man I'm with is the first potential new major-money client

I've had since the firm and I parted company. His name is Clinton Hodges and he's permanently paralyzed from the chest down with a spinal-cord injury. He can move his head and neck freely, talk and swallow, and he's got limited hand and arm mobility, but not much. Not enough to hand-push his new Everest & Jennings wheelchair. He had to get the motorized version, the one that lets you do all the work even if you can only move one finger. If you can't move even one finger, sometimes you can learn to drive the chair by blowing into a tube. Clinton's not that bad off; he can move his fingers. People like Clinton learn, over time, to count their blessings in tiny increments.

He's learning how to drive the wheelchair; some days he does better than other days. Some days he drives the machine into the wall and can't turn it around. His wife or the technician will find him spinning his wheels like a stuck wind-up toy, pinned up against a corner.

Forget his functioning normally again; this poor fellow won't even have the ability to have a regular bowel movement. He'll need constant attendance and monitoring for the rest of his life. If he's lucky, he'll be able to feed himself—if someone hooks the food tray onto his chair, places the utensil in his hand, and folds the hand closed.

He's thirty-three years old. When he was able to stand on his own two feet he was six-three, 215 pounds. His wife is terrific-looking, a statuesque brunette. Their oldest kid is eight, and the baby is just a year old.

Before the accident last year, Clinton coached his son's T-ball team to a league championship. He's one of those extremely physically-oriented guys—owns his own construction company, with sixteen full-time employees, which he built from scratch. Last year they netted over a million dollars, and he'd still be out at a site on the weekend, personally pouring concrete. His company's built up so much business all over the Four Corners he had to get a pilot's license and buy his own airplane. It was delivered less than six months ago, while he was in intensive care, being fitted for a halo brace.

Now he's strapped into a wheelchair, straining every muscle that still responds, just to try to scratch an itch on his nose. Sometimes the itch goes unscratched.

Personal-injury cases are how lawyers get rich. Lawyers like me, who don't have clients like Mobil or IBM. A $3 million liability judgment, which isn't so outlandish these days, can net the lawyer for the plaintiff a million bucks or more. A couple cases like that and the bills take care of themselves.

What happened with Clinton was, he's out riding his bike one bright, sunny morning. A Sunday, it's the one day he allows himself personal recreation, while the wife and kids are at church—they're Mormons, pretty devout, but not smug assholes about it. He's out there with a bunch of his hard-core biking buddies, all strong athletes, they're racing a hard 50K, he's somewhere in the middle of the pack, trying to catch another group ahead of him, so he's about twenty-five yards behind one group and the same distance ahead of another, momentarily separated from a bunch of riders. He's a good rider but some of these guys ride six days a week, plus they're five to fifteen years younger, still he's holding his own, as he's crossing a thoroughfare the light's about to turn from green to yellow to red, he's barrelling through on the yellow, he's clearly got the right-of-way, several witnesses will attest that the light had barely hit yellow when he started through the intersection at thirty-five miles an hour or so on his new boron-graphite racing bike, customized for him at a cost of over two thousand dollars. As he's pumping through, head down, intent on catching the leaders, a lady trucker who's hauling a load of drilling equipment is driving in the opposite direction, on the other side of the road. Now this lady truck-driver just had a fight with her husband, who told her to go fuck herself and the horse she rode in on, if she doesn't like it she can lump it, which means he's out of there for a couple-three days, he's done that before, lammed on her and the kids, drunk up his paycheck on Jim Beam boilermakers, the usual domestic grief. So she's out there on the highway, she's late on her delivery and when you're late for her boss you hear about it all afternoon, she doesn't need anyone else bitching at her, she's had it up to here, thank you, she's trying to light a Virginia Slims, drink a cup of take-out coffee, and she's wrestling through the gears of her twenty-five-year-old Mack, the old-fashioned kind of tugboat no one manufactures anymore. And she's not doing a good job at any of it, the clutch is almost shot, the brakes are metal on metal. She's halfway through the intersection before she realizes it's her turnoff, it's two miles to the next place she can turn around, she sees that the light is changing, no cars coming from the opposite direction, so she does a fast spin of the steering wheel, down-shifting like her arm's on a piston, fishtailing a sharp left across the divider, and there's Clinton. And it flashes through her mind if I stand on the brakes I spill coffee on my new stone-washed jeans and scald the shit out of myself. So she kind of half-brakes, half-swerves, and slides sideways into Clinton, who never saw it coming.

Now he's a quadriplegic the rest of his life, the insurance company won't pay more than the $250,000 policy limit, which won't even cover his rehab, much less take care of him and his family for the rest of his life, and the driver's company is balking at paying anything above the benefit. Why? Because they're claiming he ran the light, citing the traffic regulation that a left hand turn can be made on the yellow-to-red configuration but that a vehicle coming straight through, after the light hits yellow, is at risk, and they're claiming it was yellow long before he hit the intersection, that he had ample time to brake, but chose not to. Which is a lie, and they know it. It's a bullshit reason, a cover for the real reason. The real reason is that Clinton is a rich white Mormon and the lady trucker who hit him is Hispanic. And in this neck of the woods rich white Mormons are not well thought of. Even if they're good family men, hard-working, industrious, and have the right-of-way at a traffic light.

The company won't pay because they figure a jury will vote the issue on race, and around here the race not to be in this kind of trial is white. Reverse discrimination at its ugliest.

But what they're forgetting, which they do all the time because they're not only rich and arrogant, but stupid as well, is that I won't be trying my case against Izela Munoz, Hispanic mother of four. I'm trying my case against a ten-billion-dollar energy company. If there's one thing juries around here hate worse than rich Anglos, it's rich energy companies. I'm going to show that jury that it's not Izela's money they're taking, it's a billion-dollar conglomerate's.

I'm with the Hodgeses for a couple hours, going over details. Preparation for a trial such as this costs money, a lot of it. By the time you're finished with the models and investigators and background and everything, all the hours, it'll be over $50,000. I pay for all of it, out of my own pocket because I don't bill them hourly, like in a normal case. I'll take a percentage. Thirty-three percent. Some lawyers take fifty percent. It's money well-earned, because you're working without a net, essentially. You can make a fortune, but if you lose it's all flushed. High risk, high reward. Up on the high wire—my kind of case. If I win, I'm solid again, triple-A rating. I can hold my head up anywhere, including the watering holes frequented by my former partners.

It's after lunch before I get back to Patricia. She picks up her private line on the first ring. I get the feeling she's been waiting for my call all this time.

"Will," she says. She's been crying. She isn't now, but I hear the tears that she's shed.

"What is it?"

It better not be about Claudia, that's all I ask. I know she reassured Susan, but it could have been a con to get me to talk. She knows I don't like to talk about her personal life any more. I'm finally over that, and I don't want to get sucked back in.

"I've been fired."

"What?"

The tears start. I can hear them, hear her trying to stop me from hearing them. She doesn't pull it off.

"Fired. I've been fired from my job."

"Why?" I'm surprised; stunned, actually. If there's one thing I know about Patricia it's that she's a good, conscientious worker. And smart. Who fires a smart woman six months after she's been hired and relocated at company expense?

"Because . . . oh shit, I'm so embarrassed." More tears. She blows her nose right into my ear, a good healthy honk.

I know, then. Exactly why. She's been looking for love in all the wrong places.

"I've . . . oh God!" She cries again. "I feel like such a jerk," she says, talking and crying at the same time. "I'm sorry, this is stupid. I'll call back later when I'm . . . when I'm . . ."; and she cries.

"Don't be silly," I counsel her, "and don't hang up," I add quickly, before she can. "I'm not going to judge you no matter what happened, so don't worry, okay?"

"Okay." Sniffle sniffle. Honk! I jerk the phone from my ear before I lose an eardrum. This woman is not demure and lady-like when it comes to emptying her sinuses.

"So . . . are you going to tell me?" I could fill in the blanks for her, leaving out only the specific names and places. I know this road like the back of my hand. But I wait for her to be forthcoming; that's why she called: to tell me, not to be told by me.

She calms down. I picture her in her office, taking a deep breath, getting under control, sitting up straighter. She allowed herself a good cry, now she's going to be an adult.

"I've been having an affair," she informs me.

"I see," I reply neutrally. The 'I see' you use in trial when you're coaxing information from a reluctant witness. The 'I see' that helps lubricate the tongue.

"With one of the senior partners," she continues. "Joby Breckenridge."

"He's the one that hired you," I say, remembering.

"You've got a good memory," she says.

I know Joby. He's a straight shooter. Affairs aren't his style. Certainly not casual ones. But there are always exceptions.

"Serious?" I ask.

"Very," she answers. "Was," she modifies. "Was very. At least I thought. Now it's . . ." she tails off.

"Over."

"Takes two to tango," she says. "He isn't interested in dancing anymore."

"Well . . . these things happen."

"They never happened to me."

"I'm sorry."

"I was in love with him." A silent pause. "I *thought* I was in love with him. Maybe I just wanted to be in love with him. It doesn't matter anyway; not now."

"How did he feel?"

"He said he was." Another pause. She's hearing herself as she tells me; some of this may be coming to her for the first time, even as she articulates it out loud, now. "He probably was. He's not much of a dissembler, even if he is a chicken-shit son of a bitch."

That's the girl—get mad. Healthiest thing in the world. It isn't your fault.

"Okay," I say. "You had an affair . . ."

"Not just an affair, for Christsakes! An affair with a married man, who happens to be my boss."

"It generally isn't considered an affair if one or both of you isn't married," I inform her. "Otherwise it's just fucking."

"Oh . . ."

"So you had an affair with this guy at work . . ."

"My boss . . ."

"With your boss, which, by the way, is the most common kind . . ."

"Thanks. In other words I'm not even special," she complains, starting to fall back into self-deprecation.

"You're special, Patricia," I assure her. "It's just your affair that isn't."

"Whatever. I don't see much difference."

"You will," I say. "Someday, when you're over it."

"Wonderful," she exclaims bitterly.

Fuck. Why are you laying this on my head, lady? We're divorced, remember? Long, long time. I'm not supposed to have to put up with this kind of shit anymore. I've got enough shit of my own to handle.

I don't say that. I can't. She is the mother of my child, now and forever. I will always be there for her, if only because I have to be there for Claudia.

"So you and your boss had an affair," I continue, bringing it back to the center, "and it's over. What does that have to do with your being fired?"

"Because we both can't be in the same workplace anymore," she says. "It's too uncomfortable."

"Too uncomfortable? Come on."

"It is. That's what he told me."

"*He* told *you?*"

"When he told me he was letting me go."

"Which was when?"

"This morning . . . last night . . . I mean we talked about it last night but then we talked about it again this morning. That's when he said he was going to have to."

She starts sniffling again. I wait until she gets it under control.

"He's firing you because he's uncomfortable having you around?" I ask, as gently as possible.

She nods over the phone. "It's too hard on him. He says he can't work with me around. He can't take the guilt—that's what he tells me—told me," she says, putting it already in the past. "He feels uncomfortable whenever he sees me. Because he still wants me," she adds. "He told me that."

"Well. Isn't that a crying shame."

"What?" she asks.

"What about you?"

"What about me?"

"Is there an echo on this line? You. How do *you* feel?" I say to her.

"Awful."

"Besides that. Could you still do your work? Seeing him around, still wanting him?"

"It's hard."

"Can you?"

"Yes," she answers finally. She had to think about it. "I'd still get my work done."

"So the bottom line is he's firing you because you make him uncomfortable. Nothing to do with your performance on the job."

"Yes."

"Well, then," I say, "I've got a very easy answer to this problem."

I hear the pause.

"You do?"

"Yes." I take a moment; I am, first and foremost, a litigator. "Let *him* quit."

"I don't think I heard you."

"Yes you did."

"Did you say 'let *him* quit'?"

"See? You did hear me."

Another pause.

"That's . . . impossible."

"Why?"

"Because . . . it just is."

Again: "Why?"

"Because. It's his firm. He's the boss. He hired me. He can fire me."

"The fuck he can!"

"Will. It's his firm. He's the senior senior."

"I don't give a shit if he's the fucking Pope," I tell her. "He can't fire you for that."

"Well," she says timidly, after another pause. "If you're talking legally . . ."

"That's exactly what I'm talking. I'm a lawyer, that's the talk I talk."

Silence.

"Who hit on who first?" I ask.

"Who . . ."

"Come on, Patricia. If you want me to help you, don't waste my time."

"He did."

"It wasn't mutual."

"I liked him. I found him . . . I find him attractive. Still. But he's married, I wouldn't start something." She pauses. "You know me."

Do I ever.

"Yeh. It's not your style, going after married men."

"No."

"Just wanted to make sure. You've been going through lots of changes this past year."

"Not this," she assures me.

"Yeh, I know." That goes too deep. "Okay. So your married boss made a play for you, you turned him down . . . did you?"

"The first time."

"Right. You turned him down but he kept trying. Because he couldn't help himself. He had to be with you."

"That's what he said. Practically word for word," she adds, hearing the ironic cynicism.

What mortal shits men are.

"And his marriage was starting to go bad," I continue.

"It is bad," she says.

"This is public knowledge?"

"He told me."

Fucking Joby. No straight shooter he after all.

"He was going to leave her," I say. "Whether you were in the picture or not. His marriage was over."

"You know all the lines, don't you?" she asks, anger in her voice.

"I know them, but I've never used them. Not those."

"Sorry."

"And you believed him," I continue.

Total honesty: "I wanted to."

My heart breaks for her, long distance.

"I'm sorry, Patricia."

"It's not your fault," she says softly. I can hear the tears starting to creep into her voice again.

"No crying," I plead. "Not now."

"Okay." Gathering herself. "All right."

"My gender," I say. "I'm apologizing for my gender."

"Yes. For that, yes."

"Patricia . . ."

"What, Will?"

"Do you want to hold onto your job? Keep working there?"

"Yes, of course. It's the best job I've ever had."

"And you can do quality work even with him around? Even with him in your face?"

"Yes." With some determination, the first time I've heard that in her voice. "It wouldn't be easy, at least not now, but of course I could. I'm a professional."

Where have I heard that line before?

"Who knows about this?" I ask.

"The affair? Or that he's firing me?"

"Either. Both. The affair."

"No one . . . that I know of," she says. "I mean *I* didn't tell anyone. We were extremely discreet."

But of course. Married senior partners having affairs with co-workers are usually extremely discreet.

"I'm sure he didn't tell anyone," she assures me; perversely assures herself.

"Including his wife," I say.

"Definitely not his wife."

I nod; I feel good, talking to her like this, giving her wise counsel.

"You should tell his wife," I inform her.

"Will!"

"You owe it to her," I say. "As one woman to another."

"I don't think so," she answers reluctantly, after a decent pause. I'm setting wheels turning.

"You don't think she should know that her husband's fucking around on her?" I ask.

"Well . . ."

"With a junior member of his firm? Who he personally hired, from hundreds of miles away?"

"He didn't hire me so he could . . . have sex with me," she says.

I can hear the bell going off in her head: did he? Was that why? How far back does this go? Was I always just a piece of ass, from the first time I walked in his office, looking for a job? Was it any part, even one percent?

"Of course not," I say reassuringly. "But it did happen. And as one caring woman to another, maybe she should be told," I tell Patricia. "For her own good," I add.

"I don't know how good it would be for her," Patricia says. "I think it would devastate her."

"Then maybe ol' Joby should've thought of that before he started having an affair with you," I say.

She doesn't answer.

"What about the other senior partners? Shouldn't they be told?" I ask.

"Are you serious?"

"As a matter of fact, I am," I say. "This is the kind of thing that can ruin a firm. Not the affair per se," I add, "that happens, we're none of us perfect. The lying, the bullshit. Taking advantage of a junior partner."

"He didn't take advantage of me . . . not really. I went into it with my eyes open," she says.

"The hell you did," I say. "You fell for him and you had every reason to believe he fell for you and he played you for a fool and now that it's over he's dumping you, and not only dumping you, but depriving you of your livelihood. If that isn't fucking somebody over, kiddo, I don't know what is."

I can hear her thinking. "If you put it that way . . ."

"This is the twentieth century, Patricia. Practically the twenty-first. Haven't you heard of sexual harassment?"

"Of course, but . . ."

"But me no buts. He can't fire you because he doesn't feel like fucking you anymore . . ."

"Oh he still feels like doing that . . ."

"Because of whatever. He's afraid to divorce his wife, he's afraid he'll get hurt in the firm, he's afraid it'll cost him money, whatever. It doesn't matter. He flat-out can't do it."

"So . . . what do I do?"

"Has he talked to anyone about firing you?"

There's a pause. "I don't think so," she says, somewhat tentatively.

"Maybe?"

"No." More positive. "We talked about it over drinks last night."

"Over drinks?" I blurt.

"I didn't know," she answers defensively. "I thought it was same as always."

"What a prick. I'm sorry," I say, "but that's crap."

Softly: "I know. I felt like throwing my drink in his face."

"Good you didn't. For now. Anyway, so far it's just you and him. And me," I throw in.

"Yes. He wants it to be as smooth—that's wrong, as *contained* as we—he—can make it. He doesn't want to hurt my career . . ."

"Ha!" I interject.

"He just doesn't want me in the same firm. He's going to help me get another job first. And then . . ."

"A nice smooth-over, amicable parting. For the public."

"Something like that." Even as she mouths the words, she hears their hollowness, their hypocrisy.

Shades of my own experience with Andy and Fred. There is symmetry in the universe, more and more I'm convinced of that.

"So . . . what should I do?" she concludes, practically begging me on her hands and knees over the wire. "I can't stay here, Will. Not for long. It's been hell, just this one day. I can't take a week or however long it takes me to get another job. If I can get one," she adds, "remotely as good as this one."

"Very simple," I say. "What you do is, you go into his office, you close the door, you tell him politely to ask his secretary to hold all his calls, which he will do with alacrity, and then you tell him that you like your job and you've decided to keep it. That you *are* keeping it. You have no intention of doing him harm in any way. You don't want any money, you don't want his wife to know about what happened, ditto his partners, all you want is to be allowed to do the job he hired you to do without being discriminated against because of the difference between the two of you, the difference of the one XY chromosome. That if he acts professionally in this matter, so will you, and it will be a closed chapter. Very calmly and professionally, you tell him this. And very calmly and professionally, you also inform him that if this is not acceptable to him, for any reason, you will have no alternative but to tell his wife what happened, and his partners, and the Washington State bar association, and maybe even a reporter or two. You don't want to do this, make sure he knows that, because you don't, but you're not going to let him fire you. It's your job and he can't kiss you off because he wants those perfect tits and his Protestant guilt won't let him. He's got a problem, and you're not going to let him compound it by scapegoating someone who's doing her job, who uprooted herself and her child, who destroyed her child's ongoing relationship with her father, who misses her terribly . . ."

"Will," she says, interrupting. "You know I feel awful about that."

"Yes, I do. I'm saying I want him to know." And you, too, Patricia. You, too.

"In other words," I conclude, "you are not going to put up with this shit. Not one ounce worth. If push comes to shove, you will file a sexual-harassment case against him and his high-falutin' firm. Period, over and out."

"I don't know, Will . . ."

"You'd rather be fired."

"No! . . . I mean . . . I'm scared. You know how I hate confrontations."

"It's your life."

"Maybe I should have stayed in the appeals division," she laments. "Maybe that's where I belong."

Ah so. Now we're getting at the truth behind the truth. The innate fear that deep down she is an unworthy piece of shit who doesn't deserve this. She's been doing government work all her life, you start to think that's where you belong forever. You lose your balls.

But it isn't true. Any of us deserves it as much as anyone else, I swear to you, Patricia, you do. You wouldn't be there otherwise. So don't crap out on me, Patricia, I beg silently. Don't crap out on yourself. On our daughter.

"I don't know," I tell her. "But I don't think so. That's just my opinion, but I don't think so."

There's a pause.

"All right," she says finally. "I'll think about it."

"Good."

"I'm glad we talked," she says.

"So am I. And I know you'll come to the right decision. Whatever it is."

"I hope so . . . I hope so," she says. I hear the fear in her voice. It's a hard transition. Some people never make it.

"Let me know what happens," I tell her. A polite way of ending the conversation.

"Will," she says, before I hang up on her: "thanks."

"Don't be silly," I say. "You'd do the same for me."

"For being there for me," she says.

"Sure. Let me know."

"I will."

"Take no prisoners."

"I'll try."

"Good enough," I say.

" 'Bye, Will. Thanks again."

" 'Bye."

I cradle the receiver gently. When you share a child with someone, you are never completely divorced.

"IS THIS LAWYER ALEXANDER?"

You could cut the accent with a knife—a deep southern mountain drawl.

"Yes," I answer, smiling to myself. This voice coming over the telephone conjures up memories of the people I spent my summers with, back in Alabama and Mississippi. I haven't been in either of those states since I left for college more than twenty years ago, and I have no conscious expectations of ever going back. But I love the sound, the music.

"Glad I finally got ahold of you," the voice says. "I've been trying two-three days now."

There's no complaint in his tone, just doggedness.

"Sorry about that," I apologize, not really feeling a need to, more a politeness, since he's being so civil about it. I already knew it wasn't a client, Susan told me that much when she passed the message on a couple days ago, that a Willard Jenkins who she could hardly understand had called and left a message for me to call him at my convenience. I return clients' and potential clients' phone calls first; the rest have to wait their turn, particularly when they say there's no emergency to it.

"I was about to call you back," I tell him. Which is true, sooner or later.

"That's all right," he drawls, his voice about as slow as molasses and almost as thick. "County pays for mine, so I don't mind dropping the dime."

I locate the message, buried among others on my desk. An area code I don't recognize.

He speaks again, as if reading my thought.

"I'm the sheriff down here," he says. "In Raley. That's in West Virginia? Near the Virginia–Kentucky line? You prob'ly never heard of it. Nobody ever has 'less they from here."

I remember that southern inflection, ending a declarative sentence with a question mark.

"Yes?" I say.

"Anyway, this case of yours up there in New Mexico, the one with them biker fellas killed that guy and cut his dick off and so forth?" he continues. "I got this fella come in my office t'other day says he's the one did it."

After all this time I still feel a momentary rush of blood to my head. Maybe because I want something else to take into the courtroom with me besides Rita. Even though I know it's going to be bullshit.

"Hello? You still there?" comes the drawl.

"Yes, yes. I'm still here," I answer.

"Okay," he says in his soothing voice. "Don't want to lose you over the phone," he adds. "Ours go out pretty reg'lar, what with the antique equipment we've got this neck of the woods, could be another couple days 'fore we make contact again," he chuckles.

"I'm still here," I repeat.

"Good," he says. "Comforting to know somebody's equipment's working properly."

By now I'd figured the crazos would have stopped coming out of the woodwork. We kept the file of phony confessions on the case, which Susan has presciently placed on the desk in front of me. There have been seventeen confessions to this crime, but none in the past year.

Why this one, the specifics of which I yet know nothing, should have given me pause to feel differently, I don't know. But there was a definite tingle.

In all probability, however, five minutes after I've hung up from this call, the tingle will be gone. It's not the first time: hope springs eternal in the human breast. Mine, anyway—occupational hazard.

"So someone came in and confessed to this crime. What did he do, just come in right off the street, or what?"

"More or less," Sheriff Jenkins replies. "Him and this preacher friend of his, they walked in, asked could they talk to me? And then this ol' boy just up and says 'well, I did it.' Meaning the crime."

"What did he say, precisely?" I ask. "Was there anything specific?"

"It was all specific, what there was of it," Jenkins answers. "He didn't say all that much," he goes on, hedging a bit, " 'cause he said he wanted to tell it to you, fresh, since you're the lawyer on the case, but he said enough to get my attention, I'll tell you that, Mr. Alexander. I know you get these kinda confessions all the time," he says, as if reading my thoughts, "but this fella talked some real specific stuff. I mean stuff you couldn't know by just watching TV, you know what I mean?"

The last thing I want to do is go to nowheresville, West Virginia.

"Yes," I say, "I know what you mean." I reach for a pad and pencil. "First things first. What's his name?"

His name is Scott Ray. He's a floater. Been in Sheriff Jenkins's area three, four months. More or less normal-looking, maybe a little on the girlish side, not bad-looking actually, I'm being told, making my notes, some of the women seemed to find him attractive enough, although most men here would think him too dandified, this is a hardworking, conservative area. In his twenties, maybe late twenties.

What happened was, Scott Ray got religion. He's a disciple of the

Reverend Reuben Hardiman. Reverend Hardiman's got himself a reputation in these parts, Jenkins tells me. He's a charismatic preacher, a saver of souls, a faith healer nonpareil even for the southern West Virginia area, where there's a slew of quality faith healers and soul-savers. He's a wild-looking so'bitch, nobody knows how old he is exactly, probably forty to fifty, lives up in the hills in the midst of his congregation, hill people, hardscrabble folks. One of these real intense preachers who would scare just about anybody into accepting the Lord to save their souls. Yes, this Hardiman's quite an intense figure of a man.

Anyway, Scott Ray somehow wound up back in the hills where Hardiman's church was, and he got religion. Hard. And now he wants to square himself with Jesus, and to do that he's got to confess his sins. And the biggest sin he's got going is that he murdered Richard Bartless in New Mexico and he can't let some innocent men go to their deaths for a crime they didn't commit.

"That's the story. You think there's anything to it?" Jenkins asks.

Fuck. One thing I do know—the tingle's gone. I put about as much stock in religious confessions, conversions, and faith healers as I do in swamp real estate in Florida.

"I doubt it," I admit. "I don't put much stock in confessions of the soul."

"Yeh," he says, "I know what you mean. Still . . ."

I wait.

"Still?"

"Oh, I don't know," he says. "It's just sometimes . . . you get a feeling. You know what I mean?"

Susan books me on a flight to West Virginia, through Dallas. It's another bullshit lead, I'm sure it is, but I'm going. I have to.

THE TOWN OF RALEY, West Virginia, is about two hours and forty years in distance from Charleston, where my plane lands and I pick up my Avis Toyota. The drive is picturesque and hilly, wooded up-and-down crests and ridges interspersed with small towns, all of which saw better days long ago, when coal and John L. Lewis was king. It's cold out, spring has not yet arrived, here and there patches of snow still cling to the hard-clay ground. The occasional faces I see on the streets of the towns as I pass through are pale and pinched, bundled up in layers of flannel and wool against the wet wind. Years ago, fresh out of Vietnam, before law school, I traveled through Yugoslavia and northern Greece. The faces here remind me of the peasant faces from those hills, but with less color. Nobody looks optimistic.

The town of Raley, which is also the county seat, is like the rest of the area, very hilly and drab. You'd have quite a set of legs on you if you walked these streets all your life. I stop in a local cafe for a coffee and instructions to the sheriff's office. The men sitting in here, all older men, glance over at me. I'm sure they get visitors in here, but I don't fit. My clothes are too good, they lay on my body too well, my skin has too much sun. I'm dressed casually, in khakis, turtleneck, a warm jacket, and running shoes, but they're of a different quality. My Patagonia parka probably cost more than any suit of clothes you can find in the best men's store in town. Kids here that want quality and style have to travel. And once they're out of high school most just keep going.

Sheriff Jenkins's office is in a small cluster of county buildings just off the main drag. An overly made-up woman deputy, probably a good half-decade younger than she looks, her tight polyester uniform pants snug against an ass more than an ax handle wide, smiles cheerfully upon hearing my name and asks how I take my coffee as she immediately ushers me into the sheriff's office. Southern hospitality. She has a pretty face, even if she does subscribe to the Tammy Faye Bakker school of makeup.

Jenkins pumps my hand vigorously. He's the antithesis of the prototypical southern sheriff; he's so thin, as the saying goes if he stood sideways he'd be invisible. Tall, angular, younger than I thought he'd be. It dawns on me that I have an unconscious prejudice about southerners both in general and in particular, fueled by the media. It reminds me of the negative, knee-jerk reactions people have about lawyers.

"No trouble finding us?" Jenkins asks solicitously.

"No trouble at all." He's a nice guy; he wants to help however he can.

The lady deputy brings my coffee.

"I hope you like it sweet," she says, smiling. Her voice is more country even than Jenkins's, a combination of nasal and honey.

"Can't get enough sweetness," I banter, smiling back.

She blushes. She's not used to strange men from distant parts teasing her.

There are at least four teaspoons of sugar in my coffee, and it's lightened with condensed milk. I manage not to gag as I swallow and nod approval. She smiles again, happy that the coffee is to my liking, and leaves, closing the door.

"You got here quick," Jenkins says. "A busy lawyer like yourself."

"I had a hole in my schedule," I tell him. "And this is an important case to me." No being cool, no bullshitting.

"I can understand that."

I look at him. There's no guile to this man. I can trust whatever he tells me.

"What do you think about this Scott Ray?" I ask. "You're a professional, you have a sense of when people are telling the truth and when they're not."

He regards me with an unwavering eye.

"I think he's telling the truth."

Oh, baby.

"As far as he knows it," he qualifies.

"Meaning?"

"Religious people can be peculiar ducks, Mr. Alexander."

"Yes, I know."

"Especially the newly-converted. Especially," he says, "when they've been exposed to a pile-driver like the Reverend Hardiman. That man could squeeze blood from a stone and then some. He's pow'rful."

"So what you're telling me," I venture, wanting to make sure the words are right, "is that this man Scott Ray truly believes he's the killer of the man my men are on Death Row for. But it could be that he's saying this because he's been . . . let's say, convinced . . ."

"You can say brainwashed," Jenkins says. "Certainly manipulated. These preachers are sometimes not of our world. They interpret gospel real literal. Sometimes so much that what anyone else calls the truth comes out some other way."

I nod. He may be stuck back in the woods, but he's no rube.

"Manipulated," I say. I'm half-thinking out loud. "All right. He's been manipulated, or convinced, through no devious intent but out of passion to cleanse himself, to believe that he did it. Or if he didn't, that he could have, and that it's the same thing, and so if he confesses to even an imagined crime he'll be cleaner when he goes to heaven."

"That's what the preachers tell their congregations," Jenkins says.

"What about this Hardiman?" I ask. "What's he like? What should I know about him? He sounds like a real character."

Sheriff Jenkins leans back in his swivel desk chair. A smile of pure enjoyment crosses his face.

"Let's let that be a surprise," he says, still smiling. "A pleasant one. 'Cause there's nothing I could tell you that would prepare you for the Reverend Hardiman. I mean there is no one in the *world* like this man."

He laughs, a good belly guffaw.

"Damn. Hardiman." He laughs again. "That man can flat-out *preach!*"

"Is he dangerous?"

"Oh hell no! No, not at all. He's an honest, God-fearin' country preacher. It's just he's . . . you'll see."

I don't need any more surprises, but I have no choice. It'll come when it comes.

"When can I meet them?" I ask.

"Tonight. They're expecting you."

HARDIMAN'S CHURCH IS thirty miles away, deep into the hills, over tortuous twisting roads that appear to have not been paved since the Roosevelt administration, or at least LBJ's. My little Japanese car hits potholes so deep I'm afraid for the axles, my head on several occasions bumping against the roof, even with my seat-belt fastened. But the car holds up, a mechanical mule.

Although it's night, there's an almost-full moon, so I can make out details as I drive. This is backwoods America of Margaret Bourke-White lore, bare-wood clapboard houses, the paint long since cracked and blown away, many of them with no plumbing or electricity, you can tell the ones that have electricity by the TV antennas sticking up from the tarpaper roofs, old rusted-out cars up on blocks, Chevys and Mercs and some old Hudsons and Packards, too, hard soil by each dwelling that in the first genuine thaw will be planted as a kitchen garden, in most cases providing the only fresh vegetables these families will have; clothes hanging on lines, no fluorescent colors or designer labels, time stood still here from the thirties until the sixties, then stopped again when Vietnam took all the money, and none of it ever came back. Those that stay here stay because they don't have it in them to move; all the ambition and dreams and power have been bred out of them, by location and some inbred genetic deficiency. This area reminds me of Indian reservations at home: a third-world living inside the richest nation in history. And as in a few other pockets of western countries, like northern Ireland, there are many families in regions like this one who have been sucking at the public tit for three and four generations.

I hear it before I see it.

The sound at first is like a buzz, sharp, as I get closer it gets louder, more differentiated, a sound made up of lots of different sounds coming together. Voices together, not yet understandable, like a loud wailing.

The road curves sharply and I'm in a large clearing, bare hard ground. Cars are parked all over, mostly older clunkers like the ones I've been passing on my way here, but some newer ones as well, lots of pickup trucks, too, some of the newer cars fancy ones, Oldsmobiles and Buicks. I notice that while most of the license plates are from West Virginia there are also some from Virginia and Kentucky, North Carolina, and even some from farther away, Tennessee, Maryland, New Jersey, Georgia.

The church is a large, wooden one-story building. Not a traditional-looking church with steeple and stained-glass windows, more like a big wooden tent. As I get out and walk towards it the sound becomes louder. It isn't amplified, but it's loud as hell. Hundreds of voices at a high pitch. It's obviously prayer, but I can't make out a word of it; it isn't English or any other language I'm familiar with.

I am not religious, and my family wasn't either; given our socio-economic background we were odd in that respect. Except for compulsory service in the army I doubt that I've been inside a church of any denomination two dozen times in my entire life. But I've seen enough on television, Jimmy Swaggart and Ernest Ainsley and the rest, to know what's coming.

So much for being cool. I open the church door, and every preconceived notion I have is blasted out the window.

Talk about religious ecstasy! This brand of fundamentalism will *never* be on television, unless it's in a Frederick Wiseman documentary. There are a couple hundred people crammed in here, and they're all speaking in tongues. They are enraptured, in another world, gyrating and dancing in a frenzied symphony, heads rolling, eyes closed, calling and shrieking.

I'm standing in the back of this barn-like place, with an altar way up at the front (partially obscured by all the bodies moving around, there's people up there but I can't make them out). The sound is so intense it feels like waves of energy coming at me, a tidal wave of prayer.

I'm glad Jenkins hadn't prepared me for this: being taken by surprise is part of the excitement of the experience.

I take a moment to adjust to my initial jolt, start looking around. This is a country place; these are country people. White, Anglo-Saxon country people. Bereft of color, their skin almost transparent, veins popping in foreheads, lank mouse-colored hair plastered about faces from the sweat of prayer, washed-out pale blue eyes. Many, both men and women, are thin, not the thinness of fashion but of poor and inadequate diet, their bones jutting out at odd angles, big-knuckled hands, twisted fingers, receding chins, drooping noses. Those that aren't thin are pasty-fat, the blubber of heart attacks and cancer. They all look old, in parts like these you're old at forty.

My age.

There are few young people in attendance. Middle-aged or old. The kids have better, more modern things to do.

"Do you believe in Jesus!" suddenly booms a voice.

The voice comes from the altar, rising above all the others, a rich bass-baritone, loud and full and commanding.

The praying dies down almost immediately as the congregation turns its collective attention to the front, where the altar is located.

"Do you believe in Jesus!" the voice calls out again, his rich voice resonating throughout the old wooden building.

"Amen!" replies the congregation.

"Do you believe in Jesus!" he asks a third time. A purely rhetorical question, the essential call and response of the preacher.

"Amen!" the answer back, "well!", "yes!", "Lord!", similar answers, loud and throaty.

I'm taken by all of it; the rhythm, the fervor, the ceremoniousness. It brings back memories of my forays into the Native American Church. They, too, have taken me down some pretty strange paths, but not like this. That is about spirit; this is gut-level worship, ecstasy and subservience in one.

I move around to get a look at the man behind the voice, up at the altar, hidden from my sight until now.

Again, I'm blown away.

To begin with, Hardiman is black. Not coffee-with-cream African-American black, but jet-black, coal-black, blacker than a starless night. Absolute black. I don't think I've ever seen an African this black, let alone an American. And he is American, his voice is southern American to the core; not sloppy or slurry, just deep and resonating.

Moreover, he's huge, immense. I can't tell from back here exactly how tall he is, but he's got to be at least six-nine or more, maybe seven feet, and he weighs at least three hundred pounds. His hair, also black, sticks straight up from his head à la Don King's, except there's a lot more of it.

He's dressed simply, white shirt and dark pants. He holds a Bible in his left hand, brandishing it aloft, the well-worn book almost disappearing in his large hand, a hand festooned with gemstone rings on three of the four fingers.

"Amen," he says in response to their 'amens,' "amen," softer now, one more "amen." He doesn't have to shout; it's quiet now.

The congregation starts to sit down. I find a seat in the back. A few turn and look at me; it's obvious I don't belong. I smile at them; they regard me as a curiosity for a moment, then disregard me.

I get a better look at the assemblage. The first thing that strikes me is the number of cripples that are here. Several people in wheelchairs have been placed in the aisles, while others, supported by crutches, are scattered about, positioned so they have easy access to the altar.

I know what's coming; this I've seen on television. I've never believed any of it. Now I'll get a chance to see the real McCoy in action.

Hardiman opens the Bible and looks out at the congregation. There is a shuffling of feet, a clearing of throats. These people, most of them, are regulars. They're settling in for the good stuff. The lame shall walk again, eyesight shall be restored to the blind, various and sundry afflictions incurable by modern medicine will be cast out in the name of the Lord.

But I'm wrong. I'm off by such staggering proportions that whatever cool I had left is gone, and all that remains is wonder and astonishment.

Two boxes are carried up to the altar. Big, solid wooden boxes, the size of orange crates, with airholes randomly punched in them. I can feel the electricity in the congregation—something's about to happen, and it's not going to be preaching and testifying.

I'm disconcerted by the boxes for a moment, trying to figure out what's inside them, and then it hits me: one of the two box-handlers is as out-of-place here as I am. He's young, certainly not yet thirty, he's dressed in relatively hip clothing, his hair is cut modern. As he places his box upon the altar he looks up at Hardiman with a look of awe, of worship, of complete submission.

It's my man, Scott Ray.

He melts into the choir that stands to one side, at the back of the large altar. I keep my eyes on him. He sure doesn't look like a killer, he looks like a choirboy, only from a more contemporary congregation.

I turn my attention back to Hardiman as he opens one of the boxes and plunges his hand in. There is a moment of hushed electricity as the congregation leans forward. Then his hand emerges, holding a rattlesnake.

It's a big one, thick around the middle as a baseball bat, with a six-inch-long set of rattles. Hardiman holds it up, not behind the head where it can't strike at him, but in the middle of its body, the snake twisting and writhing, its triangular head with the poison knobs above the eyelids darting this way and that, the forked tongue sliding in and out of its mouth almost too fast to see.

If this snake bites him in a vein on the face or neck, he's gone in sixty seconds.

People are opening their Bibles. I steal a look over the nearest shoulder, following a dirt-encrusted finger as it traces in the old King James Bible the Gospel of Mark, chapter 16, verses 17 and 18: *"In my name shall they cast out devils; they shall speak with new tongues; They shall take up serpents; and if they drink any deadly thing, it shall not hurt them; they shall lay hands upon the sick, and they shall recover."*

Take up serpents. Talk about literal belief. I'm rooted, on my feet, watching Hardiman holding this snake a couple inches from his face, his eyes and the snake's eyes boring in at each other.

"Do you believe in Jesus!" he cries.

"Amen!" they answer back in a roar.

He flips open the top to the second box, reaches in with his other hand, comes out holding a water moccasin. A smaller viper, but just as deadly. Again, not behind the head, where he can stop it from striking, but in the middle of its scaly body.

He holds the two snakes up in front of him, level with his massive head, thrusting them out at the congregation, the two vipers undulating in his hands, looking at him, at each other. Somewhere I remember reading that different species of poisonous snakes hate each other. If they get into a fight he's right in the middle.

The only thing that keeps me halfway okay in all this is that I know he's done this before.

Somewhere near the front a woman starts keening, a high, thin, banshee voice, and it hits me where I've seen these people before—these people are Richard Bartless's mother, all of them, relatives if not in the blood and flesh, then in the spirit, which is even stronger. It's her voice I'm hearing, a cry of anguish from the trial. I'm alone with all these kin of the mother of that dead man, all alone except for their minister and his acolyte, Scott Ray.

The keening is at first a sound. An animal cry. Then it changes, going into what I heard when I first came inside, a praying in tongues.

'They shall speak with new tongues.'

Others join her, a few, women at first, then more, men and women, until everyone is speaking in tongues again, everyone except Hardiman, who is dancing around the altar like his shoes are on fire, dancing like a dervish, dancing up a storm, but he's in control, he's holding firmly to the snakes in his hands, whipping them like bullwhips. It's the scariest and most electrifying thing I've ever seen.

The only others who aren't caught up in the rapture of tongues are Scott Ray and me. He's silent, his eyes fastened, as are mine, on Hardiman.

And then Scott Ray turns and looks right at me. It's a long way between us, from the front of the church to the back, but his look is unmistakable. He frowns for a split second, then smiles broadly, as if my being here is confirmation for him of something that has to be.

Then he turns away, his eyes back on his mentor.

For a moment the spell is broken for me; I remember why I'm here. There's a coldness to it, a sadness. This is all so extraordinary and compelling that the incursion of the secular seems petty, wrong.

I turn back to the altar. Two women, younger and more attractive than most of the others, have joined Hardiman in his dance. The snakes in his hands are undulating as if to some unheard song, their tongues fast slithering in and out of their mouths, and the women have taken up their undulations, slipping their own tongues in and out, dancing not only with Hardiman now but with the snakes, dancing to their rhythm. One of them, on Hardiman's right, sticks her head up to the rattler's, right next to it, inches apart, and starts darting her tongue at the snake, even as he's darting his tongue at her, and the snake rises in Hardiman's hand to his full length, and even with all the din going from the speaking in tongues the sound of the rattles can be heard, and he strikes, and hits Hardiman dead-center in the chest, right at his heart.

Somehow, I don't know how (I can see from here that there's nothing under Hardiman's cotton shirt but flesh), the fangs don't penetrate, but are blunted by Hardiman's massive body, and the venom dribbles out from the fangs onto his shirt and down it to his belt.

"Amen!" the congregation voices, coming out of their ecstasy.

"Amen!" Hardiman answers them, slowing down his dance.

"Amen!"

He hands the now-harmless serpent to the woman who kissed it. She holds it tight with both hands, struggling with its weight, and puts it back in its box, shutting the lid tight on it.

Then he turns to the water moccasin. The congregation becomes quiet again.

"Hello, devil," he says to it.

"Satan!" cries the assemblage.

He holds the viper up to his face, inches away.

"Satan! Your brother tried to bite me! He tried to poison me! But I repelled him! God repelled him! And now he is without poison. And I mock him!"

"Amen!"

"And I mock you. Satan in snakeskin. Are you also foolish like him?" he cries. He's smiling, like he and the snake have some inside joke going on just between the two of them.

The snake is two inches away from Hardiman's face, which is not as strong, as tough, as his chest. But the snake doesn't know that. The snake knows only that it's in the hand of someone, something, much more powerful than it.

It doesn't strike.

Snakes' brains aren't very sophisticated, but I'd swear on a Bible that this snake chickened out.

Hardiman stares it down, then he puts it away. It was cold when I came in here, but I'm sweating now, and it isn't from the church's old-fashioned coal-burning heating system.

The choir breaks into song, an old hymn I vaguely remember. No matter what else happens tonight with Hardiman and Scott Ray, what I've just seen has been awesome.

While the choir's still singing, one of the snake-dancing women comes back to the altar with a large towel and a mason jar half-filled with a murky thick liquid, which has the look and consistency that I remember from my childhood as moonshine.

Hardiman wipes his perspiring face with the towel. He picks up the jar.

My curiosity gets the better of me. I lean forward to an old man sitting in the row in front of me.

"What's in the jar?" I ask.

"Cyanide," he answers, like he's saying 'lemonade.'

"What's it for?" I ask again.

"To drink." He turns around to look at me.

To drink? What the fuck. Guy drinks poison and plays with poisonous snakes? I mean okay, he's charismatic as hell, maybe the most charismatic man I've ever laid eyes on personally, but I've got four men on Death Row whose fate could be hanging on him and some street kid he's recently converted. What if he actually drinks this shit and it kills him?

"He drinks cyanide?" I parrot dumbly.

"When God tells him," comes the answer.

When God tells him.

Up at the altar, Hardiman grabs the jar of cyanide, holds it aloft. *'And if they drink any deadly thing, it shall not hurt them.'*

I've seen people, holy men in India, walk across a bed of white-hot coals that should have burned their feet up to the ankles, and stroll away without even a hotfoot. And yes, in my forays into the Native American church, I've seen (actually not with my own eyes, but heard from extremely reliable sources) miracles as farfetched as drinking poison from a mason jar.

Hardiman regards the poison in his hands. He brings the jar to his face, sticks his head in, takes a deep breath.

"Lawdy!" he exclaims. "That cyanide do burn the sinuses."

His followers laugh.

"Amen," they cry. "Say it!"

He takes a long, almost regretful look at it; then he places it on the side of the altar.

"Later for that," he says. "Maybe later."

He steps to the center of the altar, looks down at the congregation.

"Do any of you know Jesus?" he asks softly.

"Amen," calls back his flock. "Yes, well, Lord."

"But do you *know* Jesus?" he asks again. "Does He live with you, in your heart?"

"Yes!"

"Amen!"

"Do you *know* Jesus, in your *heart?*" he asks yet again.

"YES!"

"AMEN!"

"You know Him!"

"Yes!"

"In your heart!"

"Yes!"

"You know Jesus!"

"Yes!"

"Completely!"

"Yes!"

"Without reservation!"

"Yes!"

"In your heart!"

"Yes!"

"Completely!"

"Yes!"

Near me, a woman faints. Her neighbors lay her on her chair, turn back to Hardiman without missing a beat.

"What a friend I have in Jesus," Hardiman starts to sing, a rich basso-profundo worthy of Paul Robeson. The congregation joins in, singing lustily.

I don't know many of the words, but I, too, join in. It feels like the right thing to do; not from obligation, but from belonging. I'm beginning to understand why a man who would kill another man (so Scott Ray claims), stab him forty-seven times and cut off his cock, would readily, willingly confess. The Reverend Hardiman is a powerful force.

We sing several more hymns. One thing I've realized is that there are no other blacks in here besides Hardiman, and that this fact seems not to matter at all. He is their shepherd—that's all that counts.

The testifying begins. Those that have been saved, and those that haven't but will be, here and now, come forward. They talk fervently of their conversion to Jesus, how Jesus took them out of the pit of darkness and loneliness and sin and put them on the path of righteousness. It's moving stuff, but I've seen it before, it isn't as novel and unique as dancing around with two poisonous vipers. I'm not going to be saved, not tonight anyway, despite what I've seen, so I'm antsy. I want to sit down with Scott Ray and find out if there's anything to him beyond this.

These services are obviously long and drawn-out. I look at my watch; it's already ten-thirty and the end is nowhere in sight. As quietly and unobtrusively as I can, I leave my seat and go outside.

The cold air feels good. I sit on a damp, worn railing, look up at the sky. It's become cloudy, I can feel the rain closing, see the moon veiled by drifts, stars banked in the fog. The voices from inside recede as I let my thoughts wander, submerging into the chalky darkness surrounding me and the church and the clearing.

"Too much for you?"

I turn with a start; I hadn't heard anyone coming.

"No," I answer, looking up at her. "I needed some space. I'm new to this."

She approaches from the closed door of the church, wearing a man's old car coat to ward off the chill. I recognize her as one of the snake-dancers. Up close she's pretty, probably about my age, her face unlined, freckled even in winter, large green eyes flecked with hazel set in milk-white skin, her middle-of-the-back-length auburn hair now done up in a demure bun. No makeup, not even lipstick. A little work and she'd be close to beautiful.

"Evelyn Decatur," she says by way of introduction. "Welcome to our church."

"Will Alexander. Thank you." Very formal we are.

She nods politely, her greeting.

"They've talked of you," she informs me.

"They?"

"Reverend Hardiman . . . and Scott."

"Oh." My guard goes up; was she sent out here to birddog me?

From her coat she takes a crumpled pack of cigarettes, lights up without offering me one, inhales deeply. She smokes like a European woman, like I imagine Simone Signoret would have smoked, fully and without apology.

"Scott's a good boy," she tells me, taking a long drag. "Now that he's found Christ."

"Uh huh," I say noncommittally.

"He made his confession last month," she continues.

"To everyone?" I can't hide my surprise and concern. A public confession to several hundred born-again Christians could taint the case somehow. It feels strange; all of this does.

"To God," she answers, taking another long pull on her weed. She turns, fixing her gaze on me, her open coat revealing her full, shapely woman's body under her wool dress. I was wrong—she doesn't need any work, she's fine just as she is.

"Are you a Christian?" she asks me abruptly.

"No," I say, almost jumping. It's not a question I'm used to being asked. "I was born of Christian parents," I add, feeling some guilty compulsion to explain, "but no, personally, I'm not." I feel myself flush.

She leans against the railing, her body close to mine but not touching, smoking her cigarette down to the filter, looking up at the now clouded-over starless sky. Men dream, at one time or another, of chucking it all, starting a new life, a new identity. In that imaginary new beginning they meet a woman. When I have those thoughts the woman is earthy, grounded, not a captive of the moment, but timeless. She is this woman next to me, leaning against the railing.

Despite myself, I check her ring finger. Unadorned.

"Are you going to come back in for the healing?" she asks.

"Should I?"

She holds me with a look for a moment, without answering. Then she finishes her cigarette, flicks it into the darkness, goes back inside. I watch her, her bare white legs under the coat, her piled-up hair. They sent their best-looking woman out to make sure I didn't get away, that whatever they were doing didn't scare me off.

She was the right one to send. I stand up, follow her in.

"BEFORE YOU SAY ANYTHING, let me explain something. I am not your lawyer. Anything you say to me is not privileged. I can use it against you. Do you understand what I'm saying?"

Scott Ray looks at me, unblinking.

"I killed him."

We're in the church, down front. Scott Ray, Hardiman, and me. Everyone else has gone. Most of the lights are out.

I'd sat through the miracles. They went on for a couple of hours, healing the lame, bringing sight to the blind, what I'd expected. They were good, but I'd seen such stuff before. I was antsy for my own show.

Finally, it had ended. There was an offering, much hugging and kissing, more testifying. I'd waited in the back until the church was clear so I could hopefully get at what had been tormenting me for more than a year.

Ray and Hardiman are sitting in a first-row pew. I've got a folding chair, opposite them, the altar to my back. The only lights left on are coming from some unseen alcove tucked in behind the altar, up high, giving their faces the look of vampire faces in silent movies. It feels like we're inside a big, drafty cave. I check the time when we start: 1:30 A.M., eastern standard time.

"Until you tell me otherwise," I inform Ray, "this is going to be off the record. For your protection. Whatever notes I take will be my work-product notes. The state can't touch them, I promise."

Ray nods. "I got nothing to hide."

"Even so, I don't want my case tainted because of a procedural mess-up. I can't have some technicality screwing this up, you understand?"

"I ain't concerned with no technicalities," Ray says, looking at Hardiman for approval.

"He wants to walk with the Lord," Hardiman says. "That's all he wants now."

"I want to get straight with Jesus," Ray affirms. "I can't go to my Maker with a murder hanging over me."

"He's got to live by holy scripture," Hardiman says. "He's got to square himself with the Lord's commandments."

"Thou shalt not kill," Ray tells me, his face expressionless.

"I agree," I say. "Even if it didn't say so in the Bible I'd still feel that way; wouldn't you?"

"He's got to do this by scripture," Hardiman says again.

What the hell does that mean? Maybe you do it that way in the Middle East, where the Koran is literally the law, but this is America, where the courts are secular. Do they understand that?

"I hear what you're saying," I tell them gingerly. "But what you've got to understand is that getting straight with the Lord, Jesus, whoever, isn't the same thing as being on trial in the United States. Religion isn't part of the judicial system in this country. I realize you're intelligent men and you know that, but I have to make it clear. We can't be muddying the waters by making this a religious experience."

They look at me dubiously.

"God may forgive you, but the state of New Mexico may not, is what I'm saying," I tell them.

"God's forgiveness is all we want," Hardiman says. "If the state demands its pound of flesh, so be it."

"Render unto Caesar that which is Caesar's, and to God that which is God's," Ray tells me.

"As long as we understand that," I say.

"And by thy confession will ye be cleansed of your sins," Hardiman says.

Shit. I should've taken a crash course in the Bible before I came here. They're going to scripture me to death. I've got to get this on track before we fall off the deep end. I look Scott Ray right between the eyes—hold him with my stare.

"You were in Santa Fe," I say.

He nods.

"When did you arrive?" I ask. "How many days before Richard Bartless was murdered?"

It's like swimming in molasses. Wearying to the bone. But little by little, the story emerges. And the more I hear, the deeper and deeper I'm sucked in.

"I'd been drifting around, not doing much of anything, just bumming around. I'd been down in Mexico, Texas, Arizona, all over the place, hanging out. Dealing drugs was what I was doing mostly. Nickel-and-dime shit, nothing big, nothing could get me in trouble with the big boys. That and getting laid, more than anything else. Fucking. Any cunt would let me stick my dick into. Fresh young snatch, the younger the better. Sometimes I'd do a daughter and her mother, too. The older ones, they really like it. They appreciate a young, hung stud. One time I did two sisters and the mother. Better'n a three-dog night in the Yukon. Dealing drugs and scoring pussy, life in the fast lane . . ."

"It was an abomination unto the Lord," Hardiman says fiercely.

"Amen to that," Scott replies. "I know that now; if there's one thing I know it's that. I was evil, pure and simple."

"To fornicate outside the vows of marriage is a sin," the preacher intones.

"That is for sure," Scott affirms. "Which is why I am now celibate," he tells me, "and will be until the right woman comes along, who is willing to forgive this sinner and join me in marriage."

He says it all with a straight face. I'm having trouble keeping one; that he actually believes what he's saying makes it even harder.

From somewhere in the back, Evelyn Decatur materializes, so quietly she's almost upon us before I notice her. The other woman who had been on the pulpit, dancing with the snakes, is with her. They carry trays of coffee and sweet rolls.

Hardiman puts a massive arm around the other woman's waist. She smiles down at him.

"This is my wife, Rachael," he tells me.

"Hello," she says, turning the smile on me.

"And this is her sister, Evelyn, who you've already met, I presume."

"Yes," I say, looking at her, smiling politely, being smiled politely at in return. My guess is she's younger.

"She is herself unmarried," Hardiman says.

"That's too bad," I say. "For the men around here."

He laughs the appreciative laugh, the mutual knowing of two men who understand women and the need men have for them.

"That's true. That's very true. But her standards are high." Teasing her: "very high."

She smiles at him. No blush, no girlishness rising to the bait.

"How do you take your coffee?" she asks me.

"Black," I tell her. "At this time of night."

She pours for me, hands me the cup, our fingers touching for the briefest of seconds. She doesn't notice. I feel like a schoolboy, trying to screw up the courage to ask the prom queen out for a date. Hardiman has his arm firmly around his wife's waist. His wife snuggles close to him, a happy and contented woman.

We have our coffee and rolls, the women joining us. Everyone else takes cream and sugar with their coffee, heavy on the sugar. The rolls are homemade, very sweet. I eat two; Evelyn eats half of one, gives me the other half. I try to taste her fingers on it where she tore it, but it's too sweet.

The women leave, as suddenly and quietly as they came.

Scott turns to Hardiman. The preacher nods. Scott starts his account again, where he left off.

We go until dawn. Slowly, laboriously. As the hours pass Hardiman gradually becomes more central to the narrative, interjecting, reminding, changing. Scott acquiesces at every turn. And the biblical shit is maddening, it's like a mind-fuck, like whatever is real isn't, unless there's a biblical quotation or phrase to buttress it. And then it'll turn back on itself, every argument has a counter-argument, because in scripture you can find two sides to virtually any issue or problem, it's kept millions of scholars in business for millennia: In First Corinthians so-and-so said this . . . but then in Jeremiah, so-and-so said this, which is the complete opposite. On and on, all night long, I have to strain to separate the wheat from the chaff, what is acceptable in American jurisprudence and what will have to be settled by an authority higher than all of us.

Slowly it comes, inch by inch, detail upon detail. By the time Ray finishes telling his story, I'm convinced beyond the shadow of a doubt that he's the killer I've been looking for.

What's worrisome is Hardiman's complete control over him. It could be a real problem if and when I ever get Scott Ray into a courtroom. He is no more acting out of his own free will than Rita Gomez was when she gave her original testimony. If Robertson picks up on it, and he's no dummy, he'll see this for what it is, it could blow us all out of the water. I'm going to be doing some fancy dancing to keep Hardiman buried in the background.

But that's not the issue. Scott Ray is guilty. His story is utterly convincing; he knows too many things only the actual killer could know.

Sheriff Jenkins puts me in touch with a local lawyer. He seems like a good man, small-town, but knows his stuff well enough. I explain the situation to him, and after his initial shock he agrees to represent Scott Ray so far as taking his testimony goes.

They meet alone for an hour. Hardiman wants to sit in, invoking clergy-parishioner privilege (I'm surprised at his knowledge of the law), but the attorney and I refuse. I'm not sure of their relationship,

Hardiman and Ray, but I don't want to take a chance on anything's being thrown out on a technicality.

Hardiman and I cool our heels in Jenkins's office, down the street. After fidgeting for several minutes, Hardiman turns to me.

"I don't want to lose this boy," he says to me, his voice anguished. "He's a soul worth saving now."

I nod but don't answer. I don't know how much of him there'll be left to save when this is all over.

The lawyer formally tape-records Scott Ray's testimony. It takes most of the day, by the time the transcribing is done. He locks the tape in his safe, gives me two cleanly-typed, notarized copies.

Hardiman and Ray escort me to the Charleston airport.

"Good luck," Hardiman offers, shaking my hand.

"Thank you. For all your help." I mean it sincerely.

"It was the only thing to do," he says.

Scott Ray shakes my hand, too. He seems fine, unworried, not a crease in his brow.

"Thank you for coming," he says. "I'm going to be able to get straight with Jesus now, because of Reverend Hardiman and you."

I nod. He's probably crazy, certainly his brain has gone through some major hoops, but I know he's speaking with complete sincerity.

"I'm glad," I say. "And my clients will be, too. Very glad."

As I walk across the tarmac to my airplane, Hardiman calls out to me.

"He won't run," he shouts. "He'll be here when you need him. I'll see to that personally."

I nod, wave as I'm climbing the steps into the plane.

I take my seat and look out the window. They're still watching.

I LEFT IN WINTER; I come home to spring. It's not like in most parts of the country, where trees are suddenly green, flowers in bloom. It's more a feeling, partly a smell, warm spring high-desert smell, warmth in the air.

There's a surprise waiting for me right out of the box as I walk off the airplane in Albuquerque. Mary Lou's there—that's expected, I'd called ahead and told her my flight. It's nice to see her; she looks good, even across the blacktop, I'd forgotten what a fine-looking woman she is. A week out of town and I forget something that important.

Claudia's the unexpected one. She's standing next to Mary Lou, her head rising above Mary Lou's shoulder, she wasn't that tall the last time I saw her. It hits me that she's almost a teen-ager; it's a jolt. A middle-aged father and his teen-age daughter. And what's she doing here, it isn't school break yet.

"Mom quit her job," Claudia announces before the kiss.

I look at Mary Lou. She shrugs. Claudia hands me a sealed envelope.

"She took off," Claudia continues, dancing around me as we walk to the car. "So I'm going to live with you for the rest of the school year. Isn't that great?"

Yes and no. For me, yes. For Patricia, I don't think so.

Mary Lou drives, Claudia in front with her, the two of them listening to Elvis Costello on the tape deck as we drive north in Mary Lou's Acura. I sprawl across the back seat, digesting Patricia's letter.

Patricia hadn't, in the end, been able to hearken to my call. She'd resigned. The firm gave her a great parachute, considering the short amount of time she'd been with them: three months at full pay (a blatant payoff, some of which, I'm sure, is coming directly out of Joby Breckenridge's pocket), and had gotten her another job, relatively similar, at least as far as pay is concerned, at another Seattle firm, starting when her sabbatical ends. It wasn't, strictly speaking, a mercy fuck—smart female lawyers don't grow on trees. She won't have to move again, and she unexpectedly has the sudden wherewithal and security to take her first grown-up vacation in years. She's in Paris, then on to Rome, Milan, parts north and south. Open-ended, but she's gone for awhile, so Claudia's with me, from now until the end of the school year. Everybody's happy, at least temporarily.

(All this is contained in the letter. It's more formal than I would have expected, as if she feels guilty about it—all of it, the quitting, the sudden taking off: it all happened in a week's time, dumping, her words, Claudia on me, the works.)

It's amazing how lives can change so much in a few days. Hers and mine both. I guess she's happy—she's not confrontational, she's always run from a fight, the daily game-playing would have devoured her,

her nerve ends are too raw. Still, I wish she had stayed and faced it down. For her, for her daughter.

The three of us have dinner together, then Mary Lou drops us off at my place. She misses me, I can feel it even though she didn't say anything, and she's dying to know about the trip, every single detail. I give her the highlights, enough to satisfy her curiosity. She'd love to hear it all, right now, but she won't intrude on Claudia and me tonight. I kind of wait to see if Claudia will include her in, but she doesn't. She wants me to herself, she's been with Mary Lou two days. Patricia had detoured to Santa Fe on her way to foreign locales, and finding that I was gone, had brazenly asked Mary Lou 'since her father's gone and I didn't know, would you mind?' To her credit Mary Lou had said 'I'll be glad to,' even though she was under no obligation, she did it out of love, so they spent two nice days together, my daughter and current woman; but now, for Claudia, this is at the heart of the treat of being back here: her and daddy, a twosome.

Mary Lou and I kiss goodnight. There's real hunger on both sides. We'll have breakfast tomorrow, after I drop Claudia at school, where she'll be reunited with her old friends, which thrills her no end. I missed Mary Lou; maybe it took some juvenile lusting after another woman to make that come clear.

My daughter is more like me than she is her mother. This is not revelatory, it happens in the best of families, I've known it since she was an infant, practically. It's more logical in our case than most, because Patricia and I separated when Claudia was very young, and she's played the other role in the relationship. There have been times when she's had to be too much of an adult for Patricia, too grownup. With me, a man, she was always a little girl. There's less stress. She doesn't know this, but it's part of why it's always been easy and comforting for her to be with me.

On the other hand, even though she lived close by until a year ago, I didn't have to do the daily day-to-day. I got more cream and less skim than Patricia; but also less gut stuff, the making of the person. It's a price you pay for divorce that's immeasurable. She will always, at heart, be Patricia's child.

After we polish off our pizza she wants to talk. About her mother, what happened from her child/woman point of view, about herself and what's going on there. Gently but firmly, I stop her. She's been too much burdened with adulthood, she thinks she likes it, the responsibility, but I don't. We'll talk; we'll talk long hours about it; but tonight I want her to be eleven.

I read aloud to her before putting her to bed. We get lost in books, we're both essentially loners and books are easier than the world sometimes; certainly more alive.

She wants to read something new, something I particularly like that she would like, also, something more 'grown-up,' so I find my Lattimore translation of *The Odyssey*, which I've had since college, dog-eared and underlined, start with Book I: "*Tell me, Muse, of the man of many ways, who was driven far journeys, after he had sacked Troy's sacred citadel. Many were they whose cities he saw, whose minds he learned of, many the pains he suffered in his spirit on the wide sea, struggling for his own life and the homecoming of his companions . . .*"

We get through half a Book before she fades. I mark the place, put the book on her bed-table. We'll resume tomorrow. Maybe she'll dream tonight of sailing, of water, this land-locked child of mine. Perhaps she'll dream of her mother, who looks every day upon water.

I kiss her goodnight and close the door, and sit in the darkness with two fingers of Johnnie Walker Black and my thoughts.

I am searching for the perfect woman, and the perfect woman doesn't exist, except in my fucked-up childish desires. I blew it with Patricia, granted it was both of us, but I was the lead player, we might still be together if I had worked harder at it. Strike that, it's bullshit. We wouldn't have stayed together, but we should have worked harder at it anyway, I didn't know shit about staying together; 'it isn't working? *Adiós*.' Holly, of course, was the disaster of all time, I don't blame myself for that, but what was I doing with her in the first place? I fucked around on both of them, I fucked around in-between, finally a terrific woman comes into my life, practically throws herself at me, and the first piece of exotic pussy that crosses my line of vision, a born-again semi-virgin no less, stirs my loins. I'm going to be making love to Mary Lou tomorrow night, she's going to do me better than Delilah did Samson, and I'd bet healthy money Evelyn Decatur will slip into my stream-of-consciousness. 'You can't always get what you want.' They should engrave it on my tombstone. And of course when

I do get it (which is more than I should, I wanted Mary Lou much more, didn't I?), that *it*, whatever that is, isn't what I wanted. Or thought I wanted.

By and large, I think therapy's a crock of shit, all that inward narcissism, but I should go into it. I need to know why I'm such a bridge-burner, why I trash what's most important to me. I did it to two wives, to the firm; what's next, Mary Lou, my new practice, Claudia?

I keep thinking about how Patricia's not such a good role model for Claudia, negatively comparing her to other women. Yet what right do I have to talk, to compare anyone to anything? What the hell kind of model am I as a man for my daughter? I'm a womanizer and a boozer; talk about being a role model, I'm a prize loser in that arena. And she has to know, she's old enough now, she's seen me lose jobs and relationships.

I have to change. For her sake if nothing else. I can't let her see her old man go down the tubes; forget success in the marketplace, that's shallow, that I can do in my sleep, it's the waking world I'm inadequate in. I have to show her that there's beauty and honesty in men.

Two fingers begets two fingers begets two fingers, before you know it you've killed the better part of a fine bottle; I resolve to put Johnnie-boy away so as not to pour that second drink. I want to sleep without a buzz. I want to lie awake, if that's what it comes to, clear-headed. So if the thoughts come, they'll be real.

But I am a weak-willed motherfucker, that I am. I manage to hold the line at two, small ones, mere sips, really, boon companions against the night.

Shit, I've become good at deceiving myself. A fucking master. I don't even bother with pretense anymore.

And of course, when I do put the bottle away, I'm full of petty self-disgust. Scott Ray is the real thing, I should be flying, instead of dying in little shitty bits, not even heroically, but with the lamest of whimpers.

PART FIVE

"IN THE EVIDENTIARY HEARING for a new trial in the case of *The State of New Mexico* versus *Jensen, Paterno, Hicks, and Kowalski*, this court is now in session, Judge Louis Martinez presiding. All rise."

Finally. After all the twists and turns and blind alleys and disappointments, after having door after door slammed in our face, after being told it would never happen, we're here, back in the same courtroom with the same players we were with for the trial, a trial that feels like it took place a long, long time ago. Which it did, well over two years since that night Robertson first called, a damn long time, time enough for me to have blown off my firm, gotten a divorce, seen my child move away, and lost the most important case of my life. But what goes around comes around, with luck this time for the better, because this is it, I have no illusions, there will be appeals for years, but if I can't do it this time, if I don't spring these men here and now, with the new witnesses and information I have, I'll never do it, and they will die in the penitentiary by the hand of the state.

"This is not a trial," Martinez says, instructing us. "We are not here to judge innocence or guilt."

I look over at Robertson, who's presiding at the prosecutor's table. He's neatly pressed in one of his good courtroom pinstripes, his hair freshly trimmed, a week-end tan giving him a healthy, robust air. Moseby is with him. His attire is not as sartorially elegant.

Robertson had accosted me outside in the corridor a few minutes before the hearing started.

"Enjoy it while you can," he'd warned me. "I'm not going to be content with just beating you this time, Will. I'm going to humiliate you."

I'd kept my cool. I won't rise to his bait; our side will conduct our case and not worry about his. He doesn't have one, doesn't need one. He can sit back and take pot-shots at our witnesses. As far as he's concerned we're fishing without bait, one last desperate attempt to pull one out of the bag.

"In a proceeding such as this," Martinez is saying, "the burden of proof is not on the prosecution to prove guilt beyond a reasonable doubt. That happens at the trial phase. We're here today because new evidence has come to light that may make us reexamine our findings at that trial; evidence that, if it is deemed sufficiently important, would compel us to grant a new trial."

The bikers, manacled and in prison-blue jumpsuits, are sitting at the defense table with Mary Lou and me.

One last time.

"CALL RITA GOMEZ."

Once more to the stand she comes, our Lady of Perpetual Sorrows. No hinky dresses and beehive hairdos like she wore on her first ascent to the scaffold, no inch-thick mascara or fuck-you ankle-strap high heels. She is being presented au naturel: acne, chapped lips and all. This baby's come a long way, and it's been all downhill.

"Do you swear . . . ?"

Her hand on the Bible, she does. Like she did the last time, with about as much conviction.

In front of me on the table is her transcript from the trial. Her pack of lies that sent four men to Death Row. I lift it for a moment, feeling the lying, incriminating pages sift through my fingers like dead, brittle leaves. Somewhere in the wilds of Washington state a tree was cut down to make the paper for this bilge, maybe a mature tree hundreds of years old, that provided shade and oxygen. A life-sustaining organism, now dead and riddled with shit.

Lone Wolf looks at her, seated on the oak chair, dwarfed by her surroundings; a frightened figure in a large, forbidding cave.

"She ain't changed a damn bit," he exclaims.

"Yes she has," I answer him. "You don't have a clue how much."

"She looks the same to me," he says. "Same dumb cunt."

"You'll see how much she's changed once she starts singing," I tell him.

"I'll believe it when I see it," he answers dubiously. She's already burned them twice—first at the trial, then when she bailed out of the court hearing. Their only expectation of her is that she'll somehow wind up fucking them over again.

She studiously avoids looking at them. She's going to try and save them, but she doesn't want any contact, eye or otherwise. She's probably more scared of them now than she was then; she's had two years to build the terror.

But she's going to talk straight. Mary Lou and I have spent countless hours and days preparing for this moment. We did it ourselves; Tommy and Paul, our partners at the original trial, are no longer with us. Tommy was available for a long time, even though Mary Lou and I were carrying the ball he wanted to be part of it, but a couple months after the riots he was offered a great job with a firm in Albuquerque, and he couldn't turn it down. He'd paid his dues and more, and he left the Public Defender's office with his head held high. His new firm expects a lot of him, and he'll deliver; of that I have no doubts. But with the workload of the new job, he couldn't take the time to come up here and be with us.

He regrets it, feels he's let us down; I assured him that isn't the case; he pulled his oar and more for a long time. Life goes on. We'll talk over the phone. He still sees Goose, it's a relationship that will endure. Goose understands Tommy's absence; he paid for a bottle of champagne to be delivered to Tommy's new office his first day on the job.

Paul, on the other hand, flat-out disappeared. He and I'd been in sporadic contact for awhile after the trial, but it had become less and less frequent, and then one day, he was gone. His office empty, a new tenant occupying his space. Both his office and home phones had been disconnected, and there were no forwarding numbers or addresses. He just wasn't there anymore.

My feeling is, he got tired of it all. He'd been in so many of these circuses over the years that to have been part of the losing side, after so much effort, took whatever starch there was left out of him; particularly since he had been the one to commit the only blunder—the opening of the 'hot knives' issue—that our team had made. We never talked about it, but I think that deep down inside he felt he'd been responsible, at least in part, for our losing.

He wasn't, of course; any one of us could have made that same mistake. And that wasn't why we went down. We were victims of symbols, not of logic and evidence.

He had his demons; like mine, they were fueled by drink. Too many gray cells finally burned off. It impairs the ability to take the shit and keep coming back for more.

Maybe that's a blessing. If I don't change my ways, I'm going to find out someday, undoubtedly the hard way. It's a sobering thought.

I stand tall, smooth my lapels, taking my time. I pause for a sip of water, turn to face the bikers and Mary Lou, offer them a reassuring smile, and then I walk forward towards my witness, who sits perched on the edge of her chair, as wary as a possum caught in a trap, awaiting an unknown misery.

'I have met the enemy, and he is us.' (Pogo, one of my childhood heroes, said that.)

Time to engage the enemy.

Martinez had heard much of the documentation at the earlier hearing, but he can't keep his eyes off Rita. Not now the dispassionate jurist, even-handedly dispensing justice, above the fray; he is a man who has to find the truth, the real truth, because of the circumstances under which he'd thought he'd found it back then.

Robertson, too, is riveted by her, making copious notes as she talks, constantly referring to the affidavit I submitted with her sworn testimony, the same bombshell I'd dropped in his lap when I'd first found her in Denver and she started her song of crime, punishment, and betrayal. At the beginning, when she starts telling how she was whisked out of town without bothering to leave a wake-up call, courtesy of Sanchez and Gomez, her father confessors, and when she talks about how the brainwashing started, he's all over the place with objections. Martinez sustains some, over-rules others, but as we get deeper into her narration he shuts Robertson down.

"This is not cross-examination, counselor," he admonishes Robertson. "Please let the witness tell her story in her own fashion. You'll have ample opportunity to question her."

Martinez turns back to Rita, abruptly dismissing Robertson, who slumps in his chair, fuming, turning to look over at our table, shooting poison daggers. The bikers nudge each other, stare daggers of their own back at him. Lone Wolf flashes him a wide smile that clearly says 'fuck you where you eat, asshole, you shit all over us, now it's our turn to reciprocate.'

She's been on the stand for two hours, telling her story. The version she'd told me in the hotel room at the Brown Palace. It's been grueling; she's still scared to death of the consequences.

"So," I say, "after all that time up in the mountains, they brought you back to Santa Fe. The police."

"Yes."

"And you gave your statement. Officially."

"Yes."

"And they told you—they impressed upon you—that if you changed your statement, recanted it in any significant fashion . . ."

"Did what?"

"Recanted . . . went back on it."

"Oh. Right."

"If you went back on it, they'd book you for accessory to murder. They said that to you directly."

"Yes."

I look at the prosecution table. Robertson's scribbling feverishly. Moseby, who's been intent on Rita and me, looks away with a start. The two cops, Sanchez and Gomez, stare forward stoically, two cigar-store Indians; see all, reveal nothing.

Martinez is looking at them as well. It's a look I can't decipher; but one thing I do know, he believes her. Maybe not completely, but enough that he's become extremely unsettled. Four men were sent to be executed in *his* courtroom, in large part because of her testimony. Now she's saying it was all lies, worse, not only lies, but crimes of deception, of corruption, the worst nightmare an honest jurist can have. In his courtroom, with him in charge.

He had read her new testimony. But that was words on pages; here it's alive, from her own mouth.

I look at him. His expression is almost one of grief, of being stricken unawares. As if he personally was the one being lied to, as if *he* was the one, personally, who gave life to those lies. I feel for him; he's an honest man, this isn't supposed to happen. The ground is shifting under his feet, threatening to swallow him up.

He's afraid for his reputation, for that of his court. I sympathize with him; it isn't his fault. The system failed him, as it failed John Robertson. The difference is, he's willing to see it, acknowledge it, make amends. Robertson isn't.

"When they brought you back to Santa Fe," I continue, turning again to her, "did they offer you the services of a lawyer?"

"No," she answers, flat.

"Even though they'd warned you that you might be charged as an accessory to murder if your story didn't hold up."

"Yes."

"Did they ever at any time read you your rights, that you had the right to an attorney, and that you had the right to remain silent?"

"No."

"Your honor." Robertson stands. "Miss Gomez was not a suspect, she was a witness. We don't Mirandize witnesses."

"You do if they may be indicted as accessory to murder," I shoot back.

"Your honor," Robertson says, his voice starting to rise, "there was never any intention on the part of my office to indict Miss Gomez. None whatsoever. So Mirandizing her was never an issue."

"All right," Martinez answers. "We'll hold that in abeyance for now."

"Until what time, your honor?" Robertson asks.

"Until such time as we determine the veracity of Miss Gomez's statements, counselor. Then and now," he says.

Robertson starts to say something more, thinks better of it, sits down.

Martinez turns to me.

"This is the extent of your written affidavit, Mr. Alexander," he says. "Is there anything further you wish to ask your witness?"

"Yes, sir," I answer. "There is one more thing."

I turn to Rita again.

"The four men sitting at this table," I say.

She forces herself to look at them; then quickly away.

"Yes."

"You said at the trial that they raped you."

Hesitantly: "Yes."

"Did they?"

She looks at them again. They look back at her, their eyes cold, expressionless. Even though she's on their side now, they can't bring any compassion, it isn't in their nature. They are, at heart, bad to the bone, men for whom raping her was nothing but a diversion.

"Yes," she answers.

"Repeatedly?" I ask.

"Yes."

"It must have been terrifying," I say.

"Very."

"And painful."

"It hurt like hell for days."

"Did you go to the hospital?" I ask. "To be examined, taken care of?"

She pauses. "You mean, by myself?"

"Yes."

"No."

"Why not? If it was so painful?"

"I was too scared."

"That the hospital might tell the police, and then you'd have to tell about the bikers, and they'd make good on their threats to come back and kill you," I elaborate.

"Yes."

"When the police . . . when officers Sanchez and Gomez . . . when they found you, were you still experiencing pain?"

"Yes."

"Bleeding?"

"Yes."

"Did they do anything to help you?"

"Yes."

"What did they do?"

"They took me to the hospital."

"Objection!" from Robertson, on his feet, his arm outstretched.

"Over-ruled," Martinez barks, never taking his eyes off Rita.

"And they saw to it that you were taken care of," I say.

"Yes," she answers.

"And only after that did they take you up to the mountains and start to get your story."

"Yes."

I stand in front of her. Our eyes meet. I look at her with as much warmth and reassurance as I can muster.

"You lied before, didn't you? At the trial."

"Yes." Eyes downcast, her entire body shaking. If I've ever felt for her, it's now.

"And you're telling the truth today."

"Yes."

"Absolutely and without reservation and without any coercion or promises from me."

"Yes," she answers, in a firm, clear voice. "I ain't lying now."

"Miss Gomez."

Robertson stands in front of her, poised on the balls of his feet. He leans in towards her. She draws away from him, pressing her back against the hard oak chair.

"Why should anyone in this room believe what you've told us today?"

"Because it's the truth," she says, defensively.

"I see. The truth."

"That's right," she answers, more aggressively. I'd coached her to be prepared for this, and not to back down. She has right on her side, and she shouldn't be afraid to stand up for herself; in her case, easier said than done.

"And what you said at the trial, that was the truth, too, wasn't it?"

"No."

"But you said it was. You swore on a Bible that it was."

"I swore falsely." She looks up at Martinez. "I had to, judge. They would've sent me to jail otherwise."

"So you say," Robertson barks at her. His voice echoes through the courtroom.

"It's the truth," she protests, jumping in her seat, startled and frightened.

"You seem scared, Miss Gomez," Robertson tells her. "I barely raised my voice. Of course, you should be; you're involved in a pack of lies here, a web of deceit that makes this courtroom stink to high hell!"

"I am not," she answers gamely.

"Why should anyone believe a word of what you've said here?" he thunders. "Of what's in these raggedy-ass pages," he continues, holding her new testimony in his hand.

"Because . . ." she starts to say.

"Because it's the truth," he answers for her, cutting her off, the sarcasm dripping. "Because you, an admitted liar and perjurer, say so."

"It is," she whimpers.

"Sure," he comes back, "and the moon's made out of green cheese."

Martinez leans down from his perch.

"Counselor," he tells Robertson, "lay off the hyperbole, okay? And stop browbeating this witness."

"Browbeating this witness?" Robertson exclaims. "Browbeating . . . what's there to browbeat, your honor, this woman is completely without credibility!"

"That's for me to decide," Martinez tells him.

"That's right," Robertson says. "It's for you, the court, to decide." He's fighting to keep in control, and it's hard, because he's a true believer. "And may I remind your honor that your decision must be based on clear and over-riding evidence, hard evidence. It's not enough that a witness says she's telling the truth now and was lying then. You have to be convinced that what she's testifying to now is the truth, beyond the shadow of a doubt, virtually, and all the rest is lies. You have to be completely convinced of that.

"And you also have to be convinced," he continues, turning away for a moment to give my clients a look of utter contempt, "that if her testimony today is true, her sworn testimony, then several officers of this court have committed criminal acts. Grievous acts, acts that could imprison them. They are flat-out liars, and Rita Gomez sits at the right hand of the Virgin Mary."

"I'm aware of my duties," Martinez tells him, his voice cold with anger. "But thank you for reminding me."

"I mean no disrespect towards you, Judge Martinez," Robertson tells him, eating a little humble pie, "but I just can't believe her. She is the most unpredictable and contrary witness I have ever encountered in all my years of practicing law."

Martinez looks at him through hooded eyelids.

"When she was your witness you believed her well enough," he says.

My argument exactly.

"Because her testimony was consistent with all the other facts in the case," Robertson protests. "What we're hearing today is utterly without foundation."

Martinez shakes his head. "I can't agree with you."

"Let me give you a specific example," Robertson pleads.

"That would be helpful," Martinez tells him dryly.

Robertson turns to Rita.

"You've said that when detectives Gomez and Sanchez located you, you were still in bad shape from being raped."

"I was. Real bad, still."

"And that they took you to the hospital and got you fixed up."

"Yes."

"What hospital was that, Miss Gomez? Do you recall?"

"I'm not sure. I was kind of in a daze. I wasn't paying attention."

"But a hospital with an emergency-room facility. They took you to the emergency room."

"The emergency room, definitely."

"And the hospital was in Santa Fe."

She nods. "We didn't have to go very far."

"Who paid for this, Miss Gomez? Did you pay?"

"No, man. I don't have that kind of money."

"Well, maybe your insurance company paid."

"I ain't got no insurance," she says, almost laughing; she virtually lives on the street, to her the thought of having luxuries like insurance is simply ridiculous. "I can't even afford a car or a decent apartment."

"Maybe the policemen paid? The detectives who allegedly brought you there?"

"They must've. I never thought about it one way or the other."

Robertson turns to the bench. And I suddenly realize where he's taking this and I kick myself for not following through properly.

"There are three hospitals in the Santa Fe area with emergency facilities, your honor. We have gone to all of them and checked out the date in question when Miss Gomez would have been admitted. In fact, we checked from the day she said she was raped until the day she voluntarily gave her statement about this incident. None of those hospitals have any record of a Rita Gomez being admitted to their emergency room or any facility of theirs."

He crosses to his table, picks up a large envelope, hands it to Martinez.

"Do you have a copy for me?" I ask, testily, glancing at Mary Lou. I'm really pissed at myself, I should've been prepared for this.

He hands me a duplicate envelope. I pass it to Mary Lou, who rapidly skims the contents, silently hands it to me. We both feel dumb as stones.

Martinez reads his more carefully.

"These appear to be in order," he finally says.

"They are, your honor," Robertson replies. "My staff double-checked them personally. We had to be sure. She was never in a Santa Fe emergency room on any of those dates."

He takes a hard look at Rita, then turns back to the bench.

"Plain and simple, your honor, she lied about going to the hospital. She was never there."

"That appears to be the case, yes," Martinez says.

"It's her pattern, your honor. She's a liar. And if she lied about this, which, although important, is not critical, who's to say she isn't lying about something else? About everything else? Who's to say that what she's told this court today, and in her so-called sworn statement that this testimony is based on, is nothing more than a desperate pack of lies?"

"It's the truth!"

Martinez bangs his gavel.

"Please restrain yourself, Miss Gomez," he warns her.

"I have a different theory about these events, your honor," Robertson says. "It's much more in keeping with the facts that were developed at trial, and with the personalities in this case."

He turns and stares at our table, at the four convicts sitting there in Death Row overalls.

"These four men here, in front of us, are scum. They are the worst kind of cancer in our society, and they have committed crimes from here to eternity, practically. They were convicted in a fair and square trial. And they were sentenced to their just rewards."

"So what about this hospital shit?" Lone Wolf asks in a whisper, leaning close to me. "Is that for real?"

"I don't know," I answer. "I'll try to find out."

I'll try to find out as fast as I can; this is blowing a big hole in our case.

"But they couldn't accept that," Robertson continues. "They were going to get her to change her story, one way or the other." He turns to the bench. "We all know the horror stories about men like these. And we know that they spread their poisonous tentacles all over the country. That their comrades-in-arms from other chapters stand ready and waiting to assist them."

The truth is, he's right. Not in this specific, but in the general mix of things he's right.

"Someone got to her," Robertson states flatly. "Another Scorpion, Hell's Angel, one of them. Somehow, despite her best efforts to get herself out of harm's way so she could start a new life, they found her. And they scared her to death so that she'd come up with this story she's brought in here today. Not only that . . ."

"Objection!" I'm on my feet. "This is supposed to be cross-examination of a witness, your honor, not a formal summation."

"Agreed," Martinez says. "Sustained."

"I'd like to respond to that, your honor," I continue.

"What is it?" Martinez asks.

"Someone did get to Rita Gomez. I did; initially. I found her—let me correct that, my colleague Ms. Bell found her—and I took her statement at that time. Later on, when she was about to appear before this court, someone did get to her. According to her, it was one of the officers who had originally corrupted her."

"Bullshit!"

We all turn. Moseby's standing, his face beet-red.

"That's a lie, your honor!"

Martinez slams down his gavel.

"Sit down and shut up," he commands. "Or you will be forcibly escorted from this courtroom *right now!*"

He turns to all of us.

"This is not the proper time to be discussing these allegations," he warns us. "We will deal with them at the right time, which is when I say it is."

He turns to Robertson. "Are you finished with this witness?" he asks, taking no pains to conceal the anger in his voice.

"Yes, your honor."

"Then she may stand down, subject to recall." He looks up at the clock. "This court stands adjourned until ten o'clock tomorrow morning." He stares at Robertson, then at me. "Let's try to conduct the remainder of this hearing with less rancor and hysteria—from both of you."

With a sweep of his robes, he storms out, leaving us all hanging.

At three o'clock in the morning, Ellen, my intrepid researcher, walks into my office with a geek. She's done a great job of finding a needle in a haystack. She preens as she introduces him. We shake hands. His is cold and wet.

Then the geek, a pimply-faced computer nerd in his late teens, sits at my desk, opens a Toshiba T3100SX mini-computer, hooks his modem up to my telephone, and starts to type.

AT ROBERTSON'S INSISTENCE (and what seems to be my and Mary Lou's grudging acquiescence) Sanchez and Gomez are brought to the stand. Each categorically denies having taken Rita to any hospital at any time, or to have in any way brainwashed her or caused her to alter her story in any fashion. They stand on their previous testimony and on their combined service of more than forty years as deputies in the Santa Fe County Sheriff's Office, during which time they have received nothing but accolades.

A ridiculously skewed stand-off—the sworn testimony of two highly-decorated police officers against that of an admitted liar.

"CALL LOUIS BONFIGLIO to the stand."

The geek shuffles down the aisle, crosses to the dock, languidly raises his hand and takes the oath. He's dressed out of Central Casting; polyester shirt, the clear plastic penholder in his pocket stuffed with ballpoints, gabardine pants belted halfway up his chest, Birkenstock sandals. Short, unkempt hair, a complexion fish-belly-pale from never being outdoors. He's a good fifty pounds overweight: the prototypical computer nerd.

I scoop up a pile of printouts that are laid out on the table in front of me and approach him, smiling as if to put him at ease. He smiles back; his is the smile of the smartass co-conspirator whose greatest pleasure in life is to fuck over the authorities.

We establish his bona fides, such as they are: he's a student at Saint John's College here in Santa Fe (the Great Books school, home to the far-out geniuses who don't fit into places like Harvard or Princeton), he's one of their top math and physics students, and he's president of the campus computer club. He is famous in the underground hacker world for having broken into the computer that monitors the nuclear power plants that supply the energy to much of the Four Corners, shutting the entire operation down for several hours last year. (Famous not only for the deed but also because he was never officially charged; the authorities didn't want what would have been overwhelmingly negative publicity, they let him go with a severe warning. And they watch him like a hawk.)

Since then he's played it straight, more or less. Until last night.

"Did you recently obtain these documents for me?" I ask him, passing across the sheaf of printouts.

He gives them a cursory glance.

"Yeh, I did."

I hold them up for Martinez to see.

"These are the raw, unedited records from the computer in the emergency room at Saint Mary's Hospital here in Santa Fe, your honor, for the date that Rita Gomez says she was taken there by detectives Sanchez and Gomez. If you'll notice, the name Rita Gomez has been entered." I put my finger on her name in the middle of the page.

Martinez's eyes bug open.

"Let me see those."

I hand them up. He starts reading them.

Robertson spins in his chair, looking at the two cops seated behind him. They look away. He jumps to his feet.

"I want to see those myself."

"In good time," I tell him.

He stands in place, fuming. Martinez flips through the pages, turns back to the one I'd ear-marked for him.

"Are these for real?" he asks finally.

"Very real," I assure him. "The only real hospital documents that have been introduced in this courtroom."

He hands them to his bailiff.

"Place these in evidence," he commands. As an afterthought: "see to it that the District Attorney's office gets a copy."

Mary Lou gets up from our table and tosses a copy on the prosecution table. Robertson grabs it, quickly starts reading.

"How did you get these?" Martinez asks me.

"Mr. Bonfiglio obtained them for me, your honor. At four o'clock this morning."

The judge stares at me, conflicted.

"Were they obtained legally?" he asks reluctantly, feeling compelled to, not wanting to.

"To be truthful, your honor, it's a gray area. They are not public documents per se, but Saint Mary's is a publicly funded hospital, so a case can be made that their records are public records, as long as releasing them doesn't breach doctor-patient confidentiality, which in this case I clearly felt did not happen."

Robertson, meanwhile, stops reading and strides forward.

"With all due respect, your honor, I have never seen these documents. Until this moment, I didn't know they existed. But it's obvious to me that they were obtained illegally, and should not be allowed to be placed in the record of these proceedings or used in any fashion here."

Martinez shoots him a look that would stop a rhino in its tracks.

"This isn't a trial, damn it. We're trying to find out what the hell's going on." He turns back to me. "Explain how you got these, and why they aren't part of the official record."

"I'll let my witness explain, if I may."

Martinez turns to the kid.

"Explain."

Bonfiglio smiles. The kid is in his element; he's going to savor this.

"Sure, judge. I'd be happy to. It works like this."

I step back; I want all the attention to be on him. All eyes are on this geek: the bikers, Martinez, Robertson, Moseby, everyone.

"This patient came into the hospital. They got all her information, blood type and so forth, entered it here." He points to places on the printout. "Every patient who ever comes into a hospital goes on the record. They have to, in case they get sued later by some ambulance-chasing lawyer looking for a quick buck." He smiles maliciously at me. Let him—he may be a geek and an asshole, but he's my asshole.

"Then they treated her. According to this," he reads, "they did the following procedures: a D&C, administered blood-clotting medication, antibiotics by injection, sterile after-care measures."

"Standard medical procedure for treating rape and vaginal bleeding," Mary Lou interjects, standing at our table. "We can have a gynecologist testify to that if you so desire."

"I'll take your word for it," Martinez tells her. He turns to the nerd. "Continue," he says impatiently.

"Okay. After they fixed her up, which took, let's see, five hours, see here," he points, "this is the time they admitted her, and this is when they discharged her, it's military time, that's why the twenty-four-hour stuff . . ."

"I understand that," Martinez interrupts. "Stay with the records."

"Okey-doke. Now . . ." he stops, grins. "Here's the funny stuff." He points to an asterisk at the end of her chart.

"Then she disappeared."

"What do you mean, 'disappeared'?" Martinez asks.

"They wiped her records out. Like she was never there."

"They can do that?" Martinez asks.

"It's done all the time."

I glance over at Robertson. His jaw is open in absolute disbelief.

"It is?" Martinez says.

The nerd looks at him with disdain.

"Judge . . . haven't you ever heard of computer crime? Hacking?"

"Yes."

"Well, that's what this was. They just did it in-house, instead of someone like me doing it from the outside. Same difference. Now you see it, now you don't."

"I see . . . I think," Martinez says slowly.

"You don't. Not really," the nerd tells him. "But it's okay. All you have to know is, somebody erased the files. Rita Gomez? She was there, then she wasn't. Instantly."

Martinez looks at Bonfiglio like he's a species never before seen on this planet.

"All right. But if she was erased from the records, how did she show up again?"

Mary Lou and I exchange a secret smile. We had asked the same question as the sun was coming up this morning.

"They screwed up," the nerd tells him.

"How?" Martinez asks.

"They erased her off the regular computer. But they didn't erase her off the backup computer." He smiles triumphantly. "Probably 'cause whoever did it, some nurse or some other flunky, didn't know there was one. But there was."

Martinez steeples his fingers.

"Is this common?" he asks.

"Backup computers, or erasing files?" the kid counters.

"Both."

The kid nods.

"Erasing official files is common?"

"CIA does it every day," Bonfiglio informs him. "Couple million times a year. It's the modern way to rewrite history, judge."

Martinez nods dumbly. He is not of the modern age, like this snotty punk.

"What about backup computers?" he asks Bonfiglio.

"It's common in institutions. The police, FBI, military . . . and hospitals. Too easy to lose information. It's a fail-safe method, like Dr. Strangelove."

"Dr. who?"

"Never mind. Inside joke. You're obviously not a Kubrick freak, judge."

Martinez pops the $64,000 question.

"I would assume these backup computers are not open to public use," he says.

"Nosirree. Definitely not."

"Then how did you get in?"

The nerd puffs up like Jose Canseco after he's hit a home run.

"The computer hasn't been built that I can't get into, judge. Not if I work at it hard enough and long enough."

"How long did it take you to get into this one?" Martinez asks.

"Thirty seconds," the nerd answers.

"Thirty seconds? You must be a genius at this," Martinez exclaims in open admiration, which is pretty interesting considering the nerd just admitted breaking the law.

"This is true." Bonfiglio pauses. "Of course, I already knew the password. I happened to have needed to get into that particular computer last year to help some friends check their records regarding prescriptions for certain pharmaceutical substances."

If I ever have the need for designer drugs I'll have him put a prescription into the computer for me like he did for his friends at Saint John's. He must make a pretty penny off that little scam.

Martinez lets that pass.

"So you got into this backup computer . . ." he pauses.

"That has lots of raw data the regular one doesn't, that's it, you've got it," the nerd finishes for him. "And there was little Rita Gomez, front and center. The computer doesn't lie, judge. Just the people who screw around with it."

"It's simple. The police couldn't take the chance of officially admitting Rita Gomez to the hospital. Because someone else might have questioned her before they could program her."

It's the following morning. I'm standing in front of Judge Martinez. Everything's as it was yesterday, except Sanchez and Gomez are absent from the proceedings. I'll bet dollars to doughnuts they won't be seen in here again unless they're under subpoena.

"That's pure conjecture," Robertson says. He's glum; his objection comes without force.

"We'll find out soon enough," Martinez replies. To me: "Continue your thought, Will."

Familiarity from Martinez. We're definitely getting somewhere.

"That is my thought, your honor. If she had gone public at that time, who knows what she would have said? She is telling us now that she was forced into making a false statement. This new information indicates to me that she's telling the truth now, and lied at the trial because she was scared for her life, literally. If they did what she says they did, who knows how far they would have gone?"

Martinez nods in agreement. He turns to Robertson.

"Do you have anything to say about this?"

"This doesn't prove my people were lying," Robertson says, grasping desperately at a straw, "it merely shows that records were tampered with at some unknown time. Somebody could have put this entry in later, to try and discredit us."

"You really expect me to believe that?" Martinez asks in astonishment.

"I'm saying it's a possibility," Robertson insists stubbornly. "If this hacker that the defense presented yesterday could get into confidential files that easily, and add material as he said he did, he or someone else with his expertise could have inserted her information in there."

"Yes," Martinez says. "But I don't think that's the case here." He pauses. "I don't think you do, either."

Robertson doesn't reply. He sits down heavily, glancing at Moseby, then away, in disgust. He's starting to doubt his own people; it shows clearly in his face.

That doesn't mean that he thinks my clients are innocent. Short of Jesus Christ Himself coming back to earth and proclaiming it, John Robertson will go to his grave convinced that they murdered Richard Bartless; not because of hard evidence, but because of *who they are*. And no evidence that I can present will ever change his mind, because he's bought into it too deeply.

DR. GRADE SETTLES HEAVILY into the witness chair, his dour demeanor a clear indication to me that he'll be attempting to maintain his attitude of condescending superiority; but that posture's wearing thin, and the good doctor knows it. This case is changing, the ground beneath him is less secure than it was before. His unusual, daring medical opinion had dovetailed beautifully with Rita's testimony, the one authenticating the other, but now her support is gone, and his findings will have to stand on their own. That has to be undermining, even for a man with his overweening ego.

Once again, the pictures are placed in front of him. Once again, he gives the impression of studying them carefully. By now I'm sure he's memorized them.

"Same pictures as before?" I ascertain.

"They are."

"Good."

There are copies in the courtroom. Martinez follows along with his, Robertson with his, Mary Lou and the bikers with ours. I touch various wounds on Grade's set with my ballpoint pen.

"Knife wounds," I say.

"Yes."

"Here . . . here . . . here . . ." Showing where I'm pointing to Judge Martinez, to the prosecution table. Tracing them on the black-and-white pictures, everyone tracing his copy along with me.

"Yes."

"Caused by knives that were heated to the cauterization point."

"That is my testimony, sir."

"And you first learned about this theory in a medical journal which you unfortunately are unable to this day to remember the name of."

"Unfortunately, yes."

I give him the photos to hold, walk to my table, where Mary Lou takes a magazine out of a manila envelope and hands it to me. I walk back to the stand, hold the magazine out to Dr. Grade. *Modern Abnormal Pathology*, March 1983.

"Could this be the magazine in question?" I ask.

He opens it, skims the table of contents, flips to the article in question.

"Yes. This is it." He turns to Judge Martinez, a look of relief combined with arrogance spread across his face. "There can be no question now of my truthfulness, your honor"; swiveling back to face me: "or my integrity." He smiles again. "I'm glad someone finally found it. Where, may I ask, did you find it?"

"In a medical library." I answer casually.

Ellen, my intrepid researcher, found it. She's been looking for the goddam thing since the trial. She sweated blood to find it—it's an obscure publication, it was a one-in-a-million fluke that Grade had come across it in the first place, particularly since the magazine had folded a few issues after this article came out, and had no circulation in the profession to begin with. She'd found it just a few days ago, in the University of Idaho Medical School Library. It was the two hundred and forty-third source she'd checked.

Judge Martinez doesn't come out and say so, but I know that he's baffled. He's at a loss as to why I'm seemingly happy about discovering a piece of evidence that is so damaging to my case, and then compounding the problem by introducing it into evidence, which I'm under no obligation to do. I'm sure he was expecting us to hammer at Grade about this article, claiming that it never existed and was part of a collusionary effort to frame my clients. Now I've legitimized Grade's theory and seemingly hurt my cause.

Robertson stares at me in almost euphoric disbelief; you just blew your brains out, asshole, his look says, I didn't even have to, you did it for me.

Martinez calls for a recess so he can read the article.

"We'd like to see it, too, your honor," Robertson asks.

"Make him a copy," Martinez instructs his bailiff. "Make a mess of them—we're going to need them." He looks around. "If no one has anything further to add we'll recess for one hour."

I speak up before he gavels.

"One more question for Dr. Grade, your honor."

Testily: "Go ahead."

"To your knowledge, Dr. Grade, have there been any other articles published about the 'hot knives' theory."

"Not to my knowledge," he answers.

"You keep current with these things—these developments in forensic pathology."

"I am as current as any coroner in the country," Grade replies icily. "Any reputable coroner or pathologist will attest to that."

"I'll sleep better tonight knowing that," I reply with an equal share of contempt as I turn my back on the flatulent asshole.

Mary Lou and I hang out with the bikers in the otherwise empty courtroom while we wait for the various interested parties to read the article.

"They must think we're crazy," Mary Lou observes.

"You hang with fuckers like us, you got to be," Roach tells her. "But it's okay . . . we still love you."

"Are you sure you want to introduce this evidence, Will?" Martinez asks Mary Lou and me. He's summoned us to his private chambers.

"Yes, your honor," I answer.

"It's hurtful to your argument. An argument, I might add, that's been going well for you." He looks pained, like we're undercutting him. "You can withdraw it from the record," he adds. "We're not at trial here."

"We want it in. We want all the cards laid on the table," Mary Lou says forcefully.

Martinez sighs heavily. "It's your hearing. I hope you know what you're doing. I hope your clients know."

FRANK SUGARMAN, M.D., Ph.D., coroner for the city of Saint Louis, noted author and lecturer on causes and effects of violently-produced death, strides down the aisle and takes the stand, his 'I do' in response to the oath booming through the still courtroom. Sugarman's a robust fifty, a tall, burly hell-raiser, kind of a medical Gerry Spence in terms of courtroom notoriety, one of the top forensic pathologists in the country. He often testifies as an expert witness in important murder cases, and his opinions are taken seriously. He's a gun who carries major weight.

He'd flown in last night; Mary Lou, Ellen and I spent several hours going over the original trial transcript (especially Grade's testimony), reviewing the crime photos of the body, and dissecting the article I would later that day introduce in court. Sugarman had been alternately bemused and angered.

"I know Milt Grade," Sugarman had told us, "his reputation is okay, although in my opinion out-dated. But this," meaning the conclusions Grade had drawn, "is terrible. It's every coroner's nightmare. Makes us all look like a bunch of snake-oil faithhealers."

I think back to Hardiman, to his prowess at healing using snakes and faith, but keep my mouth shut. This isn't the time for arguments about religious belief versus scientific inquiry.

"So you'll have no qualms about refuting him, on our behalf?" I ask.

"None whatsoever."

I place the packet of photos of Richard Bartless's mutilated body in front of Sugarman. He looks at each in turn, studies them carefully, hands them back to me.

"These wounds, Dr. Sugarman." I point to several of the wounds, in various pictures. "What would you judge them to be?"

"Knife wounds. Either a hunting-type knife or something from a kitchen. You can see serrated-edge marks on several of them," he says, pointing to different wounds in the pictures.

I look; I don't see the distinction. Martinez motions to me to hand up the pictures, squints at them.

"I'm not seeing what you're referring to, doctor."

"It's hard for a layman. Get me a magnifying glass and I can show you."

We wait while a marshal hunts one up. He hands it to Sugarman, who stands at his chair so he and Martinez are on the same level.

"Here," Sugarman says, pointing with a wooden match he's taken out of his pocket, which he uses to light his Macanudos. "Here, here, and here."

Martinez squints, concentrating.

"Yes," he says. "I can see that." He turns to Sugarman. "What does this mean?"

"Couple of things. First, all the wounds were inflicted by one knife. The serration marks are closely-enough identical to say that with pretty fair certainty."

"I'll accept that," Martinez says.

I'm not looking at the photos with them; Sugarman and I covered this ground last night. Robertson, on the other hand, is poised on the edge of his chair like a hound pointing, waiting his turn to get a look.

A door opening in the back of the room catches my eye. Grade has quietly entered, sits down in the last row of benches. When he sees me look in his direction he turns away.

I turn back to Sugarman.

"Anything else, Dr. Sugarman?" I ask.

"They weren't made while the victim was alive," Sugarman says.

I look back at Grade again. He's staring straight ahead, his face bloodless.

"Not alive," I repeat.

"No."

"Because the victim didn't bleed from his wounds," I say.

"Yes, but that's not the important reason."

"What is the important reason?"

"All the wounds are identical," he says. "Same size, same shape."

"But that's because only one knife was used, isn't it?"

He shakes his head in irritation.

"The reason the wounds are all the same size and shape is because the guy was dead. Corpses don't move."

"But what about Dr. Grade's 'hot knives' theory? That the wounds were cauterized."

"Impossible."

"Why?"

"You're alive," Sugarman says. "Somebody's trying to stick you with a white-hot knife. I don't care how many people are holding you down, you're going to struggle like a madman. And when you do get stabbed, you're going to twist and writhe like a fish trying to throw a hook. You're going to tear your skin where that knife's sticking in it. Your wounds are going to be torn, ragged, especially from the serrations. It's going to tear you every which way until you're too weak to fight. None of these wounds were lethal in one shot, which would be the case if the knife had penetrated the aorta or carotid.

"They didn't kill him," he states firmly. "A bullet through the brain did. Those stab wounds occurred some time after the victim was killed. They're all the same size: they had to be."

Martinez is riveted by Sugarman's testimony, while Robertson frantically studies the pictures.

I walk to the defense table, pick up a copy of the magazine article that had turned Grade on to the 'hot knives' theory. I hand it to Dr. Sugarman.

"Have you ever seen this article?" I ask.

"You showed it to me last night."

"Before then."

"Yes."

"Do you remember when?"

"When it was initially published. Shortly after I assumed my present position."

"What was your reaction to it?"

"After I stopped laughing? I thought it was the most irresponsible piece of garbage I'd read in my professional career. Dangerously so."

"Did you give it any credence?"

"Of course not. It was written by an obvious crackpot. It has no substantiation whatsoever in medical fact."

"What was the consensus in the field of pathology?"

"What I've just said. A tale told by an idiot."

"Did anyone in your field of forensic pathology—anyone well known—do anything to rebut this article?"

"Yes. I did."

"What did you do?"

"I conducted a series of experiments that proved beyond a shadow of a doubt, not only to me but to several colleagues, that the theory was impossible, without foundation. It couldn't happen."

"Did you publish your findings?"

"Yes, I did."

I cross to the defense table, pick up a medical journal, hand it to him.

"Is this your article?" I ask.

"Yes, it is."

"I'd like to submit this to the court, your honor. It is from the *American Journal of Pathology,* dated November 1983."

I hand it up to Martinez, who looks at the title.

"This magazine is considered one of the benchmark journals in your field, is it not?" I ask.

"It is," he replies.

"They wouldn't publish anything they didn't believe was factual and correct."

"They would never have published something this sloppy," he says, brandishing the 'hot knives' article.

"How would you categorize the 'hot knives' theory, then, doctor?" I ask.

"If it's me and you and a couple ol' boys sitting 'round the campfire swapping lies, I'd categorize it as a crock; no offense meant, your honor," he says to Martinez with a smile. "In scientific terms, it's up there with the flat-earth theory. Pure uninformed bunk. You couldn't find another reputable pathologist in the country who would think of subscribing to it." He pauses. "I hate to say this about a colleague, especially one with Milt Grade's reputation, but I was shocked when I heard he based his testimony on it."

"Especially since there had been your follow-up article," I say.

"I guess Dr. Grade didn't see it," he says. "Although I'm surprised, because everyone in the field reads that journal."

"He must've missed that issue," I volunteer.

"Pretty unfortunate if he did," Sugarman replies. "But he must have. He never would have used that bogus theory otherwise."

Robertson buries his head in his hands.

I look to the back of the courtroom. Grade is gone, the massive oak door slowly swinging closed in his wake.

"WE MOVE THAT THE RESULTS of the original trial be over-turned, your honor, because of tainted, coerced, and falsely-obtained evidence, and that all charges against our clients be dropped."

Robertson objects. He's a pit-bull, he'll never let go.

"I'll give you an answer in the morning," Martinez says. He's dragging; the testimony we've introduced has knocked him for a loop. He presided over a false trial, and it's killing him inside.

He withers Robertson with a look as he walks out.

"I hope I helped," Sugarman says.

"You definitely did," I assure him.

"Grade." He shakes his head in disgust. "They ought to put his sorry ass out to pasture."

Mary Lou and I gather our papers, head back for the office. We have hours of work ahead of us, and when we go home neither of us will sleep a wink.

WE'RE IN JUDGE MARTINEZ'S CHAMBERS. Robertson stands apart from Mary Lou and me, ramrod-straight.

Martinez turns to me. "My hands are tied, Will. I can't dismiss outright, much as I want to. Miss Gomez says she lied before; she probably did, but it's one statement against the other, which you know under these circumstances is considered subjective evidence and not legal cause for overturning the verdict, certainly without going to trial again. Neither is Dr. Sugarman's testimony, although I devoutly believed it."

"What about the falsifying of the hospital records?"

"That's a separate issue." He turns to Robertson. "Which I hope the authorities will vigorously pursue."

"We're looking into it, your honor," Robertson tells him.

"Don't take your time," Martinez snaps. He turns to me with real compassion.

"I'm sorry. My hands are tied," he reiterates. "Unless the prosecution wants to consider dropping charges," he says pointedly.

"We don't, your honor." Ever the righteous man.

Martinez is trying; I give him credit. Better a late convert than never at all.

He looks over our witness roster.

"I see you have only one more name on your list . . . Scott Ray . . ."

"Yes, your honor."

"Will his testimony be addressing anything that gets to the heart of this case? Otherwise I believe I have enough information on which to base my decision."

"I think you'll find him an enlightening witness, your honor."

"All right then. Let's have him."

"CALL SCOTT RAY TO THE STAND."

He walks forward, this pretty-boy hustler/Jesus freak in a fresh-bought Sears, Roebuck suit.

Robertson looks at the witness. He doesn't know who Scott Ray is, but he won't waste any time trying to find out.

Let him try. By the time he knows, it'll all be over, one way or the other.

Scott Ray solemnly swears to tell the truth, so help him God.

I approach my witness.

"Mr. Ray. Could you tell this court where you were and what you were doing on the night Richard Bartless was murdered?"

It was a couple days before the killing. Maybe three. Driving from down south, West Texas, Lubbock, Mule Shoe, crossing into New Mexico at Clovis, where Buddy Holly and the Crickets recorded "That'll Be the Day" and "Peggy Sue" at Norman Petty's studio. Buddy Holly—the guy was a fucking musical genius, no question. Detouring there, looking at the old place like visiting a shrine, thinking if it hadn't of been ol' Buddy done it, it could've been me. That's the way my luck always runs, too late and bad.

The idea was to drive up to Denver and look for a straight gig, chill out from OD'ing on the fucking and dealing, that shit will ultimately lead to an early grave if you don't give it a rest occasionally. But the car was fucked, it was fucked when he bought it and it was fucked ever since, piece of shit, fucking salesman saw him coming, unloaded his primo lemon. That's what happens when you trust human nature, it'll fuck you every time. He was able to limp it as far as the outskirts of Santa Fe, then it just up and died completely, leave it to the vultures. Nobody'd pick him up hitch-hiking, he had to walk four miles into town in the heat and dust.

On automatic pilot he made his way to a high-class gay bar and set up for business in the men's room. By closing time he'd worked half a dozen sorry faggots into sucking him off behind the closed door of the shitter, at fifteen bucks a pop (he could always get it up, no matter how often he came, it was natural to him, something he was born with; it came in handy in circumstances such as these), then to top off the evening he tailed the last cocksucker, a middle-aged drunk, to the parking lot in back, where he mugged and rolled him. Candy from a baby, motherfucker never knew what hit him. He came away with close to three hundred in cash and a shitload of credit cards, which he used to rent a car (he'll abandon it on the street when he's ready to split), secure a decent room, buy a new wardrobe, and withdraw a thousand dollars in automatic teller cash advances before dumping the hot plastic down the sewer: the dumb shit had his secret code in his wallet, folded up next to his driver's license. The way to do stolen credit cards is to not get greedy, use them and lose them fast before they're reported.

Flush with cash, decent wheels, and new rad threads, the following night he's at the Dew Drop Inn, looking for pussy. (He's not a gay, no fucking way, he'll let them suck it but he won't do them, you close your eyes it could be a chick, it's like a whore fucking; a job.) And in walked Richard, and it was like 'hey dude, let's party,' 'cause it was obvious they weren't like the usual clientele that hung in here, they had some class, him and Richard, that was obvious from the get-go. He had the money, when you've got it, spend it, that was his motto, so they picked up a couple whores and a bottle of quality tequila, scored a lid of primo weed (Richard was well-connected locally in that regard), and drove in his rental car, a 5.0 Mustang convertible, black on black, to a nearby roach-motel, where Richard was staying.

He and his whore fucked and sucked the night away; a little bondage, some golden showers, the usual. Richard didn't do so good—his whore told Scott's whore the next morning he didn't do nothing; too drunk, too high. Scott knew better: Richard was a closet fag, an experienced hand could tell right off. He, Scott, didn't give a shit one way or the other; sex is sex, what's the difference? Whatever works for you. He personally could take it any way it came, he considered himself lucky that way.

So what if Richard was gay? Scott could swing every which way but loose, as long as he didn't have to play the girl. He drew the line there—he'd pitch but he wouldn't catch, he'd let the faggots suck him off, but he wouldn't suck, and no fist-fucking, none of that shit. He was, is, and forevermore would be, straight. A man. He made sure everybody knew that. The chicks he hung with knew it for sure; he was a cocksman supreme, they all told him so.

Okay, maybe he'd been a pussy in prison, the one or two times he'd been in, but that was inside, you're fighting for your life every second in the joint, sometimes that's the only way; to be some boss motherfucker's honey, so you can stay alive and get some priority favors. But everybody knows jail is different, the rules are suspended. Plenty of straight dudes have to be Barbie in prison, that's the way it is, pure and simple. It has nothing to do with being a man in the free world. Not a fucking thing.

The next night he motivated down to the Dew Drop Inn again, it was a righteous place to hang out, plenty of hot-to-trot chicks looking for a real man like himself. Richard was there and attached himself to Scott right away, which was okay 'cause Scott knew he'd want to score some more dope and Richard could put him with the right people. So then Richard introduces him to this skank maid from the motel called Rita who'd come with him, they'd hitch-hiked 'cause Richard's car wasn't running. Scott remembered her from the night before. She had offered herself to Scott, practically thrown herself at him. Scott had told her thanks but no thanks, he had higher standards than that, he didn't need a beauty queen or nothing like that to get him wanting to fuck, but this chick was ragged, a blind man could see she'd been to hell and back as far as who she fucked was concerned, she could be carrying every disease known to man, and some that hadn't been discovered yet. Pasadena on Rita Gomez, then and now.

Richard obviously liked her, though; maybe she could get him hot to trot, people are weird in what turns them on, live and let live, that was Scott's motto, whatever turns you on. Party forever and fuck the rest, that was another of his mottos.

Tonight was a bummer. The women weren't responding. There were enough of them, some of them pretty good, but either they were all with guys or they gave him the cold shoulder. The ones that let him know they were available were below his standards, spoiled goods. It was obvious that being with Richard and his ranked-out motel maid was a turnoff, the chick had absolutely no class and it rubbed off on him by association. If he was going to score some pussy tonight he was going to have to dump Richard and Rita and find another bar.

Before that, though, he wanted to get high, so he and Richard went outside to smoke a doobie. Richard had good weed and plenty of it; that made up for most of his negatives. Rita tagged along. She was already high, she didn't know Scott existed, which was fine with him.

It was hot, her T-shirt was clinging to her tits, she was showing through practically, like in a wet T-shirt contest. One thing she did have was good tits, he had to admit that. But the rest of the package was too damaged, there was no mystery left to her at all.

They smoked a joint, Richard and him, it was righteous weed, they were feeling mellow. The night was still young and he was not ready to go to bed with nobody to play with except five-finger Mary, so he was about to shove off when he heard the motorcycles approaching. They were Harleys, no mistaking that sound.

They pulled into the parking lot, spraying gravel, and parked their hogs, just so, lining them up symmetrically. Four beautiful machines. Be nice to ride one of those babies. But not here and now. Scott wasn't about to even get close to take a look, he knew this score, you don't fuck with the likes of these, you keep the hell out of their way. He'd known outlaw bikers from dealing dope, if you had brain one in your head you kept a wide berth.

He'd already told Richard he was splitting, so he started to his car, and as he's opening the door he hears Richard starting to talk to these bikers. He's standing in the shadows so it's okay to watch, and here's Richard talking to these guys, and it sounds like they're having a brief conversation. What it was, he couldn't hear clearly. But one of them raises his voice at whatever grief Richard's giving him, and all of a sudden another one of them slaps Richard across the mouth, hard, it sounded like a gunshot, and another one rabbit-punches him in the kidneys, and Richard collapses, and they start laughing and jeering at him, and Richard's crawling away, and then he gets up and starts running, which is the first smart thing he's done all night.

Then they all go inside (Rita's already in, she ran in when the shouting started), so Scott starts up his car and heads out down the highway, and fifty yards from the entrance there's Richard hobbling along like his ribs are broken, so out of kindness for the dumb shit Scott pulls up and tells him to climb in, he'll drop Richard back at the motel on his way to his next rendezvous.

So they're cruising on down the road and Scott asks Richard what the beef was all about.

"Drugs," Richard said.

"Like what," Scott kidded, "you wanted them to give you some?"

"Fuck no, I wanted to sell them some. I got five kilos of fresh-harvested Michoacán stashed up in the hills, where do you think that righteous weed I've been laying on you came from, I need some fast money to get my car out of repair and pay off a bunch of bills, somebody could really make out dealing this stuff."

Right away, the light-bulb went on in Scott's head. Ten kilos of primo Mex grass, he could unload that in Denver for fifteen to eighteen thousand.

"What do you want for it?" he asked.

"I'll sell the whole load of it for two thousand, five hundred," Richard had told him.

Scott didn't waste a second.

"It's a deal."

Richard looked at him.

"You got that kind of money?"

"That and then some."

"Let me see it."

Without slowing down, Scott reached into his pocket, pulled out his roll. Richard looked at it and smiled.

"Let's do some business," he said.

Scott's throat is dry from talking. He asks for a glass of water. I walk to the defense table, lean in to the defendants.

"Do you remember any of this?" I ask.

Lone Wolf shrugs.

"I vaguely remember some asshole saying something stupid in the parking lot. It could have been the way he says it was. Whatever it was, no one was dead when we went inside."

"What about him?" I nod towards Scott.

"Never saw him in my life."

The others nod; he's a cipher to them.

I cross back to Scott Ray.

"Please continue," I tell him.

They stopped at the motel first. Richard had to get something out of his room. Scott waited in the car. Richard was back in a flash with a knife so Scott could cut off a taste to check it, and a paper bag to put the money in, and they started to drive up to the mountains, where Richard had the grass stashed. Richard was enjoying himself, singing along with the radio. Scott was enjoying himself, too; he was about to shear this poor lamb for all his wool. Twenty-five hundred for five kilos. The profit he'd make would set him up for months. Richard had good weed, no question there, but he had no head for business.

Too fucking bad. For Richard.

They drove up into the mountains northeast of town. It was pretty up here. The road was winding, doubling back on itself, at times you could see the entire town and valley laid out below, the lights twinkling like Christmas ornaments, and up above the stars twinkling like more Christmas ornaments, each mirroring the other. It was peaceful and beautiful, and Scott was happy.

Three days ago he'd limped into town with nothing but dust on his shoes, and he was going to leave with new clothes, a bono car (he'd take it as far as Denver and ditch it there), and beaucoup money to be made. His luck was finally changing for the good; about time.

"Pull off here," Richard said abruptly.

They were high up now. It was a flat area, bordered by trees. Private—as soon as they pulled off the road they were hidden from view.

Richard got out first. Scott turned off the engine, followed Richard deeper into the wooded area.

"What'd you do, bury it?" Scott asked.

"Not exactly," Richard answered. He turned back to Scott. "Don't worry," he said. "You're going to get what you want. Or at least what you deserve."

I have a map in my hand. It's an aerial map of the area where Richard Bartless's body was found. I set it on an easel in front of Scott, at an angle that both he and Judge Martinez can easily see.

"Is this where you stopped?" I ask, pointing.

"Yeh. That's it."

Scott Ray is trembling now. His leg's doing a Saint Vitus dance.

"Are you all right?" Martinez asks, picking up on his nervousness. "Do you want some time to collect your thoughts?"

Scott Ray looks up at him.

"I've had two years to collect my thoughts," he says. "Let's get on with it."

"Go ahead, then," Martinez tells him.

Scott looked at Richard. What the fuck was he talking about?

"What do you mean, 'what I deserve'? We're doing business here, don't worry about what I fucking deserve."

Richard was looking at him in a funny way. It made the hair stand up on the back of Scott's neck.

"Where's the stash, Richard?" Scott asked.

"I got your stash," Richard said. "Right between my legs, man. Your pot of gold at the end of the rainbow."

The gun was in Richard's hand all of a sudden. He had taken it out of the paper sack, along with some bungee cords.

"Stop fucking around, Richard," Scott said. "I don't suck cock. Put the goddam gun down and let's do the deal."

He was scared; if you're not scared when somebody's pointing a gun at you you're either crazy or brain-dead. But he was more angry than scared; fucking Richard, the bastard was going to try and make him suck him off as part of the deal? No fucking way.

"Put the gun away," Scott said again. "Let's do the business we said we were going to do and bail out of here."

Richard smiled at him then.

"This is our business," he said.

The lamb had sheared the wolf.

"You ain't got no grass up here, do you, motherfucker?"

"That's right, baby," Richard said, grinning. "The only grass you're going to be tasting tonight is the clump growing around my root."

He cocked the gun, walked to Scott, placed the end of the barrel against Scott's temple.

"On your knees, cocksucker," he commanded.

Scott had no choice. He went down to his knees.

"Hands behind your back."

He tied Scott's hands together with one of the bungee cords.

Scott's eyes were squeezed shut. This isn't happening, he told himself. It's a bad dream.

"Open your eyes, sweetie," Richard said. "I've got that joint you've been waiting to suck. I'm going to get you high like you've never been."

Scott opened his eyes. Richard's cock was in his face. He may have been a limp dick with a woman last night, but now he was stiff as a poker.

"Kiss it," Richard said. He stuck the end of the gun barrel in Scott's ear. "Like it's the most delicious thing you've ever tasted in your life." He had a big shit-eating grin on his face. "Admit it to yourself, man. You're gay. You're as gay as I am. So start doing what comes naturally."

Scott had no choice. He put his lips around the tip of Richard's penis, and started sucking.

Richard started moaning. He sounded like a girl, almost like last night's whore, when Scott had eaten her.

Scott was a primo pussy eater; lots of women had told him he gave the best head they'd ever had. He was good at it because he loved it. But that was women; he didn't suck cock, never had, never would. Until now.

"More," Richard said. "Take more of it. You love it, goddam it—take it all."

He was moaning, gyrating his hips, fucking Scott in the mouth. With his free hand he grabbed the hair at the back of Scott's head, pulling Scott to him, pushing his cock deeper into Scott's throat. Like Scott had done two nights before in the men's room of the gay bar. Like he'd done to the sad faggot he'd mugged.

Richard started to come in Scott's mouth, spurting semen. Scott gagged, tried to spit it out.

"Swallow it!" Richard pushed the gun into Scott's ear.

Scott swallowed. And then he was crying. He didn't know when he started, he was crying like a baby.

"What're you crying for, miss?" Richard asked him, mocking him.

Scott stared up at him. What kind of asshole question . . . ?

"What are you crying about?" Richard asked again. "You liked it. You fucking loved it, didn't you? Admit you loved it."

"Fuck you," Scott said.

"Wouldn't you like to," Richard answered.

He squatted down, his face right next to Scott's.

"You loved it," Richard taunted him. His cock was still semierect, spider legs of semen spurting out. "That's why you're crying—*because* you liked it. You're gay, Scott. You're as gay as I am. You just wouldn't admit it to yourself. But now—now you have to."

Richard started laughing.

"Big macho stud. You're as queer as any queen on Forty-second Street. You're the ultimate macho queen. The ultimate phony queen."

He stood on unsteady legs, weaving his dripping phallus in Scott's face.

"You're out of the closet now," Richard said. "And you can't go back in."

Richard was staggering around, laughing, his cock flopping in the breeze, waving the gun around like a drunken sailor. He was into himself, he'd gotten what he wanted from Scott.

"I'm going to give you a treat," Richard said. "I'm going to let *you* fuck *me.* Right up the ol' chocolate highway. Something I'll bet you've had a lot of practice doing."

Scott's hands were still tied, he couldn't do anything, Richard had the gun.

"Pretend I'm one of those whores you like to fuck, except when you close your eyes you're wishing it was a man. Admit it, Scott," Richard said.

He had to do what Richard said. It scared Scott, because Richard was a gay doper, and the thought of AIDS popped into Scott's mind, but Richard had the gun on him, he had to.

He fucked Richard royally. Like he was fucking a fourteen-year-old virgin.

When he finished, Richard started mocking him again.

"Don't say I never did you no favors," Richard said. "I just gave you the ride of your young life, son."

He was sitting on his bare ass on the ground, laughing to beat the band.

And one of the ends of the bungee cord popped, and the rope went slack on Scott's bound wrists.

And he was moving at Richard, rising, and Richard didn't see him coming, in his euphoria he didn't realize that Scott had broken loose, Scott felt like he was moving underwater, in slow motion, he was off his knees, pushing up, and then Richard saw him, and his face had shock written all over it, and Richard started to raise the gun.

"*He* had the gun on *me*," Scott says in a low tone, his voice quivering from crying.

"He was going to shoot you," I say, confirming for him.

"He would've," Scott nods. "No question."

"Why didn't he?"

"'Cause I was too fast for him. He couldn't react fast enough."

"You managed to get the gun away from him."

Scott nods.

"I grabbed it out of his hand. I wasn't thinking, I just knew if I didn't he'd kill me."

"Then what did you do?"

He looks up at me, tears streaming down his face.

"I killed him, man. I blew his goddam brains out."

He looks past me, begging understanding.

"I had to. He made me. He made me! I ain't no faggot, man! He made me! I ain't no faggot! Never!"

Martinez recesses the court to give Scott Ray time to pull himself together. Scott sits on a bench in a corner of the empty corridor outside the courtroom, reading the Bible. I watch from a distance, making sure no one disturbs him.

"What happened then?" I ask.

It's been an hour since Martinez excused everyone, after Scott finished telling what he had done. We're back inside the courtroom again.

"After I shot him?"

"Yes."

"I don't remember exactly. I kind of freaked 'cause I didn't really mean to kill him. It's like I didn't have control over myself . . . over anything."

He's becoming agitated again, reliving the events up on the mountain.

"Take your time," I say. "Just take your time and try to think straight."

"I freaked out. I remember hearing a bunch more shots and wondering where they came from, then I looked down at the gun in my hand and thinking 'why is this gun going off?' And then I realized I was firing it at him, until it was empty. I don't even know if I hit him any more times, I wasn't aware of anything right then."

He looks up at Martinez, as if in supplication.

"I don't know nothing about what I was doing then," he says. "It was like it wasn't me; it was somebody else using me."

"I understand," Martinez says.

I'm watching; watching everyone—Judge Martinez, Robertson, Mary Lou, the bikers. They're all wrapped up in this, all there up on that mountain with Scott Ray.

"Then what?" I say, prodding gently.

"I sat down. My legs collapsed under me."

"You sat down next to the body."

"Yeh."

"Why didn't you run away?"

"I couldn't move."

"So you sat there. For how long?"

He shakes his head.

"An hour?" I ask.

"At least. Probably longer."

"Then what did you do?"

"I started to freak out again. I was looking at him, and he was turning white, like a dead fish, that ugly kind of dead-fish white, and I started getting angry at him again. Real angry. I didn't want to kill him. I just wanted to do some business and be on my way. I done some bad things in my life, I don't deny it, but I never killed anyone. I swear to that. You believe that, don't you?"

"Yes. I believe that," I tell him. I wait a moment: "Go on. Then what happened?"

"I took that knife he'd brought and started stabbing him with it. I was crying and cursing him for making me kill him for no reason."

"You stabbed him after he was dead?"

"He'd been dead from the minute the first shot was fired."

"More than an hour before."

"Yes."

"Did he bleed much from the stab wounds?"

He shakes his head.

"He wasn't bleeding hardly at all. There wasn't no blood coming out. It was already starting to settle."

"Okay. Keep going."

"I realized I had to hide him off the road better, 'cause he'd get found too fast where he was, and somebody might've seen me pick him up, or at the motel, or something, so I dragged him into the brush."

"And that was it?" I ask. "After that you left?"

He shakes his head again.

"I cut off his cock."

"Why?"

"Because he made me put it in my mouth! Because he made me do it." His eyes pop open. He scans the courtroom, trying to look at everyone, to make sure they see him, make sure they understand.

"He made me suck him off!" he cries. "He made me!"

"And that's why you did it," I ask rhetorically.

"Partly," he says.

"Why else?"

"Because he deserved it," Scott Ray says defiantly. "I knew he'd be found sooner or later. I'd have called the cops myself if he hadn't been." He looks at me, defiance in his eyes. "I wanted everyone to know what he was," he says. "That he was a faggot rip-off artist. I wanted everyone to see it."

"YOU TELL AN INTERESTING story, Mr. Ray."

Robertson stands in front of Scott. Considering the torpedoes that have been shot into his case, he seems relatively composed. But he's a true believer, he'll believe the bikers did it to his dying day, no matter what anyone says or does.

"It ain't a story. It's the truth."

"So you say."

"That's right," Scott says with some defiance in his voice. "I swore on a Holy Bible to tell the truth and that's what I'm doing. I don't swear on Jesus' name in vain."

"It is a good story," Robertson says. "I will admit that."

"It's the truth, damnit! I'm telling the truth."

"I don't think the truth in this case exists anymore, Mr. Ray," Robertson says. "Everything's gotten so crazy now that there is no truth. There's what you say, what she says, what my people say, what the defendants say. You all have your own truth, and none of it's the real truth, as far as I can tell."

"Mine is," Scott says doggedly.

"Really," Robertson says, mocking him.

"Yes." Firm, sure.

Robertson shakes his head 'no.' He turns to Martinez.

"Everything this witness has told us could have been learned from newspapers, magazines, and television, your honor. There is nothing new here that could compel the court to believe this man's story. It is no more credible than the recanting of Rita Gomez."

"You saying you don't believe me?" Scott asks incredulously.

"I think you're as absolute and complete a liar as I'll ever meet," Robertson says.

"Why the hell would I be coming up here and saying I did it, saying I'm the one should be in jail, maybe getting the gas chamber or however you kill people, if I didn't do it?" Scott asks.

"I don't know. Maybe someone put you up to it. Maybe you're some kind of religious fanatic who wants to save the world."

I stand.

"This is ludicrous, your honor," I say to Martinez. "This man has put his life on the line here. I'm sure you respect and understand that."

Martinez nods that he does.

"Then where's the evidence?" Robertson shoots back at me. "In all this time, all these recanting witnesses, you haven't produced one shred of real evidence to buttress these outrageous, ridiculous claims. You haven't shown this court one piece of hard physical evidence that would prove this isn't anything more than an elaborate concoction, a cluster of intricately interwoven lies. Not one real, physical fact."

I look at him for a moment, as if pondering the truth of what he's said. Martinez is looking at me, too: One thing, counselor, he's saying silently, give us one real piece of evidence.

"Where's your smoking gun?" Robertson asks.

"It was never found," I say.

"It was never found," Robertson echoes, bitterly.

I walk around the defense table, up to the witness stand. The French have a saying: 'Revenge is a dish that is best eaten cold.' After two terrible years, my clients and I are about to have our well-deserved feast. I will never sucker-punch an opponent in a courtroom as I am about to do to Robertson at this moment.

"Mr. Ray," I say. "This gun you say you took away from Richard Bartless, that you used to kill him. Whatever happened to it?"

"I hid it," he answers.

"Do you remember where?"

"Yes."

HE HAD THROWN THE GUN into a culvert halfway down the mountain from where the killing took place. It takes the police less than an hour to find it.

"YOUR HONOR. We request that the court dismiss all charges against our clients and order their immediate release."

"Objection," Robertson responds tonelessly. He is, if nothing else, consistent in his convictions.

Martinez stares him down.

"So ordered."

He bangs his gavel.

"The defendants are free to go," he states. "And gentlemen . . .

this court offers you its heartfelt apologies. I'm sure I can say for everyone concerned . . ." he looks hard at Robertson as he says this . . . "that I wish none of this had ever happened."

It's just us in the courtroom: the bikers, Mary Lou, and me. After the hugging and dancing are over, and the reality of their freedom has sunk in, Lone Wolf sidles up to me.

"Why, man? Why did you keep going? Why didn't you give up on us, like everyone else?"

It's a question I'd asked myself, many times over.

"Because one time," I tell him, "just one time, I wanted to get something right."

IT'S DARK NOW. Everyone has scattered. Mary Lou has gone home, waiting for me.

I'm in the mountains above town, near where it all happened. It's very peaceful up here; there's no suggestion that the violence and death that birthed these terrible events still linger. And maybe now, finally, it doesn't. Maybe the rains and the snows and the years of passage and exorcism have washed it all away, so that I can again bring my child here to feel, at least while we're in the moment, nothing but peace.